"An evocative mélange of history and memory, daily life and dream, spanning generations and continents, speaking powerfully to all of us who know what it is to be far from home."
Chitra Banerjee Divakaruni, author of
The Vine of Desire and *The Mistress of Spices*

"Brava! In this anthology Marianne Villanueva and Virginia Cerenio have gathered together a vibrant, diverse array of Filipina poets and fiction writers writing in English.... A wonderful new addition to the growing body of Philippine diaspora literature."
Jessica Hagedorn, author of *Dream Jungle*

"This collection of poetry, prose, and prose poem is amazing.... These are landscapes of time and memories and realities and imaginations that illuminate the past, the present and often give glimpses of the future. The beauty, the sorrows, the joys, and the incredible humor that radiate from *Going Home to a Landscape* make this book to be bought and then passed around and then bought and read again.... This is a book to be talked about. The voices in it vibrate across continents and can be recognized anywhere even in their uniqueness."
Roshni Rustomji-Kerns, author of *The Braided Tongue*

"The poems and stories in this stunning collection are poignant, raw, hip, and beautiful. A lyrically charged landscape worth revisiting again and again." **R. Zamora Linmark**, *Rolling The R's*

"In *Going Home to a Landscape*, Virginia Cerenio and Marianne Villanueva have brought together a lovely and powerful chorus of new and established Filipina voices that sing to each other and to us back and forth across the Pacific."
Elaine H. Kim, editor of
Asian American Literature

Going Home to a Landscape
Writings by Filipinas

Edited by
Marianne Villanueva
and Virginia Cerenio

with a foreword by
Rocio G. Davis

CALYX Books

The publication of this book was supported by grants from the Autzen Foundation and The Rose E. Tucker Charitable Trust. With grateful appreciation, CALYX acknowledges the following "immortal" who generously supported this book:

Nancy Nordhoff

Cover art, "Tropical Landscape II," by Dixie Galapon
Cover and book design by Cheryl McLean

CALYX Books are distributed to the trade through Consortium Book Sales and Distribution, Inc., St. Paul, MN 1-800-283-3572.

CALYX Books are also available through major library distributors, jobbers, and most small press distributors including Airlift, Baker & Taylor, Ingram, and Small Press Distribution. For personal orders or other information contact: CALYX Books, PO Box B, Corvallis, OR 97339, (541) 753-9384; FAX (541) 753-0515; E-mail: calyx@proaxis.com; web: www.proaxis.com\~calyx

♾

The paper in this book meets the guidelines for permanence and durability of the Committee on Production Guidelines for Book Longevity of the Council on Library Resources and the minimum requirements of the American National Standard for the Permanence of Paper for Printed Library Materials Z38.48-1984.

Library of Congress Cataloging-in-Publication Data

Going home to a landscape: writings by Filipinas / edited by Marianne Villanueva and Virginia Cerenio; with a foreword by Rocio G. Davis.
  p. cm.
  Includes index.
  ISBN 0-934971-85-4 (cloth : alk. paper) — ISBN 0-934971-84-6 (paper : alk. paper) 1. Philippine literature (English)—Women authors. 2. American literature—Filipino American authors. 3. Filipino American women—Literary collections. 4. Women—Philippines—Literary collections. 5. Filipino Americans—Literary collections. 6. American literature—Women authors. 7. Philippines—Literary collections. I. Villanueva, Marianne. II. Cerenio, Virginia R. III. Title.
  PR9550.5.G64 2003
  820.9'9287'09599—dc22

                                                      2003018337

9 8 7 6 5 4 3 2 1

Acknowledgments

"White Turtle" has been published as part of Merlinda Bobis' collection of short stories, *White Turtle* (Spinifex Press, Victoria, Australia, 1999), re-published in the U.S. as *The Kissing* (Aunt Lute, 2001). An earlier version of "The Mango Summer" by Lilledeshan Bose was published in *Philippine Graphic Weekly Magazine* Vol. 9, No. 21, Oct. 26, 1998. "In Late" was published in Catalina Cariaga's poetry collection, *Cultural Evidence* (Honolulu: Subpress Collective and 'A'A Arts, 1999). "Another Day" by Erma M. Cuizon was published in the *Philippines Free Press,* March 22, 1997. "Fools" by Susan Evangelista was published in *Creative Juices: Works of the Ateneo Faculty*, edited by Susan P. Evangelista (Manila: Diwa Scholastic Press, Inc., 2001). "April in Stockton" by Dawn Bohulano Mabalon was published in *maganda*, No. 11, 1999. "The Stone" by Isabelita Orlina Reyes was published in *Philippines Free Press*, Vol. 90, No. 50, Dec. 12, 1998, page 37. "Tending the Earth" by Elda Rotor was published in *New Digressions* art and literary magazine (1998, Vol. 5). "Tango" by Angelina Narciso Torres was published in the *Asian Pacific American Journal,* Fall 2003. "Testament" by Katrina Tuvera was published in the Fall 2002 issue of the *Two Rivers Review.* "Loreto, Alone" by Linda Ty-Casper was published in the *Mid-American Review*, Vol. XIV, No.1, 1993, pp. 16-21.

Contents

Foreword

Rocio G. Davis

The Philippines' history of successive colonizations and diasporic movement have made the question of place central in its people's creative imagination. Place in literature, a geography of space and imagination, binds its members in a shared sense of purpose and a common sense of belonging.

The history of the creation of the Philippines is complex and problematic. It was originally an archipelago inhabited by Malay and Chinese, centuries before the arrival of the Spanish colonizers. In 1898, the Philippines' war of independence from the Spanish empire quickly segued into another occupation, this time by America. Filipino writing thus demonstrates a desire to capture in literature a landscape that was historically written and re-written by others. It is a struggle for creative self-definition and appropriation.

In the twentieth century, the diasporic movement towards more economically solvent countries—the United States, Canada, Britain, and Australia—led to a second form of creative engagement. For immigrant writers, the landscape of the Philippines is one of nostalgia, idealized often through the myth of return. For the second generation in America, for instance, place often acquires another meaning. The need to identify with a landscape becomes a double challenge, as the physical landscape that surrounds these children of immigrants in the present often comes into conflict with the vision inherited through communal memory.

The women in this volume inscribe cartographies of personal and cultural belonging. Their highly individual representations of the Philippines have as a major feature the concern with developing, maintaining, or recovering a relationship between self and place. Writing landscape thus becomes constitutive of the process of selfhood. The Philippines, as represented by the women in this volume, is a distinctly plural phenomenon constructed out of the comparison and intersection of past and present, of colonizations and immigration, of the cohabitation of different races and cultures.

The need to orient oneself spatially has always been an almost biological need, and for the immigrant, as for the second generation who must redefine the relationship with place, cultural identity is intricately woven with the idea of location. These writers, therefore, function according to Anita Desai's description of "writers who create place. It does not exist on any map—or else, it exists in all maps and in all countries and the writer who recognizes it as his spiritual home goes straight to it out of an instinct as true as the homing pigeon's."

The challenge, and the success, of the collection lies in the way the writers experience the blending of inner and outer landscapes, of memories that intersect with national and emotional affiliations, and of carving out a voice that speaks to everyone who has ever contemplated the problematic intersection of place and self.

Introduction

Marianne Villanueva

*Luzon is a large skull-shaped island in the Philippine archipelago.
The skull appears on the maps as a profile; the open mouth is
formed by Manila Bay. The skull faces east. Invaders from the
west came here by rounding the Sea of Celebes. Here and there are
dotted numerous islands, too many to be adequately explored.
Some are only a mile wide. Deeply forested, these islands were
whispered to be the home of giants. No one knows if the stories
are true, since as far as anyone knows, no one has cared to find
out. But the Philippine archipelago is full of secrets, secrets it
would take a lifetime to uncover.*
Marianne Villanueva, "Mountains,"
Literary Review, *Spring, 2000*

*I was last home for my father's funeral. I say "home" even though
I am an American citizen now, sworn in with a twenty-piece Navy
band in the grand ballroom of the Marriott Hotel on 4th and
Mission in San Francisco. Yet, "home" for me was always that
other place, that city James Hamilton-Patterson describes as "a
parody of the grimmer parts of Milwaukee."*
Marianne Villanueva, "Sutil,"
Threepenny Review, *Fall, 1997*

The idea of landscape has always been a central one in my writing,
perhaps because I no longer live in the country of my birth. What
is this landscape that I write about? It is not only a place that exists
in real time. It is something more personal and inward, a landscape
of memory.

For Filipino women, the maintenance of this internal landscape is
vital. As Rocio G. Davis states in her foreword, it is an almost "biological need." It is what shapes and drives our moods, pulls us out of
despondency, and drives us forward. We situate ourselves in this internal landscape; we are at the heart of our own stories. The very act
of writing is a way of creating this inner space, so essential to our

well-being. It is a way of building a home for ourselves, in a sometimes hostile and alien environment. It is what helps us to survive. It is what the memoirist Andre Aciman calls the "geographical frame to a psychological mess."

When Virginia Cerenio and I first met to work on this anthology, we knew we wanted the process of putting together this book to be one of discovery. We decided to spread the net as widely as possible when we issued the "call for submissions." From my home in California, I sent out E-mail announcements. I sent announcements to *Filipinas Magazine,* to *Philippine News.* I prepared flyers and took them with me when I spent a few months teaching at my old school, the Ateneo de Manila University. Further announcements appeared in Philippine newspapers.

It is tremendously fitting that this book is published by the women of CALYX, my second mothers, who made me a writer before I even knew what it was to be one. They published *Ginseng and Other Tales from Manila* in 1991. Those were stories stuck in a drawer; I never thought to send them out for publication. It was Margarita Donnelly, the director of CALYX, who asked to see what I had, after hearing me read in a bookstore in San Francisco. What fun it was, I discovered, to read aloud to groups of people. How thrilling to discover that I had a voice that could make people *listen.* I, who had only left the Philippines a few short years before, who still considered herself not a Filipino American but a Filipina, in every sense of the word.

The last decade has been one of tremendous change in the Filipina literary landscape—many Filipina voices have emerged. Michelle Cruz Skinner's *Balikbayan and Other Stories*, M. Evelina Galang's *Her Wild American Self*, Sabrina Murray's *Slow Burn*, Lara Stapleton's *The Lowest Blue Flame Before Nothing*. There were rumblings from Australia, a heretofore undiscovered country, in terms of Filipino writers. There was Arlene Chai's *The Last Time I Saw My Mother*, and then Merlinda Bobis' *White Turtle*, published in the United States as *The Kissing*. From France, we heard from Reine Melvin, who a short time ago came out with her first collection of short fiction, *A Normal Life*, which won the Philippine National Book Award. (Evelina, Merlinda, and Reine are all included in this anthology.) Most recently there has been Tess Uriza Holthe's mesmerizing *When* the *Elephants Dance* and another book by Sabrina Murray, *The Caprices*, which recently won the PEN/Faulkner Award.

These books are part of the context of this anthology, which contains work by a remarkable array of Filipina writers who live scattered around the globe. In the end, the writing that Virginia and I discovered we were most drawn to was writing that showed a profound sense of *engagement*, writing that struggled with issues of dislocation, dispossession. Writing that examined the plight of women coping with loneliness, the burden of family relationships, and exile.

The order in which the pieces were presented was also important to our vision of the message we were trying to convey. We decided to begin with the section *"Las Dalagas,"* which celebrates the contemporary generation of Filipinas, secure in their independence in their chosen country. From this hopeful and charged present the pieces move slowly back to the home country, the Philippines, ending finally with the section called "Roots." We hope the book parallels the process of discovery that many young second- or third-generation immigrants experience as they discover the country and culture of their parents or grandparents. The process of discovery, the forging of connections with what has been, can be profoundly liberating, as many of these writings attest. The book itself is a mirror of this journey, the journey to a discovery of self through a re-discovery of one's cultural heritage.

Going Home includes fifty poems and twenty-one short stories and novel excerpts. Each individual piece represents moments when the writer struggles to describe her interior landscape. There is a disconnect, a feeling of "You are *here*, but you are really *there*." The book grows with a cumulative power, as landscape piles upon landscape. Grief, loss, longing are there, but also celebration, joy, strength. The strength that says: in spite of everything, I will write. I will assert my right to *be*.

Some of the writers have never before been published in the United States. Some are represented by their first published pieces. The ostensible subjects are the subjects of all good literature: love, suffering, power, family, guilt, failure, endurance. But peel the sheath and what you find beneath is dispersal, evasion, ambivalence.

As Cecilia Brainard's young narrator states in the story "Vigan," "Even though Lola spoke enthusiastically of the house (this remnant of our family's glorious past), I found it depressing." The past can sometimes be a burden, as the Philippines' colonial history can attest. Or the past can be a locus of sadness, as in Lilledeshan Bose's "Mango Summer," when another young narrator writes, "I am eight, nine, or ten, and my mother has left us here with the maids while she works in the city. My parents have just split up, I think. My mother is concentrating on being alone."

The present has its own challenges, as M. Evelina Galang's narrator discovers, when she is asked to chaperone a high school dance: "Isabel was not sure what she had witnessed. She could feel something was up and it made her nauseous...Why didn't she realize her girls were *Las Dalagas?*...She hated feeling like Mary Tyler Moore. She hated knowing she had more in common with the career girl from Minnesota than her own Pinay sisters who were younger than her, but just as brown. She hated that." Indeed, identity is a slippery thing, a treacherous and constantly shifting entity.

The writers may write *around* the landscape, never dealing with it directly. But the strongest and most vivid thread coursing through these pieces is the memory of a place. There is Manila, that cacophonous city, a symbol for the decadence and spirituality, ugliness and beauty that shape our culture. There is the pristine, untouched landscape of Vigan, with its old homes and old mores. There is the rugged beauty of Hawaii, the sharpened rhythms of Los Angeles, the fog-shrouded evenings of San Francisco. The loneliness of a small midwestern town. The vibrant bustle of Hong Kong.

In each piece, there is remembrance, exile, the passage of time. There is the attempt to recapture, to preserve, and to return to the past. There are many pasts represented in the work, and others are present only indirectly: the past of the *manongs* in the California farms; the past of the grandmothers who suffered through the indignities of the Japanese Occupation during the Second World War; the very personal past of each writer's childhood, which unfolds like an undiscovered country.

We begin where we are now, and we move backwards to what we think we have forgotten. There are pieces that hit us with the intensity of a blow, like Katrina Tuvera's powerful "Testament," in which, to quote from Caroline Hau's introduction to Tuvera's excellent first short-story collection, "an insomniac is driven to violence by the ceaseless deferral of her desires." There are others that lull us into believing in the utterly magical, as in Merlinda Bobis' ineffable "White Turtle," with its unforgettable conjuring trick. And there are those in which our hearts go out to the narrators, as in Reine Melvin's "Homecoming," in which a biracial narrator holds onto a fragile sense of self as she tries to negotiate a return to the homeland with her new son.

How then do we Filipinas describe landscape? The landscape is something we take with us, wherever we go. It is what we carry on our individual journeys. For myself, it is always the Filipino landscape of family, memory, culture. It is as strong as the smell of garlic in a dish of simmering *adobo*. It is, as in Merlinda Bobis' "White Turtle," a place of "turtles or dreams, or the sound of dreams in their own tongue." It is a spell, an enchantment. As strong as the feeling of "summer rain on the earth's cracked skin." It is touch— whether the gentle touch of a mother's hand or the hand raised in anger, as in Lakambini Sitoy's searing short story, "Touch." It is grief—the grief of losing one's self, one's culture, one's family. It is all these things.

The stories and poems in this collection are beautiful, which is not to say that the situations many of them describe are not painful and heartbreaking. But they are beautiful in the sense that the writer has been able to harness the power and fierceness of her vision to create a space where she might re-create her home, a home we all recognize and love.

In the end, we see that landscape is more than just a physical reality. It is also the thoughts and feelings that infuse a territory with metaphor. And how can we, readers as well as writers, use memory and imagination to recover a landscape and to understand other landscapes?

The pieces in this book will show us the way.

Introduction

Virginia Cerenio

As the diaspora of people from the Philippines has occurred throughout the world, so has the poetry of their hundred languages and seventeen hundred islands been dispersed. In some cases, the people, their language and culture, have adapted to a new geographic location and local culture, but the sensibility that is Filipino remains.

The many poetry submissions received from all over the globe reflect this truth. Global communication, whether by E-mail or by post, brought us poems by women of Philippine descent, written all over the world, yet sharing a common root culture and a singular vocabulary of vision. It is a revelation to acknowledge the dynamic presence of this global community of women who write as women *and* as Filipinas, and an affirmation of their strength, intelligence, and insight, as demonstrated by the poems to follow.

These poems are composed of pixels creating images. The images are urban and rural. Some images are the sepia-tone quality of old photographs; others are the colorful, shifting shapes of an MTV music video. For some poems, the background music is mandolins or ocean waves. For others, urban cacophony, traffic, an overamplified concert of city sounds. Still other poems ask only for silence, the silence of complete attention, the attention of a woman focused on herself and her being within the space of time captured by the poet's words.

The landscape is the Philippines, a place where nature is predominant, where woman is synonymous with Earth, as when Fran Ng writes, in "Notebook": "I graze in the belly of language..."

Crossing and traveling over water is the experience of the majority of these poems. Whether first-, second-, or third-generation immigrants, these writers have traveled across and over to a new place, a place where to be of Filipino descent is to be different and alone, where identity is both a struggle and a strength. Lewanda Lim writes, in "An Expatriate to Her Sister,"

"I think I have to trace my way home
to find the missing half."

The first generation still looks back over their shoulders, looking to the familiar landscape of the Philippines for strength, and for memories. As Jean Vengua Gier writes in her poem, "Talk Story,"

"Move from that moment to this;
knowing that a word might strike
tinder, to signal what flew before
and what dark bird still
sings after."

The second generation gives us talk story, chronicling the history, personal and public, of parents, grandparents, *barrio* uncles and aunts. The names with their Spanish music and *barrio* rhythm become a chant, a talisman to a time past. The memories are of the senses—of food, smell, sights, and sounds—documenting the rituals of a people adapting to a new land.

"april is the month of salmon head
and tomatoes and onions and hot rice"
— "April in Stockton," Dawn Bohulano Mabalon

From *chismis*/gossip/talk story that women all over the world have always used to pass the time over the labor of cooking, laundry, and factory work, to the spoken word of the millennium generation, we create a new horizon.

"my mama's so brown
she's inherited the bamboo skin
from my *lola*'s crown
perfected the art of weavin untold stories
through her eyes..."
— "The Dozens—Pinay Style," Pinay M.A.F.I.A.

We are very proud of this selection of poetry and thank all the Pinay poets, both those represented in this collection and those whose works were not selected, for according us the great privilege of sharing their work.

two women planted dreams
through a year of seasons
the dreams grew stories
traveled vmail to email
down the coast highway
gambled in vegas
jetted to hawaii
island *balikbayan*
coming home to a landscape
time to harvest
our stories

Section I Las Dalagas

The Big I Am

Maria Stella Sison

Sometimes it's hard to be American, girl.
People ask why I am not blond enough,
Christie Brinkley or Pamela Anderson.
American Girls are supposed to be tough
We wear last year's European styles
We pay for our own meals on dates
English makes us too accessible.
I am a slut because you say so.
I laugh without my hands.
Sometimes I want to kill Hollywood.

It's Hard to be an American Girl.
There is violence in our own neighborhoods
And our own movies and
especially in our own beds.
We have no religion,
Only feminism.
Time makes us worthless
In the end.
We only get foreplay the first time.
I don't want to marry or bear children.
Sometimes men say they love me.

It's hard to be a Pinay
Living in my parents' grand design
Why is my English so good? And, no, this is no tan.
Every day I seek proof for my anger.
It seems men date Orientals at least once.
And Fuck No, not all Filipinas are hospitable
especially when I work harder than you.
People say that I am different than the others,
They laugh when I talk back.
We no longer swing from them trees here
But Sometimes I still cry from broken bones.

For the Women
Dawn Bohulano Mabalon

for Concepcion Moreno Bohulano, Isabel Tirona Mabalon,
Camila Labor Carido, Asuncion Nicolas, Eleanor Olamit, Paula
Dizon Daclan, Segunda Reyes and Eudosia Juanitas, Virgilia
Bantillo, Angelina Bantillo Magdael, Leatrice Bantillo Perez,
Angeles Raymundo, and all the pioneering Pinays of Stockton,
including my mom Christine.

i was only about 12 or 13. one time i was on the top of a mountain,
very high, and i would see all of the ocean. i used to wonder, what is
on the other side of the ocean? but i never dreamed i would go to the
united states, until my father said, "you are gonna come and stay
here"

this poem is for the women
for manang lilay, manang segunda
to manang paula, manang asuncion
manang eleanor, manang eudosia
my lola conching
my lola isabel
(dead after only a few years in america)
these women of stockton
and the women of san francisco
of salinas/delano/vallejo/los angeles
before their history is buried with them
before we forget them
the way we almost forgot
their brothers

there's not too much written on the pilipinas. we should be entitled
to something. we contributed too much to this country too

these women
who traded *bakya*
for saddle shoes
and province life
for queen contests
these women who
have seen almost a century
pass before their lives
have a place in our history

before in 1929, we are diamonds. when you come over here, you are
the belle of the town! we were like gold to the pilipinos

these women
who were queens
who were like gold
women so special
a precious commodity
in a community of lonely men
these women
who were fondled
and groomed
and praised
and adored
and worked to death
these women
who created their own destinies
and were no one's victim

oh, i could have been somebody. i was going to be a dentist or an
architect. I just accepted it because I know that's impossible. i didn't
think of coming to america. that was not my decision. and my brother
cried when i left because he said our parents worked so hard to leave
us something that we can live on. i also had lots of bad luck here.
that time we could have improved our life, then grandpa got sick.
we had to buy everything when we got here. only one of us could
buy warm clothes. but i don't regret

these women
these women who stood barefoot
on a beach in leyte
and in a rice field in aklan
and wondered what awaited
them on the other side of the mountains
and on the other side of the sea
and who bucked every expectation of them
to catch a presidential liner to america

how did I happen to be here? I knew that it's hard when you go away from your parents. and my mother said, oh, you'll be the only one there. and no one will help you. so I made my mind up. I had to fight. so I was not afraid. i'm a fighter

these wild, radical
courageous women
who bucked a province of frowning *lolas*
and dominating *tatays*
to slip onto the s.s. cleveland to san francisco
almost unnoticed
only to disappear
on the pages of our history

i was confined to eight children. my gosh, the eight children is hard to take care of, with all your trouble with them. and sometimes i felt so bad. why did i come here to america? sometimes you get disappointed with your life

these women who came to find their el dorado
only to find crying babies
work in the fields
days of work neverending

we worked in the fields. i remember when I had to pick prunes. that's the hardest work, picking prunes. i cried. strawberries and tomatoes is not hard. onions are not hard. but the prunes. oh god. it seemed so long to fill up the bucket

these women
if you ask
will tell you of dreams unfulfilled
of babies lost in the asparagus fields
hands that cracked and bled
from laundry done over washboards
these women who will tell you that they
too have degrees

*i got the degree of m.d. making diapers. i tell them! sometimes they
kind of insult me cause i have no degree. in the philippines we are
not educated. we are just taught to be a good wife, darn and sew,
and cook for your husband. that is our life in the philippines, to
serve your husband even if he kills you for not doing it*

these women
with few choices
with their hands and hearts and prayers
birthed us
and fed us
and wiped our tears
with no one to wipe their own
these women
who managed
who survived

*it was really bad. we were treated bad really. but later on, i know
how to fight already. nobody's gonna fool around with me*

these women
whose joys are reno on a saturday
their grandchildren's laughter
these women
who gave their lives
and who ask for little more
than our love

*if i don't feel good, I ask god, make me well, if not, take me. i'm
ready to go. i'm 85 years old now. i've lived all my life. i've seen my
grandchildren, my great grandchildren. i just take easy now*

Excerpt from Chapter Six of What Is Tribe

M. Evelina Galang

I sabel was asked to chaperone the Tidewater Youth Dance. She felt so Midwestern, so Mary Tyler Moore. At dusk, she stepped her way around the bodies of souped-up cars. The parking lot reeked of whiskey soaking in the skin of youth. From their mouths hung cigarette butts. They grunted at Isabel as she walked by. They nodded hello.

Inside, the music beat against the walls and floated up into the rafters, banged against the pane of skylights, fighting to get out. Boom, ba boom boom—bang, bang—ba boom boom. The rhythm of bass called forth the various tribes. Several hundred teenagers bumped and shifted to the beat. Everybody danced. Everybody moved. Every beat made itself known. Underneath baggy jeans and skin-tight Lycra, hips popped like metronomes. The music made them want to explode. Led them into new levels of consciousness. The DJ, the bartender (who delivered Cokes and lemonade), the parents who chaperoned the dark corners and cubby holes of the room, the little baby sister someone had brought—all moved. It was as if everyone could understand at least this much: rhythm.

Several college boys cased the room, stood at doors—legs thrown apart, arms crossed—warriors guarding the young. They nodded to the steady boom ba boom boom—bang, bang—ba boom boom. Their jaws were set and ready for a fight. They were all business. They were the *kuyas* looking out for their younger siblings, their little cousins.

A red light floated in a shaft across the crowded dance floor— searched out trouble—caught the spinning disco ball on occasion and glittered brightly.

Outside two police cars crawled about the parking lot waiting for the inevitable—or so they thought. Last time, two rival gangs rumbled with switchblades and surgical knives they'd taken from their fathers' offices. Someone sliced an ear, scarred the apple of someone's cheek, almost killed a brother. Time before that, the sisters from one of the tribes jumped a girl for talking trash, beat her till her eyes went from brown to black and blue. And nobody had forgotten the year before when several brothers from Familia circled the Cultural Center, shooting bullets into the windows and doors of the dance hall. No one died. Several fainted. Mostly aunties.

Isa felt Arturo's presence filling the room. She wondered if the others saw him shifting among them, bumping hips with the pretty girls, swirling fast with the other break-dancers. To utter his name would validate the circle of cop cars, to mention his death a threat to everyone there. So no one named him, but Isabel knew he was there. He was a guardian angel now, he was a spirit, forever caught in the mix.

Isabel wanted to enjoy the music, but the tension was too distracting. The song floating from the speakers haunted them. No telling what would happen next. She wandered the dance floor with a camera in her hand, shooting images of teens dancing to escape.

On stage, two boys in black ski caps and basketball jerseys rapped into the microphone. The rhymes were sloppy, and sometimes they had to rush the words to make them fit the line. One boy was big, bearlike. The other was small and skinny. The small one had a loud and angry voice. The larger one was as mellow as an old-time jazz singer. They swung one arm low, leaning their bodies down to the crowd as they spat words out. They hid behind dark glasses, but every now and then one of them peeked over the top of his shades, winked out into the crowd. The dancers cheered the rappers on, even though many of the words were lost to the deafening beat of the music. DJ Boy spun records, scratched vinyl against the boys' rap. Every now and then Isabel picked up a line: "Lookin at me you think I'm a Chino, but I am (beat beat) FIL-A-PEE-NO." Backup rappers chanted "Brown is the power, now is the hour" in between the bleeding of bass and the thick strokes of a steady electric beat. In the center of the gym, break dancers tumbled like a set of children's jacks, whirling in different directions, twisting limbs, knotting bodies.

She shot photos of JoJo perusing the crowd. He stopped at the doors and checked in with the college boys. She saw how they deferred to him. He placed a hand on one of the boys' shoulders. Patted each of them on the shoulder or arm, moved on. Every now and then he nodded at her. His face remained expressionless. He walked laps around the youth and she shot pictures of him moving constantly, waving at kids—hello, watch out, stop that. At one point she asked him how he was doing. Too worried, he said, too anxious. He wanted to know where Elliot was.

"Why?" she asked.

"Just wondering," he said. He was rocking on the heels of his running shoes, looking over his shoulder, his hands still waving at kids around him.

"Is he picking you up or do you want a ride?"

"I have a car," she said.

"Great," he said, his face breaking into a smile. "Then, can you give me a lift or what?"

She told him, "Okay, find me later," and then she wandered around the dance floor, counting the youth. Must be two hundred, maybe more.

Fifteen years ago, Isabel and her friends worried about stupid things—dance routines, crepe paper for the gym, in-depth articles on submarine races and cartoon strips that would catch the essence of their class. They had hall passes, yellow slips of paper that granted them permission to go to the bathroom or the library or nurse. They'd steal a pack of passes and get Jody Anderson to place counterfeit signatures on the bottom right corner. They dealt with teachers—not security guards.

Her students at Westover had to walk through metal detectors every morning, just to get to class. She'd been there at lunch when security guards announced random searches, frisking freshmen for scissors and blades, for guns. They lined the students up along a wall, spread their legs and arms wide like they were sure the kids had something on them. They checked everything, even the insides of their socks and shoes, the lining of their jeans, the spaces along their inner thighs. All this, just to have lunch.

There was never that kind of trouble when Isabel was in high school. Out in the north parking lot, they got high on pot or made out between periods. They divided themselves, not by the color of skin, since that would have meant Isabel against all of them, but into categories—jocks, freaks, actors, and video nerds. Isabel floated in and out of the categories depending on the season, defying labels. During her last year they drank or cut classes, because they were seniors. The behavior was traditional, expected.

The dances she attended plastered boys too cool to move against the walls, while the girls were the ones scattered in the middle of the floor, moving without pattern, in many cases without rhythm to the likes of "American Pie," "Brown-Eyed Girl," and any song by the Eagles. What a change, she thought.

She heard voices coming from the stairwell, so she stole up the stairs in her soft-soled shoes. Two female voices hissed to each other in a mix of Taglish and street talk. She had a hard time understanding so she hurried to see what was happening.

On the third landing she found two girl crews. Lourdes, Maya, Mercedes, Angel, and Marilena stood with other girls from Westover. Tough girls, they clenched their fists, their jaws. They stood with their feet spread apart, claiming territory. The other girls from Norfolk faced them with equally strong stances, equally beautiful faces filled with hate. They didn't notice Isabel right away; they didn't see her spying them. She caught a word or two. Someone trash-talked someone. Someone's getting jumped for something—a boy, a comment, most likely an attitude.

They faced off, but only Lourdes and another girl were speaking. They glared at one another, growled like two cats threatening to fight. For the first time since she'd moved to Virginia, she realized that her girls were part of something larger.

"Sup?" Isabel said.

The tension fell away as the girls leaned against banisters and bricks. Some of them smiled at her. Some walked past her, down the stairs.

"Nothing," Angel said. "Girl talk is all."

"Yeah," Maya said. "You know—boys an shit."

The stairwell was dark and only a light from the floors above illuminated their shadows, threw expressions on their faces. Isabel had a hard time recognizing her girls. She felt their attitude more than anything, knew something bad was going down. Lourdes and the girl from Norfolk smiled. They flung an arm over each other and passed Isa silently. Slowly the girls descended the stairs, one and two at a time. They whispered to one another. Chitchatted as if they were all sisters. They left her standing there alone.

Isabel was not sure what she had witnessed. She could feel something was up and it made her nauseous. She uncapped a bottle of water and drank long and slow. Why didn't she realize her girls were *Las Dalagas?* She stood for a minute and listened to the fading sounds of their shoes as they flip, flip, flipped their way down the stairs. A small army of girl soldiers mad at something. Someone. She hated feeling like Mary Tyler Moore. She hated knowing she had more in common with the career girl from Minnesota than her own Pinay sisters who were younger than her, but just as brown. She hated that.

That Age
PERFORMANCE POETRY MEMOIR, EXCERPTED FROM "SUNGKA"
Alison de la Cruz

When you get to be that age, they'll say
You be princess Leia and I'll be Han Solo, wait here...I'll rescue you.

When you get to be that age, they'll say
Pssht, *hoy*—getting too big to run outside by yourselp'. Take your cousin wit' you.

When you get to be that age, they'll say
Barbie's dumb. GI Joe's better! Go Joe!

When you get to be that age, they'll say
Wow! Getting so big now. I remember when you were dis e'small. (Holds her hand at knee height.)

When you get to be that age, they'll say
(Teasing) I can see your panties!! I can see your panties!!

When you get to be that age, they'll say
Stop playing outside. Gonna get too dark.

When you get to be that age, they'll say
I heard you could get pregnant by tongue kissing. (Sticks tongue out and wiggles it.)

When you get to be that age, they'll say
Now class, let's talk about great American leaders, let's talk about great American men.

When you get to be that age, they'll say
(Whispering) Eh! I heard Susie got her period, yuck!

When you get to be that age, they'll say
Come on, come on. Eat some more! Eat some more! Plenty of *pancit*. (Pause) *Hoy* wait. Not you! Getting too big now...no more eating!

When you get to be that age, they'll say
You're a tomboy, not a girl.

When you get to be that age, they'll say
I told you. Come home straight after school. I need you to watch your sister.

Then they'll say
Ha'come you don't play with us anymore?

When you get to be that age, they'll say
Why haven't you clean yet? Look at this mess.

When you get to be that age, they'll say
Dang, everybody has a bra, but YOU!

When you get to be that age, they'll say
Honey, don't worry, you'll pind a good husband to take care of you. You'll get married, you'll be okay.

When you get to be that age, they'll say
My brother told me, you're not REALLY Filipino. You're only HALF!

When you get to be that age, they'll say
Don't you have any respect for the family?

When you get to be that age, they'll say
(almost chanting or song-like) Girls who sit like this get none (holds out left hand with middle and index fingers crossed like legs), girls who sit like this get some (uncrosses fingers, but keeps them together), and girls who sit like this (spreads 2 fingers apart), get this (flips off the audience), like this (snaps fingers).

When you get to be that age, they'll say
Thanks for the suggestion, but we're going to go with Eric's idea.

When you get to be that age, they'll sign your yearbook
(as if holding up to sign the book) Oh mah god! I can't believe the year has gone by sooo fast. Okay truth?! (pause) When I first met you, I thought you were such a bitch, cuz you talked sooo much... but like now I know you and you're cool. Take care, cuz I care! K?!!

When you get to be that age, they'll say
Wow, look at your cousin: just crowned Miss Sampanguita, she's going to UCLA, she's gonna be a doctor. What about you? What are you gonna do?

When you get to be that age, they'll say
Hey baby, what's your name?...Damn, you look good...I think you
and I would look good together...wait, i just wanna talk to you for a
minute, just for a minute...I said, just wait a MINUTE.....eh!! I'M
TALKIN TO YOU........WELL FUCK YOU THEN BITCH!!!!

When you get to be that age, they'll say
Dar-ling. It's not that we don't trust you...it's the crazy people out
there we don't trust.

When you get to be that age, they'll say
Come on, baby, please. I'll just die if I don't get some...it's like
biological, guys just need it me. PLEASE. (pause)....I love you!!!?

And when you get to be that age, sometimes you say, "No."

The Dozens—Pinay Style

© *by The Pinay M.A.F.I.A.**
(*Mad-Ass Filipinas Infiltrating Amerikkka:-)*Emily Porcincula
Lawsin, Stephanie Velasco, Dawn Bohulano Mabalon, Allyson G.
Tintiangco, Myra Dumapias, Alison de la Cruz, Faith Santilla,
Rikka Racelis, Maya Santos, Darlene Rodrigues, Lilyann Bolo
Villaraza, & Pamela Gil

Em:
"Hoy, my mama is so brown,
She can smoke a Marlboro, Dunhill, AND Benson & Hedges
BACKWARDS at the same time!"

Steph:
"*Ano ba*...my mama is so brown, she can work a nine-hour job,
cook *sinigang* and rice, handwash clothes to hang-dry,
raise her feet & *tsinelas* in the air and still have time to ask me
'Did you eat yet *anak*?'"

Dawn:
"oh yeah, well check this:
my mama's hella brown,
a teacher/artist in da Flip nation
don't got an accent
'cause she's second generation!"

"my *lola*'s so '*tigas*
nothing ever trips her
her favorite question is,
'*hoy boang*, belt or slipper?'"

Allyson T:
"Yo, My mom is so Pinay
she gotta life-size Santo Niño in our family room
that tells her to work 60 hours a week
just to make ends meet
dance cha cha so on beat
all night long till she got bruises on her feet

cook mad portions of *pancit*
so the whole barrio can eat
and wear hella superhold hairspray so her hair always looks neat."

Myra Dumapias:
"*Ay*, whateber! My mama's so Pinay,
no matter what I do,
In her eyes,
I'll always be her baby,
with milk still in her cheeks,
and she'll cook us 'ros caldo,
come *noche buena*,
and russian salad
like a familiar ballad,
and other yums and all the rest
under curlers and make-up
that never sweats."

De La:
"Psst *Hoy*. Dat's noting. My *tita* is so brown,
She's got soy sauce in her circulation
she e'sweats vinegar and if she ever cries: it's *patis!*
(*Tita* don't need a market!)"

De La2:
"I met my *lola* when I was five
but I remember her as so Pinay
cuz she'd point with her lips
with a baby on her hips
while eating rice off her fingertips."

faith santilla:
"my mom is so brown
brown like añejo rum
as brown as the brown of the philippine flag sun
brown like *palay* floating above / a banaue rice terrace
brown like *kalamay* or / honey from the cordilleras
as brown as a ripe/ or not yet quite / banana
and as brown as my blue-eyed *mestiza* grandma"

Rikka:
"My Motha's so Brown,
Gave her 22 years
     of fights bruises guilt social workers psychologists psychiatrists
     bills tuition slapping smack talk Disrespect
And she's still down."

"My Pinay is SO Bicolana Brown,
That one look
runs my females out of town
Raised me no fool and
Makes my Black Daddy look good
when they cruisin,
Taught me love only woman can give.
Momma's so down she still aroun
Even with the life I live."

Maya:
"my mama's so brown
she's inherited the bamboo skin
from my *lola*'s crown
perfected the art of weavin untold stories
through her eyes, she writes them down
and i read them every day
in my reflection tapestry
they will stay
tagalog/spanish/inchik/portugee
drawin line after line
i can't find the boundary
cuz the stories remain residual
like the sistas in my life be situational
leavin sentences fragmented and partial
like i am with my reflection
and between the lines that we speak
all i have are questions
like how it all ends and where did it begin
when i started to see my mama's stories
and my *lola*'s mama's soul within?
is she the reason why i am passive aggressive
is she the reason why i try to be 'progressive'

is she the reason why i draw boundaries in the sky
is she the reason why i can't look you in the eye?
is she the reason why i am closer to the brothas
is she the reason why i forget to say i love her?
in all the forms she come to me
with that same 'pinay pride' it's hard to be
collectin the molecules of love she brings to me
once in a blue moon she sings to me
like through these computer chips
outline my mind to my lips
i speak of her
my *lola*'s mama she never knew
but you know, from reading this
she looks a lot like you."

Darlene:
"Howzit,
sistahs,
My maddah,
she so
brown she
grew her own *toscani,*
and when she quit smokin'
we still had *talong, kalamungay* and *kamote!*"

'kay den
titas,
me kea
aloha,
Darlene

LBV:
"Hey, my momma's so brown
she putting 3 kids thru college
got Tatay on Direct Deposit
works 12-hour days
in a job that hardly pays
looking forward to those weekend *chismis* fests

where she brags that she's got the best
  lecheflan
        man
    smooth 'n' creamy and oh so sweet
beatin out auntie baby's *kuchinta* any day of the week!"

"Oy, my *inay's* THE Pinay
Cause if you break it down
you will have found
that the "p" in pinay
is only before "inay"
to denote
perfection, pure and PILIPINO...."

map:
"well, yo mama dis
'n' yo mama dat
but what they don't know
shuts up
the wisest-wise crack
'cause my mama
she is PINAY
yeah, she got it
all
like dat
carryin' the weight
of the world
on her back
so step of jack
fruit nimble 'n' quick
'cause she sip sip
da *balut*
without suckin' up
to da chick
'n' she bring home
da *baboy*
without sizin' up
to the dick

tearin' up
its *tenga*
wit' her verses
like it ain't
no trick
but an artform...
you've been forewarned
about this PINAY
callin' out all others
with her swing, boogie,
'n' cha cha
now what can you say 'bout
yo' mama?"

Em 2 / All:
"*Hoy! Talaga, talaga!*
Our mamas are so brown
They're the Presidents of their own
Pinay **MAFIA***—
*Mothers Against Filipino Ignorant Assholes."

A Poem/Tribute for Olivia Malabuyo on Her 22nd Birthday

Dawn Bohulano Mabalon

(Inspired by her poem, "83 Years," and written at the Philippines: Global and Local Perspectives Conference, UC Berkeley, May 2, 1998)

as I sit here and listen to debates
about Manuel Quezon's attitudes towards
Japanese invaders
the nature of American colonial government
and whether or not the Moros consider themselves Pinoy
with 50 other concerned scholars
 of P/Filipina/o studies
I think of you,
your *lola*'s red hat
and your question

I too wonder if
there is enough time
time for me to know and think
but also feel
to resist and struggle
but to also love
is there enough time
to just be?

this afternoon I thought of you
newly 22 (but with an aged soul)
I thought of you and your *lola*
laughing today over hot rice and fish
somewhere in South of Market
and of my own grandma
who bears burdens so unlike mine:
heart disease, diabetes, and disappointment

and as I sit here and theorize
about the meanings of slavery
in Filipino historiography
my own *lola*
whose struggles weigh so heavily upon her back
(though they say it's osteoporosis)
cries because I never come home
and as I live my comfortable city life
she slowly withers

each time I cross those yellow hills home to Stockton
I wonder if this will be the last time
I will taste her *torta*
her *kare kare*
or take her to bingo
she tells me she won't make it to the next Easter
I tell her she will never die

like most flips
i'm on time for being late
and wasted so much time
chasing other people's dreams
trying to be a *babaylan* warrior priestess
but I am no heroic pinay
can't lead no revolution
the *barrios* burning are inside my head
and my *lola*
only asks
that I take her to bingo
every once in a while

you asked if there's enough time
and I watch the clock tick
seconds, minutes, hours of my
confinement in a tower
I built myself
with a weary pen I write
of pinays long gone
and the history collected
in the dirt under my father's fingernails

and me, a historian
wishing I could destroy
those enemies: clocks, calendars, and age
we watch as history is buried with our ancestors

today I think of you
your *lola*'s red hat
and your question
and I pay tribute to your
22 years
and to your wisdom
which knows no age

Some Women

Bunny Ty

some women color their lips red.
not me, i like to color mine with good words instead.

some women curl their lashes hard.
not me, i want mine soft to catch my tears.

some women need to blush their cheeks pink.
not me, mine blush by themselves when i'm tickled pink.

some women close their eyes to show off their eye shadow.
not me, i want mine open to see the world.

some women take pains to pretty up their faces.
not me, i would rather take pains in prettying up the world.

some women think i look plain and dull without color on my face.
not me, if you look hard enough, you'll see I am wearing a rainbow.

Pinay Pioneers

Holly A. Calica

I have always wanted to be
as strong

A light to those old farmers
staring as you passed
the only Pinay for 200 miles

What a wonder you were
so pure, walking with your head held high
through the dusty fields of every valley from California
to Washington

So lonely were they
but happy to find food
a warm room, a good story in your home

They looked for love
in the blondies of the dance hall
Rare was he who found it

Even now the *manongs* sit silently
reliving the rink-tink rhythms
of you dancing with them before the watchful eyes
of your husband

but you never gave them more than a thought
they didn't know that you longed
for a woman to hold your hand

as you walked down the street
that you were almost, though no one knew it
as lonely as they were

Section II Landscapes

Going Home to a Landscape

Shirley Ancheta

My cousin Orlino shows me the Big Island
for the first time.

At Kapulena, we stop at our uncle's house.
We tell him the names I am from
Until the old man remembers
and nods at my grandmother's name.

I want to tell him we've forgotten
the oyster mushrooms I brought from the Mainland
but I've forgotten how to say it in Ilocano.
My island pidgin is even worse
so my uncle doesn't understand
what it is I'm trying to say.

All the way to the Kona side
my cousin and I try to name the mushroom
that grows wild on certain trees
after a good rain
but we are far away from remembering
and turn instead to a Hawaiian *mele*
on the radio and sing together
the words that tell of the mountain
that towers to our left,
this place that rose up from the sea.

Between Waimea and Waikoloa he says, *"O'ong."*
"O'ong," he laughs because he's known it all his life.
In this world I know
the smell of burlap sacks
the sound of rain and my father's voice
near a river years before
harvesting mushrooms
in a place far away

    from this light fading on the slope of Mauna Kea.

Chinatown, Moon Festival

Luisa A. Igloria

The streets branch
like narrow harbors.
During flood-time,
the waters rise here,
the color of dry crusts,
old amber, verdigris.

We tell ourselves we have come
in search of curly tree-fungi, seared
eggplants, bamboo shoots—a different
way to return vividness to the jaded
mouth. And, because it is the moon's
festival, we will return bearing
tins of cakes heavy with lotus
seed paste, a thin oil
oozing from the yellow of ducks
eggs, their gilded secret.

In the drugstore down the way,
vegetal roots and animal horns
lie peaceably curled in their liquid
solutions. A wave of scent
washes over me—ginseng, hawthorn
root, dark plum, licorice stems.

I breathe it all in, and, breathing, walk
over the little footbridge with torn
paper lanterns, over the creek
with its layers of scum
and human refuse.

Later, one evening, I will lift
the last sliver of cake from its box
and my insides will bruise
from a sweetness mingled of all
these forsaken colors. The tongue
will withdraw a little, anticipating
release and remembrance, what it knows
of experience passing away with such
indifference.

The simplest acts, also the most
extravagant: what we take
into our bodies, the small
gestures of ordinary life—
that knocking at the door of a deeper
hunger; how, after we have entered the foyer,
we want to know what it is that shines
so warmly from behind
the other closed doors.

April in Stockton

Dawn Bohulano Mabalon

april is the month of asparagus
of old uncles with bent backs and tired eyes
of hot sun on my back and shoulders

in april
my father greets the sun
and stays in the fields long after sunset
in dirty flannel and worn Dickies
for more than forty years he has cut and packed
a detestable vegetable
white people love to eat

april is the month of salmon head
and tomatoes and onions and hot rice
Easter Sunday
new clothes
kneeling to pray
in ghetto churches

after Mass
the old Pinoys shuffle home alone
and I ride my bike down Charter Way
past narrow streets
Little Manila's
abandoned storefronts
Flip and Chicano lowriders
yellow and green houses
banana trees, rosebushes
iron-barred screen doors and barking dogs

tatay says it's all the same
nothing new here, he says
april is the month of asparagus

and when am I coming home?

Mang Tomas

Victoria Sales Gomez

Tomas Padua comes to the ICU on a gurney from the Emergency Room one night, neck and shoulders tense with every breath, ribs marking his chest like waves in a pond, nostrils opening wide then closing like the gills of a fish out of water, what they call respiratory distress. Caridad and Nita move his frail body onto the bed by pulling on the edges of the bottom sheet and are immediately over him, brown arms like the tentacles of an octopus in a tangle of chest leads, cables, and plastic tubings. In the SF General Intensive Care Unit the graveyard shift is all Filipino.

"Welcome to Manila General," laughs Nita as she punches keys on the monitor that displays Tomas' heartbeat tracings. "How long have you been short of breath, Manong?"

"*Ewan ko*...lately I cough at work...so I always have to stop making beds...or whatever else I'm doing," Tomas says between gasps, his voice muffled by an oxygen mask.

"Any chest pain? Palpitations?" asks Nita, pounding her chest with her fist like an act of contrition.

"It hurts all the time...I have to lean against the wall...to catch my breath..."

"Do you have any family?" asks the other nurse, Caridad.

"No. They're all in the Philippines...my cousin who lives here in America for many years now...he got me this job at a hotel downtown."

"Then who should we notify in case of an emergency?" asks Caridad.

"*Hindi bale na*. There is no use. I haven't seen my wife in many years."

Caridad knows she won't get any answers from Mang Tomas, which reminds her of when her father left home years ago in the Philippines, before she became a nurse. She searched for him all over Manila, riding jeepneys and buses in the dust and sticky heat. "Certain things cannot be forgiven" was the only answer she could get that afternoon she found him in an office building in Ermita. She had reached over piles of papers at his desk and wrapped her arms around his neck, staining his shirt with tears and mascara. He was the same father who called her funny names like *ting-ting* and played with her as if she were a boy, before he and her mother stopped speaking to each other. He had still smelled like pomade and cigarettes, but he was like a stranger, stone cold.

As days go by, Mang Tomas does not improve; he becomes increasingly dependent on the different intravenous drips that maintains blood pressure and heart tone. A corrugated plastic tube coming out of his mouth connects his lungs to a respirator. Caridad threads a thin catheter into the breathing tube and aspirates frothy secretions, tinted with blood. Tomas gurgles and sputters in a spasm, but surrenders with a raising of eyebrows, as if to say, "*Sige na*, let it be."

Caridad pulls Tomas up in bed and turns him like a log. A small and thin woman, she has a surprising strength. Her age can only be guessed by a few strands of gray on her dark hair, pulled back into a ponytail, not a hair out of place. She puts a stethoscope in her ears and places the drum lightly on different spots on Tomas' back.

"His lungs are turning into mush," says Caridad to Nita as she pulls the stethoscope from her ears. "They sound like rice crispies. I bet he's had this cancer for a while."

Tomas often raises his hand and inserts a thumb between his fingers to signal "pain shot." Morphine must feel like a giant tub of cold water from heaven, putting out the fire that spreads from the center of his chest to his ribs, Caridad thinks. But after a while Tomas cannot make any more gestures. He slowly falls into a deep sleep and becomes another faceless collection of vital signs and heart rhythms, a body cloaked in the mild fetid odor of those who begin to decompose in life.

"*Alam mo*, Doctor Rosenthal, the head of Ethics Committee was here today," says Nita to Caridad one evening over dinner break in the nurses' lounge, sipping coffee from a Styrofoam cup. "They say Mang Tomas' cancer is so advanced they're going to take him off the vent. I guess no family ever showed up."

"How about his cousin, the one who got him a job? Did they get a hold of him?" asks Caridad. She pulls a Tupperware of leftover *kare-kare* and rice from the microwave oven and slams the door shut. "Have some," she says to Nita, whose mouth has started to water at the smell of oxtail and garlic.

"Yes, but he doesn't want to make any decisions for Manong. He says, *Bahala na sa Diyos*, it's up to God. Besides, Mang Tomas is undocumented. I bet they think it's costing the hospital a lot of money," says Nita.

Later in the evening, the last of the visitors has already left. The nurses sit at the central station, scribbling notes on charts, occasionally glancing at the patients' cardiac tracings on the big screen. Heavy footsteps suddenly thud on the linoleum floor.

"O.K., Jim, let's extubate!" says Dr. Rosenthal to Dr. Watkins, the lung specialist. Dr. Rosenthal is short and elderly but has the sure steps of a man of authority. He looks at the board where patients' names are written in black marker pen beside their bed numbers, and glances over the rim of his glasses at the name Padua beside bed number three. Dread overcomes Caridad like the heat rising from her chest to her neck and ears. But years of nursing training, of postponing weariness and bladder relief when situations demanded, keep her nailed to her chair while she regroups and devises the next strategy.

Dr. Watkins, his graying blond hair carefully in place, his discreet scent refreshing the odors of human waste, approaches Mang Tomas. He removes his coat from his lanky frame and hangs it by a chair. Guided by the report in the chart that the patient is comatose, they don't bother to tell Tomas what they are going to do. Just as Dr. Watkins begins to fold his sleeves over pale and hairy arms, Caridad springs from her chair and darts around for the last bag of morphine. She screams in her head, "*Putang ina!* Son of a bitch!" Dr. Watkins begins to remove the tape that secures the breathing tube to Tomas' mouth, pulling one strip at a time. Caridad inserts the tip of the intravenous tubing into the bag, hangs it by a pole, and opens the drip chamber, the miracle fluid flowing freely into Tomas' veins. As the doctor pulls the tube out, Tomas coughs into a spasm one last time, his skin turning from a rich brown to a deep purple, eyes wide open, fixed on Caridad, eyebrows raised as if questioning.

"*Huwag*, Tatay!" Caridad says to Mang Tomas, imagining instead her own father across the ocean. But she cannot stop the doctors; she can only pull a rosary from under Mang Tomas' pillow and shove it into his hand. As Tomas takes one last breath before closing his eyes, the doctors stare at Caridad, puzzled, as she mumbles the "Our Father," choking back tears, the only ceremony other than the ripping of tape by carefully trimmed fingernails, as the cardiogram widens and then turns into a flat line.

At 2:00 in the morning, the patients who are not unconscious drift in morphine-induced bliss. The events of the evening drift across Caridad's mind like the patients' cardiac tracings on the screen. She hates losing her composure in front of doctors, but she couldn't help herself, she thought. When she and Nita were wrapping Mang Tomas' body in the plastic shroud, she remembered words her father had spoken that summer long ago: "Over the years I built walls around my mind so nothing could hurt me."

Nita breathes softly, her head on the desk; a few minutes of light sleep will be enough to keep her alert for her morning drive to the suburbs. Her legs begin to twitch slightly when her mind slips into a timeless dream of minutes that seem like months. She is back in the Philippines, digging roots in her mother's garden. Her father works alongside her in silence, in shorts and T-shirt, pounding the soil with his hoe.

At 2:05 the Intensive Care Unit is silent except for the faint clicks and dings of monitors and intravenous machines. For a moment, Caridad thinks she hears Mang Tomas' respirator, now clean and stored in a corner, hiss like a draft of wind, as if Tomas has just taken a deep breath.

Cartographer

Conchitina R. Cruz

You think I am all
mountain and valley,
your mouth
probing forests,
your tongue
climbing peaks.

I am small,
a landscape defined
by the space
within your arms.
Your palms
journey
and memorize me.

You are lost.
My terrain extends
to sky, spills
over the points
of constellations.
I tell you, take you
to stars
yet you choose
to wander.

You think
the only earth
is skin,
coloring me
with your kiss,
marking territory.

Kauai 1 and 2

Barbara J. Pulmano Reyes

KAUAI 1

Here
I am literally
In between
Two homes

Both of which
Consider me
An outsider

It is in this place
Where I have come
As a visitor
To an island
Populated by
The historically
Displaced
That the people
Tell me
I belong

KAUAI 2

An Ilocano bus driver
Mistakes us
For locals
Vacationing
From Honolulu

Our skin is
Naturally
As dark as his

My family
Is Ilocano too
I tell him
In English

He smiles
Forgives me
For not knowing
How to speak
My own
Native language

Homecoming
Reine Arcache Melvin

As the plane touched down at Manila's international airport, Jinky made the sign of the cross. The baby, who had hardly slept during the flight from New York, began to cry. Jinky slipped his head under her blouse and guided his lips to her nipple. It would be a few minutes before she realized she had no milk. Until then, the sucking would silence him.

All around her, passengers were clambering onto seats to unload suitcases and cardboard boxes from overhead compartments. Jinky decided to remain seated until everyone else had left. Being surrounded by Filipinos always made her feel conspicuous. She was too tall, for one thing. And not fashion-model tall. Almost six feet, big-boned, broad-shouldered—and white. It had been painful growing up like that in Manila.

When the cabin was empty, she tucked her son into his pouch and attached the straps around her waist and shoulders. She piled his stroller high with an assortment of hand carried luggage and enough baby supplies to last her through several weeks of volcano eruptions, coups d'etat, or hijackings. Then she edged her way down the aisle, trying to hide her body behind the baby and stroller.

She had not wanted to come home again, but there was no way out of this. Michael had always wanted to see where she grew up. He had told all his friends that his wife was Filipina. That was important for him. So she had let it be. Played the role of a foreign wife, different from his friends' wives. As long as no other Filipinos were around, she could pass as Filipina.

She had three weeks to prepare a home for him, to make him believe she really was from Manila. In the meantime, she waited. She leaned against a pillar in the luggage-claim area, surrounded by *balikbayans*. Dozens of suitcases and rope-tied cardboard boxes emerged from the ramp. She watched the couples around her—tiny Filipinas with their strapping American husbands, and the gaggle of babies in tow. *Mestizo* babies were almost always beautiful. She was sorry hers was not.

Epifanio de los Santos Avenue was a mess. Clogged with cars and ancient buses and hundreds of people spilling out onto the highway at each bus stop. Potholes everywhere. She remembered Makati when it was full of blank spaces, her childhood punctuated by empty lots with high grass and trees waiting to be climbed. Now the smoke from the cars in front of her filtered in through the taxi's air-conditioner, and she feared for her baby.

She reached into her bag for a bottle, then gently inserted the rubber nipple into his mouth. He began to suck, one side of his face buried against her, one blue eye staring calmly up at her.

She had wanted only to breastfeed. As if the act of giving milk, of feeling her child's mouth against her nipple, would bring Michael back to her. But every time she looked at her son, she saw the white skin and broad features of Michael, and it renewed her sense of loss.

She should have married a Filipino. She should have had a dozen children, each darker than the last, so that the whiteness of her skin would finally be washed away by the color of her children. That was the only way back to her country.

At a stoplight, beggar children scampered up to the car and pressed their palms against the window. Jinky checked the locks on the door.

"Which way, ma'am?" the driver asked.

Without thinking, she answered him in Tagalog.

He glanced at her in the rear-view mirror. "Where did you learn to speak our language, ma'am?" he asked her, in his best imitation of an American accent.

She hesitated. A little girl was staring sadly at Jinky's baby, her nose flattened against the pane.

"I grew up here," Jinky murmured.

A big golden-toothed grin. "*Kaya pala,*" the driver said. "And your parents are what? American?"

"Sort of," she said finally.

Another beggar came and pulled the little girl away.

She had spent years regretting the marriage that created her. Her father had stumbled upon the Philippines in the late sixties, looking for a drug scene more idyllic than the one in Goa. Instead he found Estella, a convent-bred heiress who lured him off drugs and into her family's shipping business. They were happy enough in the beginning, Estella often said. Then Jinky came along. While most Eurasians possessed a strange and unsettling beauty, Jinky had inherited the worst of both parents: Estella's nose, Hans Joachim's complexion and bulky frame. *Mestiza bangus,* her playmates called her: half-human, half milkfish. When the time came, Jinky was dispatched to university in New York. "At least she's bright," Estella sighed over mahjong.

Jinky learned about her parents' breakup over a dormitory pay phone. The details came through sporadically: Estella had wrested the house, Hans Joachim was keeping the golf club membership and stock options. The house in Forbes Park continued to run on its own energy for a few more years, the maids cleaning up after themselves, the drivers sitting in the garage next to cars that no longer ran. Then even that came to an end. The house sold, her mother moved—literally carried by the servants—to a small apartment on the fringes of Makati. No one visited her mother anymore, and the thought of that bitter woman in the shuttered room frightened Jinky into avoiding Manila.

She stayed away fourteen years. Enough time to find a husband, have a child, grow nostalgic for what she had left behind.

As the light turned green, Jinky thought she saw her father in the Mercedes in front of them. She craned her neck, wanting to be certain. It could not be him. He had assured her he would be away on a business trip, but you never knew about Hans Joachim. He had his own life now, and very little time for dabbling in his past.

The man in the car ahead turned to look out the window, and Jinky saw his profile. Too young to be her father. She thought of Michael, on his own in the streets of Bangkok. A Westerner in Asia was always vulnerable. There were the bars, the stage shows, the banana trick. And God help any white man who caught the eye of an Asian woman.

Jinky closed her eyes, trying to calm the constrictions in her chest. Michael would see her, for the first time, in her own country and realize that she was as much a misfit there as she was in New York. He had thought she was vaguely exotic, with her black hair and narrow eyes, but he would see how false that was once he arrived in Manila. Or he was already seeing how false that was, perhaps right now, in some squalid room in Bangkok, where a tiny brown body with small breasts and dark brown nipples was leaning over him.

The driver turned into a side street off Ayala Avenue and navigated the bumps to the condominium building where Jinky's father lived. Cement and concrete, glass doors, plants everywhere. A security guard helped her out of the car. She tipped the driver—too much, she knew—then unfolded the stroller and locked the baby into it. He was almost asleep, beginning his night after the restless trip. His fat, pale body seemed curiously vulnerable in the harsh sunlight. She was ashamed of him, as she had always been of her own body. She would never feel at ease in this land of narrow-hipped, golden-skinned women.

The security guard carried her luggage to the reception desk. The woman on duty was armed but polite.

"Can I help you, ma'am?"

"I'm Mr. Breuer's daughter," Jinky replied. "I'll be using his apartment while he's abroad."

The receptionist excused herself and entered the office. When she came back, she was smiling. "He left you the keys," she said, handing Jinky an envelope. "And there's another set for the *yaya*. She's waiting in the apartment. Do you want me to tell her to come down and help you with the luggage?"

Jinky nodded, relieved that her father had found a nanny for her visit. Beyond the glass walls of the lobby, coconut trees lined a green-tiled swimming pool. Jinky gently lifted her baby from the stroller and carried him out to the poolside. No one was around. She settled into a plastic chair under a thatched awning. High walls all around her, and beyond them, soaring blue and silver buildings. She held the baby closer to her, longing for the lush gardens and high-ceilinged rooms of her childhood.

"Miss Jinky?"

A pretty young woman, barely out of her teens, dressed in a short skirt and faded T-shirt. There was an evasiveness in the girl's eyes and a hardness in her mouth that distressed Jinky. She knew instantly that she could not trust her baby to this woman.

"I'm very sorry, ma'am," the girl whispered, staring at the ground. "The agency your father called, they couldn't find a *yaya* for only one month. So the secretary of your father, she asked me. I'm the cousin of her maid."

"No problem," Jinky said, forcing a smile. "What's your name?"

"Sol, ma'am." The girl reached for the baby.

Jinky held onto him. "It's okay," she said, wondering how she was going to find another nanny on such short notice. "I'll bring him upstairs myself."

After a moment, the girl said: "Your suitcases, ma'am?"

"Next to the desk. Could you ask the guard to help you bring them up?" Sol nodded, still avoiding Jinky's eyes. Head bent, she disappeared through the sliding doors.

The baby began to whimper, pressing his head against Jinky's blouse. No answering tightening in her breast. How long would it be before the milk dried up completely? She remembered the nights spent holding the baby against her, letting him suck, as much as he wanted, as often as he wanted, hoping the milk would flow. And Michael had been there beside her, urging her on. He hadn't wanted his son to be bottle-fed. He kept telling her that it was natural to breastfeed, that there was always enough milk, as long as the woman kept trying. She had kept trying, until her nipples bled. And still her baby screamed. She was ready to do anything to calm his cries, to gain a few hours of sleep.

A security guard, fully armed, was sitting on a high stool inside the elevator.

"Where are you going, ma'am?"

"Mr. Breuer's apartment."

He pressed the button for the twenty-seventh floor. She looked more closely at him. Tall and muscular, with the military bearing that had come into fashion during the numerous coups d'etat.

As the doors were about to close, a young man in cheap black pants and an ID pinned to his *barong* tried to enter the elevator. "You have to take the service elevator," the guard told him firmly. The man retreated, and the doors slid shut in front of him.

"He could have ridden with us," Jinky said. "I don't mind."

The guard turned slightly towards her, his face softening. "That's not the problem, ma'am," he said. "It's for your safety. You know how it is here." He patted the gun on his hip, then aimed an imaginary pistol at her. "Many of the people living here, they have bodyguards. We don't want any kind of shooting in the elevators. Especially, we don't want innocent people like you—and your baby, ma'am—getting caught in a shooting."

"Does that happen often?" Jinky said, more calmly than she felt. She remembered suddenly that the ex-dictator's wife lived in the building.

"Oh, no, ma'am. Maybe once a year. Not every year. We have very tight security. But that's why we ask the bodyguards and messengers and maids to take the service elevator."

Jinky leaned against the back wall, feeling the cold metal through her blouse.

When they arrived at the penthouse, the guard pressed the button to keep the door open. "You let me know if you need anything, ma'am. I'm Johnny."

"Yes, Johnny," she whispered, turning the vowels over in her mouth.

Jinky rang the doorbell, the keys in her pocket. Sol opened the door. Behind her was a sweeping view of Makati's skyscrapers, marred only by wicker furniture and bright batik prints.

Sol followed her into the spacious kitchen. "Do you want me to change the baby, ma'am?"

Jinky shook her head.

"Can I unpack your luggage, ma'am?" Sol asked hesitantly.

"No, thank you." Jinky took a deep breath. "Sol, my father was supposed to hire a *yaya* for the baby."

The girl was instantly defensive. "Yes, ma'am. I mean, his secretary tried to find someone else. And she did. But that woman, she never showed up. So what could we do, ma'am? Don't be angry at me. She asked me to come instead. I like babies very much, ma'am."

"It's okay," Jinky said, without conviction. She opened the kitchen cabinets. A few cans of imported olives and salted mixed nuts. In the drawer next to the sink, a pile of take-out menus.

"Are you sure, ma'am?"

"We'll see how it works out. But I'm sure it will be okay."

All these formulas, Jinky thought. Save face, let the other save face. Even if the other was a nervous young woman who would certainly drop her baby in the bath.

She didn't know what to do with Sol. The girl was hovering beside her, eager to be useful.

"We'll need food," Jinky said suddenly. "Can you go to the supermarket?"

Then Sol was gone, the baby asleep in the guest bedroom. Jinky watched the curve of his cheek against the sheets, then propped pillows on each side of him. His mouth continued to make a sucking movement.

She unzipped the side pocket of her suitcase and retrieved her address book. All the people to contact in Manila. How many were still there? She had crossed out so many names. And she was in no hurry to speak to Estella.

She tried to enter her father's bedroom. The door was locked. She inspected the other rooms in the apartment—two guest bedrooms, three bathrooms, a study. A shoebox-sized safe in the bottom drawer of his desk. She fidgeted with the numbers on the lock; she had read somewhere that most people selected birthdays as their combination. What would Hans Joachim have chosen? Not his birthday—that was too easy. She tried it anyway. Estella's? Not that, either. Jinky shut the drawer. Probably the birthday of his stockbroker.

She remembered rummaging through her mother's closets years before, when the marriage was beginning to unravel and Estella had dragged Hans Joachim to a Couples for Christ weekend. The nightgowns were pretty—satin and silk sets that her mother had bought during her monthly shopping trips to Hong Kong. And the clothes, of course, were impeccable—suits from Chanel and Dior and evening dresses from local couturiers. Dozens of imported bags and matching shoes were arranged by color in another closet. But the underwear was a disappointment. White synthetic bras and pastel-colored polyester panties that must have reached up to Estella's waist. Jinky had been ashamed for her mother, and for herself. She thought of the huge bed her parents shared, each stretched out on opposite sides, so that at least four adults could lie down in the space between them. Her father with his stack of detective novels by his bedside, her mother with a mini-shrine under her lamp—a wooden bust of the Virgin with a rosary strung around it, framed images of various saints, and tiny pamphlets of her latest novenas.

No wonder Hans Joachim had strayed. And strayed repeatedly.

She wondered what Michael was doing now. On a tricycle in some narrow alley, his body too large and white for these Asian travels. What women were surrounding him? She imagined them tiny and slender and beautiful, with long black hair and slits up their dresses.

Again the regret that she was not exotic, not Asian, not different enough to keep him with her.

She walked barefoot around the apartment. So little trace of her father. Had he bought it furnished from some other German cutting his losses before moving out?

Why had they bothered to have her?

All those years in school, cramming her head with facts and figures, when all it came down to was an image she could look at—or not—in the mirror.

Mestiza bangus.

Jinky the fish.

Jinky the whale.

And now the whale had a baby.

She slid open the glass doors and stepped into the terrace. A barrage of horns and screeching wheels from Ayala Avenue. Air-conditioning—in the taxi, then in the apartment—had insulated her. But here there was no protection. She leaned over, inhaling. How the city smelled. And that noise. And the black smoke shooting like snakes from the backs of speeding buses.

How was she going to aestheticize this for Michael?

Suddenly she realized that she could not hear the baby cry from the terrace. She stuck her head back in. Only the whir of the air-conditioner.

Outside again, she wondered how she would ever manage to cross Ayala. To get to the other side, where the malls and restaurants and hotels were, she would have to join the crowds outside the building and walk—or run—across the avenue. In all her years in Manila, she had never crossed Ayala on foot. None of her friends had, either. A chauffeured car had always taken her everywhere, dropping her off at a cinema, then picking her up at the designated time to take her to a restaurant across the street. Now she would have to go down to the lobby and find a way to cross Makati's principal artery—without anyone noticing her. That was impossible. Once she left the condominium building, people would stare.

It didn't matter. She didn't have to leave the apartment just yet. Sol could do her errands. And there was no need to see anyone until Michael arrived.

Now she was certain. The baby was crying. Above the din of the traffic. Jinky rushed inside, not bothering to close the glass doors behind her. As she entered the bedroom, she saw Sol kneeling by the bed, barefoot, her legs short but well-shaped. The girl picked up the baby and cradled him to her breast, rocking him and singing—she looked like a twelve year old playing with a doll. Jinky observed her quietly from the doorway. The baby calmed down and reached out for Sol's face. His fingers rested briefly on the mole under the girl's eye.

Jinky walked briskly into the room and took the baby away. "Could you prepare some lunch, Sol? The carrots and *calabasa* I told you to buy? You can chop them and boil them."

The girl nodded eagerly, her dark gaze fixed on Jinky's lips. Jinky wondered if she knew how pretty she was. Those big eyes and thick lashes, tiny nose and sensual lips. The kind of face Westerners raved about.

Jinky smiled at the young girl, who was still watching her lips. "You can go now," she said.

She watched the line of Sol's body as she left the room—the short skirt, the fake Tommy Hilfiger T-shirt that outlined her breasts. I'll have to get her a uniform, Jinky thought. Some navy blue outfit with a frilly white apron, like those worn by the maids in her house before her mother stopped caring.

Eventually the food was prepared, the baby fed and lulled to sleep on the bed. Sol sat on the floor next to him, her head tilted, cheek on knees, long black hair falling over her calves. Jinky could not bear to look at her.

Time to cross Ayala, she told herself.

Then the elevator again, and Johnny. "Good afternoon, ma'am. Where's the baby, ma'am?"

"Sleeping," she said, glancing at his wide, eager face. To her dismay, she felt herself flushing.

"And where's your husband, ma'am?"

Jinky was taken aback. She had forgotten how direct Filipinos could be. "He'll be here soon. He's traveling."

"On business, ma'am?"

"Yes, on business." No need to tell him about the naked girls in Bangkok. She had a hard time remembering Michael's face—a vague recollection of his chest, his skin. Remember this, she admonished herself: He loved you. Or at least wanted you.

Who else had?

She leaned slightly towards Johnny. She sensed his body, all muscle, underneath that uniform. She wanted to hear him talk again, to feel the soft rhythms of his voice under her skirt and blouse.

"I wanted to ask you," she began.

He stared into her eyes, as innocently and artlessly as Sol. He wasn't aware of what she felt, then. Suddenly she imagined what he must be seeing when he looked at her. No Filipino had ever found her attractive.

"Ma'am?"

"Nothing," she snapped, taking a step backwards, marking the boundary between them. He understood immediately, drew himself up and stared straight ahead.

She counted the diminishing numbers on the panel over the elevator doors. Why couldn't she have resembled her mother? Why did she have to have a Filipino soul in her father's body? It would have been bearable if she were a man. Tall, broad-shouldered, muscular. But not like this. Even Johnny didn't see her as a woman.

The doors opened. She could not walk out. Could not cross Ayala, could not bear the staring faces. Not just yet.

"I forgot something in the apartment," she murmured, not looking at him.

His silence accompanied her back to the twenty-seventh floor.

As she entered her father's apartment, she told herself, I have to get out of here.

She glanced at the living room mirror. Suddenly she lifted her skirt and stood sideways, watching her stomach in the glass. Almost flat, no stretchmarks. She unbuttoned her blouse and lifted her breasts out of their cups. They didn't look bad. She wondered if there was something wrong with the mirror.

She lifted her head, listening. No sound from the bedroom. She hurriedly slipped her clothes back on. Suddenly she was terrified. And if something had happened to the baby while she was out? Sol could not be trusted—she was a child, a frightened child.

Jinky rushed into the room. Her baby in Sol's arms, the young woman's brown breast exposed, a dark nipple in her baby's mouth.

Sol gave a small cry when she saw Jinky. She tugged her blouse over the baby's face. "Ma'am, ma'am, I'm sorry, ma'am."

Jinky felt her heart pounding. A slow, silent tightening in her throat, a rabbit running blindly towards the headlights.

"Ma'am, he was crying so much."

Jinky tried to speak. No words.

Sol looked up at her, her eyes bright.

"He was hungry, ma'am. I didn't know where you kept the milk."

A massive effort. What would Estella have done?

"No problem," Jinky said, trying not to stare at the young girl's small, perfect breast. She wanted to cry. The milk was dripping, staining both sides of Sol's blouse.

Jinky reached for her baby, wiped the drops of milk from the corners of his mouth. She sat on the bed. Sol turned away and quickly buttoned up her blouse.

After a moment, Jinky asked gently, "You have a baby?"

"Yes, ma'am. Two."

Her son's eyes, watching her.

"How old are they?"

"One is three years old."

"And the other?"

Sol didn't answer.

"The other?"

"Two weeks old, ma'am."

A long silence.

"The same father?" Jinky said, surprised at her question.

"No, ma'am. I'm not married."

The baby strained his body forward, eyes closed, lips searching a nipple. Jinky could not bring him to her breast.

"Take him," she said, thrusting her son into the girl's arms. Sol pressed her finger over his lips, and Jinky strode out of the room.

Half an hour later, Sol tiptoed into the kitchen. "You should go home to your baby," Jinky said, emptying a cup of tea into the sink. "You really shouldn't be working yet."

The girl's eyes filled with tears, her body taut, as if she were going to run away, into the bushes, away from the relentless glare of the headlights.

"Give me a chance, Miss Jinky. I promise. I won't do it again."

"It's for your own sake. Your baby needs you."

"I'll prepare the bottles for the next time. Where do you keep the bottles, ma'am?"

"I don't use bottles," Jinky said angrily. "I give him my own milk."

The girl looked confused, pretty and soft. Jinky imagined men gazing at her from benches in front of their shanties, desiring her, sweet-talking her into their beds. And simple, beautiful Sol would have other children with other men, never really knowing what had happened.

"Does the baby's father help you?"

"Ma'am?"

"The baby's father. Do you see him?"

"Oh, no, ma'am. I don't know where he is. It only happened once."

Jinky removed a few five hundred-peso bills from her handbag—easily the equivalent of a month's salary for a *yaya*. She pressed them into the girl's hand.

"No, ma'am." Sol tried to give them back to her.

"It's for the baby. Not for you. A present."

The girl's fingers tightened over the bills.

"And you promise you'll take care of your baby? Not try to look for work for at least a month?"

The girl nodded.

She'll be on the streets tomorrow, Jinky thought—and then the snake lifted its head—but at least she'll be gone when Michael gets here.

Sol stood silently, head lowered.

"Go now," Jinky whispered, then impulsively embraced her. The girl's shoulders were fragile under her hands, the black hair fragrant. Jinky lowered her head and slid her lips lightly across that hair.

The girl hugged her. "Thank you, ma'am."

Sol looked up. Jinky was taken aback by the coolness in her eyes.

"You'll be okay, ma'am?" the girl said, with a perfunctory smile.

And then she was gone, and Jinky returned to the air-conditioned bedroom. She carefully removed her clothes and stretched out beside the sleeping baby. Her hands ran over her body, as if it belonged to someone else. The strangeness of that flesh, slightly goose-pimpled in the cold room. How much warmer Sol's body had been, how much softer. Her baby had been happy with Sol in his mouth.

Time to sleep now, Jinky told herself. There was much to do. Before the week was over, she would have to cross Ayala. Find a travel agent to change her ticket. Flee this country, take her baby with her and return to New York. Let Michael deal with it when he arrived in Manila. He could follow her, or he could stay on.

And Johnny? Did she dare invite him in, make one last attempt? The mirror in the living room had been kind. He could watch her image there. Only one night, Sol had told her. And the timing was right. She would take her chances and then run away. And if she had another baby, it would be a girl this time, a real Filipina, with a face like Johnny's. And people would stare at her wherever she went, because she would be tiny and beautiful and not too bright, with a perfect body and long black hair and a mole under her eye, and she would have small breasts spouting milk, whenever she wanted, wherever she wanted.

Jinky rolled to her side. She guided the tip of her nipple into her baby's mouth and tapped gently on his cheek. He began to suck in his sleep, erratically at first and then more steadily, his tiny fingers curled against her breast. She cupped the back of his head, holding him to her, protecting him from noise and light and her own stirrings, adjusting the rhythms of her breathing to his. For an instant, just before sleep, she was happy to be home.

We Go Back to Manila in 1999

Angela Narciso Torres

What will my children remember
of the shape of that year? Perhaps
the city skyline, swathed in blue
smog, a plane landing at daybreak,

arms reaching to encircle their small,
flight-weary bodies as they melted
into the waiting crowd. But those
were fleeting glimpses, through eyes

still fogged with sleep. More likely
the sticky heat and stench of fumes,
a van weaving through early traffic
to the village that housed their mother's

memories, verdant still, a jungle-green
deeper than California's silver-sage.
Most certainly the tile-roof house, where
they learned to call their grandparents

Lolo and Lola, learned to say *ulan* for rain;
rain filling potholes and gushing in gutters,
drumming on the low eaves, on windows
slammed shut to monsoon winds. Breakfast

of sweet sausage and rice, the clatter of pans
begun long before morning's hushed light,
punctuated by the calls of a bread vendor
peddling hot *pan de sal* on a bicycle.

Come Sunday—Mass, lunch, and
cousins, all honey-brown, coal-black eyes
shining with a primal fire they recognized;
a pilot flame igniting the ring of kinship,

amber like lamp-lit panes glazed with rain.
Older ones leading, they roamed the dark
rooms like a pack of young wolves—
rummaging through cupboards and drawers,

prowling the backyard rubble to unearth
the stories from which they grew. In years
ahead, lulled by an electric fan's whirr,
their dreams will be peppered with strange

names of fruit—*guava, caimito, siniguelas.*
The sudden sound of rain will rouse what's left
of distant, half-remembered trees: the heft
of rough branches, their slippery embrace.

Odysseus Cripple at Bantayan Island

Merlie M. Alunan

The light, the light here how pitiless
it burns from the vast skies at noon.
All day the heated wind
presses its salt kiss on the skin.
Bantayan Island, not such a way
from home, West of Leyte where I come.
Straggler though I am, this isle still
is my own—the starveling dogs, the armies
of sandcrabs guarding their holes,
the children too, brown and thin
with sunburnished hair, lilting seasounds
in their speeches, my bittersweet familiars.
Not that one—white and blue-eyed traveler
hefting himself by his two good arms
on crutches of steel, dragging his body
on shriveled legs inch by careful inch,
Odysseus cripple, wandered from his own
ice-locked continent to this atoll
east north west south of nowhere.

He squints past the breakers
to the rims of farther shores,
his bald pate with its blond fringe
glistening in the cruel noon glare.
Dense on that very chair, on borrowed space,
he sits in a cripple's infinity of patience,
speaking to no one, and thus
not a word spoken to him in return.
Children gape at his odd gait
as he makes his way slowly, painfully,
under the shadow of the palm trees
meeting nobody's eyes.

What's to gain by asking his name,
whence he came, why he's here?
Inquire by dint of what resolve
he'd vanquished space for these shoals?
When he leaves (obliged, who knows,
by some splendid Nordic design
that he alone may satisfy), anyone could see
it'd be a simple matter for wind
to blow sand over his tracks.
The sandcrabs scamper to their burrows
in their perpetual habit of reticence
as he draws by, but they'd be back
to resume their sovereign claims in a while.

Stranger too, I will pass on as he does,
never perhaps to return. Still, after us,
over this island at nowhere's end,
this light, this constant peerless light,
would pour down merciless and blinding
from the vast and eyeless sky.

Cicada Song

Alma Jill Dizon

HONOLULU, 1982

Tim was already lounging in front of the TV, wearing her short kimono, when Mel got up and went into the kitchen to find some food. The rest of her family had already left for work and school. Still a little deaf from the Waikiki nightclub where she worked with Tim, she felt like a bat, sensing the vibrations of late morning instead of hearing sounds. Her hair smelled thickly of cigarette smoke, and she sang "Thriller" to herself as she opened the refrigerator door, even though she was sick of the song. But these were minor irritations to her, like the one business course she took every semester at the community college, in the hope that she might eventually move up to manager. Someday, she told herself, if she and the man of her life worked hard enough, they might be able to get a small condo with parking.

When she looked in the refrigerator, Mel decided that they were going to have a good day. One of her nephews attended a school that had just had a *huli huli* chicken fund-raiser, and there were two barbecued halves lying on a shelf. She slid each half onto a plate and had begun rinsing some raw rice when she heard a car pull up in the driveway to drop someone off. She shut off the tap and walked into the living room in time to see her mother swing open the front door.

Marina Tanod stared at Tim, one hand over her heart while she leaned back against the door. Tim stared back, one hand clutching a cushion over his unmentionables.

"Tim," Mrs. Tanod said, "where is Imelda?"

"I'm right here, Mom," Mel said too loudly from the doorway. For the past year, she'd told herself that her parents would eventually find out about Tim's visits, but she hadn't planned it out. At least, she told herself, they wouldn't have to listen any more for her parents' a cappella snores, amplified by the master bath between their bedroom and hers.

Tim looked from one to the other and flashed a disarming smile. He shook some hair out of his eyes and said, "I'll go get dressed." Then he hurried past Mel, still clutching his cushion.

Mrs. Tanod sank into an easy chair and shut her eyes. She was unusually pale, and beads of sweat clung to her brow and upper lip. Her heavy eye makeup had run a little, making her look monstrous.

"Mom, are you OK?" Mel asked, worried and irritated at the same time.

"I had to leave the school," her mother responded. "Another secretary and I are in the middle of teaching the graduation hula, but I feel like an elephant is standing on my chest."

Mel frowned. "The last time we took you to the hospital, they said nothing was wrong with you."

"The doctor cannot see that my children are killing me," Mrs. Tanod announced dramatically.

"Stop putting us down. We all help pay the mortgage. What's killing you is that you're fat," Mel said, exasperated. "Why don't you use that exercise bicycle we got you for Christmas?"

"I can't believe you speak to me this way. I would never have spoken to my mother like that."

"You talked plenty bad to Grandpa all the time." As always in her mother's presence, her English seesawed between standard and pidgin. Marina Tanod, née Rungsot, had been valedictorian in one of the English standard schools, and even though none of her offspring had finished college, they could all speak like her when necessary.

Mrs. Tanod chose to ignore Mel's last comment. She opened her eyes and stared at her daughter. "Are you going to marry Tim?"

"I don't know. I guess so."

"What kind of an answer is that?"

"It means that I don't know." She wondered why everyone, even her friends at the beach last week, had to ask her this question. At twenty-eight, she'd had a ring picked out for six years already, but she didn't want to end up in another unit of the extended family compound.

"You are utterly shameless and ungrateful," her mother moaned. "Who would think that children would cause such pain? But then if we knew ahead of time, no one would have children, and there would be no more people."

"I don't think so," Mel said sarcastically. "People like doing it too much."

Her mother raised an eyebrow and said, "Don't think that I don't know that." She snapped open her purse and took out a tissue. As she dabbed at her face, she asked, "So what is Tim anyway? He looks *hapa*."

"He's *hapa haole* and Chinese Hawaiian."

Her mother sighed. "That explains those lovely dark eyes. Well, could be worse. He could've been just *haole* trash."

"I don't get it, Mom. If he was just *haole* or just Chinese or Hawaiian, he wouldn't be good enough, yeah? That's the way you are, you talk stink about everybody, but then you see somebody who's got a bit of everything, and it's not as bad."

"I've never said anything like that," Mrs. Tanod answered. *"Hapa haole* kids are better looking, but they're not necessarily better than what they came from."

"So, do you want me to marry him and have some cute kids?"

"No, we don't have the space."

"I wouldn't stay here," Mel said angrily. "We'd live with his mom in Nuuanu. They have a beautiful old house with lots of room, and it's much safer."

"Why aren't you two sleeping there then?"

Startled, Mel didn't know what to say. She went to Tim's place occasionally for dinner, but they always ended up back in her bedroom surrounded by her stuffed animals.

Satisfied with her daughter's silence, Mrs. Tanod hoisted herself back to her feet. She smoothed her short hair, which was dyed and sprayed until it shone like black lacquer. "I'm going to lie down for a while," she declared. "Bring me a glass of juice."

Mel went back to the pot of rice in the sink, fuming over how their conversations inevitably ended with her feeling like a teenager. One of her uncles had let it drop that her mother had abandoned her studies in New York to become a hula dancer in a swank hotel, far from the chaperones at school dances and from work at the pineapple cannery. But Mel found that hard to believe. Even if she had lived a dissolute youth, Marina Rungsot had returned home not only forgiven but even proud and on the arm of Barney Tanod, a local boy with a chest draped in medals after his service in Europe. The Tanods had gone on to produce hard-working children who were now raising grandchildren in various apartments all clustered around a garden and a statue of the Virgin. Except for Mel, of course, who wanted and wanted but remained strangely ambivalent.

∽

NEW YORK CITY, 1948
Mel and the other children who have yet to make their entrance into Marina's life will never understand how Marina Tanod loves to dance.

What Marina loves most about dancing is the complete movement of her body. She has never been able to decide if the music throbs through her limbs and hips or if she, through its notes and beats. The music is silly and twangy. Mostly in English with the chorus in Hawaiian, the lyrics give her hands almost no story to tell. This is safe music, the kind that kept hula alive after the missionaries failed to outlaw it. Yet even while her fingers have to take poetic license with the words to give them a shimmering quality, the back and forth swing of her hips acts out an ever-present base. They took away the pagan chants, but the sway is still there in the "Cock-eyed Mayor of Kaunakakai."

The musicians and dancers are an odd lot from Hawaii who have found and cling to each other in Manhattan. The city is vast and busy with banks that stay open all night. There are so many people, endless waves of little faces that wash through the avenues like fish looking for safe holes in a coral reef. There is a breathless, frenzied joy in the young people who are trying to amuse themselves after five war years of trying to be serious. Women have stopped wearing military-style suits and are buying clothes with curves. For the group from Hawaii, there is the added freedom from gas masks and martial law. And for Marina in particular, her apartment on the upper West Side is filled with an enchanting and liberating air even though it's the size of a drunk tank. There is no line of ever smaller brothers and sisters, demanding food and clean laundry from her. At night, she pulls a sheet across a clothes line to shut the bedroom off from the living room where her roommate sleeps, so that she and her lover can have some privacy.

Stuart is a GI back from the Pacific where he got in the habit of seeing dark people, and he tells her that she is most beautiful when wrapped in a sheet on a chilly spring morning. He prefers even her raffia hula skirt to her street clothes. On Sundays, they lie in bed all day, and he tells her how funny the pale-faces look with their blue veins and blemishes glowing in their skin. She rubs the scruffy beard that darkens his very white skin and can't imagine that he was once as tanned as he claims. He is fairer than the *haole* boy she had lunch with once in Honolulu, the one for whom her father beat her with a belt.

Stuart is a waiter whose impeccably starched collar belies the time he spent unshaven and crawling up beaches while under fire. He makes jokes about the "monkey suit" he has to wear with white gloves. There are late afternoons when over bright red spareribs and chow fun, he talks about a new twist to add to his jitterbug.

She asked him once what it was like to kill someone, and he refused to talk about it. He is younger than her and has many plans for the future. Next fall, he says, he will start classes at N.Y.U., and he doesn't plan to stop for about seven years until he has a law degree. Marina can't think that far into the future. She wasn't able to imagine that much time some six and a half years ago when she saw the dogfighting above Pearl Harbor, and now she doesn't want to picture herself in her mid-thirties, still waiting for her music to start.

It is late in June when Marina finally tells Stuart that she has missed two periods. They have been as careful as possible, but now that they know it's pointless, they make love with abandon. Her moods flow quickly from exhilaration to anxiety to bleak hopelessness and then back again. She hasn't written home about any of it. Her parents think she has completed her first year of graduate school. When she cries, he holds her on his lap and tells her that he will provide for the three of them. Old laws are being overturned; in some places they can even marry, although in others they still can't live together. They will have to choose well when they look for a home, so that Stu will be able to find clients in spite of having mixed children. But he says that the laws are going to keep changing, and one day she will be able to go with him wherever he goes. He assures her that he's a mutt anyway—Scottish, French, and a touch of Algonquin on his mother's side, he whispers conspiratorially. She takes the part about the Indian blood seriously. Only later will she realize that she can't know when to believe him.

On the drive up to his parents' summer house on the Connecticut coast, she makes him pull off the main road, and they find a hidden spot to lie down in some tall grass even while he warns ominously about deer ticks.

Afterwards, they lie still, pulling their damp clothes loose from their skin to let in a little humid air. The sky is hazy, and as Marina lifts herself up on an elbow to look for her compact in her handbag, she finally notices a buzzing that she didn't hear with her face in Stuart's chest. The sound is like an electric throbbing in the air that rises and falls in uneven pulses. She looks about the field towards the line of woods but sees no poles.

"Stu, what's that noise? A power line?" she asks him.

"No, city girl," he murmurs back drowsily. "Those are cicadas."

"I'm not a city girl. I'm a Hawaii girl," she corrects him. Then, "Cicada," she says slowly, trying to spell the word in her head. "I think I've seen the word in books, but I never knew how to pronounce it. Are they crickets?"

"No, something else. They're ugly, like big flies," he says. "But in a way, they're very romantic. Some of them hibernate for seventeen years, and then they wake up for one summer of singing and love-making before they die."

"Like us."

"Not at all. We raise our kids," he smiles and stretches lazily. "Look at you," he lifts one of her wrists admiringly. "You're already getting browner."

As they turn down a series of smaller roads and creep closer towards the Long Island Sound, Stuart describes his parents' beach house. They won't be able to sleep together, and the floorboards creak too much for him to sneak into her room. But he assures her that she won't want to spend much time in bed. The bedrooms are tiny and cramped, stuffed with mismatched cast-off furniture from their other house. After all, the whole idea of a summer place was to spend as much time as possible outdoors. The little cove that lies a stone's throw from the porch would not be like Waikiki Beach, but he promises her that she will appreciate it after a winter in New York.

They round a bend, and Marina sees the water at last. The sound is a deep blue-gray, and, through the haze, she can make out a faintly deeper line of gray that is Long Island on the other side. Near the shore, there are islets, each one barely large enough to hold the house that summer residents have built on them.

Stuart pulls into a gravel drive and parks the borrowed Chevrolet beside a small, white house with a screened porch. Planted around the side of the house are bushes with pale pink and lavender flowers in clusters. Over the pulsating of the cicadas, Marina hears another layer of sound—the giggling and squealing of the neighbors' children as they play with a dog across the street. But as she gets out to help Stuart lift their bags out of the back, the game stops, and all she can hear is the insistent hum of insects. She looks across the road, and a row of faces are gawking at her. The dog, a red setter, wags his tail and barks once.

Stuart waves and shouts a hello at the kids who giggle and shriek. They run into their house with the dog following. Marina struggles to make a tense smile and turns to find a grimace on Stuart's face as he waves to the gray-haired woman at the porch door.

"Would you like some more green beans, Miss Rungsot?" asks Mrs. Weston, lifting the serving bowl beside her plate.

"Yes, please," answers Marina. She has had some of everything and is still starving. She hasn't had any of the morning sickness everyone talks so much about, and she doesn't have any particular cravings, but what she thinks of as the strange little squid inside of her seems to want to eat as much as a shark. She has a long waist and doesn't show yet, but she knows her dancing days are numbered.

"Stuart told me that you're studying for a master's degree in English," Mrs. Weston says.

"That's right," interjects Stuart.

Marina says nothing, a little surprised. She had lain down for a brief nap after their arrival, but her nap turned into a deep, dreamless sleep lasting over four hours. In that time, a wind must have blown her biography back a few pages.

"He also said that you wish to teach high school English."

Marina chews a mouthful of beans and can only offer Stu a meaningful look.

"She'll make a fine teacher," Stu says. "Her grammar is perfect."

"Do you have a favorite author, Miss Rungsot?" Stu's mother pronounces her last name in a way that makes it sound like a ladder part with alcoholic tendencies.

Marina shakes her head and swallows. "It's hard to choose one in particular," she murmurs. She read everything that was assigned, no more nor less, and wrote the required papers as well, but the words always remained on the paper.

"I have always liked Melville." Mrs. Weston dabs her mouth with a napkin.

"*Moby Dick* always made me a little seasick," Stu says, smiling.

"It's unfortunate that Mr. Weston passed away last year. He had a great respect for learning. Stuart was a miserable student in high school and caused his father a great deal of pain, but his military service has been good for him." Stuart's mother studies him, her expressionless eyes finally straying from Marina, who takes advantage of the moment to pick up another dinner roll and smear butter on it.

Stu smiles, but a little weakly, Marina will think later. He looks from his mother to her and then back again.

"The GI bill is going to pay for my schooling," he tells his mother, "and I'm sure Marina will help me with my study habits."

"Yes, I suppose so," his mother replies, "when she has the time away from her own students. She'll have to help support the two of you."

"Won't the government pay him a stipend?" Marina asks, surprised.

"Dear," Mrs. Weston looks at her in a way that showed she doesn't mean the word as an endearment, "he only served one year. Of course, he's been back two years and hasn't applied yet."

"I see," Marina says, not knowing what else to say.

"You would be wise to wait a little before starting a family," Stu's mother goes on. "I know that every young girl wants to have a baby of her own, but it's hard work and too often idealized."

"She's the oldest of six kids," Stu smiles brightly. "She knows a lot more than I do about changing diapers and burping babies."

"Then you understand precisely the kind of squalor I wouldn't wish on the two of you." Mrs. Weston's unsmiling gaze falls back on Marina, who chews slowly and swallows, all rhythm and appetite now gone.

A week later, Marina boards a ship for Havana with her roommate. Her friends ask what happened, but she only says that Stu isn't ready yet to be a father. She refuses to explain more, to say that he will never be ready to be a father to *hapa haole* children. His mother did not have to say what she would not accept. It was enough for her not to say it at all. Marina can't really express how sharply she now sees edges around her body, how clearly separate she is from the disjointed cadences of pedestrians and the tuneless blare of traffic. Leaning over the railing of the boat now, she breathes deeply of the sea air to clear her nausea and suddenly longs for the small island she grew up on, where she never once even stepped into a canoe.

Another woman at the hotel lounge where she works has told her where to go for a cheap vacation and an abortion. She will drink fruit drinks laced with rum and learn to mambo to Yoruba rhythms that will drown out the plaintive notes he leaves in her mailbox.

∽

HONOLULU, 1982

Mel strode back into the kitchen, fuming over her mother's way of knowing the worst things. Now, she would have to mull over why Tim and she never stayed at his mother's place.

Tim walked in while she was running fresh water into the pot. He pulled a leg off one of the barbecued chickens and began gnawing on it.

"Honey, why do we always sleep here?" Mel asked.

"I dunno," he said. "You're the driver."

"But where is this going?" she insisted. "Where are we going?"

"Like I said, you're the driver." He laughed and hugged her.

"That's what I'm afraid of," she said softly.

The Stone

Isabelita Orlina Reyes

We grew used to packing boxes, rearranging
furniture, ourselves, flying, leaving
a one-car firetrap on an alley in Pasay
for New York, making our way to choices

of churches, restaurants, everything
plural. My sister and I, home, kept looking
for Rockefeller Center and snow. In lieu of kin,
we'd had windows on 5th Avenue.

∾

    She collected junk
in an old box, motley
tokens like people
she knew. I was a stone, flat,

elliptical. With a flick of the wrist,
a stone could skip across water ten times
before sinking. I taught her
the trick of making it dance.

∾

She buried her box outside
our house, marked the spot
with rocks, marked the time promising

she'd come back
for the box, if Mom would leave it
alone. We made a bet.

∾

Long distance from Hong Kong, her voice
ached for our room, I'd grown so used to
living alone, the ringing like glass
breaking. She said I'd become

a craggy old rock. I searched in the yard
Mom cleared of weeds. I might have won
the bet. But it was all there: tangled
string, whistle, sheet of music, stone.

At twelve, my sister had played cards
for money, in her twenties, played
with choices. She always won,
except the last time she flew
home, she laid odds a rest was all
she needed, when she knew well
her blood flowed too quickly
and too much. That last bet, we all lost.

I shuffle cards at my desk, think of Queens, my sister and I
make snowballs we don't throw at each other. I spread out
solitaire, she sits on my sofa with husband and daughter,
fills up the square meters of my flat. At Mom's house,
I see her in the yard, the den, asleep
I see her. Someone drops a glass, I answer the phone. But no tricks,
no bets. All I have left of her is a box and knowing
when it crosses water, a stone can dance.

Summer Rains

Fran Ng

Summer rains
mean naked children
slipping on their laughter,
splashing each other with cold
from a rusty drum
or a cloud
or a little milk can with holes.

They bathe in the pit-a-pat
and clap and poke
of darts from heaven
that make the earth
glisten and sing.

The patter of their feet
marks the flitting of summer,
their laughter sparkling within

the earth's cracked skin.

Cold

Noelle Q. de Jesus

The heart is an adaptable muscle. That is what she's read. But Katrina, who is weak and cold with homesickness, decides it's about skin. The resilience and adaptability of skin. She imagines herself a creature emerged from massive boulders of ice, her skin still intact, pulsing, vibrant even after the mighty winds of an ice age. But as she shops for thermal underwear and a warm winter hat at Beller's, the only department store in this small Midwestern university town she has come to, Katrina suspects that she might just belong to one of those species that becomes extinct when an ice age strikes. Her skin will not toughen up, rather it will shrivel, confused. Her skin will do only what it knows to do back home in the Philippines. The pores will open up, expecting sweltering heat, her skin poised to perspire, but the sweat will freeze instantly and she will transform into a block of ice.

The letters Katrina writes home are filled with these sorts of observations. To amuse her family, she composes lists of the things that happen here that don't happen at home. Here in America, she writes, the mail comes twice a day, the afternoon light has a pink cast, and the air smells of wood. It was not as though she had not expected the differences. She had known it was going to be cold. She looked forward to seeing the green leaves change color, wanted to see snowflakes drifting from the sky, and dreamed of molding snow into the snowmen of her childhood books. But when confronted with the cold, she is anxious at how her skin refuses to adapt.

"How cold is the winter going to be, really?" Katrina asks Alison, a small, curvy, rather girlish woman with blonde hair cut high on the nape of her neck, sleek as a velvet cap on her shapely head.

"You're in the freezer, with like, the door closed," Alison replies, amused but highly matter-of-fact, her tone exacerbating the forlorn homesickness in the pit of Katrina's stomach.

"Even in a coat?" Katrina persists, thinking of the plush, black wool jacket she bought at Beller's.

"Sure, you've got a coat on, but like, the door's still closed and all." Alison laughs at her and Katrina longs to laugh as easily. The sound reminds her she has not laughed in a long time. Instead she has an inside face where her eyebrows furrow, puzzling over the things these Americans say, the jokes they find funny. But she hides that with her outside face: a smooth smile. The result of a controlled command from brain to lips.

Her mother's letters lecture. "You need to make friends." But there is no one. Katrina feels like a stranger, even to herself. She met Alison the day of registration at the graduate school. The American had laughed out loud, delighted by Katrina's remark that no one so far fit any of the ideas she had about Americans. The two registered together, confirmed their mutual nervousness about being teaching assistants, and even exchanged tentative stories about their childhoods. Katrina heard herself manufacturing an American drawl and hoped they might have dinner together as she hated eating alone. But Alison hopped on her bicycle, waved good-bye, and disappeared.

They have the evening Shakespeare survey together, and after class, Katrina joins Alison and another young woman named Jennifer to go out to a bar to "party." They walk clickety clack on the pavement. Jennifer's hair is a rich red brown that sets off eyes that are an amazing green; her skin is milky white. Under the streetlights, Alison's yellow hair and bright blue eyes seem to glow. Katrina stares at all their vibrant colors and feels sad and drab with her shock of black hair and her black eyes that she says, for the record, are brown (since someone once told her that no one really has black eyes).

It is a crisp night in late September. The air bites, nibbles at Katrina's ears. The smoky warmth that surrounds them as they enter the bar is mildly intoxicating. Through two bottles of beer, she sits and laughs at the appropriate times, even as she feels a strain in her cheekbones and her eyes water with the stress of exaggeration. She is thankful to be with others, but cannot help feeling terribly alone.

In late October, the sunlight is no longer real. A chilly white cast arrives in the morning, and warmth only teases for a few hours in the afternoon. Not the heat of home that draws drops of sweat from her scalp, trickling behind her ears. At the end of her day at school, Katrina marches down one of the two main streets and again, the air is cold, the sun, gone. Wind pushes her with a strange force, sliding her down the street. Her nostrils dry up, and the strands of her own hair sting her face like miniature whips.

What frightens her is how the cold seems to have numbed her brain, frozen her speechless. English is suddenly clumsy and hard to her tongue. She has come all this way to teach freshman composition so that she can pursue her literature degree, and yet she feels it is she who must learn it all again. Sentences and paragraphs are now strung together in liquid American drawl. Unconsciously, she finds herself enunciating, speaking slowly and setting her words apart as though she were picking tiny stones from grains of rice.

"You speak English so well," they say. But she is lost, always grasping for the right word, faltering in her lectures, tripping into Tagalog. She sees her students frown and raise their eyebrows at each other, but she is helpless. Her English is stiff and clumsy, breaking down in its natural habitat.

Katrina recalls her sense of panic the day she first arrived. The two-hour drive from the airport to the town she was surprised to hear people call a city was a shock. The airport sedan meandered through miles and miles of cornfields, spreading out towards a domed horizon in every conceivable direction. Katrina had an eerie thought: what if something should happen to her, who would know? It made her feel cold, like pebbles plopping one after another into a pool in her stomach.

In November, the people seem cold as well. Even their good-natured inquiries, *How ya doin? How are you?* are just questions tossed in the air that don't wait for any answers. In her classes, the faces are aloof or absent. They have their own lives to live, of course. When she speaks, they seem to know what she will say and have no patience to wait while she struggles for the words. She senses eyeballs rolling so only the whites show; she feels judging glances. She must not be so sensitive, her mother writes, and Katrina reads the slight reprimand in the dashes and lines of her penmanship. But in Modern Poetry, George Hunter sighs. Tracy Wallace and Kay Petrocini whisper. An older bearded man, whose name Katrina always forgets, shakes his head. Helen Mitchell is kind, however, and listens to Katrina with such rapt, wide-eyed attention it makes her feel much worse.

One day John Markman, with whom Katrina shares an office, invites her to his house for Thanksgiving. His wife, Janie, calls her on the telephone to finalize the details.

"We're having a traditional turkey dinner with all the trimmings. You haven't had that, have you? And I've asked someone from my office as well. A very nice fellow from Korea. I just know you two will hit it off."

Katrina is polite. She is sure they will get along nicely.

She brings as gifts the packets of dried candied mangoes that her mother packed in her suitcase for just these occasions, and feels a pang of homesickness as John takes her coat at the door.

"Oh, what's this, now? Something from Korea?" John Markman asks, then without waiting, "You didn't have to."

"Just something from the Philippines," Katrina forces herself to say.

At the table, she is seated next to Mr. Sonhai. He is about her height and on the heavy side with a genial smiling face. He is a graduate student in engineering. "He's single, I think," Janie whispers to her.

He shakes her hand. "You from Philippine?" he asks.

"See?" Janie chimes in as she sets down a dish of creamed onions. "I just knew you two would get along." Katrina is irritated by her cheery tones and how she and he are lumped together. Two complete strangers who don't even speak the same language. She imagines Janie thinking, "*Whatever.*"

John hands her wine in a crystal glass as delicate as the icicles that hang over the window.

Finally everyone is seated at the table—John and Janie and their six-year-old boy, Max, and another couple that they know.

For a moment, the warm colors hypnotize Katrina—the centerpiece of leaves and dried flowers and ears of rusty brown corn with kernels like colored beads. The golden turkey and the burgundy cranberry sauce and all the shimmering side dishes, green beans, orange sweet potatoes with puffs of marshmallow, and creamy silver white onions. A tangerine pumpkin pie sits on the sideboard. All these dishes Katrina has only read about in books but never eaten. For once, she is glad that no one pays attention to her, and she does not need to speak. Mr. Sonhai too is silent beside her.

"How are you both doin'? Mr. Sonhai? Eat up now." John asks, patting the back of his guest's chair.

"Is very good. This dinner...this with the Indians and the Pergrims, yes? And that, that is..."

Little Max bursts with laughter. "Pilgrims—not Pergrims!"

"Now, Max," Janie chides, shaking her head.

"You have it exactly right, Mr. Sonhai." John smiles broadly. "Eat up now. But remember, we still have dessert!" he warns. Everybody laughs as though this is a hilarious joke. Katrina finds the smile on her outside face still smooth and secure. But when she glances at Mr. Sonhai, she sees the same frustration in his nothing-else-but-black eyes. They *do* speak the same language.

Saying good-bye, Katrina feels her face is wearing thin. Her smile is bright, but she fears it is cold like the crystal wine glasses.

On her walk home, streets and streets away, wind stabs at her bare ears, thundering cold. As she finally winds her way up the concrete pavement towards her small studio apartment at the end of the town's first main street, she slips on a glassy patch of ice and falls on her knees like a child. Later, under the light, she finds them skinned. With numb fingers, she presses the flesh around it, but the blood is frozen and will not flow.

The first day of December is blanketed with a new glistening snow that bounces with sunshine, that for once feels warm like a layer of hope. Katrina feels inexplicably lighthearted. She lets her students off early, and they return her smile. She has had a good class.

While she gathers her papers together, one of the kids in the back, Bruce Forrester, saunters up to her table. He missed the last class and wants his paper, he says. He looks at her without blinking.

Katrina finds it in a pile and hands it to him.

"You need to revise this, Bruce," she says with a firm tone.

"What for?"

"It won't do," Katrina starts. "I can't pass this. You need to do it over. Work on...developing your ideas. And your sentence structure." She pauses. "It needs—you need to—" She falters as Bruce Forrester stares at her almost brazenly with gray eyes. She shivers. The light hairs on his face shine white from the sunlight flooding the classroom. She stares back at him.

"So?" he says, "You tell me what I have to do."

"Read my comments. Read that paper. Study the model and rework it according to that. It does not pass the way it is."

Bruce is silent and sullen.

"You can turn it in on Wednesday. That's two more days," she says more gently.

Then out of nowhere, "Fuck you." It is quiet. Almost under his breath. But there is no mistaking the words. Bitter shock and humiliation stir in Katrina's stomach. She looks at Bruce Forrester. What is he thinking? That she would not hear? That she would not understand?

Katrina shakes with anger. She wants to hit him. Bring her fist to his face. Her hands are freezing, clenched like packed snowballs. She reaches for the words.

"*Putang Ina Mo!*" she says.

Bruce Forrester looks confused.

He shrugs, takes his paper. He mutters, "What the hell?" Then walks out of the classroom. Katrina sits, still trembling.

Your mother is a prostitute. A whore. She sleeps around and no one knows who your father is. You animal! she wants to scream. But he will not understand. The words in English are all wrong. They are not what she wants to say. She wants to say, *Gago! Hayop! Tarantado! Putang Ina Mo!* And have those words strike him across the face.

When Katrina finally leaves the classroom, the sky is dark. It has begun to snow once again.

That night, after Shakespeare, Alison asks her to join them for drinks. Katrina shakes her head no. "Come on. You need a break." Katrina says no again.

As she puts on her coat, Alison asks, "Is something wrong?"

And Katrina longs to answer. To really answer. To tell her everything. About Mr. Sonhai and the Markmans. About the people and the cold. About Bruce Forrester. She wants to explain about the words that run from her clumsy tongue, which seems coated with the same ice she slips on. How she would like to hear her own language and speak it, peel off the layers of clothes and thaw out her brain and hair and skin and be warm again.

"No, nothing's wrong." She shakes her head, careful to keep the hot tears frozen in her eyes.

Later that night, Katrina cannot stop shaking with the cold. She curls up in socks and dons a sweater over the flannel nightgown that was sent to her in a box by an aunt in another frozen town somewhere in America. She tucks the ends under every inch of her body, pulling her arms into her sleeves and holding them closed so no cold can enter. Awkwardly, she pulls the blanket over her body, over her head, and does the same with the bedspread. Everything over her head, over her cold nose. But she cannot still the shaking.

So Katrina begins to count. She inhales at one-two and exhales at three-four, her breath whistling through her gritted teeth. Slowly, the shivering stops. She continues to warm herself with her breath, no longer counting. Only whispering. *Kailan?* When? When will it happen? She breathes to warm her skin, and waits for her heart to make the proper adjustments.

Tired

Maiana Minahal

Not demon nor god
just my tired father
who snaps off the useless bulb
burning above me.
Home from another night shift
at the machine shop,
grimy at midnight,
he finds me
half asleep,
face down in a book, tired
from trying to cram
too much in one night.
Too young, he thinks,
to work so hard.
But he wants me to work hard
and ace this American country.
His footsteps fade away
as I try to shake off sleep
to tell him,
no American dream drives me,
but fear,
fear of failing to conquer words
I don't
understand.

Meteors

Terry Rillera

I hugged myself tight against
4 a.m. November cold and
scanned the sky remembering
a summer night, a New Hampshire porch
and so many falling stars Sharon and I
couldn't wish fast enough but she's
years and miles and lives ago
and a winter star fell, its tail
chromatic white against blue-black
just above the trees
*one for me
make a wish*

"Every 33 years" these meteors and
Lauren gave me an amused/alarmed look
last week in Las Vegas when
a little girl stated that "old" was 33
so we were on borrowed time
so why not enjoy our old age
play arcade games and get our fortunes told
see an Elvis show and get a schoolgirl crush
on Trent Carlini the Dream King
together
old age is a wonderful thing
and a star arced high in the north
*one for you, Lauren
make a wish, chica*

It had to be the Dream King who woke me
knowing I wanted to see the meteors
and even though he's probably
a Cowboys' fan, smokes cigars, hates baseball
has seven kids for all we know
he helped me and Lauren discover
even after years of friendship
we could still surprise each other
and a star like a gossamer white scarf
trailed the November sky
*one for you, Trent
make a wish, Dream King*

Section III Traveling Over Water

White Turtle

Merlinda Bobis

> "I'll dream you a turtle tonight,
> cradle on her back
> bone-white;
> I'll dream you a turtle tonight."

Lola Basyon listened intently to the translation of the final lines from her chanted story, then to the palms, which met in loud approval in the foyer of an art deco building in Sydney. She was very pleased. Her translator, an Australian anthropologist, was doing an excellent job. They must like the story or turtles or dreams, or the sound of dreams in their own tongue, the seventy-year-old chanter from the Philippines thought as she bowed politely to the crowd, hand on her heart.

Filipina storyteller and chanter Salvacion Ibarra, a.k.a. Lola Basyon, was on her road to fame, but she didn't know this, nor did she care. Her main concern was to get the night over with.

"Please, can't you sing those last lines again in your dialect—Bikol, isn't it? It's beautiful," said the woman at the other end of the stage.

Ay, the oriole with the books that made people laugh. Lola Basyon turned towards the bright yellow streak on black hair, which was neatly combed back from a half-awed face. Of the three authors who read from their books that night, the old woman liked best this vivacious young writer with her silver bangles and vivid gear. She reminded her of a rare bird in the forest back home. A glossy oriole.

But the novelist seated next to her, who sported a cowboy hat and snakeskin boots, disturbed the old chanter. She kept an eye on his boots under the table, worrying that any time they might slither all over the stage. He had a way of running his fingers over the crisp pages of his book, almost lovingly, before he began reading. He hardly looked at anyone or anything except the fine print of his text. He stared at the words so hard that Lola Basyon had wondered whether he had a problem with his eyes, poor man.

The other author, a middle-aged man with gray sideburns and dark, heavy spectacles, was very polite, she observed, as he, half-smiling, nodded to whoever had finished reading. He himself had read for more than half an hour and Lola Basyon wondered whether they would ever get to her turn. She was very nervous; she felt she didn't quite belong. With no book or even paper to cling to, she hid her hands under the folds of her *tapis*. She imagined the audience could hear them shake; she had been worried since the program began. How in the world will they see the white turtle if I can conjure it only in my dialect? *Ay, Dios ko,* this is very difficult indeed.

The old woman rubbed the fabric of her *tapis* between her fingers for luck. She had chosen to wear her dead mother's fiesta clothes because they had always made her feel as if she were wrapped in a cozy blanket but, at the same time, dressed for a special occasion. The *tapis* was home-dyed in various shades of soft green. The blouse, a kimona made of *piña,* the fibers of pineapple leaves, was embroidered with tiny *sampaguita* blooms and intricate loops at the neck and sleeves. But this finery seemed to lose its old power of bestowing comfort and confidence when the storyteller stepped into the big building of strange, white faces. For a while, she did not know what do with her shaking hands.

Oriole's reassuring smile from the other end of the table had eased her anxiety, and now the black hair with its vibrant yellow plumage was nodding towards her. "Please, I'd love to hear it again. It's very beautiful."

"*Salamat*...thank you...." Lola Basyon bowed once more. She understood "beautiful" but couldn't quite comprehend the request in the foreign tongue. She turned to the anthropologist who immediately came to her aid. The chanter obliged.

"*Ngunyan na banggi*
ipangaturugan taka ki pawikan,
duyan sa saiyang likod
kasingputi kang tulang;
ngunyan na banggi
ipangaturugan taka ki pawikan."

All palms, especially Oriole's, responded with enthusiasm once again. Except Cowboy's. He was still glued to his book, scanning it for the next round of readings. There was a faint buzz of praise in the room. Lola Basyon felt the warmth rippling in her stomach, then invading her arms, flushing her hands to their fingertips. She abandoned her *tapis* and lay her hands on the table.

"*Salamat...maraming salamat*...thank you very much." They saw the white turtle after all, thank god. They're talking about it now.

"Imagine, doing harmonies in her throat."

"It's like listening to three voices singing. Amazing."

"I've never heard anything quite like that before. An unusual way to produce sound, don't you think so?"

Lola Basyon was tired though exhilarated. She had just flown in from the Philippines the day before for this writers' festival. The Australian anthropologist, after much fussy discussion with the board, had arranged that she be invited to this event. He had met her during his research on the mythologized genesis of native peoples and was undoubtedly charmed.

In her village of Iraya, he had fallen in love with her chant about the white turtle. Its story is pure poetry, he had explained to her in broken Bikol, his blue eyes misting over, growing as bright as the sea where the turtle swam. A mythical tale—once the turtle was small and blue-black, shiny like polished stones. It was an unusual creature even then; it had a most important task. It bore on its back the dreams of Iraya's dead children as it dived to the navel of the sea. Here it buried little girl and boy dreams that later sprouted into corals, which were the color of bones. After many funerals, it began to grow bigger and lighter in color; eventually it, too, became white, bone-white. This was Lola Basyon's story told in a chant. When the anthropologist first heard it, he felt as if the white turtle had somersaulted into his eyes.

The night of the readings, it dived into him again, down to the depth of his irises as he acted as interpreter. After she sang each scene, he would read his translation. Theirs was a dialogue in two tongues blending in counterpoint. Strange to hear the turtle voice in English, Lola Basyon thought. She rather liked its sound, though.

"I am your cradle
rocking
your babydreams
past anemone;

the hundred fingers
curling
around sleepgurgles
passing..."

What an exciting version of performance poetry, someone from the back row thought, listening more to the chanting than to the translated story. Notice how she sings with no effort at all. She doesn't even blink her eyes. *"Ako ang simong duyan / napasagid / sa puting kurales..."*

"I am your cradle
brushing
against white corals;

porous bones
draw in
your bubblebreath
humming."

Oriole's eyes were closed. She was engulfed by the chant, lulled into it, falling into the sea with the anthropologist and a few keen listeners. Wonder how this feels in her dialect for someone who is born to it.

"I sail your cradle home.
Be water.

I sink your cradle
deep beyond grief.
Be stone."

The bespectacled writer was slightly impatient. Her act is a multicultural or indigenous arts event, definitely not for a writers' festival. And those organizers should have, at least, printed and handed out the translation to the audience. That anthropologist's reading is painfully wooden, dead. And this could go on forever, heaven forbid. He looked at his watch, shaking his head.

"But warm. Skin-smooth
and promising wings.
Be bird.

And hear your flapping
from the navel of the sea."

Cowboy was bored; he was suspicious of all performance poetry. He thought it was invented to disguise pedestrian writing. Where he came from, he had seen too many performance poets outshouting, outstyling each other. He fixed his gaze at the cover of his latest crime fiction.

"Nice performance—and what a fabulous top." A woman in black and pearls whispered to her companion in the front row as the anthropologist ended the reading of his translation. She could not take her eyes off Lola Basyon's *piña* blouse.

"Wonder what it's made of."

"Very fine material, I'd say."

"I love your story. It's poetry—where can we get your book?" A teenaged boy wearing a ponytail addressed the chanter directly, in order to drown the clothes-talk at his elbow. He's about the age of my favorite grandson back home, Lola Basyon couldn't help but notice. Earlier, right after her chant, he had placed two fingers into his mouth and whistled, then he had clapped vigorously, stamping his feet. She felt embarrassed, but pleased. Did you see the white turtle? she wanted to ask him.

"I'd like a copy of your book. It would be a treasure."

A faint titter issued from the back row.

Book, book. Lola Basyon recognized the word, but what was he after? "Book?"

Cowboy rolled his eyes to heaven then back to his latest crime fiction and the bespectacled author raised his brows towards a tall woman in cobalt blue; she was the chair of the readings.

"Yes, book—your book. I'd like very much to buy it."

The anthropologist tried to intervene, but Lola Basyon was just beginning to speak, so he kept quiet.

"Book..."

"Yes, book..."

"*Gusto niya raw bumili ng libro mo.*" A shrill voice from the audience interrupted the exchange. "Excuse me, I'm a journalist from the Philippine community paper here in Sydney—and I was just translating for her that young man's request," she addressed everyone before taking a photo of Lola Basyon and sitting down. The anthropologist-translator felt censured.

"I'd love a copy, yes," the young man pressed on.

The storyteller sensed the blue sleeve at her shoulder. The chair of the readings explained that the audience would have enough time to chat with the writers during drinks later and that they were running out of time, but she was interrupted by the young man's seat mate. "Do you have a publisher here?"

Cowboy suppressed a giggle, the spectacles adjusted and re-adjusted itself—she shouldn't have been in this panel in the first place—and Oriole looked very disconcerted.

"I like your white turtle very much."

All heads turned towards the origin of the very young voice. A girl, about six, stood on her chair at the back of the foyer and made her own statement. "Oh, yes, I do."

Her mother shushed her, but she was very determined. "Is it really white?"

In broken Bikol, the anthropologist tried to explain to the story-teller just what was happening, while the cobalt blue dress took the floor and, with admirable diplomacy, introduced the second half of the readings. The embarrassed mother had to drag her protesting daughter out of the building.

"But I've got lots of questions," she bawled.

Cowboy caressed his pages again and cleared his throat before launching into his old spiel, with improvisations this time. He rhapsodized over more details on the writing of his latest novel. How he was converted to crime fiction, but not the genre writing kind, mind you. He was a committed antigun lobbyist. His heroes were good cowboys like him, someone like the Lone Ranger without a gun. Oriole and the older writer seemed very amused, while from the audience the Filipina journalist took another photo of Lola Basyon staring at the speaker's snakeskin boots.

After the reading, a lively exchange filled the foyer. The exquisite poetic style of the bespectacled writer, the quirky plots in Cowboy's fiction, and Oriole's comic eroticism were notable conversation pieces. And, of course, Lola Basyon's extraordinary chanting was also a favored subject. "Almost like three voices harmonizing in her throat, remember?" A few referred to the awkward moment when the boy asked about the old woman's publication. "How silly, how ridiculously dumb," the woman in pearls complained to the anthropologist. "He had put that poor thing in an embarrassing situation."

The drinks taste very strange, but these colorful bits are so delicious—*siram sana!* Oblivious to all the murmurings about her, "the poor thing" was having the time of her life sampling all, from the wine to the orange juice to the trays of canapés and fruit as the crowd wandered towards the three authors' book signing.

I wish I had understood their stories, she thought, shaking her head while biting into a strawberry. They must be very important ones considering how fat their books are. *Ay,* impressive indeed. She ran her fingers across the books, imitating Cowboy's loving gesture, then parked herself beside the food trays.

"*Marhay ta* enjoy *ka. Su kanta mo* very good." The anthropologist offered her another glass of orange juice. He said he was glad to see her having a good time and that the audience loved her story.

"*Kumusta,* I'm Betty Manahan, a Filipina journalist originally from Manila. *Ang galing mo talaga*—great performance!" She hugged and kissed the chanter, then shook the anthropologist's hand before adjusting her camera. "I'll put you on the front page of my paper," she gushed at Lola Basyon. "I can make you famous in Sydney, you know. Isn't she fantastic?"

"She's very special," the anthropologist agreed. "Her turtle story is just—just beyond me. I must say I—"

"I liked your translation, too—could you take our photo, please?" The journalist handed the camera to the enthusiastic translator before posing beside Lola Basyon, who looked a bit baffled.

"Picture *tayo,*" the journalist flashed her most engaging smile at the old woman and towards the camera, putting an arm around the waist of her greatest discovery.

A quarter of an hour later, after many more compliments, Lola Basyon found herself alone beside the food trays. I must memorize the taste of this wonderful feast, so I can tell it to my grandchildren. Imagine, they put pink fish on biscuits and what's this yellow thing that smells like old milk, I don't like it, *ay, ay.* And what's that blowing bubbles over there? Someone had just popped a champagne bottle open. *Aprubicharan ngani,* I'll try it, too. *Hoy, luway-luway daw,* Basyon, easy, easy, she chided herself, or else they might think you're very *ignorante.*

"Thanks for that fabulous performance."

In the middle of gulping the bubbly stuff, Lola Basyon recognized the pearled woman who had kept staring at her kimona blouse earlier. The chanter smiled up at her. *Aysus,* how very tall.

"That's beautiful, very delicate." The woman gestured towards the kimona.

"Beautiful." Lola Basyon bowed and pointed to the other's pearls.

The woman smiled graciously. "What's it made of?" she asked, squinting at the kimona.

"*Sige, kaputi ngani*...touch...touch..." The chanter held out the edge of her blouse towards the manicured fingers.

The pearls leant forward and fondled the floral embroidery. "I say, so dainty, so..."

"Mother...my mother..." With little success, the storyteller was trying to tell her about the source of the heirloom, when the ponytailed young man appeared. He had just extricated himself from the long book-signing queue.

"Thank you very, very much for your story..." he began.

"I guess I must join the queue now," the woman with the pearls said, laying a hand on the chanter's arm. "See you."

"I do like your song immensely." The young man's face was unabashedly radiant.

Somehow, Lola Basyon understood this overflow of enthusiasm and youthful confidence—the way he opens his hands towards me like my favorite grandson. She managed the widest grin; her jaws ached pleasantly. He smiled back.

"I wish I could tell you how I feel about the burial of dreams of dead children. How I really feel about your story—here," he said, cupping his hand to his chest.

"Story...sad...happy." She searched her head for more English words.

"Sad-happy, you're quite right, and very disturbing."

She longed so much to understand the full meaning of his earnestness. And she wanted to ask whether he saw the white turtle, but how to say it. She looked around for the anthropologist so he could translate for her, but he was chatting with the chair of the readings. And the Filipina journalist was busy "networking with my Aussie V.I.P.s, you know."

Again, the young man opened his arms towards her. "I like the sound of your dialect, too. I wish I could have a copy of your story, but—"

"Story...?"

Ay, my son, why don't you speak my tongue? Lola Basyon longed for a proper conversation with this beaming face.

"I know, I know, stupid of me. Of course, that was an oral story... how could I have made a fool of myself then? And look at me now trying to—"

"Excuse me, please—"

Lola Basyon felt a slight tug at her skirt from behind.

"Is it really white, your turtle?"

She turned to face the bold little girl who had asked about the turtle earlier. Her eyes were shining.

"Really white white?"

"White turtle...." This Lola Basyon understood.

"There you are. I thought I'd find you here." The mother took her daughter's hand. "Thanks very much for your performance. We loved it."

"Big turtle?" The girl drew a large circle with her little hands.

Lola Basyon chuckled, nodding vigorously. "Big...big big."

"White white, too."

"White white," the chanter repeated, squatting before the child.

"And beautiful?"

"Beautiful." She opened her arms towards the girl as if to embrace her, but the girl clung to her mother.

"You're all shy now, hey?" The mother laughed.

"Beautiful," Lola Basyon laughed, too, pointing at the daughter.

For the first time since she boarded the plane from her country, the old chanter felt very relaxed. She was making a real conversation at last. She will tell her grandchildren just how nice these people are. And they saw the turtle, after all, they really saw it. *Ay, I could sing for them forever.*

With her second glass of champagne and amidst this comforting company, the old woman was transported back home, close to the forest and the sea of her village, among her grandchildren begging for the old story, waiting for her to take them for a swim on the turtle's back. All in a night's chant.

"Ngunyan na banggi,
ipangaturugan taka ki pawikan,
duyan sa saiyang likod
kasingputi kang tulang;
ngunyan na banggi,
ipangaturugan taka ki pawikan."

The warmth in her stomach made double-ripples as she began to chant again, filling her lungs with the wind from the sea and her throat with the sleepgurgles of anemones. Her cheeks tingled sharply with saltwater. "I'll dream you a turtle tonight." She sang softly at first, then steadily raised her volume, drowning the chatter in the foyer.

Three harmonizing voices reverberated in the room with more passion this time, very strange, almost eerie, creating ripples in everyone's drinks. All book-signing stopped. People began to gather around the chanter. By the time the main door was pushed open from outside by a wave of salty air, the whole foyer was hushed. An unmistakable tang pervaded it—seaweed!

"White white...oh, look...beautiful white!"

The little girl saw it first, its bone-white head with the deep-green eyes that seemed to mirror the heart of the sea and the wisdom of many centuries. It was as large as the four-seater table from where the three authors stared in bewildered silence. Taking in the crowd, the white turtle raised its head as if testing the air. Then it blinked and began to make turtle sounds also in three voices harmonizing in its throat and blending with the song of the chanter. Everyone craned their necks towards the newly arrived guest.

Six voices now sent ripples through everyone's drinks. *Hesusmarya-hosep*, the Filipina journalist muttered under her breath, a miracle! The mother and daughter and the young man gasped as the immense creature came very close, while at the other end of the room, the anthropologist stood riveted, all movement drawn in, pushed to the back of his eyes. A hundred white turtles somersaulted there.

What a gimmick, a regular scene-stealer, Cowboy thought, peeved, but as curious as everyone, as he left the book-signing table and strode towards the very late guest. Meanwhile, the middle-aged writer, sideburns strangely tightening against his cheeks, peered from behind his spectacles, and Oriole sensed the salt-sting behind her eyes. *Ohs* and *ahs* traveled the foyer while the hand of the woman who loved the kimona flew to the pearls at her throat and the cobalt blue dress swayed to the chant. The skin around everyone's ears tingled.

As if in choreographed motion, all bodies began to lean towards the two chanters, arms stretched out, palms open, wanting to catch each of the six voices. Even Cowboy had succumbed to this pose, which was almost like a prelude to a petrified dive or dance. For a brief moment, everyone was still.

"Can I pat it?"

The girl had wriggled free from her mother. "Can I?" Her voice, in its foreign tongue and timbre, wove into the long, drawn-out vowels of the chant.

But the mother heard her daughter distinctly above the alien ululations. She grabbed the eager hand and held her close, hugging her tightly. The dreams of dead children, the mother remembered, goose bumps growing on her arm. Why am I being so silly?

"I want to pat it. I want to touch—it's a good turtle, a beautiful, good turtle," the child protested, beginning to cry.

The spell was broken. Everyone started moving and speaking in unison, some in wonder, others with the deepest unnamable emotions, but a few murmured their doubts. Dreams? Dead children? Suddenly, they remembered the story. Funerals. One man contemptuously dismissed this foolishness and argued instead against cruelty to animals. "It was probably flown all the way here." "Part of the act?" "Just look at that poor, strange, beautiful thing, an endangered species, no doubt." "But what if it had been smuggled in," speculated an elderly woman. "It might not have even been quarantined." The crowd began dispersing. In the din, the turtle stopped singing and Lola Basyon swallowed her voice.

Silent now, the massive whiteness crawled towards the table where the books were displayed. Passing the snakeskin boots of the Cowboy, it seemed to shudder and hesitate before moving on. The chair of the readings rushed out of the room to ring for help.

When the police arrived, they found it nestling its head on the old woman's lap beside the table of books. They were dumbstruck. What whiteness, what extraordinary, beautiful whiteness. Color of bone. With eyes full of understanding, the turtle stared at the last two people in the room, Lola Basyon and the anthropologist.

Lola Basyon wanted to explain to the men in blue that the turtle did not mean to cause harm or any trouble, that perhaps it came to the reading because she did not have a book. Because the story that she chanted was written only on its back, was never really hers. Only lent to her in a moment of music. She wanted to plead for them to be gentle with it. It was very tired after a long, long swim. But how to be understood, how to be heard in one's own tongue.

The turtle blinked its emerald eyes at the police. It seemed sad, as if it were in mourning. Its white back stirred, then rocked like an inverted cradle. The anthropologist sensed the burial of dreams. Gloved hands steadying the creature, the police wondered about the unnamable emotion that stirred in their wrists, a strange, warm ripple of sorts. They lifted it with utmost tenderness, as if it were a holy, precious thing. It was as large as the table, but oh, so light.

The Painting

Cristina Pantoja Hidalgo

While they waited for the storm to spend itself, the stranded travelers had sought shelter in a small roadside noodle house. It was not particularly clean or comfortable, and its wooden shutters were such flimsy protection against the strong gusts of wind and rain that puddles had formed all along the room's walls.

But, as often happens when people find themselves in this sort of predicament, a kind of intimacy had sprung up among the travelers, and this partly made up for the inconvenience and the anxiety the storm was causing them.

The thin man with a cane had suggested that the hours would pass more quickly if they were to take turns entertaining the group with stories. And they were thus now pleasantly occupied, sitting around a long wooden table, which had been cleared of the remains of their supper.

No one had expected the young priest to speak. He had been sitting so quietly at the far end of the table that they had forgotten he was there.

But when the laughter had died down after the tale told by the large woman in a green dress, he suddenly said, "I have a story. I think it's an interesting one, and I've often wanted to tell it."

This startled his companions, not just because his speaking out was so unexpected, but because his voice was so deep and resonant. It did not seem to come from him at all, for he was slight of build and unprepossessing in appearance.

"Have you never told it before, Father?" asked the bald dentist.

"No, I have not," the young priest admitted.

"Why not, Father?" asked the elegant old lady with the sleeping grandchild.

"I think...because I have never quite believed it myself," the young priest replied.

"Did it happen to you, Father?" asked the aging ballerina.

"Have not all the tales we tell somehow happened to us? And do they not happen again in the telling? But now, with your permission, I shall tell the story. I feel that it is time."

So, the young priest began his tale. And as he spoke, complete silence fell upon the little group, for his voice was compelling, and the tale he told stranger than any they had heard that night.

I come from a very old and distinguished family. I shall not mention its name, but I think you will recognize it as I go along. One of my ancestors is revered as a great hero of our people. Not everyone agrees that he deserves such an honor. In fact, brothers have been known to become alienated from each other as a result of such disagreements. But that is not really relevant to my story. I personally have never doubted that my ancestor was the kind of man rarely born on this earth. And there are those who actually believe him to be a god.

You will understand that it is not easy to belong to a family like mine. In fact, it can be quite a burden. People expect heroism to be passed on, or at least to be reflected in some extraordinary form, like intellectual brilliance or singular talent or exceptional ambition. In fact, most of us are quite ordinary. Therefore, to save myself some embarrassment, I have made it a practice not to reveal my lineage, particularly to my illustrious ancestor's ardent admirers.

But, as it is part of the human condition to be unable to escape one's identity even while one rebels against it, I have always been drawn to those people who have made a cult of my ancestor.

There are numerous groups all over the islands. They call themselves the *kapatiran*—there is no exact translation for the word. I think I have at some time visited them all. And I have studied many of them closely. Though I have never myself become a believer (as you know, I serve another God), I think I have a little understanding of what lies at the heart of their faith. It is nationhood, which to them is simply the kingdom of God on earth. Therefore a man who gives his life to attain it is not just hero, but saint, or even god.

It was at one of their rites that I first saw the woman who is the real subject of my tale.

I had gone to visit a little chapel at the foot of what believers call the sacred mountain. Perhaps some of you know the mountain of which I speak. It is a place of great beauty and enchantment. Before the white man introduced into these islands the religion that most of us now claim as our own, the mountain was the heart and soul of the land, the center of life, the wellspring of legend. Even today it is said to shelter deities unknown to us for whom those early creeds are lost. And there are many among our own kind who, disillusioned by what we have made of our world, seek and find sanctuary within its deep groves.

I had witnessed (you note I say "witnessed," not "participated in") the rites held in the modest wooden chapel. These rites were finished, and the congregation had dispersed. But a few people still lingered, hoping for a word with the *Suprema*.

I wonder if any of you have ever seen these priestesses. They are impressive individuals. All have a commanding presence, and some are strikingly beautiful. This one was very tall and very fair, with strongly chiselled features in an ageless face, large, penetrating eyes, and long hair drawn back in a bun. She had changed from her vestments into a loose white robe and was sitting on a wooden bench to one side of the chapel, where she always received people who wished to consult with her.

The *Suprema* was speaking with someone whose appearance was a striking contrast to hers—a woman in her late forties or early fifties perhaps, of medium height, plain looking, and a little on the stout side, her hair cut short as though she did not wish to be bothered with it. She wore thick glasses and a simple dress of some unfashionable color—I believe it was purple. One of her shoes had fallen off, and she was swinging a bare foot as she talked. They appeared to be having a good time, for their conversation was punctuated by laughter.

The woman in purple had a hearty, uninhibited laugh and a rather loud voice, which carried to where I sat, observing them from one of the pews. When I began to pay attention, I found that I could understand quite clearly what she was saying. She was speaking of her classes, so I gathered with some surprise that she was a teacher.

At a later occasion, I learned that she was, in fact, a university professor, and moreover, held a position of responsibility in the university's administration. This was even more astonishing to me, for she did not look in the least either like an academician or a bureaucrat. I had by then known her enough to learn that she was quite a disorganized person, the sort that always misplaces and forgets things, mixes up dates, arrives late for appointments. She was also, however, disarmingly unpretentious. And this made me like her instantly.

I do not remember now who introduced us, or when we became friends. There are persons one warms to immediately, perhaps because they are so open and trusting themselves. Consuelo was one of them. She was also truly unaware of any distinction of race or class or creed. She was exactly the same with everyone she met, as much at ease with bishops and bankers as with beggars and bums.

At first, I took her for a very simple woman. That is, I thought she was not particularly intelligent. Later, I realized that she was indeed simple, but only in the sense of being completely honest and good hearted. I also found her to be very funny. She said comical things; she behaved in a comical manner. Later, I discovered that she had the gift of making people laugh because her own heart was so full of joy.

But I am getting ahead of my story.

I think I may say that I made a favorable impression on Consuelo myself. One of those connections was established that are difficult to explain, because they are not based on any actual experiences shared. Some people call this the meeting of kindred spirits. Others believe it is simply the picking up of a relationship begun elsewhere, perhaps in another lifetime (like the unusual bond between the young man and the beautiful woman in your story, Madame). I do not know the explanation. But I am certain that such connections occur.

When Consuelo learned I was a priest, her treatment of me changed subtly. She became at once protective and respectful, motherly and deferential. I have found that some Catholic women react this way to priests. You will probably think this presumptuous of me, but I have sometimes thought that in just such a manner must the Virgin Mary have regarded her Son, our Divine Lord.

Consuelo told me that she herself had been a nun, and somehow this did not surprise me. She had known quite early that she had a vocation and had chosen a contemplative order. She confided to me that her happiest years had been those five years in the convent. But the sudden death of her only brother forced her to return to the world. He had left behind their elderly mother and a young widow with two children and no means of support.

Her Superior had consoled her with the thought that this was probably God's way of testing her vocation. But if trial it was, it was a long one. When I met her, Consuelo had been away from the convent many years, and there seemed no likelihood that she would return to it in the near future. Her family's needs had grown rather than diminished. She had come to think that perhaps this was God's way of telling her that she belonged in the world, that she was to serve Him in another capacity. But she had not yet discovered what this other role might be. Until she did, she was simply trying to do good in whatever way she could.

This way, I was to see, was multifarious. For aside from her work as teacher and administrator in the university, she was involved in all kinds of efforts to ease the plight of the less fortunate—the imprisoned, the insane, the bereaved, the terminally ill, the hopelessly poor. Not to mention the numerous individuals, friends and strangers alike, who constantly sought her counsel and her intercession. Consuelo made time for them all.

But her work in the university took precedence. She saw her teaching not as a job, but as a mission. And though she could not explain the exact nature of this mission to me, I could sense the vision behind it.

Unfortunately, not everyone could. Within the academic circles, she was regarded with much ambivalence. Many of her own colleagues thought her a figure of fun and were openly contemptuous. Consuelo was aware of this and was human enough to be pained by it. She may have derived some comfort from the fact that these same people did not hesitate to approach her for her help when they needed it, help that she never denied them. In any case, she must have known that there were many others who not only admired and loved her dearly, but believed her to be a saint.

One afternoon, when we had known each other for a little while, I permitted myself the liberty of appearing unannounced at her office. She seemed delighted to see me.

While we talked of this thing and the other, over cups of rather indifferent coffee, I looked around me, hoping to gain some new insight into my friend's character from the appearance of the rooms in which she worked. But what struck me was only their impersonality. I have seldom been in rooms so little revealing. Consuelo had left no mark on them. It was as though she did not belong there and was only using them as a way station.

In fact, she struck me just then as looking somewhat like a strange, slightly dishevelled bird poised for flight, dressed now in bright green, sitting at the edge of her chair behind her large, cluttered desk, jumping up every so often to attend to something or other.

During one of these interrruptions, my attention was caught by a painting on the wall, which I had not immediately noticed. It was a portrait of my famous ancestor.

Desiring to examine it more closely, I stepped around the desk and nearly stumbled over a capacious bag squatting just behind it. It was half open, and I could see that it contained, besides an assortment of files and papers, what looked like some articles of clothing and a pair of shoes. This amused me, as it confirmed my impression of Consuelo as poised for flight.

The painting was unsigned, a curious fact, particularly as it was a strikingly good one. The unknown artist had captured something that most others had missed, perhaps because they had never known their subject personally and worked from photographs or other portraits. They painted the hero—a stiff, somewhat pompous-looking visionary, in a neat little black suit, staring fixedly at his destiny. But this artist had captured the man and an ineffable quality that must have been recognized only by those who knew him well. There was the resolve, but it was a courage born of sadness. And the eyes revealed confusion as well as resignation.

I questioned Consuelo about the painting: Whose was it? Where had it come from? She seemed pleased at my interest. It was hers, she told me. Her grandfather had left it to her when he died. But she had no idea who had painted the portrait.

She remembered standing at the foot of the staircase in her grandfather's house as a child and gazing raptly at it. "I thought it was so beautiful," she said. "I thought he was so beautiful. I don't know if I said anything to my grandfather. Perhaps I did." Later, she forgot all about the incident. But her grandfather apparently didn't. For upon his death, many years afterwards, she learned that he had left the painting to her.

Her more affluent relatives were locked in a vicious struggle over the old man's properties. But, strangely, none questioned the fact that he had desired Consuelo to have the painting.

It was too large for any of the walls in her mother's little house, so Consuelo thought of donating it to her old convent. The Sister Superior thanked her but told her gently that it did not belong in a convent, it was of this world. Consuelo decided to bring it to the college where she was teaching at the time, and a suitable place was found for it in the office of the Dean.

When she accepted a position in the university, she left the painting behind. But some months later, her former colleagues brought it back to her. They had grown uneasy with it, they told Consuelo. Somehow, it no longer seemed to belong in the college.

"As you can see," Consuelo said ruefully, "I couldn't get rid of it."

She hung it up in the cubicle that was her office in the university, where it dwarfed everything, including the room itself. But it kept her company while she worked, and it seemed comfortable with her students. She fancied that it had a good effect on them. They seemed to think more clearly, to express themselves more easily in its presence.

Then Consuelo was appointed to an administrative position, and she and her painting moved to this office.

I asked whether she felt the portrait was content in its present perch, and, laughing her hearty laugh, Consuelo said, "Well, he's helping me a lot with my work, so he must be."

I noticed the shift in the personal pronoun, but did not comment on it. Consuelo guessed my thoughts. "Oh yes," she said, "I have a very intense personal relationship with him. My friends think it's all part of my craziness. They kid me about it, calling him my 'boyfriend.'"

Consuelo and I did not meet often. Her work and mine were too demanding to enable us to attend the gatherings of the *kapatiran* with any regularity. And even when we did manage to go, it was rarely to the same group at the same time. Nonetheless, our paths did cross now and then. And whenever they did, we would find ourselves slipping with ease into a close camaraderie, as though the intervening periods had never been.

However, I kept from her my own connection with the man in her painting. To this day, I am not sure why.

I was curious about the circumstances, which had led her, a former nun, to the *kapatiran*, assuming that she was as aware as I was of the established church's opinion of these "sects." And she told me that, initially, she had indeed taken them to be esoteric cults. Later, she had discovered a wealth of material unsuspected by most scholars and had gradually become involved in the movement, not as a researcher but as initiate (this being the only way to truly understand them). Eventually, she had decided to do her doctoral dissertation on the *kapatiran*. She was fortunate in having for her adviser an elderly anthropologist, himself a great scholar, who understood the originality of her mind and the importance of her research, and encouraged her to be as unorthodox as she pleased.

But what was it that had so intrigued her in the first place? I asked Consuelo. And what was it that bound her now to the *kapatiran*?

She replied that she honestly did not know. It was simply a strong force drawing her deeper and deeper. She had resisted at first, having some doubts about the nature of this force. For she well understood that there are malevolent forces in this world, as powerful as the benevolent ones. But she had become convinced that there was no evil in the *kapatiran*. Only this mysterious drawing power. It touched something within her, the existence of which she had not been aware of. It was like listening to a melody one somehow recognized, though one had forgotten the words, she said. She thought that perhaps by listening longer, she would remember the whole song, remember perhaps the entire symphony.

For their part, the *kapatiran* had welcomed her into their midst as one of themselves. In fact, they saw in her the prophetess of whom their own traditions had spoken, the woman who would deliver their message to the world.

And that, indeed, was what her dissertation came to be: both testimony and prophecy. What in the *kapatiran* is called *patotoo*.

"Why you?" I asked Consuelo.

"Oh, Father," she cried, "don't you think I have asked myself that question again and again? Why me of all people? Perhaps because I am open. Perhaps simply because I am here. You know better than I the strange ways in which God works."

And, though she had not intended it, I felt justly rebuked.

Consuelo's field work had taken several years. The writing took no more than a couple of months. After she had successfully defended her dissertation, it was immediately published.

"I feel he was behind it all," Consuelo told me, indicating the painting. "And do you know something funny? My publishers decided to launch the book on his birthday. And at the last minute, they decided to launch it in his house, yes, the national shrine in his old hometown. Can you imagine that? I had never dreamt of writing a book, much less launching it in my hero's ancestral home."

The memory appeared to have set in motion a train of recollections, for presently, Consuelo continued, "Now that I think of it, I realize that his birthday and his death anniversary have always been special to me. Somehow, I find myself always getting involved in some way with some ritual or the other every time those dates come around. It's almost as if I were compelled to do so."

And then we both recalled that the following day was my ancestor's death anniversary. There was to be a big *kapatiran* celebration in the city, at the monument honoring the hero's martyrdom. Consuelo had been invited, and as I too was planning to go, we agreed to meet there.

It was one of those perfect evenings, unusual for the city even in December—cool and cloudless, the stars more brilliant than jewels, the breeze blowing in from the sea redolent of old galleons and far-away lands.

A large crowd had gathered at the park, mostly members of the *kapatiran*, and a few curious tourists. I did not immediately find Consuelo.

There were the usual speeches, songs, trance dances. I watched without attending too closely, more engrossed (as I always am) by the participants than by the ritual itself.

After a while, I spotted Consuelo. She was standing a bit to one side, not part of any group, but apparently as enthralled as the others.

I made my way towards her, but before I could reach her, another man detached himself from the crowd and approached her. Something—I am not sure what—prevented me from walking up to them.

The man was dark-skinned and not very tall. His clothes were clean, but faded. And he had the rough features and heavy build of a factory worker.

He said something to Consuelo, and she turned around abruptly, a startled expression on her face. What she saw must have reassured her, for the alarm receded, to be replaced by her customary attentiveness.

I was close enough now to overhear what the man was saying, without calling their attention to my presence.

He was asking Consuelo what she thought of the celebration. I did not catch her answer. Then he said: "Why does it center on the monument? Have they forgotten everything else?"

Consuelo looked puzzled, but she allowed him to lead her away from the main crowd.

I followed at some distance, making sure that I was within earshot, but never intruding into their line of vision.

The man was showing Consuelo some slabs of unpolished marble in which were engraved passages from the hero's writings. "There was a time," he said, "when these words were lit up. Now they are left to darkness and oblivion."

"If this place is as sacred as they all claim it to be, why can't they clean it up?" he added, and I was struck by the sadness in his voice. "Do we not clean the graves of our dead at least once a year in November?"

Consuelo had stooped to read the engravings, but she could barely make out the words. The man began to read them out for her: "A nation wins respect not by covering up abuses but by punishing them and condemning them... All people are born equal. Naked and without chains. They were created not in order to be enslaved. They were given intelligence not in order to be led astray...I wish to show those who deny us patriotism that we know how to die for our duty and our convictions..."

I noticed that he was looking at her, not at the marble slabs. Was he reciting them from memory? I wondered.

"What is the point of making fine speeches?" the stranger asked, gesturing towards the crowd around the statue of the hero. "They will change nothing, nothing." And now, I caught the anger beneath the weariness.

"Are you a member of the *kapatiran*?" Consuelo asked him.

"I am a Filipino," the man replied shortly.

They were moving now towards another part of the monument. The stranger had taken hold of Consuelo's elbow and was helping her over the low fences that separated the various sections of the monument. The steps here were littered with pieces of paper and other rubbish, and in the darkness, it would have been easy to slip.

I was puzzled by Consuelo's willingness to follow a strange man in the gloom of that park, and at her allowing him to touch her at all. I knew that she did not generally permit any kind of physical intimacy, a bit of prudishness which I had attributed to her years in the convent. But even more astonishing to me was my garrulous friend's unfamiliar silence.

The odd couple had stopped now before the fountain that had been brought over from the European country where the hero had spent part of his exile. Consuelo was examining it curiously. But the mysterious stranger's gaze had wandered to a group of people nearby—a little boy with blank eyes, his bare skin showing through his rags, moving his limbs mechanically in a small, grotesque dance; and beside him, three elderly men, sitting idly on a stone bench.

After watching them for a while, Consuelo's companion said, "Look there. That boy has lost his mind from being half-starved all his life. And those old men are on the prowl for young street girls who will do anything to get a bite to eat and a roof over their heads for the night."

At the skeptical expression in Consuelo's face, he said, "You are wondering how I know that. Believe me: I know. This park is my home. I literally live here. The problems have not changed. It was all for nothing. All useless!"

Once again, taking Consuelo's arm, the man guided her towards the spot where the hero had actually fallen. The slabs on which were engraved the various translations of the hero's final poem, written from prison as he awaited death, were as mildewed and grimy as everything else around them.

Silent himself now, the stranger pointed to one verse. Consuelo read it aloud in a strangely soft voice.

"Y *cuando ya mi tumba de todos olvidada / No tenga cruz ni piedra que marquen su lugar, / Deja que la are el hombre, la esparza con la azada, / Y mis cenizas que vuelvan a la nada, / El polvo de tu alfombr que vayan a formar (And when my grave is wholly unremembered / and unlocated [no cross upon it, no stone there plain]: / let the site be wracked by the plow and cracked by the spade / and let my ashes, before they vanish to nothing, / as dust be formed a part of your carpet again)...*" *

When she had finished reading, Consuelo turned to the stranger. And I saw that her eyes, as she looked at him, were filled with compassion, and that his were bleak with pain.

I felt a shiver go through my soul. Who was this man? Who was this woman? They were standing in the shadows, very close to each other, frozen in that pose of immeasurable suffering.

As I gazed at them, the world around them seemed to fade away—marble slabs and piles of rubbish, idiot boy and lewd old men, devoted members of the *kapatiran* and idle onlookers—all vanished. They were alone together in a young land over which blew a gentle wind. He was a lean young man in a dark suit, his face bright with the promise of all his gifts. She was a beautiful young woman in a gown that swept the ground, pale with the passion he had just awakened. Shyly she gave him her hand. Humbly he clasped it in his, and raised it slowly to his lips.... But now the wind was rising. It shook the trees, whipped her skirt about her legs, rumpled his hair. It was turning into a gale...

Then the vision was gone. The spinster schoolteacher stood before me, and beside her, the stocky worker in his faded workclothes.

I stared at them in consternation. Had they felt it? Did they suspect...?

But now, someone was calling to Consuelo. A member of the *kapatiran* walked up to her. As they talked, the man beside Consuelo quietly withdrew. I watched him slip through the crowd and disappear into the shadows of the trees in the distance. When Consuelo remembered and turned around to look for him, he was gone.

I saw the perplexed look in her eyes. And then she recognized me, and hailed me with her usual enthusiasm, her recent adventure slipping away from her mind. But I could not forget so easily. Feeling immensely drained, I left the gathering early. My mind was too agitated, my heart too heavy, for prayer. After undressing, I simply went to bed.

You must understand, my conscience does not allow me to believe in reincarnation. My religion forbids it. But all my instincts told me that the mysterious man in the park had been none other than my own ancestor. And that Consuelo, poor Consuelo, was the great love of his youth, the woman he had lost, and whom he had sought both to punish and to save in his literature, since he could not do so in his life.

It seemed to me I was gazing at Consuelo's life now as at an anagram that suddenly begins to make sense. It seemed to me I understood now what drove her, understood her groping, her searching, understood why, though she thought she worshipped Christ the Redeemer, she could not be his bride, but must bind herself to the followers of another savior whom she knew only from his portrait, faithful at last to the man she had betrayed in the willful ignorance of another lifetime.

It saddened me deeply that their sufferings were not at an end. That as she had failed him, he had failed himself, and, it seemed, his country. Or was it his country that had failed him?

What karmic force had yet to be worked out before his work could be considered done, his destiny accomplished? How long before he and she could finally find peace?

The following evening, there was to be a banquet given by a historical society to honor the living descendants of the hero. I assumed Consuelo would be there, and I had planned to be absent. But now, I decided to go. I felt that it was time for Consuelo to learn who I was, though I did not know what I hoped such a revelation would achieve.

After I had decided, I felt a great desire to give her something, something she could keep, something that had belonged to him. I think I entertained the notion that it would serve her as a kind of talisman, give her strength until the next, and perhaps the final meeting.

But my family no longer had anything that had belonged to him. Except for a few very small articles—and I had no idea where those might be—everything that had ever been remotely connected to him had become part of the national heritage.

And then I remembered there was one thing, and it was in my possession.

As you probably know, we take the vow of poverty when we enter the holy priesthood. I had therefore left behind everything that had belonged to me—everything save one small object. This was a little silver medal that had been given to me by my mother. She told me it had come to her from her grandmother, who had received it, along with a few pieces of jewelry from my famous ancestor's sister, in exchange for some money urgently needed by him in his exile. He had won the medal for an essay he had written as a schoolboy.

My mother had presented me with the medal upon my graduation from the university, the same university that had graduated him.

When I received the Holy Orders, this was the one thing I had been unable to give up, perhaps from some idea that it might someday earn me my ancestor's forgiveness. (All of you must remember what he thought of priests.)

But now I felt I was being given this chance to truly earn that forgiveness.

During the banquet, I was seated at the presidential table, along with the other members of our family. Consuelo arrived late and was given a place in the opposite side of the room. It was therefore only after the banquet was over that I found the opportunity to approach her.

If I had expected her to be offended at my having kept my identity a secret for so long, the broad smile with which she greeted me was proof of how I had misjudged her.

"Oh, Father, you are a sly one!" she exclaimed, her voice ringing out in the stately hall and causing several people to glance at us in amusement. "I should have known you were hiding something up your sleeve. No wonder you kept questioning me about my painting and everything. Now, confess, Father: what's your excuse for this great deception?"

I humbly acknowledged my guilt, offering no excuse save the usual one of finding people's reactions, when they learned the truth, acutely disconcerting.

And then, because I knew that we would soon be carried off by opposite currents, as always happens at large social affairs of that sort, I hastily dug into my pocket and produced my gift.

"It was his, Consuelo," I said in a low voice. "I think he would want you to have it."

Consuelo stared at the little silver medal in my hand. She did not ask who "he" was, or why I was giving her this little relic. Perhaps she thought I meant it as a reward for her years of fervent study of my ancestor's teachings.

I had nothing else to say. Somehow I could not bring myself to mention the sad man in the park. Or my own strange vision.

After a long moment, Consuelo took the little medal from my hand. I waited for her to speak, expecting one of her usual voluble outbursts. Instead, she threw her arms around me and clasped me in a fierce embrace. Then, without a word, she turned around and walked swiftly out of the hall.

The young priest had finished his tale.

In the silence that followed, the stranded travellers became aware that the storm's fury had abated. There was now only a cozy patter of raindrops on the roof of the roadside noodle house.

The bald dentist rose to open the windows.

The thin man with a cane shifted in his chair. "But, Father, was it really him in the park?" he asked.

"I do not know, sir," the young priest replied. "I only know what I saw."

"But why did you not speak to him, Father?" cried the ageing ballerina.

"Ah, I could not," said the young priest.

"And Consuelo, what has happened to her?" asked the large lady in the green dress.

"Why, nothing," the young priest said. "She is muddling along as she always has, watched over by the portrait of her hero."

"Only now she also has his silver medal," said the elegant old lady with the sleeping grandchild, wiping away the tears that had come to her eyes.

"Yes," said the young priest with a smile, "now she has his silver medal."

Author's Note:
* *The lines are from* El Ultimo Adios *by Rizal, translated into English by the National Artist, Nick Joaquin.*

The man referred to is perhaps Dr. Jose Rizal, the Philippines' national hero, who, after graduating from medical school in the country, went to Europe for further studies, like other young men who came to be known as the ilustrados, *and became the leader of the expatriate Propaganda Movement, which sought reforms from the colonial government of Spain. His writings, particularly his novels,* Noli Me Tangere *and* El Filibusterismo, *were an inspiration to his oppressed countrymen, particularly to the revolutionary movement. When he returned, the leadership of the revolution was offered to him, but he refused it because he believed his countrymen needed more education before they would be ready for independence. The Spaniards nonetheless arrested him, found him guilty of treason, and executed him.*

His young sweetheart, Leonor Rivera, who had been pressured by her family into marrying another man, died at childbirth. She was believed to be the inspiration for Maria Clara, the heroine of his first novel, who succumbs to family pressure and betrays her lover to the authorities; but then chooses to go into a convent, rather than marry a suitor she does not love. In the convent, she becomes the victim of an unscrupulous priest. The hero returns in the second novel, and, while plotting the revolution, plans also to rescue Maria Clara from the convent. She dies shortly before he gets there.

The phrase "...once a year in November" is a reference to All Saints' Day, celebrated on the first of November, when Filipinos clean and repaint their relatives' tombs, bring fresh flowers, and spend the day in the cemetery.

Grandma Sakamoto's Gun

Arlene Biala

grandma sakamoto's gun
was nestled in a blue felt crown royal liquor bag, stashed inside her
sewing machine case and found beneath heaps of boxes in the hall
closet of her waikiki apartment where she lived alone. it was three
weeks after she died. a rusted 38 revolver and silence. this was
surprising to no one.

*nam myoho renge kyo   nam myoho renge kyo   nam myoho renge
kyo*

a black and white photograph: *wahine* at 28, stunning and striding
down punahou street with sailors eyes tracing her beauty and a seven
year old daughter trying to keep up as her mother pulls her by the
hand. a local-girl marilyn monroe of sorts. her gaze straight ahead,
clear as the ala wai river running towards the sea. scent of *pikake*
and a hint of fear.

she was born amidst cane fields and a waikiki with no hotels. she
remembers when ala moana was a swamp, and all she could see
were the smashed shards of white coral reef, like the crushed bones
of *kapuna* drying in the sun. she remembers being left at the docks
when she was five years old, and her mother sailing back to japan.

*nam myoho renge kyo   strike the prayer bowl   vibrate through the
body*

how she outlived four husbands: hayasaka, kinoshita, silva and
sakamoto. visits in her living room. how she spoke of the difficulty
of compassion. love is easy, she'd say. it's close to hate. compassion
is what you have to work at. how she placed dry cat food and fresh
water on her porch every morning, for the stray she named brownie.

how she bought the gun for safekeeping, with or without intentions, or came upon it somehow and hid it. how she collected things: quilt squares, monkeypod bowls, tupperware of all sizes.

she would chant every morning and evening. to be a
bodhisattva: to cultivate virtues, to do something good for society.

after her first stroke, her grandson from the mainland came quickly to be with her. in her hospital bed and in front of him, she yanked the tubes out and whispered to him that she was hungry and would like to go home.

on the night she died, her closest granddaughter, on the road somewhere in new orleans, saw her in dragonfly wings and prayer beads.

laid to rest in punchbowl cemetery. how she prays for her loved ones to kiss the earth and worship *the great 14th*. to look beyond the telescopic eye.

Author's note:
Nam myoho renge kyo *is a Buddhist invocation chanted every morning and evening which covers all laws, all matter and forms of life that exist in the universe.* Bodhisattva *are those in Buddhism who have a mission to propagate true teaching and establish world peace.* The great 14th *refers to the Dalai Lama.*

Tall Grasses

Henrietta Chico Nofre

He was the handsomest man I'd ever seen. Japanese soldier at the end of the war. Kind to my family, to my sister, my mother, my father, smiling and quiet even when he knew the militia were looking for Japanese, for him and three others like him who were hiding in the grasses by the river. So handsome, so handsome, most beautiful man I'd ever seen. And so young.

"No good. Just trouble. Take in their clothes to wash and mend their knapsacks? Give them fish for soap and cigarettes? Militia will kill them, then you, leave me two small girls by myself, they catch us," Mother said.

"Just wash, woman. Take the tobacco and the lighter fluid. Militia is stupid and isn't it nice to have soap again?" Father went out to catch more fish.

Playing with us sometimes, handsome, young Japanese soldier who came sometimes with his three privates, sometimes not, but gave me and Kutoy gum. Helped us carry the drinking water into the house.

Mother, behind Father's back, throwing the handsome Japanese soldier's soap into the river. "Go away, child. Militia will kill us if they find this in the house."

Then one day, more towards real end of war, right before we moved back to our house in the city, handsome, young Japanese soldier came to my family's house. Knock, knock, small knock. Japanese soldier alone and no longer smiling. Spoke to Father, could not look him in the face.

"Sir, please, the militia is coming. I have three privates waiting in the tall grasses. Could you..."

No looking at Father.

"...please, sir..."

Eyes on ground, beautiful Japanese soldier.

"...hide us?"

Mother was quiet. Father looked kindly. "Son, our house is small, no room you can see. But maybe room for just one. Just you."

Beautiful Japanese soldier looking at feet. My feet, Kutoy's feet, Father's feet, finally say, "Thank you, thank you, sir." Smiling small, still eyes on ground. "But I cannot leave my men."

Handsome, young Japanese soldier, most beautiful I have seen in my entire life, left our feet and our door. Tall grasses.

Next day, Mother, Father, Kutoy and I, we heard gunshots. Loud. Bang, bang, bang, bang. Then, no more.

Mermaid

Conchitina R. Cruz

Your invitation
is a promise
dangled before me
like a charm.
In response,
my shell of water
ripples into cracks.

For you, I rise
above the womb,
turn amphibian,
crawl on unknown earth.
I shred my voice
into silence to learn
the syllables of your own.

Breathe new air
into me
with your kiss.
Scale my fins
into limbs
with your touch.
Break me open

as I cling
to the pieces
of a promise, hooked
to the end of a line
that was cast out to sea
one lazy day
to kill some time.

In Whispers

Michelle Macaraeg Bautista

You travel on soft breezes
shielded by cupped hands
for the unwritten rules
that were broken.
Your name floats
on these winds
that glide lightly from
lips to ears.

"She is the bad daughter
masamang babae,"
they say,
the one who rots
the family name
with her disease of dishonor.
Her fruit is spoiled.
Her seed is unholy.
Yet still, it grows from the tears
of shame from her
grandparents' eyes.

I look at her
she turns away
never again to allow
our eyes to meet
as if she will turn me into stone.
The clouds that enshroud her
walk in her eyes

Her baby cries to her
from shadowed branches
never understanding the burden
given to her from birth
never truly able to feel
the warmth of the sunshine
because of the winds that howl
in her mother's womb.

I am the good daughter
she must not soil from her stare
I can never speak to her
only of her.
As the wind travels between us
my heart too
freezes from the chill.

Haze

Fran Ng

We collide on purpose
not our own
leaping into orange

then I am red
and you are yellow
circling
a solitary fever.

We make rings of fire
in dim spaces
stroking time

Poet Traveling Over Water

Merlie M. Alunan

befriend the wind
let it ride easy
in the hollows
of your bones
open your skin
for wind to go through
storm rising
from the abyss
could pitch you
on the rocks
blow skull apart
for darkness and sun
coldness and heat
to flow in
without staying
salt-caked and split
your tongue
would breed
words of the wind's
secret
singing

now then
will the wind
command the billows
to bear you
the tide
to lay your bones
under the moon
to bleach without
rancor without bliss
everything forgiven
your name
the wind spells
on the water
the syllables
so very kindly very
gently leave
where it will

Notebook

Fran Ng

I.
I talk to words not through words
and strangely, they speak
in a bonfire of butterflies
shaping my voice luminous.

II.
I graze in the belly of language
deepening the earth's flavor
emerging from a book
spread open.

III.
I graze in the belly of language
rotating laughter's spheres
dreaming a dead star burning white
like a kiss time-traveling.

Section IV   Testament

Picture

Marianne Villanueva

She's leaning forward, as if to kiss him. There's a mark on his cheek; perhaps she's done it already. They are both smiling.

These were my parents in Manila, circa 1956. They were happy; they had always been happy. The happiness of their marriage was like a reproach.

I didn't think he looked that ugly. "*El unica problema es que no es guapo.*" Who said this? My grandmother's cousin, Lola Paching. This, at least, was the family story.

But there was a certain kind of attractiveness in my father's face. My mother, I saw now, looked like me. Or like I might have looked, if I, too, had been happy. She was wearing a white scoop-necked gown. Her breasts looked heavy and full, but her arms were thin. She was looking up at my father and smiling.

I am collecting old pictures now. I don't know what this tells me about this stage of my life.

My husband and two children are far away. My husband said, as he packed their things, "Don't call us. We're happier that way." I may have murmured something in reply, compulsively polite, even under such circumstances. I didn't know whether I meant to say, *Good Riddance,* or *I'll be seeing you,* or *Have a pleasant day!* I stood on the driveway and gave a little wave as I watched my two children's faces, grave in the back seat.

Marco is ten; his sister, Maya, is four. I had them a long time ago, when I was a different person. Now I find it hard to remember that person who changed their diapers without complaint, who gave them heated milk in the middle of the night. They lived in a neat house then.

Two nights ago, my sister-in-law called from the Philippines. The phone sounded shrill in the empty house.

"And how are you?" she asked. It seemed to me that she rolled her *r*'s unnecessarily.

"Fine," I said, and decided to say nothing about my husband leaving.

She probably knew already but pretended she didn't. Instead, she asked me a string of questions, and I deflected them all by saying, "Ben is not here right now. He took the children for some ice cream."

I'd been gardening, and my hands were muddy. I looked at my black-rimmed nails as I sat cradling the phone against my ear. "Uh-huh, uh-huh, uh-huh," I said, not really sure what my sister-in-law was saying. Her words were like a stream, their forward motion unimpeded by any barrier.

Finally I said, "And how is Dad? Is he all right?"

"Fine, he's fine," my sister-in-law said. She sounded abrupt. She said she had to go. Even before I lowered the receiver, I heard the line go dead. I sat there, the receiver in my hand. After a long while, I stood up and decided to get myself a drink.

The refrigerator was empty. It seemed my husband had taken even the last two beer bottles that had been on the top shelf. There was a mess of soggy lettuce in the vegetable crisper, moldy salami in the meat bin. A smell of spoiled milk wafted from the refrigerator shelves.

I went to the bed and lay down. What, what, what would I do now? There was the telephone, black and still. It refused to speak to me. And anyway, when it did speak, it was always my sister-in-law or a solicitor or someone else I didn't want to hear from. No one nice, like my mother or my brothers in the Philippines. Or even my uncle or cousins in Daly City. I got up and thought, I'll hide it. There was a plastic garbage can in the living room. I took the phone and put it there. I didn't unplug it yet, though. I might like listening to the sound of it ringing.

The first night, I watched an old Douglas Fairbanks movie on one of the cable channels: *The Thief of Baghdad*. The hero had black-rimmed eyes. Ha, ha. I laughed and laughed. Everything about him was side-splittingly funny. I thought, Tomorrow I will go to the video store and rent this film. The sound of my laughter was deep and throaty, and I realized this was one more thing that was changing, along with everything else.

After a long while, I got tired of watching old movies and eating moldy salami. Perhaps I had lost track of time, but it did seem that there were more newspapers collecting on the driveway, forlorn in their yellow plastic wrappers. It seemed to me that I should pull myself together. I should at least let my mother know what had happened. I didn't know where my two children were, but that was all right; their father would take care of them. I remembered the way they had clung to him as they walked out the door.

"I love you," I said, and the boy turned his head, but only a little.

"What's that?" I said, thinking he had been about to say something.

When he heard my voice, my husband turned his head. "What did you say?" he said. His face, as he turned towards me, had that familiar look: that irritable, crumpled look. A look that completely altered his features, so that I couldn't think of him as my husband, not the husband I thought I had married. When I didn't answer, he continued walking towards the sidewalk.

My son was in a hurry, trying to keep up with his father. "Dad's leaving," he said, shrugging his shoulders apologetically before turning away.

I watched his legs—skinny brown legs—in their too-large sneakers go stumbling down the front walk. My little girl clutched her father's hand. I couldn't see her face. Oh God! I thought. I suddenly wanted to scream. But the neighbors, the neighbors, I thought. And at that moment while I was standing in the driveway, my hands clasped together, the children got into the car and zoomed away. I remained standing there, watching the car round the corner.

The first days alone in the house, I thought I heard voices: when I worked in the garden, when I lay in bed. I thought I heard a voice calling, "Ma?" A voice that seemed familiar. Later I realized that this voice was a combination of the boy's and the girl's, a double strand. And I answered to the house, to its shuttered windows. "I'm all right," I said. The house breathed back its silent, moldy spaces at me.

For the first time, as I walked in and out of the empty rooms, I noticed the window frames, how the wood had warped. The paintings my husband and I had collected on our various trips home to the Philippines hung crookedly on the walls. Now and then, if I happened to think of it, I would reach out a hand and straighten one or two. I would step back, judging the effect.

In the hallway were a long row of framed prints of Old Manila. These prints depicted eighteenth-century scenes: the plaza in front of the Dominican convent in Intramuros, strangely devoid of people; a view of the Pasig River, crowded with boats. The borders were red, the frames gilt. Why were they here, hanging in the dim upstairs hallway, where no one, not a single guest to our house, could see them?

Eventually I thought, I will adopt a new family. It's easy. All I need to do is advertise. So I took out the *Pomona Weekly* and looked in the classifieds. And before I'd turned more than a few pages, I saw it: a picture of a smiling little boy, about seven or eight years old, and Filipino, too, from the looks of him. Underneath the picture was the caption: WILL YOU FEED ME?

Sure! I thought. Sure, little boy! I'll bring you to the land of milk and honey, where you'll never ever have to scrounge around in garbage cans ever again. Not if I can help it.

And I didn't know why, but looking at that picture brought a terrible pain to my chest, so that I couldn't rest until I'd gone to the store and bought paper and pen and stamps to write to the boy. And all that night, I tossed and turned, waiting for the mailman to come so that I could run right out and give him the letter, the letter for the little boy. And then I took all my son's things, the old toys he'd left behind in his room because they were too old or too broken or too dirty, and I arranged them in a neat row on the floor and said, "These will be for you, little boy. Come home soon!"

And every night after that I sat looking out the window at the empty street, expecting to see a thin shadow come running up the front walk, a shadow that hopped and skipped, the way my son used to do when he'd run home in the evenings from a day spent playing in the park or at a friend's house.

In the evenings, there was a strange kind of knocking sound from a corner of one of the eaves facing the side yard. And eventually, after sitting and listening to the sound for what seemed like hours on end, I took the aluminum ladder from the garage—my husband had not taken everything—and leaned it against the side of the house. I climbed gingerly, carefully, and there, in a corner of a rain spout glutted with dark brown leaves, was a fat green toad. It looked at me mildly with its yellow eyes.

"Oh, you poor frog. You poor, poor frog," I said. As I said it, there was again that ache in my chest, an ache that was rapidly becoming familiar, as familiar as the sound of my shallow breathing when I lay in bed at night, waiting for sleep. I backed down the ladder, cupping the toad carefully in my right hand. It sat still. Its skin was slimy and cold. I could feel the pulse in its throat against my fingers.

I thought, I will put it in the children's terrarium. I looked and looked for the terrarium, but it was nowhere to be found. Standing in the middle of the dimly lit garage, I wondered, Could they have taken that, too? I hadn't known it had meant so much to them. For years it had sat on a high shelf in the garage, after their last lizard had died. The one named Ed.

And still I wandered about with the toad cupped in the palm of my right hand. I couldn't put it down. The beat of its heart reminded me of other things, things unconnected to my present life. A baby underneath my ribs. The rip and tear between my legs that also meant happiness. The smell of soap.

Think, think, think, I thought. Did I happen to sell the terrarium during our last garage sale? Was it in among the things I sent off to the Salvation Army, along with the crib and the other baby things? The truck came yesterday: a powerfully built black man had come to the door. He said nothing as he carted the stuff away. There goes my life, I wanted to say.

I watched him fling the clothes into the back of the truck. The truck lumbered slowly down the street, and at the second corner made a slow right turn.

I put the toad in the bathtub. Its color seemed muted and muddy against the white enamel. I remembered leaning my daughter over the edge of the tub, her hair cascading over my hands as I lathered her head with shampoo. The feel of her tiny skull between my hands, the depression at the base of her head, her narrow neck. Before I knew it, my hands extended, as if there really was a shape between them.

My daughter could never keep still, even for a few seconds. Squirming, she would gasp as the water trickled over her head and face. She was a happy child, never despondent, even when I told her she couldn't have certain things she wanted very much. Now the toad gazed up at me, not moving.

Things were happening now, in that house. First, the water stopped. The toilet was beginning to give off a smell. My hair stood up stiff and straight from my forehead, and I was surprised, really surprised, to see so many strands flecked with white. If I turned my head to one side, I could also see bare patches of skull above each ear. My hair fell down the sink—where else could it go? And the water moved increasingly sluggishly down the drain.

Now, when the mailman came up the walk, I ran anxiously to the front door to greet him. Wordlessly, he would hand me the pile of supermarket flyers and turn his back. He was Asian—perhaps Chinese or Vietnamese. He didn't seem to understand English. His steps seemed to quicken as he left the front porch.

One day—it must have been spring—I looked out the front window and the roses were suddenly all in bloom along the verandah. It was a tremendously sunny day.

I decided to take a walk around the block. I put on shorts, a T-shirt, my favorite sandals. I noticed the wisteria was in bloom at the corner of the front porch. When I crossed the street, I saw the top of Mrs. Olson's head, behind a tall hedge. She was mowing her lawn, stopping every now and then. I dragged myself along. I felt I couldn't move without breathing heavily. The hair stood up wildly from the top of my head. The bald patches at the side of my skull stared up at the sun.

I stopped dead in my tracks. At that moment, the street was wide and empty. There was a tall house with a brick front directly in front of me. The shutters were drawn at all the windows. A large black dog glared at me from behind an iron gate. Had that family always had a dog? It seemed I had never noticed it, or even the iron gate, before.

Suddenly I felt, this is the way it will be forever: me, the empty street, and the sun.

Longing

Luisa A. Igloria

I want to be almost indistinct,
to recede into the grain of objects, become
salt, one of the seeds in a bitter melon, a bud
flowering briefly: memory which water
or ink can release from the tongue

I want to be the simple, companionable
wood of a doorknob whose face, completely
unadorned by eyebrows, betrays
no allegiance, turning easily
in each direction—

        The runny print
drying on a newspaper that someone
has left on a park bench in the rain,
its pages rising to the slightest
touch of wind with the recklessness
of a deprived lover—

        The delicate
streaks of mold, the old velour
of scum in corridors of train stations,
the moist lining of a sleeve that sticks
to the insides of your elbows and clings,
like the last days of an illness,
before finally letting go—

In your side, a tiny laceration
you never notice until you arrive at your
doorstep, your life a stain marking the spot
where something tipped you over:

A cup, surrendering
its contents, a crumpled envelope falling
from a window ledge, a veil that a woman lifts,
the robe that she opens to disquiet the wind—

O to travel in open country and arrive
at your body; to enter its gates, perforate
the air like light or a familiar smell

Like any ordinary sound you think
you might have heard before

An echo
awakening you before sleep
can settle clear as lake water
over which the notes of a bell,
wide-hipped, have broken
open—continuously
inviting answer

Loreto, Alone

Linda Ty-Casper

Loreto notices the wind drifting across the fishpond, carrying with it the sun and pieces of leaves: tiny plants no bigger than pinpricks, on which the *bangus* feeds. Just a river, she thinks, the way the river in back of their house in Gulod is held between its banks.

She watches the sky behind the wind that sweeps around the guava tree, heading back across the land towards the hills. Bending the light, the sky runs along the dikes that intersect long distances, sectioning off the ponds like rice fields. It makes her think of night, though it is only midafternoon.

By now, she thinks, they are sitting around the table at home, dishes untouched, wondering if her brother should be notified. Her mother might already have called him: Loreto has not come home. With whom? We don't know. Do you think we should wait? By evening?

And then? What if?

When does it become too late, her mother means by those questions, too late to restore things to the way they were, like the river.

Loreto knows how it is to be worried into silence, then into fear that mobilizes irrationalities of all kinds. They could be thinking of her already dead, floating on some *estero*, deep marks of assault decorating her body. Her mother might have already sent for the tabloids that run photos of victims on front pages, exposing wounds and grief.

And Emilio Luna is taking his time trying to reach the fruit from the tree a storm has blown over the pond; its roots are barely holding it to the edge of the water, its branches too slippery even to hold nests in place. He has reached a guava by leaping. She holds this deep in her pocket while she waits for him to get another for himself. She hates fruits with seeds, tiny seeds that get between the teeth.

She watches him against the sun, which has begun its descent, while she thinks back to that morning, earlier, when Emilio Luna stopped for her on the highway and opened the door of his sister's car. She got in as if it was Emilio Luna she was waiting for, as if they have gone off together before, or ever talked. She had assumed he was offering her a ride to where she was going, was thinking of how to tell her mother that Mrs. Luna's son gave her a ride, when she noticed they were heading north, away from Manila. Not wishing to appear alarmed, to presume an intention he did not have towards her, she said nothing.

What are they to do in this place?

They had stopped for *merienda* at a roadside restaurant. From there she expected they would head back, so all she asked for was *halo-halo*. Ice had not been delivered, so they waited, watching the traffic on MacArthur Highway. He asked if she was going to school.

"Not anymore," she said, without explaining. When the glasses of *halo-halo* were served, each glass wrapped with a paper napkin to catch the drip, they stirred the shaved ice into the milk and preserved fruits without looking at each other.

She was not used to looking at him, except unseen behind the window whenever he walked by with his mother. Nor he, being looked at. He looked quickly away when she lifted her eyes. After some silence, he said, "Instead of school, it is better to read books. Everything can be learned from books. One can learn to fly. Aerodynamics. Whatever one wants to know. That's where teachers get what they teach."

She smiled, but not at him. She smiled, watching the *pinipig*, newly roasted still-green rice, disappear among the white and red beans, the green *mongo*. The *ube* jam colored the glass purple.

Until they reached the fishponds, he did not speak again. On the way she looked for landmarks, so she could find her way back if she had to. She is always afraid of being lost, even in her dreams. They passed a schoolhouse with a separate building for Home Economics. Then a chapel facing the road, altar bare, the wrought-iron door like stiff cobwebs. A rice mill. Towns with *muncipios* facing statues of Jose Rizal in the plazas. Wild *gumamelas* growing into the road, coloring the sky.

Something has distracted Emilio Luna from getting the guava. He is now facing the pond, sitting on the nearest dike with his elbows on his knees, thinking secrets.

She cannot imagine being hurt by him, being hurt in this place.

"This is how Gulod used to be," he says, not turning around to face her. "Remember?"

The single word makes her feel sought, claimed. And a shadow, like a restlessness, shakes her while she watches him sitting as fixed as a tree.

He says nothing further and she walks to the hut no bigger than a treehouse. Peeking inside, she discovers that if she stands in the middle, she can touch the walls without stretching her arms. There is nothing inside. The Luna's caretaker must use it for shelter when it rains and to rest briefly during the day. Spaced apart for air and to allow rain to fall through, the floor is bamboo, split irregularly. There is no door. The entrance is a kind of window awning, woven from *nipa*, as is the roof.

On arriving, Emilio Luna had gone immediately inside to prop the awning with a stick.

"It's like a tree house," she had said, but he did not answer.

She thinks of walking down to him, of repeating her statement to make him answer. Suddenly piqued, she thinks of throwing the guava in his direction. But what's the use? He is spoiled, willful. Everyone in Gulod says so: because they own the biggest house, have visitors coming from the city. And during elections, the candidates sleep in their house. She should have looked away when he stopped for her. What does he think? That he can have his way with her?

The sun is its own shadow in the sky.

"We used to come when the fish were harvested." He stands up to walk to another part of the fishponds. "Men brought up the fish in baskets and threw them over there. The fattest were roasted on sticks. No need for salt. They burned their hands turning the fish. But they're used to that."

He sounds as if he's describing what happened just the day before, as if she had been there as well. She waits for what else he will say, wants to say.

From the hut she cannot tell if a fish has come up to gulp air or if Emilio Luna has dislodged a pebble in the water, starting ripples that will tear up his reflection on its surface.

"The fish are big," he says. "Come look."

"How do you catch them?" When he does not answer, she sits down on the last step of the hut, both feet on the ground, to watch him walking away on the dike until in the suffusion of light he appears no wider than a post marking boundaries. The water appears deep enough to drown in, looks dark with patches of green floating slowly across, patches the shape of the sun.

How can she make her words reach him?

At the first intersection of dikes he doubles back. Once more under the guava tree's upright branches, he stares at the fruit out of his reach. Beneath the open collar of his shirt, the skin is white. She is darker than he.

Don't you climb, she warns him silently.

He goes to the hut, pulls out a long stick from an edge of the roof. It is short by an arm's length. He throws it down and starts to climb.

"Catch," he says without warning.

The fruit rolls into the pond before either of them can run to where it fell. They narrowly avoid falling against each other.

"I hate guavas anyway," she says. "I hate fish cooked in guavas, especially guavas cooked in coconut milk and sweetened with *panocha*."

"I like guavas," he says, returning to the tree. The sky and the intense light give him a partial outline, which makes him appear incomplete, someone just happening by, like the shadow of a cloud drifting on the ground. And she is filled with longing.

She wants to yield and looks over the fishponds towards the sea beyond, miles away, years away from where she stands.

He sits at the edge of the pond again, looking out to where she thinks the rivers flow together into Manila Bay. Her Lola Sula said that during the Revolution against Spain, the Spaniards from the Central Plains tried, through the rivers, to reach Manila Bay where the *almirante,* they thought, was waiting to bring them back to España; they were caught with all the gold and silver they were carrying on the boats, with the reliquaries and palms and statues from the churches they had passed.

She wonders how her Lola Sula is. It was to buy her fresh bread that she was heading for the market that morning. Bread and *queso de bola.* Just a slice of the cheese. Just for her because she remembers when every day was a feast. Just for Lola Sula because the children do not know the difference between imported and local cheese.

She is glad she did not throw the guava at Emilio Luna. Her Lola Sula likes to eat guava with *bagoong* and rice. She looks up to see if any fruit has escaped Emilio Luna's eyes.

"It's getting late," she says.

Her Lola Sula will think she has eloped. She is also hungry. Not since *merienda* have they eaten anything. She gets up, drawn to the hibiscus beside the hut. The buds are half open. Or half closed.

She can look into the red throat of one flower, which makes her think of the sun flaming as it rises and as it drops into the sea. She thinks of calling this to his attention, but he has dropped his head between his knees.

Suppose she just walks away? Does he expect her to know what's on his mind, to agree to anything simply because that's what he wants?

Thinking over the possibility of simply leaving, she picks a blade of grass. Sharp-edged, like a knife, it draws blood that fills the long cut. The pain throbs through her body, her little finger. She licks the cut, presses it to the hem of her skirt. It tastes like raw and unripe fruit.

"It's late already." She pulls sighs, deliberately slow, from her body. This is all entirely her fault, of course: she could have looked away when he stopped for her at the highway. She could have gone her way after the *halo-halo*.

He continues to sit, now watching the light playing on the surface, watching as if his mind is sorting out other things besides her being there, alone with him. What does he measure in silence?

Each time he looks away or turns, everything seems to begin again for him. How can he have a memory of her? Any memory? She might not have entered his thoughts at all, or is no longer in his thoughts.

She walks back to the hut. The *gumamela* has opened wider, the color of the pain in her finger. She wonders that bees have not found it, though ants have and are entering its red throat. She leans against the next higher step, wondering where his wounds are that neighbors talk about, how deep?

Her brother might be home now. Her mother would have told him, Loreto asked permission to go to the market. It might merely be her excuse. Her grandmother blames me for letting her go by herself.

She had passed Sally on the road but did not go to a movie with the neighbor. *Takaw Tukso* was starring Jaclyn Jose and Julio Diaz. She did not want to see a film with "wet" sex acts, and Sally did not want to see *Napakasakit Kuya Eddie*, about infidelities.

Looking up, Loreto sees Emilio Luna running towards her, hands cupped and smiling so deeply at her as if she is the only thing his mind contains. "Look!" As soon as he opens his hands, a fish drops out. Its wet body catches the dust between their feet.

"It's ugly," she says, drawing away but afraid to move in case she steps on the fish or it wriggles against her feet.

He is no longer smiling when she looks up. A shadow seems to have dropped over him. She is gone from his thoughts, his mind erasing itself at will. Is the shadow that of an intimidating dream? This thought is an echo of what she thinks he's thinking, a brutal exchange of sorts that makes her wonder if she's the one hurting inside his dream.

She's afraid to look at him again, to see the terrifying loneliness in his eyes, in his mouth. To bring back his smile, his hurrying towards her, she says, "It's hot. Look, the *gumamela* is open. It took all day. Usually, they open in the morning."

He sits below her but says nothing. He only looks over the pond, away from her.

She is close enough to touch him, touch the ear folded like a little child's, the hair darkly soft, but his silence pushes her away. It grows until they are silent together, until—just as if he's reaching for a dragonfly—he picks the flower and crushes it inside his hand.

"Don't!" She wants to tell him to go away.

"It's hot," he says firmly, making her statement final.

She averts her face, thinking of the flower still in his hand, limp like a captured bird from which life has been squeezed, while the fishponds continue on towards the sky where the sun will go down, red, like the thrust of the *gumamela*.

"It's getting late," she says without urgency.

He looks as if he's completely inside himself; the flower in his hand is a wound that will start bleeding.

The sun is now still. But something else she cannot see seems to be throbbing, whirling. Her hands are moist as if she held the wet crushed petals herself. A pain passes through her. After they leave that place, what will have changed? If she walks away, will he bring her back or merely watch her leaving? Suppose he needs her to be there? What will her mother say when she returns? Nothing happened, she will say the truth. Will her mother believe? Is it the truth?

"Go up and rest," he tells her, smiling. "Go sleep."

She hesitates entering the hut, but she does as he says, lies down on the floor of bamboo that feels like bare knuckles. She turns on her side to face the wall so she will not see him coming up. Can he hurt her while she sleeps? And if she dreams, who will she meet in the dream? She lies there, listening.

The wind picks up. She can smell the sea, the bay. She is wondering if he will remember her in his dream when she wakes up.

Moving like water under the wind, the dark is spreading when she wakes up. Everything restless has stopped. She walks down to where Emilio Luna is. Close to the guava tree, beside the pond, he is bending over a fire, turning a fish on a stick. When the flames rise, she can see his eyes almost asleep and she feels an ache and a tenderness that wants him, then and forever, safely inside her.

Kristine

Shirley Ancheta

Kristine turns a corner in San Francisco and is struck by an oncoming car. She is floating, she thinks, in the air with the seagulls. Her teeth ache. A man steps up to her and says, "Dear God, I'm sorry. What can I do?" What? She thinks he has said, "Desire...here...what will you do?" The only man she wants to reach is married or dead or related to her. She smiles. She can't remember.

She thought she was kissing a boy in the dark, in back of the house near the pineapple field. His hands could hold down a pig for the killing. They were caught by their grandmother who threw her slipper across the yard. "No do dat wit your cah-sin! Wassamaddah you kids? You no feel shame o' what? No good fo' cah-sins fo' make li' dat!"

It is cold on the pavement of Stockton and Pine. The wind is enough to pick up Kristine's skirt. She rolls her head from side to side. As someone puts a blanket on her, she hears a siren rising to meet the ringing in her ears.

After they butchered the pig, they hosed down the concrete of pig guts and urine. He had held a pan to catch the blood after Uncle had slit the pig's throat. She had stirred the blood with a metal spoon until it became foamy then thick with the odor of vinegar.

Was it desire that made her straddle him later, or was it his desire that brought the tips of her breasts into his mouth? Did they finish before Grandma saw them or after?

"Hello," says the man who opens her eyes and lets the light in. "Do you know where you are?"

Kristine wants to say the name on her tongue. If she closes her eyes, a warm rain will come. Kunia Village, Kunia Village. This is the place she is.

Cloister

Mabi Perez David

From our dark corner in the grotto
we see her clearly. She stands outside,
beyond school gates. "No Trespassers
Allowed." We sit here knees to chests,
and cover our thin legs with our skirts.
When a nun finds us, we can always say,
"There is our less fortunate
sister, Sister,"
and we will shake our clean heads
and she will clutch her rosary beads
to her flat chest.
Maybe she will leave us alone.

She is wearing black again today.
Mourning, perhaps,
Sister will say but we know better.
We feast our eyes on what is left
uncovered—thighs, arms, neck, face—
and make up stories we are so eager
to believe, willing to trade
our costumes and chaste desks
for these night tales her skin breathes.
We are sure her breasts are
like those from confiscated paperbacks.

We think we hear Sister's footsteps
Her Second Coming.
We leave our corner
and step into the light.
She will never know of how
we savor the woman's sin

               and wish it were our own.

Testament

Katrina Tuvera

Tita Gilda didn't know what it would do to me, years ago when she decided I should have a room of my own. Or, if she knew, it didn't make a difference. Her biggest worry then was summer: it was simply taking too long. All that month I stayed home. Hardly a day passed when she didn't catch me toying with something she owned—a prayer book, a locket, or her saints arranged like a chorus line on her dresser. She said as much to Father when he came home for the weekend, and before the day was over she had moved my bed to the room across the hall.

Secretly I was thrilled, realizing the liberties instantly available. I could eat in bed, or keep the lamp on for as long as I wanted. I stayed up later each night, playing cards and daydreaming, or reading until daylight cut through the sky when I would set down my books, look out the window, and watch summer taking its leave. Charmed by my solitude, I shunned sleep—and soon, sleep eluded me.

Today, I'm twenty-nine and a true insomniac. Married, for three years now, to a man who snores. Our neighbors devote three nights a week to the karaoke. "Blue Bayou" is a favorite and they render it many ways in a single night, each variation growing more peculiar with every case of beer they consume. Then there is Elmer, our dog, who won't eat leftovers and, well-fed or not, stands all evening outside our window, barking at every shadow under the moon. Roy, my husband, keeps a gun under the bed and I tell him, One of these days I'll put a bullet through that dog's head.

And the crooners next door?

I'll blast that karaoke to pieces.

Okay, he says, anything to help you sleep. Then, patting my thigh, he turns away and snores.

I've tried everything to cure my condition. No alcohol, no TV after nine. No heavy supper, even though there are times when I eat very little but still stare at the ceiling for hours. I've given up smoking, except for one cigarette I must have after climbing into bed.

That habit I can't shake off, like locking the door or turning off the light; without it, the day doesn't feel over. I've been warned against sleeping pills, but two streets away a pharmacy sells Halcion over the counter, and who am I to tell them they should know better?

At night, when I can't sleep, I make all kinds of lists—what's left in the refrigerator, the clothes I'll wear for the week, the days I visit Dr. Luna. One of Roy's uncles, an actor, formed a theater company called Footlights two years ago and he pays me to write publicity. I do that too, even if Roy finds it annoying when he wakes up and sees that I have brought work all the way to bed. He says I'll sleep better if I stop working early, and forbids sweets after supper. And he says, Stop thinking about your father—although he knows I had insomnia long before the man died.

Some nights I drop in on Tita Gilda, who now lives alone in her dead brother's house except for a maid. I eat supper there when I know Roy will be home late, but I'm good about calling first to give notice. It's always the same when I visit: I arrive and she's in her room, praying. She makes me wait on the terrace where it is cool and I can stare at the guava tree I used to climb as a girl. When she finally joins me, she asks, though she already knows how long I've been waiting.

In her fifties now, my aunt is still a fair woman, hair in soft curls, back straight as a pole. She calls this God's reward—and it could well be: the signs of aging might not be so hidden today if she'd taken a husband and had children of her own. But marriage was not for this desperately pious woman, for whom nothing is too trivial to bring to God's attention. If Father hadn't sent for her after Mother died when I was barely six, Tita Gilda might have settled for a convent, but then, Father's house wasn't far from a convent after my aunt took over with her candles and the verses she posted on every door. Then too, there were hardly men around, because Father moved away to the farm and left me with Tita Gilda soon after my mother's death.

Tita Gilda used to say she could read my thoughts, and as a youngster I was convinced this was true. She seemed to always know what I had done. If I had slammed a door or fallen asleep and left the TV on, she knew, even if all that while she had not stepped out of her room. Silences fell between us, not out of anger but simply as a matter of course. Even today our conversations end in mid-sentence, words trailing away without a hint of discomfort.

But tonight when I visit, she stops me just as I am leaving and says that I look tired. She tells me this as we stand outside the gate, while I dig into my bag for the car keys. I pause, glancing up at her. The street lights have not been turned on and all I see of her is an outline, her curls, a faint glimmer in her eyes, but she is near enough that I hear her breathing. I say to her: I have a hard time falling asleep.

Are you seeing that doctor still? she asks.

Yes. I see him every month.

She touches my shoulder lightly. Behind her, a wind stirs up the leaves of my dead father's firetree and over their sound, Tita Gilda whispers: Your mother was the same.

And yet she had me, I reply.

We say good night and she hurries back to the house, just in time for her last prayer of the day.

Driving away, I watch the house shrink in my rearview mirror. Even in the moonlight its age is clear. Tita Gilda tries, but without Father to remind her, the broken fence and graying walls are bound to remain for some time. It was always Father, though he came only on weekends, who kept the house intact. Home from the farm he inherited from his parents, he would lead me from one end of the house to the other, toolbox in hand, peering at corners, tapping on walls. Once, I asked him why he didn't just sell the house, take Tita and me to live with him. He looked at me in amazement and said, And just how do you think that would make your mother feel? He summed it up that way, so simply: in his house every screw he tightened, every hinge he oiled, carried his thoughts back to a dead woman and her stillborn son.

But I was young then and didn't see how deeply someone could yearn for the past. Only now—when I see the house he left behind falling apart, while inside Tita Gilda walks from room to room, lighting candles—only now do I begin to sense a craving of my own.

I didn't think it could get worse, but sleeping became more difficult when I married Roy. It was July, the season of rains, when we married and moved into a two-room apartment. Whenever it poured, we had to bathe quickly, because the buckets were needed in the hall to catch water leaking through the ceiling. During our first month, it rained every night.

Only a year before my marriage, Father had moved back to the city. He had sold the farm when he discovered he was ill and, when Roy and I told him we were engaged, said he wanted us to live with him and Tita Gilda. But Roy wouldn't hear of it; for my part, I didn't want to begin married life surrounded by nurses and oxygen tanks. I knew even then that Father was seeing his last days. Home from the hospital where he had been hooked to a respirator, he hardly left his bed, only once in a while walking on feeble legs to a seat by the window where he yielded his skin to the morning sun. The day I moved out we sat together, talking about the place Roy had found. He worried about our rent and the neighborhood. When I left, it seemed that we had talked of many things, but not the fact that he was dying.

There was a time, long ago when Father lived away and I was a child left with Tita Gilda, when I greatly feared his death. At odd moments, at home or in school, I was terrified that my aunt would come at any minute, to say that Father had gotten drunk, that his car had fallen off the road, and I would close my eyes tightly to drive the thought away. It haunted me so that several times, away from my aunt's sight, I dialed his long-distance number but hung up as soon as I heard his voice. Even with him home on a weekend I was never completely relieved. When I caught him asleep on the sofa, I would hold out a finger to check his breathing.

But he lingered for forty-five more years and when the end came I was calm, astonishing everyone, including Roy. Perhaps his long illness, the months spent in the hospital, had prepared me. I understood how his suffering was over. Or perhaps, in the eighteen years we lived apart, I had lost touch with my girlhood fear and no longer knew how to measure my loss.

Neither, it seemed, did Tita Gilda. Tight-lipped and dry-eyed like her many saints, at the wake she sat alone in the room where we prepared coffee and donuts. In the past, I had wondered what could happen that might shatter my aunt's repose, make her gaze down from her God to the world of men around her. But seeing even Father's death fail to do this, I am convinced, now, that nothing ever will.

Dr. Luna holds clinic on the east side of Mandaluyong, three blocks away from Footlights. He is one of those doctors difficult to trust at first sight because, though nearly fifty, his eyes have the dovelike look of a child. It is December now and I've been a patient of his for four months. He's only the second doctor I have seen. Before him was a woman who wore gold like twine, coiled many times around her neck and wrists. It wasn't the jewelry—or her high fee—that turned me off, but the way she talked about her newborn son. Somehow, lying half-naked on her examination table, my legs spread apart, the last thing I could bear was the thought of competing.

Roy is very tactful but I know that, secretly, he wishes I would stop. I tell him I like Dr. Luna, that, unlike the others, he seems to show a more intimate concern. He makes me take my morning temperature, daily, for at least two weeks, and is stern about my thyroid pills. He keeps me on a diet rich in protein, plenty of fish and eggs. And he urges me, in a voice not completely without embarrassment, to watch out for "that twinge," a discomfort in my abdomen. That, he says, is the best time for Roy and me.

But what is true for my body is not always true for my mind. Sometimes, with Roy on top of me, I try summoning a tenderness to carry me through the moment, but it is anxiety that comes instead. Then, days later when I see a spot of blood again on the bathroom floor, I press my forehead against the door, seized by a shameful urge to run away.

Wednesday is matinee day for Footlights. It is also when I go there to turn in my work. I set off from the house after lunch and arrive early enough to see the little backstage crises before the curtain rises; once, the understudy got her costume caught on a nail. If the production is a new one, I stay for the entire program, watching it from the sides. I hand over my press releases only when the performance is over.

Now and then, with no other appointment to keep, I linger in the theater after everyone has left. I sit in the back row and look at the bare stage, recalling how only a moment earlier it was crammed with scenery and people moved about saying their lines; or the way light played on the hero's face, how an actress sighed as she gazed into a mirror. Some time ago, I heard about a blinded man who asked his friend how long it would be before he stopped dreaming in color. I think of that man too, when I sit in the empty theater, and of fragments of a life slipping away—voices, gestures, moments that will not return.

And faces. One quirk my father had was that he could never manage a complete smile, only a crooked grin, with just the left tip of his lips curled in humor. Tita Gilda insists it was the right tip, not the left, that moved when Father smiled, and my confusion amuses her. But it unnerves me, this bubble of memory floating beyond my reach.

I am in bed with the windows shut and the air-conditioner on full blast, yet from outside I still hear people singing: it's karaoke night again. Somehow, they've rediscovered O. C. Smith and, for the third time this evening, are inflicting "Little Green Apples" on the rest of the neighborhood. Even Elmer is bothered—I hear him by the gate, whimpering. But Roy is facing the wall, safely isolated in sleep. He hasn't moved for some time and I know soon he'll start wheezing. It's a curious, at times comical, sound he makes: first a gurgle deep in his throat, then silence, then a barely audible whistle. Just this afternoon I was telling Tita Gilda about it and she fell back in her seat, chuckling.

She had come, without warning, shortly after lunch, bringing a papier maché angel she wanted me to place under the Christmas tree. I was in the kitchen when the doorbell rang, and it was back there that she and I sat down to talk. She told me she wanted to fire her maid; too often these days the woman ended up burning a pot of rice. Yet, Tita Gilda said, she's been with me for years, and you know what they say. Live with what you have.

Before my aunt left, she told me she had something waiting for me at her house, a picture of her and my parents. She said, I found it yesterday, and guess what? I was right about your father's smile.

One of the neighbors has begun another tune. Surprisingly, the voice is pleasant this time. A woman's, but low and full. The song must be new. I can't make out the words although the sweet, gliding melody is clear. The microphone carries her voice high above the others and for once I close my eyes, hoping to be lulled by the music. In a short while, the air-conditioner will turn itself off. Already, coolness has filled the room; I feel mind and body slowly relaxing. But all too quickly something changes. The woman next door cannot remember her lines, and her song ends abruptly, cut off by her audience's loud, collective jeer.

One of Roy's sisters is in town for Christmas, with her husband and a son, and they decide to hold, in my in-laws' house, a reunion of sorts. Another brother attends, also a niece, and the uncle from Footlights who anxiously pulls me aside to talk about his newest production. It is a comedy about a Visayan who teaches English grammar and who wakes up one morning with a genuine British accent, and because the lead actress has just played a bit part in London, Roy's uncle wants plenty of fanfare. I have a soft spot for this man; he is skinny and anemic-looking, with a way of laughing that ends in a deep sigh. But today, when he tells me what he needs for a poster, I make a vague promise and quickly move away.

Throughout lunch I am quiet, but no one notices and I am happy to be left alone. In my three years of marriage I have learned a bit of Ilonggo and yet today I find it hard to follow the conversation. Only once, when everyone else at the table breaks out laughing, do I turn to Roy for help. He then tells me the latest about a cousin of theirs, a mother of two who, several months before, fell for the charms of a stockbroker. Now her husband is demanding that she return all the jewelry he ever gave her, but she has outsmarted him at every turn. This last time, Roy says, was when the man showed up suddenly where his wife had been hiding, in her grandfather's house, and Roy's cousin, a quick thinker, shoved everything under a cushion where she made her grandfather sit until her husband went away, fuming and still empty-handed.

Shortly before sundown Roy and I head for home, everyone yelling reminders about the Christmas dinner coming soon as we drive away. In the car, minutes away from his parents' house, Roy reaches out, laying a gentle hand on my lap. I curl my fingers around his, listen to the music in the car, but say nothing. Outside, the streets surrender to the twilight. I ask myself: When, if at all, should I tell him?

Tell him, that is, the latest from Dr. Luna, whom I saw again earlier in the week. I think now, that will probably be the last time. We had sat in his clinic, facing each other across his table, going over a leaflet he had pulled out from a drawer. It was called simply, "The IVF Method of Conception," with pictures of smiling parents and their newborn babies. But I heard nothing, nothing at all as Dr. Luna spoke, and when he finished, I waved an unsteady hand in the air and asked, trying in vain to be funny, if he would please give me time to sell my husband's car and raise the money? Dr. Luna fixed his eyes upon me—for the first time that morning, it seemed. I knew he meant it when he said, quietly: I am sorry.

The music in the car grows louder and I ask Roy: Please turn it down.

Turn what down?

Why, I say, the music, of course, the music—then it dawns on me that the radio is not even working: the humming must be somewhere else. Around me? In my head? Under my skin? And that tune, timid and halting, so like the song that woman left hanging a few nights ago...

Pull over, I tell Roy weakly. Pull over.

He gives me a long, questioning look.

Please, I say. But when the car finally comes to a halt, I am unable to tell my husband why I have all of a sudden gone pale.

The three stand under the balcony outside my parents' bedroom, Mother on the left, a small, serious woman with hair pulled back, skin brown like fallen leaves. She is leaning her head on Father's shoulder. On the right is Tita Gilda, one hand raised in midair as if she was caught giving pointers just as the shutter clicked. Between them is my father, arms thrown around wife and sister. He is smiling exactly as my aunt remembers.

The photograph Tita Gilda gives me must have been taken only a short while after I was born, for the background of santan hedges and bougainvillea barely reach up to my father's waist. I can still see that actual view whenever I visit Tita Gilda; the santan plants may no longer be the same ones but I am certain about the bougainvillea. Heavy with orange blossoms, it has grown higher than the balcony rails.

So it was there that Father, Mother, and Tita Gilda had posed, a trio of young hopefuls, two-thirds now gone. Yet today, there is no sign in that corner that my parents once stood there, staring into a camera, and no hint that their presence is at all missed. But I am here, their only child, and my duty is to remember.

Perhaps I should bring Dr. Luna one of these days, to show him that part of the garden. And if he comes, maybe I can tell him how Father tried to do his own remembering, hanging onto the house while living on the farm where the spirit of his forefathers helped him conquer his loss. Then, maybe I shall ask him why all that must end with me, and why, after my time has come, everything then will be like the colors fading from a blind man's dream.

Roy is on the phone with his sister—it seems they haven't yet tired of hearing about their cousin's ploys. I signal to him that I'm turning in early and he cups a hand over the mouthpiece to wish me good night. When, minutes later, his voice drops to a whisper, I know he and his sister have ceased amusing themselves over their cousin and have moved on to worrying about me.

I close my eyes, suddenly weary. Behind me Roy's voice glides farther and farther away. In my sleep I see him wrapped in a haze, slipping out from the shadows, moving slowly as if underwater. He gestures to the wall behind me; it has slid open, and there once again is that woman's broken song. In an instant I am walking, my feet sinking deep in mud, towards a man waiting across an alley. As I approach him, he flashes a lopsided smile, then holds out a book for me to sign, only the pen I am using is out of ink and in anger the man pushes me back, but the alley is now a creek where the water has washed away my trail and over it the wind blows, violently, shattering the bedroom wall.

It is Elmer's barking that wakes me up. The room seems faintly alien, the shadows deeper, the ceiling closer to the ground. In the darkness I feel Roy stir next to me, but rather than comfort, it is a lingering sadness that steals into my heart.

How can I tell him, this man asleep beside me, why month after month I feel driven to see Dr. Luna? What reason do I offer, when even I cannot give it a name, though there are times, as I try to recall my father, when it seems only a touch away, almost but not quite taking shape? More than once already he has hinted at adopting, but how to say that taking another's child feels like the ultimate defeat? And if indeed I might begin to explain, how to make him believe me—he with his family of grandfathers and cousins, sisters and uncles: each of them, in blood and in memory, a testament to their particular, abiding past.

He is snoring loudly now, his sleep undoubtedly bothered by the crushing heat. I turn over and lie on my stomach. Outside the dog is still howling; I hear the frightened screech of a cat that has strayed into the yard. A car roars by, and Elmer runs scuffling to the gate, breaking into a long, warning snarl. Soon the noise thickens into an uproar, spreading from house to house as other night creatures join in. For a while I suffer through it, but my thoughts soon fall into a tangle and, without thinking, I push my hand under the mattress, my fingers meeting the cool tip of metal. In a flash I am at the window, throwing the shutters wide open. It is then that Roy wakes up, one brief, jumbled moment before I fire the gun.

Invasion by Jack Fruit

Isabelita Orlina Reyes

You claim friendship
by giving me *langka*—
one pellet-shaped prickly
fruit bigger than a watermelon,
enough to make my wallpaper,
upholstery, bed sheets reek.
A nauseating, sweet pungence
stings me to my eyeballs.

Take it back, I plead
and you refuse. I give it away.
Too late.
          I search
under the kitchen sink
for my can of Lysol—
empty. I call a friend,
tap the floor with one foot,
two rings, three and a half.
How do you get rid of jack fruit
   smell?
Don't know. I call my mother,
she says "Lysol." I grab
my car keys, step outside,
my hair and T-shirt stink sweet.

Returning the next day,
before entering I sniff,
pick up a faint sweetness
inside. The phone rings, it's you
asking if I want another,
insisting you're my friend.
I DO NOT
EAT
JACK FRUIT.

Later on, you send
a messenger knocking
again and again.
In one corner of my flat, I sit,
knees hugged close to my chest.
Waiting.

In Late

Catalina Cariaga

> *grunion (grun y n) n. A small fish, Leuresthes tenuis, from coastal waters of California and Mexico, that spawns along beaches during high spring tides at the time of the full moon.*

It always
comes
in a late
moment
past desire
before the advent
of some small necessity
practically speaking, stripped of its ripe light
like that time at high tide when midnight I thought of using my hands
    one
           four
                  seven
           becomes
   ten   to the power of ten
thousands of
           grunion
  flipping   rising
             shining
  silvery
             slivers
flowing from the phosphorescence of waters washed up to spawn
the warm Pacific shore at my feet;
cold panic
  sweet fear,
    a proverb
       of coming up "empty handed"

the few morsels swimming well within the grasp of my two flat palms.
But that is how the grunion run.
The white people appear merely for the spectacle, but we
bend and stoop, enamored of ritual;
   the whisper
        in hindsight reminds me
            I could have held a catch of good eatings—
                          I should have remembered;
                                it was
                        against the law
                         to use a net
                       in the hunting
                  of these peculiar fish.

No Sleep

Catalina Cariaga

for Grant

Moonlight fills our bedroom
    through slats of open blinds.
The brightness of ninety-nine horizontal candles
    reveals your expectant smile.
Don't touch my breasts
    while I'm reading,
You knew I was a writer
               when you married me.

The brightness of ninety-nine horizontal candles
    reveals your expectant smile.
I wake up suddenly
    to re-read a poem I've written earlier.
You knew I was a writer
    when you married me,
And my aunties like to talk about that interval of time
    before we married they call, "courting."

I wake up suddenly
    to re-read a poem I've written earlier,
The winning of my gaze seems more of a challenge
    than the getting of my nipple.
And my aunties like to talk about that interval of time
    before we married they call, "courting."
The getting of my nipple seems more enjoyable
    than the having of all your desires pictured in the *Kama Sutra.*

The winning of my gaze seems more of a challenge
    than the getting of my nipple.
Sometimes I'm half asleep
    when you reach between my thighs,
The getting of my nipple seems more enjoyable
    than the having of all your desires pictured in the *Kama Sutra.*
This is what happens when we stay up late
    reading to each other aloud.

Sometimes I'm half asleep
    when you reach between my thighs
Without paying attention to my aunties' gossip
    about young married couples: "inept and voracious."
That is what happens when we stay up late
    reading to each other aloud,
Explaining and writing about
    my family idiosyncrasies.

Without paying attention to my aunties' gossip
    about young married couples: "inept and voracious,"
I don't think it's unintentional when your penis
    becomes hard rubbing against the small of my back,
Explaining and writing about
    my family idiosyncrasies,
I reach behind
    and pinch the heft of your waist.

I don't think it's unintentional when your penis
    becomes hard rubbing against the small of my back,
Like the dance my cousins performed at our wedding
    imitating the mating habits of deer in the rain forest,
I reach behind
    and pinch the heft of your waist,
It's perfectly natural to rise and want something
    in the middle of the night: sex, water, rest, to walk about

Like the dance my cousins performed at our wedding
    imitating the mating habits of deer in the rain forest,
Don't touch my breasts
    while I'm reading
It's perfectly natural to rise and want something
    in the middle of the night: sex, water, rest, to walk about.
Moonlight fills our bedroom.
    through slats of open blinds.

Apollo & Junior Grow Up

Veronica Montes

"As a Filipino," he says, "I feel it's my responsibility to be a good dancer."

He's serious, but I can't help laughing. I say, "Well, dance your little brown butt over here and wash these dishes."

My son has been digging through the Chinese camphor wood chest I inherited from my *lola,* who died when I was twenty. She left gold earrings and mother-of-pearl rosaries to everyone else and though I was a little hurt at first, I was glad to be left out of the fights that ensued. They were biblical in scope and the ten years that have passed find the women in my family still in recovery, looking at each other sideways and wishing unkind things.

Lola left me the chest because, just like my son, I couldn't keep away from it. I used to run my hands along the elephant carvings, palm trees, coolies, pretty ladies; I longed to shine the tarnished brass latch, loose on its hinge; I enjoyed the medicinal assault on my nose when I opened it. And most of all I loved the pictures inside—stacks of photo albums and hundreds of loose shots covered in fingerprints.

Apollo proceeds as directed, dancing his way across the linoleum with one hand on his stomach and the other raised ear-high into the air. He swivels his hips and keeps his eyes half-closed in ecstasy. This kid is something else. Only fifteen years old and more handsome than his father, though I feel a little guilty admitting it. We named him Apollo because we were seniors in high school and thought we were playing a game. As it turns out, he refers to his name as "the gift" and thanks me every day with a kiss on the cheek.

⟳

Junior and I were married at City Hall, a two-story building that squats just behind McDonald's. We were both eighteen years old. Apollo, with his gigantic ears and perfect little cap of black hair, charmed the Justice of the Peace and spent the short ceremony resting quietly in the man's arms. Afterwards, we had a little party at my *lola*'s house where the old people whispered, "Thank God, thank God," as if the five-minute legal proceeding had washed us free of sin.

Most of the photos from that day are hopelessly dated: my girl-friends wear black cherry lipstick and have bangs that curve like huge, perfect waves over their foreheads. But the pictures of Junior and his boys, with their goofy smiles and baggy pants, still look pretty good. I keep them in the camphor wood chest; they are the only ones Apollo doesn't wear out with his touching and his staring.

We lived with Junior's parents for two years until he got a job reading meters for the electric company. Then we moved into this apartment just a few blocks from where we went to high school. These things never work out, I know that. Junior stays with me because we've been together for more than half our lives, and he can't think of what else to do. When we were growing up, he lived two streets over in a house with the very same floor plan as mine. We each had both parents, both grandparents, two brothers, two dozen cousins, and Miss Whalen for a kindergarten teacher. Leaving me would be like abandoning his only sister. I see that he can hardly breathe. I see that.

≈

Against my strict orders, I often find Apollo still awake at two o'clock in the morning, splayed on the couch watching *The Roselle Valenciano Hour* on the international channel. He loves the hilarious splendor of Filipino variety shows and who can blame him? He sits up so I can share the couch.

Tonight, shiny-haired Roselle opens with a disco version of "Mandy." Roselle—sorry, make that "Megastar Roselle Valenciano!"—and good-looking Rico Fernandez croon "You Don't Bring Me Flowers." Megastar Roselle Valenciano! and willowy Pops Reyes cover Donna Summer's "Last Dance." And for her finale, teary-eyed Megastar Roselle Valenciano! interprets "The Greatest Love of All." At the end she looks right into the camera and whispers, "Learning to love yourself—it is the greatest love of all."

"Apollo, sweetie-pie," I say, while the credits roll, "there's a reason this is on at two in the morning." We start laughing and then hush each other so Junior won't wake up.

"Mom, will you teach me how to speak Tagalog?"

He asks me this all the time, a gentle reminder that the things I never bothered to learn could have made him happier. I say, "You know I don't know how."

"But why didn't Lolo teach you? Didn't you want to know?"

"Sometimes. No. Not really."

"But Ma," he argues, "how can you know where you're going if you don't know where you've been?'

He brings this up a lot lately. It's from staring at all those old pictures, I know it. The difference between us is that he wants to know the stories, while it's enough for me just to look. We both like the ones from the forties the best. Sleek cars, sharp dressers, women in hats. "Who's this?" he'll ask. "And this?" He's so disappointed when I don't know the answer that sometimes I'll make it up. I tell him about imaginary gamblers and doomed love, about an illegitimate baby girl who became the legendary beauty of Pasay, about a boy with no tongue.

"Where I've been? I've never been anywhere but here." There's an eyelash on his cheek. I brush it away.

"You know what I mean. Where your peeps have been."

"What are my 'peeps'?"

"Your people."

"You and your dad are my peeps."

"That's not enough, Ma." Apollo sighs and goes to bed.

Two years ago, Junior stopped touching my face when we kissed. It used to be fingertips on my cheekbone, a hand against my jaw. He used to trace my eyebrows with his thumbs, or lift my chin to his mouth. But now he's bored with my face, and he keeps his hands pretty much to himself. I feel the same way about him I felt when I was fourteen, but Junior? He's growing up.

From here, it takes exactly seventeen minutes by car to get to San Francisco. Somewhere in that neat grid of long streets lives a girl who has Junior all tied up in knots. I don't know who she is, but she smells like good shampoo and peppermints and orange spice tea. She has my husband for now, but me? I have Apollo. My husband knows as well as I do that I'll just wait until this girl and her nice smell go away.

Junior tries to explain. He says, "Well, you were kind of like a sports car. You know, before."

"And now?"

"Well, now you're like a minivan."

I turn my head away and think of a dozen ways to answer him. My tongue starts to bleed, I'm biting so hard. But I don't say a word because once you do, you can't take it back. It just twists in the breeze like a *capiz* shell mobile, gathering dust.

∽

Apollo and Junior play video games together while they sit on the couch waiting for dinner. They yell, "Get outta my way," "Hey, hey, hey, cut it out," "Oh, it's gonna be like that, huh?" and their bodies twitch and twist, they lean against each other shoulder to shoulder, their legs fly up. Sometimes a friend of Apollo's will be there and it's just like when Junior used to come over to hang out with my brothers. But I'm not in my room lying backwards on my bed and talking on the phone to one of my girlfriends. I'm in the kitchen.

Junior walks in and pretends not to notice that I'm watching him. He throws his arms all over the place, grabbing plates and slamming cabinets. He sets the table every night.

"I'll do it," I say.

"It's all right, I'll do it."

"I said 'I'll do it.'"

"Okay," he says. He throws the forks onto the counter; they slide right off, and because they are cheap, they clatter half-heartedly when they hit the floor. "You do it."

Sometimes—I pick up a fork—just sometimes—I pick up a fork. Sometimes—I pick up a fork—I hate Junior. After dinner, he says he's going to his brother's place to help him work on a car. Apollo sits down to write an essay for English class, and me? I'm not sure what to do.

∽

Apollo wants to learn how to drive. "I can't wait for sixteen, Ma. I just can't."

"Do you know how old I was before I learned how to drive?"

He rolls his eyes. "Twenty-eight. But that's because Dad drove you everywhere."

True. Junior took me anywhere I needed to go. I didn't want to learn, but two years ago he taught me how to drive, and even though I've told him a thousand times that I don't want my own car, he is putting aside a little money every month to buy one.

Apollo throws himself into my arms. He's done this forever, but I can't stand it now. I'm scared I will hold him for too long and he will shrink from my desperation and walk away and never stop.

I kiss the top of his head and pull him off of me. "Ask your Dad."

He nods. "Hey, do you like my sweater?" He's wearing a chocolate brown cardigan with a maroon stripe down the center. The collar's frayed. He looks like one of the pictures from the photo albums in the chest.

"Where'd you get that?"

"It was your *lolo*'s," he says, spinning around slowly so I can get a good look. My mother must have given it to him.

"Was it?"

"Ma, why don't you know these things? Do you know *anything* about your grandfather?"

"Oh, Apollo. Go ahead and tell me something."

He clears his throat and puts on a newscaster voice. "His mother's name was Donata deGuzman and she had the most beautiful singing voice in all of Laguna, Santa Cruz. A married Spanish sugarcane guy seduced her under a mango tree and she gave birth to five of his children. He never married her, but he gave her a little house and some money and stuff."

"Why didn't my mom ever tell me that?" I say.

"She said you never asked. She says she can count on one hand the number of times you ever asked her a question. Not like me, right?" Apollo says.

"Not like you."

We smile at each other. In the silence that follows I disappear for what seems like hours, but Apollo brings me back. He scratches his head and finally says something. He says, "You did this—you had me—on purpose, didn't you? Dad thinks it was a mistake, but it wasn't. You meant to. Is that right?"

I stare at my son for a long time, wondering how it happened that he is perfect and we are not. There isn't much to say, so I just say, "Po." His baby name. He walks over and puts his head on my shoulder.

He says, "I won't tell him."

〜

"I think it's too soon for him, Jun." We're in the kitchen and I'm talking about Apollo and his fondness for steering wheels, but Junior? I don't know what Junior's talking about.

"He's not a baby."

"He's not a man, either. Tell him he has to wait until next year. Okay?" I reach out and put a hand on his cheek.

"I was a man when I was fifteen, wasn't I? I was almost a father. If I can handle you and a kid, Apollo can sure as hell handle the freeway," he says. He says all this looking me dead in the eye like he's bored, and then he moves away and leaves my hand hanging in the air.

"Is that what you do? You handle us? Well, thanks so much. Thanks a lot."

When Junior walks out of the kitchen—when he walks out of any room—nothing fills the space. Not music, not food, not even my son.

A few minutes later, Apollo has his arms around my neck. "Thank you, thank you, thank you," he says.

"For what?"

Junior pops his head in then and tosses Apollo the car keys. Before I know it, I'm following along behind them.

In front of our apartment building, a friend of Apollo's has his arms wrapped tight around a pretty, smiling girl. He grins at Apollo and Apollo holds up the car keys and grins right back.

Junior doesn't even notice them. He just gets into the passenger seat and slams the door. He stares straight ahead, waiting.

"You want to come, Mom?" Apollo says.

"No, thanks. I'll stay here."

"You sure?" he asks, already dancing away with one hand on his stomach and the other raised ear-high into the air.

"Uh-huh," I say, nodding. But he's in the car, strapping on his seat belt. I watch them drive until Apollo sticks his arm out the window to signal, turns left, and they disappear. Then I sit down on the sidewalk and wrap my arms around my knees. It's cold, but I don't mind. I'll just wait for them to come back.

Fools

Susan Evangelista

Frank's eyes burned as his daughter shrilled the familiar taunt at him: "Well, there's no fool like an old fool. And you, Pop, you're an old fool if there ever was one. You've been had."

"What do you know about anything?" Frank's retort sounded juvenile even to himself, but his mind could go no further. He hated her, this daughter who looked so much like her mother—acted like her, too, he thought, going from man to man like some common slut. No wonder her husband Sam had kicked her out, sent her back home to bug Frank to death. He probably should have done the same with Jane, but anyway it was too late now because Jane was already dead. Dead and buried. Her adultery had killed her—served her right. Before she died, she'd been like Raquel—taunting him, standing her ground against him until he'd get so mad that he'd hit her. But even then, what good did that do? Just bonded the two, mother and daughter, more strongly against him. They weren't supposed to be like this—wives and mothers and daughters—were they? Frank didn't know; he couldn't remember his own mother, because she had died when he was only three. But as he grew up, he learned that his father expected women to be obedient. Always.

Right now he had to get out of the house. Stumbling over the idea that Raquel could reduce him to such a childishly helpless rage, fists clenched, he stomped down the steps and out behind the house to the wood frame garage and got into the brown 1982 Oldsmobile. Manhandling the gear into reverse and then gunning the motor, he backed up into the gray autumn morning and drove off towards town, still fuming.

He went straight to Ernie's place, the warm little diner where Ernie and Mari, his Filipino wife, were serving up pitchers of hot coffee and plates laden with fried eggs, bacon, ham, and fried potatoes to five burly truckers. This was the morning crowd and the morning menu. Later there would be meat loaf or roast chicken, apple pie—the heavy, stick-to-your-ribs kind of food that men need in the raw cold of the Northwest in November. But it wasn't just food, or even just food and conversation, that Ernie and Mari provided. For their good friends, people they knew well, old men whose loneliness they had sensed, they ran a little matchmaking service. Mari came from one of the islands in the Philippines, a beautiful little fishing village, she said, but poor as dirt, so there were lots of sweet young girls who would be all too glad to marry rich Americans. Hell, they didn't even have to be rich, she had said—compared to how life was on Samar, all Americans were rich.

So now Frank planted himself on one of the green plastic diner chairs. Tense, knees bent, he waited for Ernie to emerge from the back, scared to ask if there was any news, wondering how to frame the question so that he wouldn't appear too eager, too anxious. Ernie was at the stove, frying potatoes with his back to the room. Mari bustled around warming the truckers' coffee and brought Frank a steaming cup with the extra sugar he always wanted, without being asked. She was certainly a gem, he thought. She had changed the whole way he thought about foreign women; he could talk to her—at least they could joke around. He had friends who were always telling him to be careful of Asians because they were so good at hiding their emotions, but what's to hide if you're talking about food and weather and trucking? Mari's English was good and she was so sweet to her husband—Ernie was really lucky. Frank had really hoped for someone like Mari, and he thought he'd found her in Angie. Now he didn't know what to think.

"How ya doin', buddy?" Ernie's sudden presence pulled him back from his reverie.

"Good news from Angie?"

"No news," said Frank. "I thought maybe you would've found something out. It's already been a month."

"Mari always complains about the mail from the islands. Are you sure you've got the address right?"

"Yeah. I got it right from the card that the nun gave me—the one who took her in. I tell you I don't like it, Ernie. I think that nun was against this whole deal. She said she'd take care of her, but...I don't know."

Mari paused in her work, reeled into the conversation by Frank's dejected tone. She pitied Frank. He was sixty-seven, tall and gaunt and partly deaf—not much of a catch, really—but he'd had his troubles, she knew, and she had been all too glad to help set up the deal with a girl in Samar. After all, life was really hard in the Catarman area, and Frank seemed a gentle old thing. A bit crusty, perhaps, but soft underneath. She had heard the rumors about the way he had treated his wife before she died, but there were stories about Jane too, and Mari believed them. After all, the accident that she died in—there she was in Bill Braddock's car, and he died too, so there was no one to tell tales, but everyone could guess what had been going on. So if Frank had hit her once in a while, she probably deserved it. It wasn't like he was just violent all the time, like some of the men she had heard of who had married Filipinas and hit their wives whenever they spoke their own language. She'd certainly be careful never to set up a match like that, out of pity for her countrywomen. But she really thought that as long as she could find good men, even if they were old and ugly and smelled of cigarette smoke, the Filipinas would be better off, even happier in the long run, than they'd ever be at home. And they made good wives too.

"But you were already married," she interjected. "I'm sure if you were married, the nun wouldn't want her to just let it go. Why, she could even be pregnant. Couldn't she?"

Ernie glanced quickly at Frank, but he didn't seem to have heard Mari's question. "Married," he said. "Married in the goddam church."

A shadow passed over Mari's face, and for an instant she saw herself in her youth, playing on the beach with her friend Celie, and her younger sister, the three of them joking about another friend who had married an old man, an American too, right there, in the church in Catarman. They had concluded that she was trading off the sweetness of love for the sweetness of riches and comfort, physical comfort, anyway—good food, nice clothes, and plenty of chocolates. They were too full of juice to even think about such a trade-off then, but less than two years later Mari had gone off with Ernie, leaving her home, perhaps forever. Ernie was a good man, though, and not that old, and he had helped Mari get used to cold weather and heavy food, and the lumberjack-type men—truckers and loggers—who were so gruff and blunt about everything as they marched around this hick town in their muddy cowboy boots. She wondered if Frank had been wearing his boots when he met Angie in Samar.

She sat down at Frank's table. "Tell me about her," she said. "Tell me about your meeting, and your wedding."

Frank felt his face heat under his leathery skin. "Not much to tell," he mumbled. "I went to her house, you know, and talked to her mother. Her mother couldn't speak much English, but I think she understood anyway. When Angie came in and saw me, she—well, she ran away. I musta scared her, been taller than she'd expected or something. She cried and said she didn't want to get married. I don't know—it was almost like she hadn't even heard of the whole idea before."

Frank had been back from the Philippines for a month, and he had come to see Ernie several times about the difficulties that had to be straightened out with the embassy before Angie could join him, but Ernie had never heard the whole story before, had in fact never heard Frank say much of anything about his own life. He glanced at his wife and then back at Frank, careful not to appear too interested.

"So how'd you work it out?" he wondered.

"I left. Hell, I didn't want to force the girl. I went back to the house where I was staying, and, I don't mind telling you, I was pretty pissed. I spent a hell of a lot for that trip, and there I was in the middle of some godforsaken spot where the kids followed me around calling me Joe, saying 'gimme cigarette, Joe,' and then laughing their heads off. And what for? I figured, if the girl doesn't want me, that's that." Resentment piled up in his throat again, but he swallowed it down with hot coffee.

"But you did get married, ha?" attempted Mari cautiously.

"Well, yeah. Just three or four hours later the mother brought her to me. I could tell she'd been crying, and she was still scared, but she smiled a little. I don't know how the mother talked her into it, but I don't think she beat her up or anything. What she told me was that Angie got ashamed and thought her English wouldn't be good enough. That's what Angie said too, later, when I asked her, but I don't really know. Anyway, she did come back, and two days later we got married."

Frank's eyes blurred and his wrinkled face sagged as he remembered how awkward he had felt at the wedding, with Angie's mother and brothers and a couple of other women in the church; everyone had been chattering in that bird-talk language they use there, and he had felt so tall and pretty much in the way, even if he had been the groom. And then later, when he had been alone with Angie, he felt foreign and strange and didn't know how to approach her. "She's so young," he had told himself. "She'll need time to get used to me, to stop being afraid. I can wait."

"Well, it's really too bad about the paperwork." The conversation was getting a little too personal for Ernie. "But it always takes some time. Whose idea was it for her to wait in Manila?"

"Mine. I wanted to bring her to the embassy first and see if we could speed things up a bit. And I wanted to treat her a little. She'd never been in a big city before."

"How'd you settle on her staying with that nun?"

"There were a couple of teachers from Manila there in the guest house in Catarman, and they kind of befriended us. Angie, really. So I asked them to help find some place where she'd be safe and well cared for. One of them knew this sister."

"And you met her?"

"Yeah. I could tell she was going to be nice to Angie, but she looked at me as if I was the devil. As if I was beating up on Angie."

Mari startled and looked at him, with the unspoken question in her heart. He wouldn't have hurt her, would he?

As if he had heard her silent query, he went on, "As if anyone would want to hurt Angie. She was so sweet. You know what she asked from me? All she asked? She asked if she could see her friends, if there were other Filipinos in this state, and if I would let her speak her own language with them. And if maybe she could go and take some classes in a school some time."

"And did you agree to let her have friends and go to school?"

"Sure I did. I figured anyway she'd forget about the going to school pretty soon. And I know Mari's the only Filipino around here. So I thought, sure, they can be friends."

"Well, okay," said Ernie. "All I can get from the guy at the embassy is that Angie's papers aren't complete. Her birth certificate isn't with them, and she needs to get a Philippine passport. After that they promised they'd give her the visa."

"But who's helping her? Don't you have anyone there who can help her get the passport? She doesn't even know how to find the damn embassy in Manila."

"Well, I guess not. Couldn't that nun help her?"

"If she wants to."

"Umm, Frank, have you thought of going back to help her your-self?" Mari made the suggestion timidly.

"Hell no. I don't know how to do anything in Manila either. I can't understand anybody and I keep seein' people laugh at me, and then they say 'hey Joe, hey Joe'. No, I never want to go back there."

Mari was a little surprised at the vehemence of his answer. She had a sudden tragi-comic picture in her mind of the tall, awkward man thumping around the streets of Ermita in his cowboy boots, lonely, stopping to buy cigarettes on the street and tilting his good ear to-wards the vendor to hear, wondering, wondering why people seem to be laughing at him and why nothing made sense. She controlled her smile; she knew well how her countrymen would react to this deaf old "Joe."

"Anyway," said Ernie, "we'll keep working on it, and maybe you'll hear from her soon."

"It may be hard for her to write to you," offered Mari. "She is probably still ashamed." And then, "Hey, Frank, we've got a good fresh apple pie cooling back here. I'll get you a piece."

There didn't seem to be anywhere further to go with that conver-sation, so Frank allowed himself to be distracted with the pie and idle talk about the weather, road conditions, the five-car accident up north on the interstate. Anything was better than going home and facing his daughter's scorn. "Mom's out," she had once said, a long time ago, in a dry-ice witch's voice that had burned into his brain and left a painful scar. "She went out with Bill. Better not stay up, Pop—might be kind of a long wait. A very long wait."

That had been the very night that Jane hadn't come home at all—the night that the sheriff's patrol banged on the door at 2:00 a.m.—the night of the accident. Jane had died and Bill had died, and that left only Raquel of the little trio who had made Frank so miserable. And then, Frank suspected, it was Raquel who felt abandoned, de-serted, orphaned by her mother's love for Bill, as she sat sullen and dry-eyed at her mother's funeral.

Since then Raquel seemed to have made it her mission to plague Frank.

Today he thought he'd just wait until she had gone off to work; she did the afternoon shift at the little cafeteria on Spring Street. A waitress, just like Mari, but with none of Mari's gentleness. Boy, she could sure learn something from Asian women! Christ, she went out with all that make-up, bright red lipstick on, looking like a whore, and then that shrill voice of hers, demanding this, demanding that, criticizing, taunting. By God, he was going to have to protect poor Angie from her when she came.

Ahh—that was something to think about! Maybe Raquel was so dead set against Frank's marrying Angie because she knew that her arrival would change the battle lines—it would be two against one. Frank would have someone on his side for once. Maybe that was it.

Frank was especially glad now that the mail delivery was in the afternoon, so his daughter was never there to witness the nondelivery of letters from Angie, the absence which began to seem a palpable presence, Angie's silent statement. At first, right after he came home from Samar, he had listened every afternoon for the sound of the mail truck, barely waiting until it had left to see if there was a letter, but by now he pointedly delayed checking the box, waiting a couple of hours, waiting, but not really forgetting.

Finally one day in the first week of December there was a letter, not from Angie but from Sister Karina. It was neatly done, typed out on a computer with the margins all straight, and a heading that was from some organization that had something to do with Third World Women, whatever that meant. It was short and to the point:

Dear Mr. Peters:

I am writing in reference to Ms. Angela Ladicho, whom you left in my care when you departed for the U.S. last April. After much prayer and discussion, Angela has decided that it would be best for her, and perhaps you as well, if she simply returned to her home in Catarman. She had no unkind words for you; she assured me that you treated her well, but she sees that her future in the United States would be difficult. She is after all just a simple country girl.

We appreciate the help you extended to our organization while Angela was with us and we wish you well.

In peace,
Sr. Karina

Frank was stunned first and then enraged. What had Sister Karina done to Angie? How had she made her change her mind? How could he get her back?

He wanted to go and fling the letter into Ernie's face and say, "See what you've done to me? Taken all my money and this is what I get." Instead he slammed the letter down onto the table and stormed out of the house. Ten minutes later he was in the little bar on Hart Street, where he proceeded to drink three straight whiskeys in a row. The letter, and Angie's actions, made no more sense now than they had earlier when he was sober. But his rage gradually cooled and lodged like a brick in the back of his mind, a heavier burden than he thought he could carry. This trip to the Philippines, and Angie, had been his last chance for some love. And now she was gone, gone back to Samar where he would never be able to find her again.

He thought about returning there. What if he went after her, back to Samar? He shuddered; he could still envision his first trip to Angie's little grass house, and how some of the young men hanging around had stared at him as if he were an evil spirit. One of them had flipped open a knife in front of him. And the children had run around giggling and calling him Joe. No one had been able to understand him—they had all just laughed. Surely if he went back, once again no one would answer his questions, no one would help him.

Frank was still in the bar when it closed. He had drunk much and eaten nothing, but he felt dreadfully depressed rather than drunk. He drove home slowly.

The bright light in the kitchen when he entered confused him for a minute, and then there was his daughter, looming up in front of him in that garish red lipstick. She was holding the letter from Sister Karina and gloating. "See, Pop, see! You'll never have your Angie! Why would that young girl want to have anything to do with you? Fool!"

Words wouldn't come—only rage. It exploded in his head, blinding him to everything but the hateful young woman standing in front of him, taunting him with a piece of blue stationery. He struck out at her then, hard, harder than he had ever tried to hit anyone before, but his fist flailed wildly, impotently in the air, and she was gone.

Excerpts from Bahala Na!

Catalina Cariaga

51.
"All around the world" "dishes, pots and pans"
"surfing on the internet" "floors and windows"

"Singapore girl" "like genuine silk; hand wash only"
"Does anyone know more about this?" "coffee or tea?"

"All around the world" "it put cockfighting on the map"
"required reading for folklorists" "please E-mail me"

"Singapore girl" "a vacuum cleaner and oven" "cooks"
"you're a great way to fly" "armed with steel spurs"

"All around the world" "combat in a circular pit"
"100% cotton; extra starch" "please E-mail me"

52.
"All around the world" "diapers and baby food"
"Lysol, Clorox and Ivory" "another Filipina maid"

"Singapore girl" "Playtex and Gerber"
"the four-year-old boy" "declined to testify"

"All around the world" "a domestic" "she was represented"
"with clemency, but this was rejected" "please E-mail me"

"Singapore girl" "because 'voices told her to do it'"
"a Professor of anthropology and folklore" "found untrue"

"All around the world" "and then, new versions came out"
"Roosters with blades connected" "die a quick death"

53.
"Singapore girl" "on her own behalf" "a domestic"
"Mercedes Benz and Jaguar" "please E-mail me"

"All around the world" "after years of study"
"submitted in appeal" "toiletries and cosmetics"

"Singapore girl" "The Philippine government has intervened"
"Tampax and Maybelline" "it was Contemplacion, who led the police"

"All around the world" "Chanel #5 and #19"
"constitutes inhumane cruelty" "new evidence"

"Singapore girl" "surrounded by male spectators" "Alabama,
Kansas, Kentucky, Oklahoma, Florida and New Mexico"

"All around the world" "it may have originated in
Southeast Asia" "no stay" "the cock itself" "a domestic"

"Singapore girl" "lasting minutes or seconds"
"men are drawn to watch" "obliged to study"

"All around the world" "two equally matched
roosters" "visit before her execution" "no stay"

54.
"Singapore girl" "Does anyone know more about this?"
"English dialect and a Malay dialect" "Hakka dialect (Chinese)"

"All around the world" "her employer was angry"
"under the circumstances" "a kind of martyr"

"Singapore girl" "a kind of national hero"
"unworthy of scholarship" "or illegal sport"

"All around the world" "Hong Kong" "Frankfurt" "Tokyo"
"Tehran" "Kuwait" "London" "New York" "Vienna" "Los
   Angeles"

"Singapore girl" "Does anybody know more about this?"
"a domestic" "bred and raised for such purposes"

55.
"All around the world" "you're a great way to fly"
"which may seem unpleasant" "as cocks are symbolic"

"Singapore girl" "please E-mail me"
"All around the world" "please E-mail me"

"Does anybody know more about this?" "please E-mail me"
"Singapore girl" "please E-mail me"

"Please E-mail me"
"Please E-mail me"

Eureka 2000

Nadine Sarreal

The machine's roar increased suddenly to a deafening level, causing the sleek maroon casing to rattle, hinge against joint. A cloud of dust issued from the plastic body, rising in the living room and causing Valentina to cough as she inhaled the particles. She kicked the power switch with her right foot and the vacuum cleaner ground to a grumbling halt, dust still sifting out, seeping through the seams of the machine's plastic shell. *"Dios mio,"* she moaned, making the sign of the cross over her heart. The machine stood like a stubbornly accusing child in a small heap of dust in the middle of Mrs. Coleson's living room.

Valentina clutched her head with her hands. You plug it in and push the power switch, the American woman had explained. Simple enough? And the young maid had nodded with some apprehension, suppressing her inherent mistrust of anything electrical. She missed the old manual carpet sweeper that Mrs. Coleson had donated to the Hong Kong Disaster Relief Society the day after she came home with the vacuum cleaner. That had been Tuesday, a week ago. Time to leap into the twentieth century, Mrs. Coleson had said.

Valentina studied the machine uneasily, walked around it and surveyed its maroon height, its model name blazoned in gold script across the front—Eureka 2000. The black handle curved efficiently from its back. A rubber cord snaked from the recess in the casing across the floor to the outlet behind the TV. Cautiously, she felt the base of the machine first with one fingertip, then with her whole hand, and pulled back in surprise. The motor inside was hot enough to fry an egg on. Her mind raced in panic and as often happened when she was faced with a problem she could not understand, much less solve, Valentina felt herself crumbling inside. She wilted to her knees, hands hanging uselessly by her sides, so that she seemed to pray to the machine. The overpowering smell of heat-stressed rubber filled the room.

What was it about her that set these appliances off? Valentina mourned as she opened up the living room windows. After the incidents with the bread maker and washing machine, Mrs. Coleson had given her a stack of instruction manuals, one for every appliance in the flat, from the radio alarm clock in the master bedroom to the heavy coiled space heater tucked neatly away under the guest bath sink. Valentina studied the pamphlets with a sense of shame and guilt, and also with some trepidation. She pored over the pages, backing up now and then to relate each instruction with the carefully labeled diagrams. She had borrowed Mrs. Coleson's pocket Webster's to look up words she didn't understand at first. Troubleshooting, for instance. The word always came up at the end of the manuals. At first she had a gleeful image of herself, short, thin Valentina, dark hair in a neat plait down her back, carefully aiming a sleek hand gun at the shadowy heart of a recalcitrant appliance. Okay, so you won't cooperate? Bang! Shoot the trouble and it's gone.

After several nights with the manuals, Valentina's dreams took on an electrical nature. In one recurring dream, Valentina was the size of an ant, on a slow motion tour of the internal structure of a video cassette player. Wheels hummed and levers clicked around her as she walked through narrow steel passageways. Electricity streamed through red and white wires now as thick as her waist. Valentina groaned and grated her teeth in her sleep. She rose before dawn, exhausted, her jaws aching from being clenched through the night. Oh heaven of heavens, there were so many things she had to plug in and use each day. She tried not to cower before the coffee maker, toaster oven, iron, answering machine, and dehumidifier. She took careful notice, too, of the larger things that fed on electric power—the jerky elevators that took her up to the Coleson flat on the forty-seventh floor, the throbbing air conditioners in the living room and in the department stores, the merciless fluorescent lighting along the streets. There was no escape. She was trapped in a web of electrical force.

Maybe she was cursed or jinxed. Her cousin, Arlette, who worked for a Japanese family in North Point, said maybe she was electromagnetically hypercharged. Arlette had two years of college in Manila and she still read a lot, even browsed Mr. Watanabe's engineering journals. He was an electrical engineer working on the new airport out at Chek Lap Kok. Arlette said there was an article translated from Nippon Magnet Trade about a boy in south Japan who made light bulbs around him glow even when the power was off. When he was around, appliances burned out, even brand new ones, and finally his parents had resorted to using generators to power their home with a special fuel of phosphorescent liquid and a gas extracted from chicken droppings.

"Phosphorescent?" Valentina repeated, trying to understand, fearing a fate similar to that of the Japanese boy. Her only connection with phosphorus was a plastic figure of a robed child, kneeling in prayer. If she held it to the light for a minute, the praying boy would glow softly in the dark. Sister Louise at St. Mary's Home in Sagada had given it to her at First Communion. The nun explained it wasn't magic that made the figure luminous but its phosphorescence, its ability to store energy when exposed to light.

Now in Hong Kong, Valentina didn't mention Sister Louise or St. Mary's to Arlette. It embarrassed her cousin that the family hadn't taken Valentina in when her parents died twelve years ago. Valentina hadn't wanted to live in Manila with Arlette and her seven brothers and sisters anyway.

"Like fireflies?" she asked Arlette instead.

Her cousin snorted in her way that meant she wasn't really sure herself but that Valentina was missing the whole point. Arlette sometimes called her "Cordillera Girl" because Valentina had grown up in the remote mountains in a small village beyond Sagada. "And you know what else," Arlette had pushed on, "he melted two Sony Walkmans, once when he fell asleep with it on and the other time just from holding it for a few minutes in a check-out line at the store. Imagine, ha?"

Valentina stood up now, trying not to think of the Japanese boy. The silent vacuum cleaner made her miserable. She unplugged it gingerly, careful not to wince at the small shock she always got when she touched the transformer to wiggle the plug loose. Already anticipating Mrs. Coleson's ire, she wound the cord around the machine's body, fitting it in the grooves designed to hold the coils neatly in place. She wheeled the machine into the broom closet.

From the general science class at St. Mary's, Valentina remembered chalk drawings of atoms, the weighty but orderly protons clinging to a stationary nucleus, and free-wheeling electrons orbiting in elliptical paths around the heart of the atom. She never had a head for science but Sister Prudence's methodical representations of positive and negative forces had stayed with her and she now understood that life was a collection and connection of charges, that all matter contained some form of resulting energy, even dead and inanimate objects. Nothing was really ever still. Bodies decomposed; metals corroded. Some materials were more suitable for conducting energy than others. Arlette said even humans had electricity in their bodies. An electrical pulse tripped our hearts and kept them hammering blood through our bodies and brains all the time.

In the scheme of her own life, Valentina imagined herself an electron, weightless and thus easily sucked away, blown by other atoms, from her old nucleus, her quiet orphan life in the stony mountains, drawn by work and money to Hong Kong. She had been here just fourteen months, long enough to pay her hiring agency debt, and now she would have to spin off the perimeter of Mrs. Coleson's employ and find another atom to move around. What happened to electrons that ran out of energy, that no nucleus accepted?

Well, she sighed, closing the closet door, thank goodness the stove ran on gas. She scrubbed mushrooms, potatoes, and green beans, salted bloody chunks of rib-eye, and pounded and minced a whole head of garlic for the Friday night stew. How could she break the news to Mrs. Coleson this time? Maybe after a good meal, the woman would feel more charitable. Valentina would tell the truth about the vacuum cleaner but she knew that sometimes, the way you told the truth could make a difference in your fate.

Then again, maybe she could get the vacuum cleaner to a repair shop tomorrow. Last week, she'd been able to pack the rice cooker and piano lamp into a cardboard box and take them to Mr. Wong, the electrician.

She sautéed the meat in a garlic butter sauce and then clapped the lid over the pot to let the beef simmer for a while. Valentina walked back in to the living room, hands planted on her bony hips. She studied the carpet. Maybe, she thought as she knelt to tug at blue bits of paper, maybe if I pick up the lint and dust and loose threads, I could brush the carpet in one direction so she doesn't notice. I'll try to get the vacuum cleaner fixed tomorrow and I won't have to lie to her as long as she doesn't ask about the vacuum cleaner directly.

Mrs. Coleson had always been patient, Valentina thought as she searched a kitchen drawer for the roll of Scotch tape. She never raises her voice. She pays me on time and hasn't asked me to work on my days off. Valentina pulled strips of tape and wound them around her hand, sticky sides out to make a lint remover glove. On her hands and knees, she worked the highly trafficked areas of the living room meticulously, changing strips of tape often. It took an hour. The steak cubes almost burned, but she finished the living room. As she poured the red wine over the shriveled meat, she heard the click of Mrs. Coleson's key turning in the front door lock. Saints in heaven, come to my aid, she cried silently over the fragrant steam of sizzling alcohol. I didn't have time to brush the carpet. Oh no. Still, she stood in the kitchen door, smiling her welcome at the large woman. "Good evening, ma'am. How are you?" Her voice was clear, free of hesitation.

Mrs. Coleson dropped her brief case just inside the door and took a deep breath. She raised a hand to Valentina, waved a weak hello. Kicked off her pumps. The odor of sweaty feet in nylon stockings rode over the smells of cooking food. Mrs. Coleson staggered to the velvet recliner near the bookcase and eased herself back into a horizontal position. "Ahhhhh," she finally sighed. Valentina clucked sympathetically and returned to the kitchen to pour the woman's first drink. She had uncorked the Australian red just before she set to work on the carpet. In the course of the evening, Mrs. Coleson was likely to drink the entire bottle (minus what Valentina had poured into the stew), nursing her drinks steadily.

Mrs. Coleson reached sluggishly for the glass Valentina offered. "How wasyourdaydear?" she asked thickly and then bent to sip rather than raise the wine to her mouth.

"Oh, ordinary," Valentina groped for a noncommittal reply. "Nothing unusual." Which, given her history with appliances, was quite true.

"Good, good, good," Mrs. Coleson closed her eyes and leaned deeper into the chair. "Good," she said again, and Valentina thought she might mean the wine and the soft, comfortable recliner.

Valentina retreated into the kitchen to stir the meat in the brown gravy. In went the potatoes and then the beans. Mushrooms last. She scooped a mound of white rice on to a rectangular Japanese porcelain platter and then ladled the stew into a large blue bowl. She wanted to skip supper, to go to her room and curl into a knot of agony. There was no escaping her eventual firing. Mrs. Coleson would have every right. Valentina would return to Sagada and if Joseph Salu-ed still wanted her, she would marry him. He was a good enough man, faithful and hardworking, although he had an extraordinary love for local gin. Valentina could tolerate a long, simple life with him, working on her loom, the *baliga* and *sikwan*, woof stick and shuttle, dancing in her strong hands. She had learned to weave when she was a young girl just from watching Betty Macalig, the school groundskeeper. Betty told her she had quick eyes and a good mind when she saw the first *tapis* cloth Valentina made. "Your work is fine, tighter and more even than mine," Betty had said, examining the skirt cloth. Still, so the girl could earn school money, she had Valentina weave endless sets of placemats, small uniform pieces that sold well in the Manila department stores. Valentina grew tired of the same combinations of threads—red, blue and black, yellow, orange and brown—over and over. She wanted to save money now in Hong Kong, to buy enough time and thread to weave special cloths that people would buy to put out at fiesta time, to wear for weddings and baptisms. It would take a while before her work caught on in the market, she knew, but surely, when people saw the new colors and felt the sturdy weave of her cloth, they would take money from their pockets and be happy to pay for something special.

Now, she set the food on wooden trivets before calling Mrs. Coleson to table. The woman set the recliner upright and stood slowly, sniffing the air as she walked to the dining room. "You're an angel, Val," she said, standing at her place at the head of the table. She sat in the heavy rosewood chair Valentina held out for her. "Where's your plate, dear?" Valentina stood at the empty space behind her own chair, gripping the high wooden back. "What is it?" the woman asked.

Valentina looked at the fine web of lines on Mrs. Coleson's pale skin. When she was upset, a small tic twitched at the corner of her left eye, making the lines there quiver erratically. There was no tic yet. "Could I be excused from dinner, ma'am? I'm not hungry. Not sick," she hurried, "just tired."

Mrs. Coleson's face registered disappointment. Valentina knew she disliked eating alone, especially now that Mr. Coleson traveled so frequently for the bank. Mrs. Coleson nodded quickly. "Go rest. I'll clear up after myself."

As Valentina tidied up the kitchen, she avoided looking in the chrome surfaces of the appliances lining the counter. She averted her eyes from the shiny side of the toaster as she put spoons and forks in the cutlery tray. The image of her mournful face would make her feel even more defeated. Her future was already bleak, even though it probably included Joseph. It would be all right to go home to the high mountains and cool sunlight if only she didn't feel like such a clumsy, heavy-handed failure.

∾

Eva Coleson pulled the shower curtain back and yanked her towel from the hook on the bathroom door. As the steam lifted from the mirror, she saw her body and the marvelous map of fine lines that criss-crossed her white skin. She patted herself dry, in no hurry. Here, she thought in awe, rubbing the towel across the soft folds of her belly, what wonderful texture, these wrinkles that are creeping up like slow, careful vines, reaching my breasts, claiming them, pulling to reach past the expanse of chest between my shoulders. My neck flesh is nicely webbed and the lines hold my chin, so interesting, furrow my forehead like plough lines in a fertile field.

Lately, there was combined fear and reverence in Charles' eyes when he held her. He seemed both repelled and drawn to her expanding flesh and the enlarging contentment that radiated from her. She desired him. Pulled him to her at night, feeling his reluctance and then yielding, his recognition of her strength and his submission to it. Things had changed. Eva, Eva, Eva, he called softly into her hair, his hands clutching her shoulders as he twitched in climax against her. She pictured his flow of sperm racing into her vagina, past the folds and crevices into the dark cave of her uterus.

Eva stood before the mirror, gleefully contemplating the lines that seemed to hold her together, like the fine weave of a fisherman's net bulging with a full catch. Her eyes sparkled richly beneath the folds of flesh on her lids. Oh, woman, vibrant woman, what a magnificent turn of flesh and bones! The muscles seek, shift and fall into place, to present this finally whole body, this ripe self.

What Eva enjoyed most lately was her decisiveness. Where Charles seemed flooded with information that diffused rather than sharpened his ability to recognize solutions, Eva's vision was finely tuned to a bright clarity so that her senses hummed in one direction and she did not falter. She had shaken off her former mist of vacillation and when action was required, she moved with razor sharp precision. Therefore, as she dressed for bed, she felt no regret or sadness over her talk with Valentina.

After dinner, she had come upon her maid weeping in the laundry room, just beyond the kitchen. Valentina was bowed over the washing machine, her head on her arms, and she didn't see Eva come in behind her. Eva studied the young woman silently, taking advantage of the moment to see again the thin frame of her brown companion, the thick black braid of hair loosening on her back. Valentina usually stood straight and her tearful posture now bothered Eva.

When the young woman finally raised her head, Eva asked about the smell of burnt rubber in the flat. She had noted the heavy odor as soon as she came through the front door, especially in the living room, and she had known, even as she settled into the recliner, that her maid had somehow shorted out another appliance, perhaps the new vacuum cleaner. Valentina had not answered at first, overcome with fresh tears.

"What is it, dear?" she asked in her kindest voice. Kindness was a skill she had strong command of now, especially after a good dinner and three glasses of wine. "Everything all right?" Valentina nodded, her head bowed as she wiped her eyes with the backs of her hands. "Back home? All well?" Again Valentina nodded, this time looking up, and Eva was surprised that there was no fear in the maid's eyes.

"I don't know why, well, the vacuum cleaner...I...it made a strange noise. It began to smoke."

Eva leaned back on the washing machine, feeling the rhythmic vibrations as the sudsy clothes churned inside. She waited for Valentina to continue.

The explanation came in bits that Eva patiently pieced together, weeding out Valentina's defensives asides, pulling out from the tangled recounting the fragments that she considered factual. She listened to Valentina's halting apologies, still not speaking. It was not until she sensed that Valentina was casting about for something concrete, a decision or conclusion of some sort, that Eva held up her hands to stop the stream of questions.

"What should I do? I'm very sorry. I didn't drop it. What should I do? I could pay for the repairs," Valentina was saying. "Sorry, sorry, sorry," she murmured and finally stopped when she saw Mrs. Coleson's hands.

Eva cleared her throat. She crossed her arms over her chest. "What do you think is best?" she asked quietly. Valentina looked at her. "I don't know," she whispered and lifted her shoulders in an involuntary shrug.

Eva cupped her elbows in her hands, tightening her arms across her chest, and tilted her head thoughtfully. She knew exactly what had to be done but it was best to appear to come to the solution slowly, to allow Valentina the feeling that she had been part of the decision. "Would you be happier at your loom? Could you return to Sagada?" She watched the young woman's face fall with a look of resignation. Her thin fingers twitched, smoothing invisible threads of an imagined tapestry. Valentina shrugged again and buried her hands in the folds of her apron.

Eva patted her on the shoulder and sighed. "We'll talk more tomorrow. Try to eat a little supper and get some rest," she said and headed upstairs for her bath, leaving the thrum of laundry and sorrow behind.

⌘

Valentina woke in the middle of the night with a painful throbbing in her head. Her eyes felt swollen and tender, too. She rubbed the sides of her head, willing the ache to subside. The Panadol was in Mrs. Coleson's bathroom and she couldn't very well pass through the woman's bedroom to get a couple of tablets. Then she remembered the small flesh-colored plasters with round black magnets that Arlette had given her sometime ago. Mrs. Watanabe suffered from frequent migraine headaches. The best cure for her was applying magnetic plasters to her temples. She encouraged Arlette to use them, too.

Valentina sifted through her medicine box on the window sill, feeling past a tin of Vicks ointment, *sebo de macho,* and an empty bottle of White Flower that she kept because the lingering smell of the lotion was so comforting. She found the plasters wrapped in a piece of paper with Mrs. Watanabe's neat handwriting. In the dim balcony light that came through her window, she read the Japanese woman's translation of the original instructions: *The bandages can use for muscle pain and headache elevation to re-align body forces. Natural position as previous.*

Valentina smiled despite her headache and peeled two disks from the paper sheet. She pressed one on each temple, careful not to tape any hair to her skin. The bandages were lightweight and caused discomfort only when she put her head sideways on her pillow and the magnets dug into her skull. She shifted around until she was comfortable. The pounding in her head seemed to subside. Magnetic Band-

Aids, she thought sleepily. Huh! What would people come up with next? What if she forgot to take the Band-Aids off and they made her stick to the elevator tomorrow, or to the sides of the subway? Valentina giggled sleepily at the vision of herself struggling to free her head from the elevator wall. She saw a queue of what-ifs, squiggly question marks before her, peering at her. They came to her, one by one, a chain of possible results—automatic doors sliding open and closing erratically as she walked by with her magnets; the watches of people she passed stopping suddenly, simultaneously; cash register drawers popping open, hiccuping out coins and creased bills; and tram cars screeching out of control, pulling suddenly in reverse so that puzzled passengers found themselves facing the wrong direction as the shaky cars hurtled back to their points of origin. Possibilities, the night shimmered with possibilities and Valentina fell into a smooth, liquid sleep.

⁓

Mrs. Watanabe drove Arlette and Valentina to the airport. Valentina's cardboard box and suitcase took up most of the back seat so that she was crushed up against the door, her face on the window. "Thank you for the ride," she told the Japanese woman as they pulled up to the departure area at Kai Tak. "You've been so kind to me, always."

Mrs. Watanabe stepped out of the car and opened the back doors to let Valentina out and help the cousins unload her luggage. "You call collect," Mrs. Watanabe told her, "so Arlette not worry." Arlette piled Valentina's belongings on a cart.

Valentina nodded, knowing that she would have no access to a telephone once she got home. She'd wire Arlette, maybe. The flight to Manila would take just an hour. It was the road trip after that that would be long and tedious, taking at least two days to reach her village just outside Sagada.

Her cousin hugged her awkwardly and thrust a small box of Chinese cakes and an envelope into her hands. "Early Christmas gift," she whispered, and Valentina knew the envelope held money, probably an advance on next month's salary. She pushed the envelope back at her cousin. Arlette was supporting two younger brothers through college and it didn't feel right to take her gift. But Arlette stuffed the envelope into Valentina's dress pocket and turned away quickly before Valentina could refuse it again.

With a heavy heart, Valentina wheeled her cart to the airline counter. The immigration exit interview went quickly, and soon she was in line for a final security check before boarding the PAL flight to Manila. She placed her handbag on the X-ray machine belt and surrendered the cake box to the young Chinese security officer who smiled and smacked his lips. "For me?" he teased, pointing to the picture of a strawberry tart on the cake box.

Valentina smiled stiffly and stepped through the security detector doorway. A high-pitched alarm sounded, startling the security officer and Valentina. He waved her over to the side. "Again, please," he shouted, his face harsh now with displeasure. The alarm sounded again as Valentina walked through the door. A female officer approached her, scowling with suspicion. She waved a metal detecting wand over Valentina's head, and along the width and length of her body. The wand beeped around Valentina's shoulders and that was when she remembered the magnetic plasters she had pasted between her shoulder and neck, where muscles ached after she had packed her boxes and cleaned out her quarters. She left the room ready for her replacement, a middle-aged Thai woman.

"Here, here, feel this, *pangyaw*," she said, taking the woman's free hand and putting it on her shirt over the round pellets. "Magnets. I forgot to take them off." She tried to smile.

The woman shook her head. "Remove, remove," she insisted gruffly. Valentina reached into her shirt and peeled the plasters off. When she held them up to the two officers, they shook their heads grimly and pointed her through the door again. This time she passed through without incident and retrieved her bag and the cake box.

❧

Eva came home to a shrieking Nittaya, who pointed at the refrigerator and cried shrilly about a sharp, quick pain. Perhaps the shock of static electricity? The Thai woman refused to go near the refrigerator, so dinner hadn't been started. Valentina had been such a level-headed companion. Nittaya was volatile and hysterical, overcome with a fear that Eva could not penetrate with any amount of reasoning or assurance. The Thai woman gestured at the appliance and scolded it. "I don't want to die," she wailed. Eva had to leave the kitchen, unable to bear Nittaya's tears. Tomorrow, she'd call an electrician to come and check the incoming voltage and power outlet wiring and all the various-sized transformers throughout the flat.

Later that night, after calling out for pizza, Eva wondered about Valentina. Perhaps she shouldn't have been so quick to dismiss her after all. Had she made it safely home? No more toasters or vacuum cleaners for her, and just as well. Sometimes she herself wished she didn't need so many appliances. It seemed ironic that she had a maid to operate these electric conveniences, which were supposed to liberate women from the kitchen and laundry and yet somehow, she felt chained by obligations to both the machines and her maid.

Valentina will pull her suitcase behind her and balance the large cardboard box on her shoulder as she climbs the steeply sloping hill that leads to the small center of her town. The air will be noticeably thinner and drier and after her months in Hong Kong, she will have difficulty breathing. Her heart will beat hard and steady but still she will put one foot in front of the other, making her way to the crossing where Joseph, her intended, and Betty, her weaving mentor, and Sister Louise will be waiting. They will meet her wordlessly, their blank expressions holding back their mix of joy and sorrow at her early return. Joseph will take the cardboard box, which is heavier than the wobbly suitcase, and lead them further up the hill, into the mist of light early morning clouds. Valentina will walk, leaning slightly on Betty's arm, glad for the older woman's silent welcome. She will notice Joseph's strong calf muscles as she follows his sure steps and she will hear the voices of children calling to each other from the mountainsides as they run down to watch her come home. Here, she will not be the same over-aged orphan weaving traditional placemats to sell in the lowland market places. Not anymore. Already, she will be plotting out the pattern of a long table runner, perhaps for a rich man's feast. It would hold the colors of lightning and fire, hot wind and cold rain.

An Expatriate to Her Sister

Lewanda Lim

When I was ten and you were sixteen
I remember guarding you like a mother hen
that was odd.
But I loved you with a filial bond
only sisters understand.

You were a beauty queen.
Men swarmed around you
like territorial birds in amorous claims.
I shooed and swatted them
with my little wings.
That was silly.
I thought they were snatching you
away from me.
You went away and found a new life.
The oldest, you chose to marry.
Mother was dismayed.
But he rescued you from easy ordinariness
and opened a new vista of possibilities.
You bore him six beautiful children.
But your mind's boat wandered
North and South
looking for an anchor
and you found it.
Found it home where you spread
your wings far and wide
helping the poor and working for their rights.

So many years have passed
and I miss you.
What is it that binds me to you,
more than the veins that tie us together?
The country beckons but less brightly.

Am I trapped in my cozy little nest?
The oceans seem wider
than they are, to me now.
And I have but one wing left
to cross them.
I don't know how I lost the other.
Along the way it must have fallen
slowly, feather by feather
flesh by flesh, bone by bone.
But like the amputee with her phantom arm
I feel the pain of a flightless bird,
wanting to soar but cannot.
I think I have to trace my way home
to find the missing half.

Prayer Rug

Lewanda Lim

In my pious home
prayer was a rug
Swept under it
were unresolved bits of grit
from the daily grind
of differences.

When mother was angry
father said, Let us pray.

This went on for years
until he turned to soft stone
and she to soliloquy.

To the wall she wailed
where I embedded my ears
I heard the hidden distance
between them widen, silent.

The rug later I would beat
and drag away
to hang.

The Color of a Scratch in Metal

Eileen Tabios

after Some Remarks on Color *by Enrique P. Barot*

She was asked to imagine the taste of "silver, nickel, chrome"—or a scratch in them. The notion of the scratch, no matter how thin, evoked the taste of mercury. She is confident at the accuracy of her memory over an act that has never occurred: she knows a broken thermometer would free the chemical that evoked black Tahitian pearls. Light transforms their luster from black to gray. Like sunlight staining his black hair with a blue sheen. And the thought makes her fingers quiet a raven as she strokes its wings.

If a pear was a color, she feels it would be how shadows glide across his unshaven chin. If honeysuckle was a color, she feels it would be how hatred or love darkens his eyes. If passion was a color, she feels it would be the surface of black sand encasing the shores of a hidden beach on the other side of an ocean. Once, he took her there and, under the white heat of a noonday sun, he flattened the air surrounding her helpless body. That evening, her cheeks mirrored the crimson lashes against the sky as well as the inner flesh along her shifting thighs.

"And what is seeing?" Once, she asked him not to touch her hand as it lay next to his on white linen surrounded by crystal wine glasses, silver forks and knives and purple lilies. It was a black tie affair and her dress was cut low, translucent in wise places and unabashedly red. He complied with her desire, even an hour later. But an hour later, she saw the sheen break across his forehead from the effort of keeping his hand frozen when what he desperately wanted to do was take her fragile fingers and crush them until she fell to her knees. And during the fall, she would have bared her throat. The tendon would have leapt. "And what is seeing?" It is how he saw her notice the strain of his effort but remained silent, offering no reprieve, so that the price he would extract later amidst twisted bed sheets would be high.

Dream

Fran Ng

I had a dream about desire:
It happened on a mountain top
where the thin air sang
into my veins
and threaded a veil
over the valley.

It happened on a sea
roaring in the light
of speckled salt
and net sinking deep
but finding nothing.

It happened on a tree house
where the wind murmured
a password to the child
inside, asleep, but keeping vigil
as she dreamed.

This desire is nameless,
fluid, and serene.
I cannot hold it
but it holds me
despite the bursting of the well.

Section V Another Day

Tango

Angela Narciso Torres

Friday night. Scent of rosin
and mothballs rises from the nest
of scarlet silk that cradles
my father's violin. Drawing
the bow with a flourish, he rubs
amber crystal against a taut
length of horsehair. The squeaking
makes us quiver and giggle.

Mother sits at the piano
clouds of Florida Water
and Vicks VapoRub wafting
from her ruffled bathrobe. She rifles
through yellowing sheet music:
considers a Thais Meditation,
pauses at Salut d'Amour—
then decides it's a Czardas night.
Father beams in agreement.

Hands poised in air, ready to strike.
Bow, still as an arrow, set to fly.
A quick breath—
A nod—

and they tango into the stars.

my father has stopped eating

Virginia Cerenio

I.
my father has stopped eating.
at 96 years
he has lost his appetite, he says
his favorite foods have no taste.
the french fries grow cold
in their grease-stained box.
the donuts lay on the plate
        eating air in their staleness.
the coffee, creamed & sugared,
        only a chaste sip.

my father has stopped eating.
he has lost his appetite, he says
and is ready to die
any time now
but God will not let him.
instead father grows gaunt.
his brown skin, stretched
tight across his cheekbones
mottled with sun kisses.

my father has stopped eating.

i remember our evening snacks
shared like a secret between us two.
buttered toast with maple syrup or sprinkled sugar
fresh sliced peaches heaped in a bowl with milk and sugar.
just last year, he brought me *alamang*
shrimp paste sautéed with garlic and eggs.
we finished off the leftover rice
with fried Spam
eating until we could eat no more
each bite another memory swallowed into the past.

II.
my father has stopped eating.
a Filipino who no longer thinks of the next meal
is either insane or close to death.
we look for excuses to share a meal.
you cannot understand us
until we have shared rice together.
to turn down food is an insult to our brown souls.

III.
my mother in desperation
buys all asian food
shanghai *lumpia*
mangoes, bittermelon,
a jar of *alamang*.

my father studies this jar
like a beautiful woman.
he says to me: "this is the good kind."
my mother pulls out garlic, onions, a skillet.
my father ignores her
favoring the jar, its pink shrimp hips
trapped inside the curve of glass.
he ambles to the microwave
with a bowl of rice.
i open the jar, freeing the plastic ring.
he smacks his lips twice
while my mother complains
she needs to cook the *alamang*
to kill the germs.
my father sticks his spoon inside the jar
a few caviar-size morsels
spread in a neat pad
next to the corner
of the small mound of rice
he eats in silent concentration
the rice disappears off his plate
my mother and I smile.

death will avoid the scent of dried shrimp today.

IV.
my father will rise at 2 a.m.
my mother will find him in the kitchen
grating onions, garlic
dicing tomatoes
to sauté with the clay pink *alamang*.
the house smells of the ocean on a hot day.

by daylight, he refuses breakfast
rice eggs Spam
he has no appetite, he protests
my mother brings the covered dish
alamang, tomatoes, onions, garlic
he remembers his cooking now
he eats and eats
my mother smiles, placing a hand on his shoulder
brings him coffee and kisses.

V.
a few days after father's funeral
my mother gives me the almost full jar of *alamang*.
i protest, reminding her how my *puti* husband
will find the jar in the kitchen.
the salty smell of the ocean
will escape the aluminum foil, Ziploc bag
torturing his Betty Crocker senses.
instead I take home a tiny jar
formerly full of succulent osetra caviar
now my father's pink caviar
sits next to the curry paste, brined olives
homemade chutney
his stories waiting only for hot rice

Touch

Lakambini A. Sitoy

When they were young, he used to beat them, rapidly, one after the other, as they scrabbled and slipped on the wooden floors. It had been one of those peculiar rituals that families often find themselves locked into. Most of the year when their father was at sea, the children could do as they pleased, but for the month or so that he was home, they had no choice but to obey him. At the slightest mistake the house would resound with a peculiar rhythmic thwacking, like strips of meat being processed on the butcher's block.

It had been a good belt, fragrant and heavy, from "abrod," as so many of her father's things had been in those days. Wound about his hand, it had been a weapon. She remembered him when she was five years old, remembered the broad brown face with the cheekbones so prominent they seemed to have been stuck onto his skin, the wide, dry lips, the long ridge of his brow bone. His chest had been massive next to his short, pipe-like legs. Without the belt his black double-knit pants would sag open; he administered beatings with his nylon briefs bulging through his fly. Her brothers must have screamed. As Ciso and Joey had grown older, the screams had turned to curses. Phrases, fragments of cries still drifted up through the layers of Dora's consciousness from time to time. She couldn't remember who'd said what, and when. The one sound that had survived the years without distortion was that of leather on flesh, like baseballs slamming into mitts in the children's park back of her apartment block, where the kids practiced on weekends under the feeble spring sun.

She felt good about falling asleep, exhausted from her night shift, to the sound of a suburban baseball game. It was a good neighborhood. No blacks, no Chicanos—it was a litany she would repeat quietly to herself several times a day. A place where for the first time in her life she didn't have to live in constant fear of having something valuable wrenched from her person.

(Though the sounds from the park—the sharp crack of the bat, the screeches and groans of the young blond boys—had unnerved her at first. A few times she had actually stood listening to the hard, high voices, the words indistinguishable beneath the strange accent, waiting for a stray curse, a sharp *Agay!)*

The letters came two or three times a year, long wilted envelopes bearing her older brother's angular Practical Arts teacher-script. Diplomatically worded requests for money, suggestions that she come home for a month or so. News of their father, how his wet, trudging feet had worn a pale path from the bathroom to the bedroom where he now slept alone, of his gratitude for their gift of the walker. How one morning he had done a little dance on the back porch stairs and slid five risers down on his tailbone, how he had sat there for twenty minutes trying to fathom a hand that urgently caressed the worn wood of its own volition.

She read these letters once or twice before slipping them into the plastic mesh berry basket on top of the refrigerator. On her way to and from the nursing home where she worked, in twilight half the time, coat bundled about her short, dumpy figure, she would think of their contents, wondering at her own silence. On Saturday mornings, the voices of children at the nether regions of her consciousness, she would take the letters down and pass her fingers over their surfaces. Vague body memories, the leather belt descending to stripe her flesh.

Dora made herself a cup of coffee, fitting the containers of Nescafé and Alaska Evap back into place on the dining table tray. She swilled the tepid liquid about her mouth, trying to work up some enthusiasm for the tasks at hand. The quiet of midmorning had descended upon the house. A singular odor pervaded the air, an odor from her childhood, a blend of the kitchen smells of dank wood, mossy earthen jars, residual detergent—and now, the rank odor of urine and antibiotics.

She nudged aside the curtain hanging in the doorway of the sickroom. On the bed that Ciso and Joey had shared when they were boys, her father lay on his side, head turned towards the wall, legs together and bent. She thought of the babies, fully formed but not quite human, floating in the formalin jars on the shelf of her long-ago college classroom.

The old man had wet himself. The fresh warm odor of bodily discharge mingled with the sharper, richer stench of the mattress. He wore a T-shirt that said Plaza Central School on the back and which most certainly had belonged to Ciso. The T-shirt was so ancient and grubby that the urine had soaked through the hem and up her father's back. She suppressed a shudder at the sight of his bare buttocks. They were round and brown, like something you would eat for breakfast. They belonged to a much younger man.

"Narciso," her father said.

Dora started; he was awake.

"Ciso's out," she said quickly.

The old man grunted. Even in his illness his voice was heavy with the old irritation.

"When will he be back?"

Dora did not answer. Of course it was Ciso he would want; good stolid Ciso, who never married, fearing the father he might become, who survived the blows to become...what? A Practical Arts teacher at the local elementary school, sunburnt from bending among rows of vegetables, the man who made the school's Christmas lanterns and fiesta tableaus, mouth set in the perpetual kindly grin of the powerless.

Dora moved to the bedside table and picked up a glass half-filled with water, last night's dinner plate with clumps of desiccated rice still on it, used syringes, a crusted face towel.

"There's a mess," the old man said.

She looked at him.

"It needs to be cleaned up," he pressed on.

It was easier when they both pretended it was someone else's body they were dealing with.

In the kitchen, she found the rags draped on the wooden shutters above the sink, where Ciso had left them the night before. She took them up, sluicing water over them from an earthen jar, as she had done when she was a child. The household had had running water for years, yet still kept these ancient relics. She felt dazed, enervated.

The urine had traveled some distance down her father's thighs, and there was a warm blot of excrement too. Ciso had forgotten to put the bed pan within his reach. There it was, she saw, partway under the bed, still gleaming dully from the scrubbing she had given it yesterday. It was amazing how incompetent her brothers became the moment she took over.

With a fresh towel she pursued a blotch of shit over the old man's skin. A fresh sore was forming in the small of his back. She found a clean edge of the towel and dabbed around her father's groin; his penis, walnut-like, wobbled at her touch. The old man suffered her ministrations with contempt. Her face burned.

A fly alighted on her lips. She brushed it off with her sleeve and felt a sensation of wetness. The creature had feasted on the clear liquid from the sores that had magically bloomed across her father's helpless limbs in the past weeks.

In the bathroom she flung the rags under the lone tap and turned the water on.

She did the laundry—hers, her bachelor brother's, a few of the soiled sheets—and took it out into the backyard, dodging the branches of the sapling guavas. Trudging across the tamped-down earth, she couldn't resist sneaking a glance back at the house. Small, and dingier than it ought to have been, the *nipa* roof bleached almost white, so that at long last it blended with the galvanized iron rooftops of the neighbors. Once when she was in college she had overheard her mother pleading for him to build a new one, the woman's voice rising to a shriek, aimed at the *lawanit* walls, the chalky dust caking the leaves of the *gumamelas*: "The field hands live better with their dollars from Saudi!"

He remained silent at this taunt, she remembered. It was he who had instilled in his family the difference between a trained seaman like himself and the ignorant workers escaping from the surrounding haciendas to the Middle East. She had known the meaning of dollars from early childhood, when her father had been away all of the year and they lived in the other house, the bigger one. He's abrod, her mother, dead fifteen years now, used to say, eyebrows arched finely, to the neighbors. He's in Germany, she might add, or in Panama. Growing up, Dora had known what it had been to be both blessed and despised.

He sent them checks, parcels, letters. He sent his brother enough money for a jeepney-transport business; his sister's property he rescued from a heavy mortgage. No one talked about his life, the years aboard ship. As a child she had been fascinated by the way he would come home every year smaller, angrier, more leathery, until one day in her teens, he fell into bed and lay there glaring up at her and her mother, unable to rise, enraged, knowing that at the end of his furlough they expected him to pull up his carcass and make his way back to the dungeon of his vessel. Not once did they ask him how he felt. After all, he was a man. Men endured.

Ciso was in the kitchen when she came back with the empty basin. Since her return, he had stopped taking a packed lunch to school; he would bike the five blocks to the house in search of her insipid cooking. He ate the watery *adobo*, the salads she insisted on, as though it were he who was to die within weeks.

Dora greeted him with a nod and, without preamble, scooped rice out of the cauldron and set the cold platter of beef on the table. She had fed the family pets with the same grudging tenderness years ago. Cats and dogs quivering in corners, traumatized by the most recent explosion: Joey, gone bad in the fifth grade, caught sniffing glue and strung up in a sack over the stove; the marmalade kitten, her favorite, thrown twisting through the air for being sick on the sofa. Brother and sister ate together, cautiously glancing from time to time at the door to their father's room, waiting for the gravelly voice to summon them. Two abandoned children, Dora thought, middle-aged at thirty-five.

"Lola Cedes will be coming tonight," Ciso volunteered at last.

"Lola Cedes?"

"The *mananambal*. The herb woman."

"What do you need her for?" she said. "Dr. Perez comes every week."

"It is only after Lola Cedes' massages that Papa can sleep."

She mulled this over for a while, before saying almost routinely, "Massages are the last thing he needs. There's so much fluid in the tissues."

"Of course. You would know; you are the nurse." Ciso laid his spoon and fork down and gave her his sad, resigned smile. She felt the ghost of an old irritation: that inability of his to hold to an opinion, even with his own sister.

He left the dishes on the table for her to clean up. Guiding his rusty bicycle through the front gate, he went off squeaking down the street, listing perilously from side to side.

When the *mananambal* arrived, it was evening, the cicadas singing in the bushes, the acacias black blurs against a murky lavender sky. She stood on the top step, an old woman in a faded print skirt and shapeless blouse, and knocked gently. A thin, staring girl, about fourteen, trailed after her. Ciso came to greet the healer and they spoke in quiet voices. Lola Cedes made her way to the sickroom, nodding casually to Dora. She had brought with her a faint odor of herbs and lemongrass; it hung in the air, mixed with the scent of her sweat.

The younger woman stood in the doorway and watched them. Ciso had gotten down on his knees by the bedside, was murmuring something to himself, or perhaps to the little chapel formed by his clasped hands. Some vernacular prayer, rote. Lola Cedes' eyes met hers over her brother's bowed head. "Your father will not be healed unless you, too, pray," the *mananambal* said. Dora took a couple of steps forward to accept a small, well-thumbed booklet from her. The prayers were in Cebuano. She would never be able to read them aloud; it had been too long.

"And how are you tonight, Tio Tinong?" the herb-woman said, making conversation, easing the thin shirt off the old man's back, manipulating the flaccid limbs with a certain tenderness. Feebly, he tried to move his arms; they flailed in the air, hands loosely balled, like a baby's. Dora had never seen her father in this room with any woman but her mother. Lola Cedes poured liniment into her palm from a brown bottle. With a hand like a piece of sentient rubber, now pliant, now assertive, the herb-woman described circles on the old man's flesh. He didn't look at her. He looked instead at Dora, eyes black hollows under the ridge of his brow bone. Dora matched the stare. The herb-woman's hand stroked him at the periphery of her vision, devoting equal time to the nerveless parts of his body; under her touch his face softened, his shoulders lost their rigidity. His eyes closed and his lips stretched in what could only be a smile.

Dora advanced upon the little tableau by the bed, cold all of a sudden, but fascinated. His face had never looked so unguarded, so content.

She would have worn the same look as a baby, and it would have been he who would have stood over her in this fashion, and perhaps tickled her smooth belly and her little furled hands tenderly. This same moment of peace, before she wriggled beneath his touch and gave out thin wailing cries of distress, and he, helpless, would have thundered for her mother to come and shut her up, berated her for allowing the infant to go hungry. Later, she would learn to quiet down at his approach and glare at him from under a heavy shelf of brow so like his own, and he would curse her, and curse his fate, for having fathered such a sullen child—such sullen worthless children, for whom he would have to go back to his ship in a few more weeks, risking life and limb.

And you would beat us! Dora cried silently. You kicked us around the floor! The arching length of that old leather belt had brought her child's flesh to life and simultaneously blanched it of all feeling forever. His eyes opened and he saw the pity and the hatred in hers, and as Lola Cedes worked gently over his shoulders, he let his head loll to one side in resignation.

Dora clenched her rough nurse's hands, brought them protectively up to her chest. An image of greenish-white hallways rose up behind her lids. For ten years, in a fevered orgy of giving, she had mopped up shit, smiled briskly into pale parchment faces, put the warmth of a lifetime's intercourse into her voice. I could make you happy now, she thought frantically, to the defeated face. I could stretch out my hands, feel you, heal you.

But she knew it was too late. It no longer mattered—she and her father were beyond all help. There was only her life, and a sense of bitter regret for never having known him. She thought of her apartment, dark and silent now in her absence, bereft of a bridegroom, its pristine air shattered from time to time with the voices of children raised in what were almost cries of love. And she crossed her arms and pressed her fists tightly to her breast, lest she burst open, spill away, bleed at the sudden contact with his skin.

Ironing

Elda Rotor

mother's fingers
quickly draw water in shallow cups
sprinkle the pile of white and pastel cotton
Thursday baptism
of dad's office shirts
the non-sound, almost like nature,
silence, space, water, gestures
a light swish of laundered shirts moved around,
pulled from the big straw bag
that seemed bottomless—PILIPINAS
sewn in green and red straw
the board wrapped with extra cloth
tightly pulled and thick
like a favorite mattress
warm from bodies and sleep

the iron hisses when lifted upright
like a dragon awakening
I peek for dragons in the skinny window
that measures water
mother's expert hands dance around
softness and heated iron
steering evenly around plastic buttons
pressing firmly into corners and
smooth across collars and edges
cloth maneuvered to make sleeves play three dimensional
mother decides final creases to form direction
hot iron half-inches away from her fingers
I always imagined the pain and the scars
but she had no marks on her hands

even the background noise from the TV
the canned laugh track
of the Thursday night sit-com
does not drown out the ritual,
the quiet chemistry

of cotton, water, and heat
mother hardly talks, looks up once in awhile
to watch the screen
barely looks at me but knows that she is teaching

sometimes she made me practice
for when she would leave us,
I never knew something so quiet could be so hard
break into a sweat the heat my arms hurt
afraid to burn myself
I'd make the shirts too wet
cotton soaked
and mother would wait for them to dry a little and do them herself

perfect shirts hung on doorknobs
and hinges and backs of chairs around the living room
crisp whites, pastel blues and yellows and cremes
my father would wear with his few
Hong Kong custom-made
dark gray and navy suits
the room well lit and warm of cotton
and the faint smell of detergent

mother knew I was learning
for when she would leave us,
now dad has married a woman
younger modern and synthetic
that taught him labels—
wash-n-wear
perma-press
polyester blend
there is no ironing these years
no labor no art
the non-sounds of childhood
that filled out more the entity of mother
remember activity as much as person
the ordinary about her is what presses
warm and permanent in my silence

Smoky Mountain (an excerpt from a novel in progress)

Grace Talusan

Tatang was having sex with his mistress Nene when Inang, his wife of thirty years, died. He had grown tired of waiting by Inang's bedside, breathing in the bitter smell of her morphine drip, the stale oil of her unwashed hair. Tatang didn't want to watch as his wife, twenty years younger than he, aged in her bed. With each month that passed, Inang aged a decade. Her hair turned grey, then a brilliant white, then a stale yellow. Her soft body became sharp as her bones pushed against her skin. Tatang started to sleep in an empty bedroom because all he could think about when he saw Inang was death. Her death, mostly, but what Tatang couldn't stand was seeing images of his own death. When he saw her body, he could only imagine his body slowly shrinking into itself. When she would lie very still, sleeping, he could already see what she would look like in her casket and then his own funeral. He tried to avoid Inang as much as possible.

Tatang knew Inang was sick, he had hints of it for a long time, but when Inang stopped cooking for the *sari-sari* store, Tatang knew this was serious. Even in her last months of pregnancy or when she was sick with fever, Inang never failed to cook *adobo* chicken in coconut milk, *pancit* noodles with colorful strips of vegetables, and *sinigang* soup for her customers. She said no one else could cook as well as she and would shove anyone in her way out of the kitchen.

"We're going to lose money," she would say harshly. "The customers only like my cooking."

That last day that she cooked for the store, Inang climbed into bed and never got out. The doctor said they had waited too long and just gave Inang some pills to help her pain. Tatang hired a maid to take care of Inang and looked to the floor when she asked about her children. He could tell she was in constant pain, but the only way Tatang knew this was because she would bite her lower lip. He had seen that expression before on his wife's face. The first few times they had sex, when she gave birth, when a vat of hot oil spilled on her thighs. But Inang, as before, had never cried out. When her lower lip was mashed and bloodied from all the screams of pain it contained, Tatang decided to give her something.

"Here," Tatang said. He braided soft clean rags and put the thick cloth between Inang's lips. "Bite this."

That last afternoon Inang was alive, Tatang looked in on her before going to visit his young mistress Nene, who lived close by in the squatter's community at Smoky Mountain.* Inang had fallen into a coma some days before. Inang's nurse sat in a rocking chair reading a movie magazine aloud to Inang. She believed Inang still could hear them. Tatang wanted to talk to Inang, but he was too ashamed to say it out loud in front of the nurse, so he spoke to her in his thoughts, like a prayer. He tried to stop the thought in his head, *Just go,* in case Inang could hear it.

Tatang left his Tondo neighborhood for Smoky Mountain and walked up the hill of trash, tripping over cartons and plastic bags. As his feet sunk deep into the muck, he thought, This must be what walking in snow is like. Inang had never seen snow and he wondered if he would ever get the chance. The shacks the squatters lived in were built out of corrugated scrap metal and wooden shipping crates from the docks. Tatang liked to look at all the different kinds of writing on the shacks. The swirling alphabet of Saudi Arabia, the boxy Chinese characters, the rounded Japanese writing. It made him sad to think how much these crates had traveled and how little he had seen of the world.

Some Filipinos believe that when a loved one dies, their soul visits you. If you were very dear to the dead relative, the new ghost would try to signal you that they were there. They would knock on the walls or infuse the air with their favorite perfume or burn out the light bulbs.

Something made him stop in the middle of having sex. He climbed off Nene's sticky body. He lay on his back next to her, staring up at the word "tomatoes" painted on the ceiling made of shipping crate. He felt like someone was watching them, but when he pulled the curtains made of old dresses from the window, there was no one there. He looked across the trash piles of Smoky Mountain where Nene had built her shack. Alongside adults dressed in rags and bandannas, naked children held plastic bags in their hands and picked through the piles of trash. The squatters were collecting scrap metal, soda cans, and beer bottles to sell or trade. He scanned the nicks and

holes in the walls of the shack for a peeping eye. There was no sign
of that Chik, the little boy who was always spying on people. Chik's
right eye was always red with styes from pressing his face to the
dust-covered walls.

"What's wrong?" Nene asked. "You were almost done."

Tatang looked at Nene's face, once smooth as the meat of a young
coconut. When they met, Nene told him that she was eighteen, but
Tatang was sure that she was much younger. During the year they
were together, while the lump in Inang's chest gave birth to more
lumps in her body, Nene developed small breasts and the ugly pimples
of a teenager on her face and back.

Tatang didn't answer, he just sniffed the air. Nene did the same. "I
don't smell the smoke anymore," Tatang said. Smoky Mountain got
its name from the constant fires that burned the city's trash.

"Maybe you're used to the smoke," Nene answered. She turned
onto her stomach and covered her bare back with the sheet. "I don't
smell it anymore either." Nene lay still like she was trying to take a
nap and then she sighed. She sounded like one of Tatang's grand-
daughters reacting to her father's reprimands.

"You complained so much about the stink and now that you don't
smell it, you are also complaining," Nene laughed. At first, Tatang
hadn't wanted to meet Nene on Smoky Mountain. The stink of garbage cooking in the tropical sun made him gag and the yellow smoke
made his eyes water, but Nene had convinced him that he would
save money on motels by using her shack for their visits.

Tatang sat on the mat, crossed his legs, and lit a cigarette. Nene
turned back over and sat up. She wrapped the sheet around her body
and on top of her head like a nun's habit, pulling the white cloth
tightly under her chin and holding the cloth with her fist. This made
her eyes look big.

"Will you still give me the money?" Nene asked. She had asked
him for some of the money he would have paid a motel. Tatang
picked up his trousers from the floor and pulled out a few crumpled
peso bills. He threw them onto Nene's lap. She let go of the sheet
and smoothed out the bills, counting each one out loud.

"You're thinking about her," Nene said. "I always know when
you're thinking of her." Tatang looked at Nene, happily counting
her money. Her face was chubby, her cheeks like steaming red loaves
of *pan de sal*. She had gained weight since they first met, her body

fattened by the fried pork, garlic rice, and sweets that he brought her.

"My wife is dying," Tatang replied.

"That woman has been dying for a long time," Nene said. "When she goes, you can marry me and I can live in that great big house of yours. I'll take care of you. I'll even help at Inang's store. And I won't give any free food away."

Tatang remembered that day when a young girl, obviously straight from the country province, had come into the store. She was thin and hungry. Tatang remembered the way she kept swallowing as she stared at Inang's cooked foods. It was after the lunch-time rush when dock workers would swarm the counter tops, standing behind the stools in impatient lines, each one waiting for the man ahead of him to gulp down his meal. The smells of *adobo* chicken stew, sour *sinigang* soup, and fried chicken still permeated the air. He had given the girl some crispy scraps from the tray of fried chicken getting hard under the heat lamps and ladled a bowl of the steaming tamarind broth. After she ate and he would not accept her pesos, he was surprised when she kissed him loudly on the cheek in gratitude. Nene continued coming to the store every day at the same time and it was not long after that they were lovers. The first time had been in the tiny pantry in the back of the store, leaning against bags of rice and sugar.

Tatang had had plenty of affairs before Nene. He was very discreet, but he still thought Inang suspected it. Inang was a good wife. She wasn't like other Filipino wives who would cry to their sisters or scream at their husbands for having affairs. She understood that men needed variety and excitement.

His wife had liked sex and that was something good about her. Tatang was afraid that if he didn't satisfy her, she might look outside to the streets of Tondo or to her customers. Many of these men were dock workers and had traveled the world to places like Saudi Arabia, Hawaii, and Hong Kong. Tatang couldn't have that. When he imagined his wife taking a lover, he would be overcome with fury and rage. His heart beat quickly and his face reddened and he felt like he had enough strength in his hands to squeeze the air out of her lover. So he made sure to satisfy her. That jealousy never left him, even when Inang was too sick to leave her bed. Tatang still made sure to stay in the room when she was being examined by her physician. He watched the doctor carefully to see if he looked too long at his wife's breasts or if he kept his hand on her skin just a second longer than necessary.

It made Tatang sad that their children had not been able to return home from their overseas jobs. They sent telegrams to Inang that said, *Sorry, Mama. Can't come home. God Bless* from Saudi Arabi where the boys were working in the oil industry and from Hong Kong, where the girls worked as domestics. Tatang blamed himself for this. He knew they were running from him. He had to make many painful but practical decisions as a father. He had sent some of the younger children to the province to live with his relatives who weren't able to bear their own children. He had heaped more food on the eldest son's plate and told the other children, *No*, when they had asked for second helpings and refills of milk. He had made a longer investment in the older son—with young children, you never knew when they would become sick with pneumonia or scarlet fever. Feeding them first was a risky investment. He told the younger children to wait their turn, that the eldest son would provide for them, but the only son who had benefited from this was the youngest, Alvaro, who was now a medical doctor. The eldest had put Alvaro through high school, college, and now medical school.

Tatang had protected his children. During "Japanese times," those years when Japan occupied Manila during the Second World War, Tatang scrambled to save his nine children from atrocities. He hid his daughters in the rice bins when the Japanese soldiers walked the streets, looking for girls to rape. He sent his sons far into the jungle province so they wouldn't be put in work camps. Tatang still had a gun and some grenades that he scavenged from Japanese Occupation. Even now, he kept those close to him, under his bed, in case the Japanese ever came back.

Tatang had recalled those nights he couldn't sleep, when the children were still young and he wasn't sure if they could eat the next day. He had stood in the living room where all the children slept on mats, wrapped in white mosquito nets like a spider's meal. Sometimes he would lie down next to one of his daughters and watch her chest rise and fall, smell the sweetness of her night perspiration. He always wanted to touch her then, hug her close, explore her warm skin. But he was afraid of being caught. There were too many eyes in the room that might catch him.

Tatang found a will on the bureau one morning. Inang wrote in her childish scrawl that she wanted her baby jars buried in the coffin with her. During her childbearing years, Inang had given birth to three stillborns. When the first dead baby was born, Inang procured great glass jars from her cousin the pharmacist. She put that and the subsequent stillborn babies in their own jars with a white label. In her childish script, Inang had written out their names. *Maria Theresa. Jose Gerardo. Maria Dolores.* The grey bodies floated in a yellow fluid, the heavy jars arranged on a shelf with a glow-in-the-dark crucifix, a Santo Niño doll in a regal red and gold trimmed dress, and a plaster blue-robed Virgin. In the only argument Tatang remembered having with Inang, she insisted on these baby jars. "I don't want my babies in the ground," she told him. "They belong here with me."

Tatang tried to ignore it when Inang talked to the babies as if they were still alive. But he was proud when he saw how resourceful his wife was. When the children were still small and not behaving, the jars were a threat.

"Do you want to end up like that?" Inang would say. The children would shake their heads in fear, trying to figure out what these babies had done that was so bad.

"Would you ever marry me?" Nene asked. She touched him on the shoulder. "You don't even have to marry me. I can just live with you and tell everyone I'm your new servant."

Tatang grasped Nene's small wrist in his large bony hand. What a disgrace to marry a Smoky Mountain squatter.

"I can't," he said. Tatang let go of her wrist and covered his eyes with his palms. "I'm just an old man. You're so young, Nene. You'll meet a young man and forget about me."

"Being young isn't so great," Nene said sadly, sitting on Tatang's chest.

"It's everything," Tatang said. He held her knees like small apples in his hand. He stared at her stomach, breasts, smooth neck. "You have a lot of life yet to live. Me, maybe ten, fifteen years. It's too fast. Do you know what that's like? And my wife's life is done. She can go at anytime."

"I don't want to hear about your wife," Nene said, reaching her hand to Tatang's abdomen. "Now promise me, no more talking." Nene was trying to make herself useful, so that he couldn't ever leave her. But Tatang knew he didn't love her enough to have her come home with him. Or maybe he did love her. Too much. Loved her so much that he wouldn't want to curse her with someone so old as himself.

Something in the air lifted. He didn't feel that strange sensation of being watched. Tatang sighed and reached out to Nene's shoulders, pulling her face down to him to kiss. This always made him forget.

When Tatang returned from Nene's shack, peaceful and energetic, his youngest son Alvaro was sitting on the front steps.

"She's gone," Alvaro told Tatang. "Almost two hours already. We tried to wait for you, but we had to remove the body. This heat is terrible lately. Where have you been?"

He saw the last few hours through Inang's eyes. Inang, released from her body and able to watch his every move, hear his thoughts. Tatang nodded and sat down silently next to his son. They smoked and drank beer without saying a word. Watching the street activities go on the same as always, waiting for the change to sink in.

Even many years later, Tatang still missed the sound of Inang's slippers slapping heavily on the floors, the chipped coffee cups she set on tables and counter tops to spit phlegm from her constant coughing, a braided rag with brown blood stains under the bed, her hair pins on the window sills and scattered throughout the house. Inang always wore her waist length hair in a heavy bun that sagged towards her collar. Tatang still found her gray hair pins under the bed or under seat cushions. Sometimes the pin would have a long strand of hair clinging to it. Tatang would take this hair and wrap it around his finger tightly until the brittle stand snapped and floated to the floor.

Tatang did not return to Nene's shack for many months. When he finally went looking for her among the burning garbage, he knew it was a waste of time. She had disappeared. Her woven mat was not on the floor and the crude windows were empty of the curtains made from her skirts. Tatang sat on the floor, his palms sinking into the ash that had blown in from the open windows. He tilted his head back, looked up at the ceiling made of shipping crates, and read the word "tomatoes," saying this word aloud, surprised at the sound of his voice speaking English in the emptiness.

Editor's Note: Smoky Mountain—Manila's shame, an entire neighborhood built on a garbage dump.

Baby Brother Grown

Malou Babilonia

My baby brother
flies to the tip of Lake Tahoe
in a single engine plane
in the dead of winter
through an inhospitable storm
with a bucket of friends from work
and almost dies.

My baby brother
rents a twin engine plane
with a barrel of friends from work
this time a batch of fishing poles accompany.
He soars into the blazing blue and yellow heat of
northwestern coastal Mexico.

My baby brother is afraid of water
of sharks and other dark creatures not seen but felt
on his slimy, underworked legs.
But unable to resist
the clear crystal blue
he lays his white belly
atop a black inner tube
dangling four pasty limbs
into the marker-less sea.
A laughing companion fastens a cheap jelly mask
onto his cheeky pale face
and my brother plops
his now heavy head
into water
breathing unsteadily
into a leaky snorkel.
His temperature adjusts slowly
body turning to liquid
as sea and blood become one.
He watches colors of fish below him
and forgets his fear.
My baby brother, a Giant Squid.

His near-white expanse of back
turns hot pink
but he feels nothing
only his primitive hunger.
His fisherfriends plane pilot too
hook large sea food
tuna and dorado.
Bringing their gourmand city sensibilities
to the Sea of Cortez,
the men chop expertly
their still-wriggling catch
plop bite-size pieces
into a wasabi-lined Ziploc bag.
Hacked body parts in plastic swirl
until evenly coated in effervescent green
the boys chomp heartily on their sea-hunter's lunch.

My brother's back tingles a little,
but he thinks nothing of it,
Man that he is.

Monday morning
the boy-group lands safely home
freewaying to work in wrinkled suits
hatchback Honda Civic their in-motion changing
    room.
My brother cannot understand
why now his head is light
why now he wants to throw up.
His perky secretary
famous scatterer of vermilion kisses
on memos minutes message slips
notices his sunburnt neck
and demands that he show her his back.

Recoiling in horror
before catching back her wind
she rushes him
to Kaiser Emergency
just as boils begin
to crack open.

He is told by Doctor
he has third degree burns
only a high pain threshold
kept him from feeling
anything but a few
misconstrued tingles
until now.

My baby brother recovers
takes a leisurely cruise along the Nile
chatting with elderly couples
from Germany, Great Britain, and even our Philippines.
The couple from Homeland
he expects to take him in like a son
but uncharacteristically they do not,
    having
    perhaps
been aNilized.

He eats well rests a lot
but knows there is more than this.
So he jumps ship,
trains back to Cairo
where he learns with great difficulty to ride camels
through a sun-baked sand desert packed
tighter than his back.

His changeable skin, neither dark nor light
his ordinary blazer
unfashionable shoes
black army-issue beret
shield and incorporate him
no matter what the climate.
He is not cheated, nor harassed
mutable brother
he is never taken for a foreigner.
Even beggars ignore him
wherever he goes, alone.

Together we scaled the Berlin Wall,
first when it stood rigid and hateful,
then again later when it came tumbling down.
We watched school children
offer up love songs to soldiers
standing above armed
with tears breaking down resolves.
We drove from and to Paris,
our tin car rental nearly swerving off
an icy embankment
carrying us to our maybe-near-deaths
into an already ghostly
blue and white winter nightie-night.

Now my brother
away from me
calls from an isolated forest road
in a moment having decided
to drive a rugged fish worker to Alaska.

I'll be back on Monday.
OK, but be careful.
Aw, don't give me that family b-b-b-beeswax.
OK, I stop.

But sister, my baby brother adds.
Can you pick me up at the airport?

I move to hang up, he stops.
Sis, he says.
What?
Just pray for me, then

My baby brother
Who learned to be a man without the slightest hint of father
Who cultivated a yearning for adventure
who belongs anywhere in the world
but loves me enough
to live here, with me, at least for a while
between journeys.

My brother
who still trusts in God
and so fears much
is the alive-liest soul I know.

My baby brother
a Filipino American cowboy.

Christmas

Henrietta Chico Nofre

The Holy Cross Catholic Cemetery of Burbank is a nice cemetery. Lots of open spaces with cypress trees and low, crinkly-leafed bushes and statues of the Holy Family close by. Not like one of those dark cemeteries—filled with tall pine trees that block out the sun, where you instantly feel cold and reach for your jacket—where they buried my godfather, Romolo. At Holy Cross, everything is in a shade of light kelly green.

We come here each Christmas to visit my brother, Virgil, born before me. On Christmas day, after midday Mass with Father Lima, my mother packs a kitchen knife, a few rags, and a bottle of water so we can visit my brother, her firstborn, properly. Each Christmas we tend Virgil's grave, leave a tiny Christmas tree filled with toys, and sit for a while with the baby boy who lived for three days before his baby lungs filled with liquid.

I once found a cardboard box sitting on a closet shelf with a pair of white terry cloth baby booties and a blue layette set still in their original packages. In the same box was a Eucharist candle, a prayer book, roses that had dried into the color of old newspaper, and pictures of a tiny baby who looked like he was sleeping inside a fancy sewing box. He was bundled up in a white robe as if someone was worried about him getting cold. You could see his small fists curled tight on either side of him.

At first he scared me with his mauve lips and strangely pale, chubby face. But the longer I stared, the more I saw that he was just a baby. He had long dark eyelashes and the black hair that peeked out from beneath his cap would have grown to feel like mine, thin and fine. Then, standing in front of this open cardboard box, a thought began to circle inside my head: If you had lived...If you had lived... If you had lived...If you had lived I'd have fought with you over the television. If you had lived, there would have been someone to play Chinese checkers with. If you had lived, maybe Daddy would not be the way he is. If you had lived, I would have been a sister to someone.

Holy Cross cemetery is divided into sections, like neighborhoods, each with a name that is printed in white letters on the curb. As we drive by, I read: Benediction Way, Holy Redemption, Immaculate Ascension. We drive until we get to the section called Holy Innocents, where they keep the babies.

Walking from the car to the grave of the person you are visiting can make your insides curl up, especially when you know you visit adults. Sometimes the ground hasn't settled and you can feel the rounded hills that outline the coffins that lie below as you walk. You know you are walking on top of dead people. But with babies it's different. When you walk over the graves of babies, your heart feels heavy and you feel like sighing. You think of all the mothers and fathers having to give away stuffed animals and bassinets.

When we finally reach him, my mother croons in Tagalog, "Virgil, *anak*, my child, we're here," and bends from the waist to place one hand flatly on the tombstone the color of pencil lead. It feels strange to hear my mother call to another child in a voice usually reserved only for me.

And then, we work. When I was younger, I'd watch my father clean my brother's grave. First, he took the knife and cut around the border of the headstone, clearing away wiry, tentacles of crabgrass. Then, he cleared an inch and a half of dirt from the headstone until it was framed by a dark brown border of freshly turned earth. Next, he dug a shallow hole to secure the miniature Christmas tree we brought with us, and then finally, we wiped the headstone with water and Kleenex from the car. This took about fifteen minutes.

I don't remember exactly how long ago it was when I stopped watching my father and squatted down to clean the grave myself, but one day it seemed right that I should be the one to polish and dig, with my parents looking down and remembering.

It was much harder than I thought. The kitchen knife (disinfected later with rubbing alcohol) must be driven into the soil very forcefully or else the knife bounces off and doesn't cut anything. After only five minutes, hot, tender spots on the inside curl of my fingers made me stop. It was eerie the first time I drove the knife blade into the cemetery earth, like a scene out of Dracula, but I forgot about horror movies as I listened to the clicking sound the steel blade made as it glanced the tombstone or felt the thud, thud, thud of my hand coming down against the ground. After doing this for a while I started thinking crazy thoughts: What If I kept digging? This little baby who could have changed my life wasn't just some sad thought pressed between the pages of a book like he was so many other days of the year. The ache in my legs as I squatted on the grass and the blisters on my hands made Virgil real. I began to think as I heard the thud, thud, thud of my blows, "There is a part of me here." Each time my hand came down, I was saying, "I miss you even though I never knew you." When I cut back the grass, I was telling him, "I'm sorry that you died."

"Clean Kerry's and Jonathan's headstones too," my mother said, looking over at Virgil's neighbors. All three had died within days of each other. Kerry was on the right and Jonathan was on the left and every time we visited Virgil, no one brought them flowers. No one tended their graves. "They're Virgil's playmates up in heaven," Mother said. She had knelt beside me, her hands gliding over the dark gray tombstone to Virgil's left. "Jonathan, where's your Mommy? Why doesn't she visit you?"

Once I am done digging the shallow hole, carving the inch and a half border around the headstone, and have wiped the granite with water and pastel green Kleenex from the car, my mother, father, and I stand there quietly. My mother stands in her cable-knit sweater, arms folded across her chest. My father looks down. As we stand there in silence, my mind flashes to the other pictures in the cardboard box: A small white coffin with a spray of carnations on top. A gaping, rectangular ditch. A priest whose white robes were whipping around his legs. My mother in a wheelchair, still weak from childbirth, her hand over her forehead. My father in a magenta sweater kneeling on one knee.

In the car my mother doesn't say anything for a while. For a couple of hours on every Christmas day I know my mother has thought sweetly about another child who is not me. My mother once said she never touched her baby boy during the three days he lived. She said she never wanted to hold his tiny foot or his plump, dimpled hand because she knew he'd be taken from her.

And as my father pulls away from the curb, the little Christmas tree we left growing smaller and smaller, I become aware as if for the very first time of the gleam of unused seat belt buckles next to me, shining brightly in the sun.

Bandit Banjao #2

Sherlyn Jiminez

lysol smell. the blankets sterile on narrow adjustable beds. deep lake, the hospital's name in english. a view of different shades of green, leaves weighed down by rain.

how we used to fight about the light in our room. off. on. off. on. a kick. a punch. on. off. a pillow between us in our shared bed. our backs turned away from each other. your breath deepening before the shifting would begin.

we hold our grandmother's hands through the night as pain returns. they escape. move down her body beneath hospital sheets. we pull her hands away. she doesn't want to go. not ready yet she begs. later, I cradle her mouth close, curl up in the next bed.

we talked about how much your child's diaper cost. boy I saw come out, head glistening, eyes closed and face crunched up. was with you through the needle on your antiseptic-rubbed back. through the swift, precise cut and the crowning, the cone-shaped baby looking like a glow worm.

when we are old, only you will remember my childhood. only I will remember yours.

Piranhas in the Kitchen

Maloy Luakian

After he left Auntie Baby and my cousins Jun-Jun and Julius for good, Uncle Boyet—who we used to call Di-Pe or Second Uncle in his more respectable days—went to live with Uncle Ernie, the exotic animal collector. No one was particularly inconvenienced. Auntie Baby and her sons had been living with us for a while now, and it was understood that my parents would take care of them until Auntie Baby returned to her family or found another man.

Most people, including my parents, were shocked that Uncle Boyet would choose to stay with Uncle Ernie instead of with his mistress, Lanie, when it was long accepted that he was renting a townhouse in Greenhills for her. My mother blamed Uncle Boyet's double abandonment on Uncle Ernie. Lanie had been a hostess at Uncle Ernie's nightclub, Flying Stallions, and my mother suspected that Uncle Boyet had succumbed to another girl there. "Those two are *sang teh,* the same kind," my mother said. "Always running after cheap women. Too selfish to think of how their wives suffer."

Since it was true that Auntie Baby did suffer a lot—she cried in her room for days after Uncle Boyet's final desertion and told my cousins that they were as good as orphaned—I didn't think that it was fair to compare her suffering to Uncle Ernie's wife's. Auntie Chari had a demeanor and a pair of tattooed eyebrows that made you understand that she was not someone who cried and gave up easily. She had immediately sued Uncle Ernie for millions of pesos and ended up living with the tomboy who sold chickens at the Aranque wet market. Elsie never had to sell chickens again and I sometimes saw her at Lim Gold & Etc., Auntie Chari's jewelry store. Elsie was a short, stocky woman with huge breasts who unfailingly wore what seemed to constitute the tomboy uniform: a baseball cap, a shirt declaring allegiance to a certain household product (in Elsie's case, it was either Lysol or Johnson & Johnson Floor Wax), and loose-fitting, prefaded jeans. She always addressed my mother as "Mrs. Sexy," but only knew me as *"Hoy,"* as in *"Hoy,* where's your mother?" Before settling down with Auntie Chari, Elsie had once asked my mother out to the movies. My mother was flattered but told me that she thought Elsie a bit abnormal.

Auntie Chari had been the one to tell my mother about Uncle Boyet hiding out at Uncle Ernie's. She had gone over to collect her alimony and had seen Uncle Boyet morosely helping Uncle Ernie feed his lizards. Our driver, Romy, had sold them to Uncle Ernie; they had washed up on the roof of the maids' quarters in our backyard during a flood. We were supposed to eat them—the pair were about four feet long and quite fleshy. Romy and my mother both agreed they were perfect for roasting on a spit, but Uncle Ernie had saved the lizards' lives by giving Romy enough money to buy a new scooter.

"Boyet is so ugly now, ha? I didn't know he had gotten so fat," Auntie Chari said. "Do you remember that he used to be good-looking? We called him the Chinese Elvis."

"He's just had a lot of problems," my mother said, loyally.

"He looks like a goldfish! His eyes are like this!" Auntie Chari bulged out her eyes. With her curved, indigo eyebrows, she looked like a demon from Buddhist hell or at least the ruby-eyed, lucky jade frog on her mantle with the Chinese coin in its mouth. "His bad luck has caught up with him. Look at your own husband. Johnny was ugly before but he looks all right now."

My mother was silenced by the truth of what Auntie Chari claimed. Usually my mother could find some excuse for Uncle Boyet, his looks and his behavior. Every time he was caught fooling around on Auntie Baby, my mother either said that Uncle Boyet had settled down too young and would naturally have some leftover urges or that he was just getting old and trying to relive his lost youth. Later, when we found out that Lanie was somewhat young, sort of pretty, and Chinese, my mother triumphantly said, of course, it was understandable why Uncle Boyet would leave Auntie Baby, who was getting old and was a Filipina, too.

⧼⧽

That my mother found hidden in Uncle Boyet's Tancho-pomaded hair and beer-swollen body some remnant of a redeeming quality was an incomprehensible act of treason to me. To us, her children, she told stories about how Uncle Boyet had been the most-favored and best-looking of my grandmother's children; he had been light-skinned then, too, not the way he looked now, like a coconut husk frayed from being used to wax the floor too much. Teen-aged girls and even matrons used to call Uncle Boyet up all the time, and this was in the sixties, when decency was a real way of life. My mother believed that Uncle Boyet's only fault was being born into an "easy life" and not having the willpower to resist its seduction.

"He must have been a pretty girl in his past life," my mother guessed. "Maybe tricked a lot of men, took their money. Now he is paying for it."

To Jun-Jun though, my mother never said anything good about Uncle Boyet. She thought it was best that Jun-Jun reject him as early as possible. "Better not to have a father than to have a useless one," she told Auntie Baby. Auntie Baby agreed. Julius, my mother left alone. He was only four, too young to understand anything important.

My mother repeated the story of Uncle Boyet, my father, and the Cobra to Jun-Jun in her crooked Filipino like an insistent cricket during rainy season. (Jun-Jun understood Fukienese but my mother never talked to him in Chinese.) The details changed from time to time; sometimes, it was during her pregnancy with Peter, sometimes it was when she married my father and first came to the Philippines. I wasn't concerned by my mother's inconsistencies. I never trusted her accuracy anyway; she always found convenient ways to exaggerate or forget details to suit whatever moral she was trying to impress on us. The gist of my mother's story involved the garage along Banawe Street, called Thunderbird, that my family had once owned. We had been pioneers: Banawe was now full of auto shops and men running alongside your car waving flags made of different-colored window tints. Back then, Thunderbird had been one of a handful.

According to my mother, with Thunderbird, money began introducing itself to the Coyutan family. My father ran the shop, like everything else, but he had to give his brothers jobs there, too. Ah-Pe, First Uncle, supervised the mechanics, and Sa-Chak, Third Uncle, bought lunches and snacks.

"Your uncle gave Boyet the best job, counting money. They used to be very close to each other." At this point, my father would snort in denial and my mother would placatingly say, "You know, Johnny also wanted time to finish university." My mother would turn to me or Peter or Penelope and frown, "He is so smart, I don't know why none of you take after him. He skipped two grades in elementary." It would turn out that all my uncles would graduate from university and that my father never would, even with a scholarship in biology.

Uncle Boyet eventually stole all the business money and sold all the customers' cars to buy a Ford Cobra. It was the first Cobra ever in the Philippines and even the GIs from Clark Air Base and Subic Bay would stop Uncle Boyet in the streets to ask for a ride. Naturally, Uncle Boyet ended up crashing the car so badly that it couldn't be resold.

"Johnny cried when he found out," my mother said to Jun-Jun in a lowered voice. I couldn't imagine it, looking at my father stretched out stomach-down on the floor, dozing with his face tucked in his folded arms.

My mother would end the story by maternally taking Jun-Jun's hand and saying kindly, "Jun-ah, your father is a *tarantado*. You know that, right? You shouldn't grow up to be like him, ha. Study hard and be a doctor. Just because your mother is Filipino doesn't mean you can't be a good Chinese son."

I always scolded my mother whenever I overheard her saying these things to Jun-Jun. "Ma! You're so cruel! Don't you feel sorry for Jun-Jun at all? This is his father you're insulting."

"He has to know. Who else will tell him?"

"His mother! Not you!"

"Baby? Hah," my mother sniffed. "She's still crazy about Boyet. Jun-Jun doesn't know anything, *la*."

"Ma, he knows about his father. Haven't you seen his thumb?" Jun-Jun's left thumb was stunted and the skin on it was chalky and prune-like. "He's thirteen and he still sucks it."

"That's because your father's family has a *lahi* of craziness. You look at your grandfather. Look at Boyet! If I was like Baby and didn't hit you at all, you'd be crazy like Jun-Jun, too."

All the same, my mother did feel sorry for Jun-Jun. She mixed Star margarine into his rice at breakfast to make up for any stress-related nutritional deficiencies. My mother also let him bully us and take our toys and comic books. If we fought back or teased Jun-Jun about his father, my mother would come rushing over with a plastic hanger and start randomly beating us, saying, "Don't talk like that about his father! Your cousin will go *siaw siaw*!"

❦

Uncle Boyet had first met Uncle Ernie through my father when my father still raced pigeons. He had no time for them now, and the pigeons that he had were just being kept for sentimental value or as exhibition racers and breeders instead of professional athletes. My father never seemed to take competition seriously, anyway. He did import birds from Belgium and he did have a Betamax tape, "Pigeon Racing: the Sport of Kings," but he never kept track of his trophies the way Uncle Ernie did. My father just left them wherever there was space in the house. We were long used to finding plaster or brass-plated pigeons on pedestals in the toilet or staring down from the top of the freezer.

Uncle Ernie kept all of his trophies in his trophy room. He had some animal heads in there, too, mostly moose and deer, but also some endangered species, like black bears and tigers. He had gotten most of them while living in England as a college student. Uncle Ernie taught his mynah bird Lucita to hide inside the open mouths of the animal heads and screech out things like, "*Putang ina!* Look at me!"

Uncle Ernie still spent a lot of time racing pigeons ("He owns an *ago-go* dancer club. Nothing to do during the day," my father said) and we found him just exiting his three-story pigeon house the day my mother took me and my siblings to visit. We quickly found out though, that Uncle Boyet had already left. Lanie had come and dragged him home.

"*Hay,* Ernie. Why didn't you talk sense into Boyet? You know he listens to you." My mother shook her head at him in disgust.

Uncle Ernie looked cornered. He was wearing his usual white boating hat—to hide his growing baldness—and his Lacoste sport shirt. He was the only man my father's age that I knew who wore shorts. "Liling, Boyet is an adult," he said weakly.

My mother sniffed. "What kind of adult leaves his wife for a hostess?"

We left Uncle Ernie glumly sitting in his living room surrounded by hamsters (to feed the snakes and lizards with) and all kinds of tropical birds. "Living in a zoo like that!" my mother scowled. "It's bad *feng shui* to keep wild animals in the house. What does he need a monkey for? Or an eagle? Or that alligator? Peter-ah, remember when you fell in the pond?" My mother shuddered.

This was when we were younger and Auntie Chari was still living with Uncle Ernie. There weren't as many animals then, only the deer, the alligator, and maybe one or two snakes, but Uncle Ernie had already begun to collect a lot of aquatic creatures. He had giant turtles, lion fish, and sharks in several ponds outside the house, and piranhas in the kitchen.

We had been jumping up and down on the wire mesh covering the alligator pond, teasing the poor creature, and Peter had fallen through a weak spot in the mesh. The alligator had been old and toothless anyway. He could only eat slop then, but my mother had gotten quite a scare. She always referred back to that incident whenever she received a shock of some kind. "Wah! That's almost as bad as when my son fell into Ernie's pond!" she would say.

My grandmother, Amah, took the news about Uncle Boyet and Lanie living together for real very emotionally. She had been quite volatile since Uncle Boyet left; she had thrown a tantrum when my father refused to let her accompany us to Uncle Ernie's to look for Uncle Boyet. Amah first went into denial, saying that her Victory—she never called Uncle Boyet by his nickname—would never turn his back on his family for a cheap hostess. Then she blamed Auntie Baby for not being woman enough to keep Uncle Boyet satisfied. "Your hole not good enough for my Victory!" she shrieked in her bad Filipino. Amah had an unusually large lower lip and as she spoke, tears made Olympian leaps from it as if from a diving board.

"And you!" Amah turned on my mother. "Telling me this news! Only a *paih lang,* a bad person, loves to spread gossip like that!" She cleared her throat loudly and spat into the Lion's Biscuit tin she shared with Angkong as a spittoon.

"Why are you blaming my mother?" I said, annoyed. "She's not the one with two wives."

My mother had to slap me in front of Amah for being rude. ("Wah! Listen to this evil child!" Amah said indignantly.) As a result, the sweet and sour pork that she cooked for dinner that night—an apology from her—became associated with my resentment of Uncle Boyet and Amah forever.

Auntie Baby received Uncle Ernie's news about Lanie and Uncle Boyet with resignation and a bit of relief. "I just wanted to know for sure what was on his mind," she confessed to my mother. Auntie Baby had already started working at her brother Oscar's real estate agency. She stopped crying in her room so much and was getting pedicures and putting make-up on again. Auntie Baby had been pretty when she was younger, plus her father had been a district judge; I didn't know why she ever bothered marrying Uncle Boyet.

My mother worried about the effect Uncle Boyet was having on Jun-Jun. He was turning into a freak, at least in my mother's eyes. My cousin had become involved with a Voltes V fan club; we had all liked the giant robot genre Japanese cartoon but not with the same intensity as Jun-Jun. The series was essentially about the alien Bozanian empire wanting to take over Earth, whose only defenders were the Voltes V pilot team: Steve Armstrong and his brothers Bert and Little John, rodeo star Mark Gordon, and pretty martial arts expert Jaimie Robinson. The Armstrong brothers were the sons of Dr. Armstrong, the Voltes V robot inventor who was presumed kidnapped by the aliens.

By the time the series went into its final episodes, I was sick of what I considered excessive sentimental drama surrounding the Armstrong boys' search for their missing father and had stopped watching. My brother and sister also lost interest, especially when The Transformers and GI Joe cartoons started airing. Jun-Jun, on the other hand, watched the whole Voltes V epic unfold to the end.

"Eh, your cousin's friends are weird. It's not right that boys their age are still playing with toys," my mother said suspiciously whenever one of Jun-Jun's Voltes V friends came over. My mother was most dubious about Humperdink Dy, who rolled slices of cheese between his fingers and ate them only when they had attained perfect spherical forms. "That boy especially. He has a funny shape to his head. Looks like—" my mother tapped her temple ominously.

My mother started keeping a closer eye on Jun-Jun. She was seriously afraid the insanity gene that she suspected ran in my father's family would surface in my cousin. "Better pray to Buddha he doesn't end up like Boyet," my mother would say ominously. "Lucky for you, you are a girl and you have my blood to fight your father's. Imagine if you were like Angkong!"

We all believed that Angkong, my grandfather, had been born senile. He was a military barber for a day during World War Two and ended his career by accidentally cutting off a recruit's ear. He never held a steady job after that. I couldn't remember a time when Angkong didn't spend all day watching television with Amah, holding a glass of Johnny Walker Black Label in one hand and a Marlboro in the other. He often went to sleep in his rocking chair in this way and woke up with burn marks and wet slippers. My mother suffered silently over this habit; Angkong was ruining all of our good glasses—wedding gifts from my mother's sister in Japan—and my mother didn't want to hurt Angkong's feelings by giving him cheap glasses to use instead. The problem was solved when there were no more good glasses to break.

As bad as Angkong was—I once caught him urinating by the gate at the spot where Totoy, Romy's dog, always marked his territory—he was a small, albeit quarrelsome, nuisance compared to Uncle Boyet. While Uncle Boyet still lived with us, he kept clogging the toilet bowls with toilet paper. Jun-Jun half-apologetically explained that Uncle Boyet wiped his *puwet* exactly twenty times. When we laughed, Jun-Jun grew angry and said, "Hoy, I wash mine in the sink after I go. It's cleaner, you know. I bet you don't even wipe yours."

Uncle Boyet always carried toilet paper around to wipe things off before touching them. He wiped everything, even the plates at the Cowrie Grill at the Manila Hotel where my mother celebrated her thirty-second birthday. Uncle Boyet also quizzed the waiters about how the napkins were washed, whether they were boiled, and did the waiters have their gloves laundered every day? Uncle Boyet was also responsible for the quick depletion of soap at our house. He washed his hands over and over until they were red and dry-looking. He was always scratching them, and when they bled, he made Julius rub garlic on his skin to prevent infection. I could always tell whether Uncle Boyet was in a room from the combined scent of garlic, Dial soap, and Tancho.

Uncle Boyet had another, almost secret pastime in his repertoire, which I managed to discover by accident. A few Saturday mornings before Uncle Boyet left, I had gotten up very early to secretly call my piano teacher, Mrs. Libag, and cancel my dreaded lesson for the day. As I dragged the telephone into the small foyer—where I could safely be hidden behind a wall in case my mother decided to wake up early for tai chi—I observed Uncle Boyet coming down the stairs without his usual sulky steps. Uncle Boyet had a slight figure with a distended stomach, like the Ethiopian children featured on *The 700 Club*. He looked suspiciously adolescent, especially compared to my sturdy, sun-darkened father, and I watched him curiously.

Uncle Boyet surreptitiously withdrew a small notebook from behind his toilet paper and started walking around the house looking at objects and writing in the notebook, making check marks or crossing out items. He listed everything, even the leaves on the plastic house plants Peter's godfather had sent him for Chinese New Year. It must have been hard work updating the lists. Our house was full of decaying pieces of furniture from the seventies and my mother was always throwing something out or giving it to the maids. Sometimes, Amah also took things to hide in her storage closet, like my mother's set of silver chopsticks or Auntie Baby's cat-shaped teapot.

At the time, Uncle Boyet's lists registered in my mind as just another of his eccentricities. But later, after Uncle Boyet had callously replied, "Why do you expect me to do something?" to my pleas as Amah dispatched Romy to drown the feral kittens in our backyard, I pulled leaves and flowers from Peter's plants in revenge. Murder was something I expected from my grandmother and Romy was too scared of her to be humane, but I had hoped that Uncle Boyet wouldn't just stand by and watch coldly as the kittens scraped around inside the rice sack and were hurled into the river behind our house. The morning after stripping the plants, I watched, vindicated, from the foyer as Uncle Boyet counted and recounted in great distress but couldn't match the new sum with the old one. He probably kept recounting until he left.

⌒

The first surprise when my mother took me and my sister Penelope to visit Lanie and Uncle Boyet's townhouse was that Lanie was Chinese and the second, that she was heavily pregnant. My mother, probably wondering why she visited in the first place, concentrated mostly on pregnancy tips and offering to introduce Lanie to a kindergarten teacher at my school.

Lanie was unabashed. She served coffee, which Penelope almost drank but my mother glared at her in time. My mother also took note of the tea that came later in tea bags, instead of boiled the Chinese way. Lanie smoked a cigarette and made conversation politely in Fukienese. My mother insisted on talking in Filipino. I was embarrassed to see that Lanie was amused by this. My mother commented later during dinner, "That girl, she's too *huana-teh*, acts like a Filipino, too Westernized. If you two don't listen to me, you'll end up like that, too."

Uncle Boyet was not home. At Lanie's insistence, he had opened a shop specializing in selling and repairing CB radios. My mother admitted on the way home that she had already known about it and had insisted that my father help Uncle Boyet with the capital.

I was ashamed to see that Lanie's townhouse was better decorated and cleaner than our house. Lanie—I couldn't imagine Uncle Boyet being responsible for it—had hung up some anonymous-looking but acceptable watercolors of Manila Bay around the townhouse. Her furniture was the heavy, dark wooden kind I usually saw in Filipino households, and they shone and smelled like Pledge. There was a bowl of potpourri in the bathroom and a seashell soap basket arrangement on top of the toilet bowl tank. I also found Uncle Boyet's slightly damp notepad, looking sad and unused, in the medicine cabinet.

On the way home, Penelope and I extolled to my mother the wonders of Lanie's house, especially when compared to ours.

"Ma! She's just a number two and her maids wear uniforms!"

"Ma! Her maids say *po* and *opo* like civilized people!"

"Hay! You two! Maids will spend more time keeping their uniforms clean than taking care of the house." My mother thought uniforms were a useless expense; they would get dirty and ruined anyway, and she didn't think that our maids—Romy's nieces straight from the province—would feel comfortable in them. So instead, our maids wore stained and mended dresses, their own or our cast-offs, and watched television with us in their bare feet or falling-apart Kiko rubber slippers, gossiping and doing their hair in plastic curlers. They were all complete *probinsiyanas*; some didn't even know how to work spray cans. They addressed us by our nicknames instead of the "Ma'am" or *"Ate"* or "Miss" that our friends were accustomed to. By the time our maids were urbanized and presentable, my mother's friends would hire them away from us and the next batch of nieces would come in.

"But Ma, Lanie's house is cleaner than ours even though her maids wear uniforms!"

My mother scowled. "Of course it's clean. It's so small and she doesn't even work. What else would she do?"

My mother was wrong though. Lanie helped out at the radio shop, and she was the one who called us when the shop was robbed and

Uncle Boyet was stabbed in the stomach (Lanie having escaped harm by locking herself with a gun in the bathroom).

⌐∾

By the time Uncle Boyet was wheeled into the emergency room, my family, including my grandparents, Auntie Baby, and my cousins, had been waiting for at least three hours for the ambulance to arrive. Even Amah had stopped crying by then.

Uncle Boyet was pale and unconscious. Lanie told my mother that they had been stuck in traffic. The ambulance driver had turned the siren on and honked his horn in vain; no one would give way. Finally, they had to open the doors of the ambulance and Uncle Boyet, holding his intestines in with both hands, implored people to let them through. The effort had been too much for him and he collapsed.

My father became even more agitated and furious by this revelation. He had driven madly from the office in the old Toyota with the broken air-conditioning to find that he was the first to reach Cardinal Santos. When I arrived with my brother and my grandparents, I found him cursing, mostly Uncle Boyet, but also the hospital staff.

"*Piaw si-ye,* you can't trust these damn Filipinos to do anything right!" Uncle Boyet and Lanie were still at the radio shop and my father had to pay off some ambulance attendants to fetch them. Later, he would apologize to the nurses, but not to the attendants.

Until Penelope said, "What's wrong with his hand?" I didn't notice that Uncle Boyet's left hand was mutilated and covered in blood. The combined smell of my grandparents—Opium cologne and Green Cross rubbing alcohol from Amah and stale cigarettes and whiskey from Angkong—had made me too carsick to be observant.

Lanie made a sour face. "One of the robbers had a gun and Boyet didn't think it was real since they were already carrying knives. He put his finger in the barrel and the robber shot it off."

My mother, after making sure that Auntie Baby and my cousins were busy trying to rouse Uncle Boyet, discreetly passed an envelope of money to Lanie. "For the baby," she said. Lanie immediately stored the envelope in her purse without comment. My mother gave me a raised-eyebrow look as if to say, "I told you what kind of a girl she is."

⌐∾

We were still there—minus Lanie, who had to go home to rest, and Angkong, who had forgotten to bring some Johnny Walker along—when Uncle Boyet woke up from his operation. Amah began a fresh onslaught of wailing. My mother, who had been dozing, jerked awake. She was exhausted from driving all the way to Caloocan, two hours away from our house, where Auntie Baby and my cousins had been visiting their relatives and then picking up my sister at school in Pasig and then taking all of them to Cardinal Santos in Greenhills.

Uncle Boyet's first words were, "I'll be damned if I'm paying for this!"

Auntie Baby, averting her eyes away from us, said to him softly, "Boyet, don't talk like that. Johnny is paying for everything. You should be grateful."

"Why the hell should I be grateful? I'm still a Coyutan even though I'm married to you! Johnny thinks he's a big shot, anyway, so let him pay! I don't care! Do you think I have any pride left? I don't care!"

At this, my father immediately left the hospital and drove home. He played the theme from *The Good, the Bad, and the Ugly* and reread Bullfinch's *Mythology* alone in the storage room he thought of as a music room until it was time to sleep.

Jun-Jun began sucking and gnawing his thumb anxiously. He and Julius had been mute and terrified the whole time; they clung to each other like orphans. When Uncle Boyet regained consciousness, they had been so tearful and happy.

Auntie Baby tried again. "Boyet—"

"Shut up! Why do you think I want to see your face, anyway? You ruined my life when you had that one!" Uncle Boyet pointed to Jun-Jun. "*Pikot!* That's what you did to me!" Uncle Boyet started making a sound like he was crying but there were no tears and his face was composed.

As we were leaving, my mother grabbed Auntie Baby's arm. "Baby, he's just scared and he doesn't know how to show it. I know he doesn't mean it."

Auntie Baby smiled unhappily. "Liling, I want you to know how grateful..."

My mother waved that away quickly, almost guiltily. "No, no. It's nothing. Romy is waiting for you outside. Take the boys home. They look tired and they still have school tomorrow."

Uncle Boyet took his time recovering. Peter, Penelope, and I had to visit him after school everyday. He watched television and didn't pay much attention to us except to casually ask how my father was. We always answered with an uncomfortable, "He's okay."

Lanie was rarely there. My mother said that she only came when Auntie Baby and Amah weren't around. I didn't know how she arranged it, probably through my mother, who was there every morning with *lugaw* for Uncle Boyet to eat. My father sometimes fought with her over it.

"Why don't you stay home and look after our children?"

"They're in school anyway! I only go when I've done everything! Do you want Amah to start saying that I don't care about your family on top of everything else she says about me? You should go, too."

"Why? Isn't it enough that I'm paying for his damn expenses? Do you see my other brothers visiting him or doing anything at all for him?"

My mother shrugged in defeat. It was true that my other uncles and their families visited Uncle Boyet only once. Amah never said a word against them. She made excuses: "They have their own families." But if my mother was late, even by just a few minutes, she would grumble, "Ay, I'm so *koh lin,* so pitiful. Nobody cares about my Victory. Why did I get a daughter-in-law like Liling, so cold-hearted? And this other one," meaning Auntie Baby, "A *huana,* a Filipina! Such bad luck!"

Auntie Baby told my mother all of this. Amah didn't think that she understood Chinese but after twelve years of marriage, Auntie Baby had picked it up somewhat.

Uncle Boyet came to visit us only once after he was discharged from the hospital. If he had wanted to speak to Auntie Baby, it was too late. She had decided to take up Uncle Oscar's invitation to live with his family in Caloocan. My mother watched her and my cousins leave with trepidation. She was worried about Jun-Jun, who had taken to visiting Uncle Boyet's radio shop and coming back with stories about being mistreated by Lanie. "She acted as if I'm the bastard. She wouldn't even let me see my father."

Jun-Jun stopped sucking his thumb and started smoking cigarettes stolen from Angkong's room instead. Auntie Baby only sighed when she found out and turned down my mother's offer to beat some sense into Jun-Jun.

"You won't see me acting that way if any of you started smoking!" my mother huffed to me.

Despite acquiring a certain worldliness from being a smoker, Jun-Jun was still involved with the Voltes V fan club, even though the series' ending was a great disappointment to him. The Armstrong children were finally reunited with their father, but had to separate from each other once more. Dr. Armstrong had taken over as leader of the Bozanians, their former enemies, and the children had to return to Earth—they were her only guardians.

⌒

The Saturday Uncle Boyet finally came to visit, no one was in the house except for Angkong and myself. Amah was somewhere playing mahjong. My family was out doing groceries; I was at home sadly waiting for Mrs. Libag to arrive. I had a two-hour piano lesson to look forward to as punishment for canceling all the other ones.

Uncle Boyet crept in from the back of the house, through the kitchen door. He didn't see me; I had hidden myself in the foyer as soon as I saw him enter. He appeared the same, pomade and all, although he was perhaps a little thinner, but not by much. He stepped into the living room and watched Angkong sleep for a little bit, then he lit some incense for our Sing Kong altar. After washing his right hand as thoroughly as usual—scrubbing with the help of a toothbrush he awkwardly held with his still-bandaged left hand—Uncle Boyet took out his notepad and, with one eye on Angkong, began counting the items in our house. He took a deep breath when he got around to the plastic house plants, almost wincing in anticipation. When he finished, he looked into his notebook and hissed through his teeth in surprise. I had replaced all the leaves and flowers when Peter started wondering why the plants looked so bald.

Uncle Boyet quickly counted and recounted. Finally, he sat down heavily on the sofa beside Angkong. I heard the same strange crying sound he made at the hospital. When I cautiously peeked around the foyer wall at Uncle Boyet, I saw that his face was contorted into what could have been a smile.

Angkong woke up, probably from the noise that Uncle Boyet was making. "Ha? Victory? Is that you?" He spat into his biscuit tin, looking for his glasses.

"*Ho*. Yes." Uncle Boyet said.

As Angkong scrambled out of his rocking chair, his glasses clattering into the tin, Uncle Boyet walked out of the house through the kitchen door. Sely, one of our maids, opened the gate for him. "*Alis na po kayo, Kuya?* Are you leaving now?" she asked, calling Uncle Boyet "older brother" with respect. The maids had heard all about his exploits from my mother. Uncle Boyet didn't respond.

The gate shuddered loudly as it was closed. After a few seconds, I heard Uncle Boyet's car start and then he was gone.

Another Day

Erma M. Cuizon

The doctor pushed back his glasses and stared at her. He was a family friend and she knew he had a way to handle her. He said there was nothing certain; he would have to see the results of the tests. But yes, it could be bad news, he said. Still, some malignant growths are "encapsulated" and early detection could make quite a difference. Or the growth in her throat could be benign.

She thought of her mother, what to say to her who was out in the province sulking. How about a friend? Was there anyone to talk to at times like this? Should it be told to anyone at all that she could be very sick, or maybe not, but even so, that she was frightened, most of all, of the pain? It was so quiet in the room, as though someone had put up all the four walls with no doors or windows and she was sealed in. She realized that the doctor was still staring at her. "Are you all right, Bibs?" he asked.

She pushed back the bleak walls from her mind and said, "Of course, Doc. I'm fine."

"The results will come in tomorrow. Want me to call you, or will you come in? It's best if you come back. We can talk right away about what to do next."

"I'll come," she said. At forty-five, she wasn't one to run away from this. Besides, it would definitely be easier for her if she came.

"Yes, easier," he said.

This jarred her a bit; she hadn't realized she had spoken aloud. The doctor talked on, his voice receding, and then she was alone again in the sealed room of her consciousness.

She left his office and stepped out into the street, surprised to find it dark. She thought she had just entered the doctor's office, but now it was night. Whatever took her so long in that office? She touched her right shoulder. There was now the familiar throb of pain that had nothing to do with what could be her ailment; it ran from her chest to her right shoulder. She had called it her psychological pain, strange as it was. It always came when she was upset or angry enough to want to cry. She had it first when her father died of a heart attack just after her twentieth birthday party. Then it came back each time she was hurt, frightened, or wronged. And that was what she felt now. But this would go, as it always did, as soon as she stopped dwelling on the thing troubling her.

Bibsy walked faster now; it looked like it would rain. In fact, it was drizzling and she wiped the raindrops from her cheeks. But no, it wasn't rain, she was crying! She shook her head and walked even faster. Yes, it was windy, but no rain. Probably this was just the cold evening draft that always reminded her of the mists preceding rain. This cold wind had given her a sudden headache too. She hurried a few blocks down to the supermart to buy the can of cooking oil that the house help had called about at the office this afternoon.

She crossed the street thinking about what the doctor had said. Nothing was certain. Tomorrow she would know for sure. It wasn't like applying for a job and the interviewer took a coffee break while she waited in a dark, dingy room. Not as simple as that. A strange thought kept coming to mind, someone unseen tapping at the door, asking: where do we go from here? If she were to travel to some far place, what would she bring with her, or leave behind? How about the many things she started that she had left unfinished up to this time? The book she was writing, the one that would say everything she wanted to say to the world—this she had to finish, close, write The End to. There had been awards for some of her poems, and good words on others, but this would be her first book. She had enrolled in a novel-writing correspondence class and her mentor wrote that the first seven chapters were good. Now she was on her eleventh chapter and there were four more to write. It had taken her almost two years to write that much; how much time did she have left to put down the remaining chapters? She would have to leave the small publishing house where she was working and go away, hide in some retreat, to finish the book quickly.

She walked faster. The can of oil, yes. She thought she should buy a smaller can instead, so that the girl in the house, Lucy, would take care not to waste it when there was only so much. Bibsy entered the supermart and was swept into a world she knew only too well—the hustle and noise, movements up and down the aisles, the cackle of men and women. Ah, this was familiar, she thought, welcoming the sight. This was real. And what the doctor said wasn't—it was a joke, or a dream of short duration. She almost skipped to the last shelf on the right side, but the lilt was short-lived. Her headache drummed like rain on a leaking roof.

She scanned the shelf with a practiced eye. The habit of years amazed her. Living really was such a routine—small, meaningless motions recurring so often without thought. She, for one, had ambled along, tripping over petty gestures, losing sight of infinity. Now she was caught unaware—she hadn't realized someone was at her back, waiting, watching—that this was borrowed time.

She knew exactly where the cooking oil bottles and cans were stacked. There should be something different, a shift from the predictable, like getting another brand this time, or going to work five minutes before a story deadline, or reading a book in Chinese. Why should she stick to the oil her mother had used all these years, as though either of them would mind—or would her mother? They were always arguing about something, the two of them; it had become easy and always tempting for Bibsy to contradict the woman. Bibsy knew there were times Dina Roska resented her, as she always said that Bibsy took after her father. Well, not really in looks; she was only very slightly Castillian. But in the love of the arts, she and her father were a pair. She knew her mother was jealous of their rapport, and Bibsy understood this feeling, but the woman could be very unfair sometimes, or critical. A few times, they gave each other the silent treatment, or her mother would pack up for Danao where her sister was. After a while, the woman would be back in the city again. She and Bibsy would be sweet to each other once more, until the next squabble.

Well, Bibsy would surprise the housegirl, Lucy, this time with a new oil brand, she told herself. Today seemed like a good day to pick a new one, yes. Deliberately, she took a Susan Baker off the shelf and put it in the cart, then moved on to the next shelves with the new intent of buying a few more different groceries—why not? But twice, she looked at the cart, which was filling up, and was surprised to see a Susan Baker there instead of the Minola, forgetting for a moment each time that she had chosen it herself. Twice, she thought of returning it and going back to the familiar brand, for a quick moment unwilling to make the change. Now her head felt much heavier. How could anyone get a head cold from deliberating on cooking oil?

Then she thought of getting herself a box of chocolates, the kind that pampered the tongue. When was the last time she stopped for chocolates? They didn't go well with her favorite coffee. It was her paternal grandfather who loved chocolates. A Zamboangeño law-yer, he had quaint Spanish names for some of the chocolates. But chocolates were one of his very few needs; instead, he had always been a giving person, from whom Bibsy had developed some endur-ing values. He defended the poor in court, and they flourished like mushrooms on humid ground in his humble *bufete*. The cases he handled increased by the year, while the money he earned stayed the same. Not that it mattered at all to him or to his wife. Bibsy was glad her paternal roots were sensible, humble family folk whose stron-gest virtues were a kind hand for those who needed help and the good sense to mind their own business. It was her grandfather who first introduced her to reading books, although they were Erle Stanley Gardner and Ellery Queen mysteries. Later, she read a few of the classics in literature, this time on account of her father, Julio Roska. Then she moved on to Dreiser, D. H. Lawrence, and Steinbeck, and her world expanded. A couple of years later, she began writing po-etry. She felt very light now, remembering. She found herself smiling.

In the house, she told Lucy to put the groceries in the refrigerator, then she turned to go. Tonight she wanted to think more clearly, but the thoughts rushed in, disorderly, one stumbling over the other forming like mold in a wet corner. They moved, too, crossing or contradicting or enhancing each other—all the time demanding.

Lucy called after her now just as she turned to go.

"*Si Glenda nitawag, ate Bib. Nanganak na siya ug baby boy!*"

"*Uy,* good!" She thought she'd see Glenda in the hospital that week, but not as soon as tomorrow.

"*Ang imong auntie, nitawag usab. Ang mama ni Anna.*"

She looked back. "Anna?" Her Gonzales cousin was her first best friend; they grew up together. But she had grown apart from Anna when they went to college. Anna was always flunking her classes and had a breakdown each time she lost a boyfriend.

Bibsy had forgotten how sad she felt on realizing at sixteen that she and Anna had grown apart. It was like losing a friend without quarreling at all. They had begun to have different sets of friends and they couldn't talk longer than a few minutes, recalling the ear-lier days. Bibsy had gotten bored retelling the same old stories about two small girls who knew how to mambo to the delight of their clan. She knew that Anna couldn't pay attention longer than a minute when Bibsy talked about Somerset Maugham in her senior year. Now, she asked the house girl, *"Si Anna?"*

"Nasakit kono, ate Bib."

"Kung mo-telephone ug usab, ingna nga mobisita ko tomorrow igpadulong nako sa trabaho. Bisan kinsay motawag, I'm out, okay, Lucy?" She walked out of the kitchen and went upstairs to her bedroom. At the door of her room, she wondered what the room would look like if it were someone else were occupying it. Perhaps whoever she was would put in more plants, which wouldn't be a bad idea, or have wallpaper all around, a horrid thought. She opened her closet and realized that she had many clothes. Old blouses or skirts that would still look very good, except that some of them didn't match. Some people were funny about colors, as though lightning would strike a pink blouse on top of a red skirt. She went on savoring the sight around her. Only later did she realize that, in an hour that felt like a lifetime, she had gone through the old and new things in the room like the pages of a book, lingering on some, passing through others, reviewing, sorting, throwing a few and keeping the rest.

She went straight to the Gonzales house the next morning. Anna was in bed and the place was dark. It had been months since they had seen each other and she thought Anna had lost weight. Bibsy herself had had an unexplained loss of weight, which was the reason she had become alarmed. But Anna was different. She was always suffering from something. Her mother said no one could drag her out of the dark room for the past three days.

"Is she sick, Tia?" Bibsy could again feel the pain in her chest and shoulder.

"No. Nothing's wrong with her. Dr. Ed was here yesterday. Nothing physically wrong."

When Anna saw Bibsy, she cried, "I'm going to die, Bibs!"

Her mother cried, too. "She has been like this since last night," the old woman sobbed.

Bibsy felt anger rising. Was this self-pity, or was Anna sick for real? "You shouldn't joke about dying, you don't know what you're talking about," she said. It was as though Anna had dared put into words her own forbidden thought. And now Bibsy wanted to get out, thinking she'd feel better towards Anna another day. But she stayed for a few minutes more. She kept quiet except to say a word or two while Anna's worried mother hovered over them. The room felt soggy like a piece of damp cloth, the kind she hated to touch. She left and told herself she'd make up for her unkindness, if truly that was what it was.

Back at her office, she went through the motions of work. But mostly, she sat quietly at her desk by the window, letting the day go by until it would be time to see the doctor. She watched the flurry of humanity at the jeepney-stop down in the street, people waiting for rides, fighting for seats. She remembered Anna in bed, also waiting—for what? If it was true that Anna thought she was dying, of course she would be afraid.

It dawned on Bibsy that what was most frightening to her was not the knowledge of what might be ahead; it was the thought of pain. Since the visit to the doctor, she had told herself not to panic. It was best to rationalize, right or wrong, to mask the pain. Don't look, she had told herself. Her rational mind had taken over at other instances in the past. She remembered how she had feared losing her hothead of a brother, who was always in a brawl. He'd made her worry each time he stayed out late; she couldn't sleep nights imagining him carried home, stabbed in the back by some irrational enemy. But one night, she told herself that there was nothing she could do if this ever happened. Thinking this, she had turned to her side and slept. Yes, even the feeling of guilt for not being there when her father died, this she was able to handle somehow, convincing herself that from the ether, or wherever God put him, he was in the best position to understand her failings and forgive her for them. That had always sufficed. Now she was facing a greater unknown. It was so real, she knew that she had no choice but to accept it. She hoped it wouldn't be too difficult.

From the window, it looked windy down there in the wet streets. It had rained earlier. Some of the men bent, walking or standing, and dipped their hands into their pockets to keep warm. One of them looked like Tasyo, but wasn't him at all, of course. Tasyo had been her driver when she had the car, which she had sold just a month ago. She had told him then that she couldn't increase his salary, but she wouldn't fire him until he found another job. After a month, he found a job. Bibsy started driving for herself, which wasn't really a problem. Now, without the car, she was riding in taxicabs, which was easier because she didn't have to think of fighting for parking space and she felt snug and safe with her thoughts. There was time while the taxi moved down the road to sit and listen to the harmony within, her mind and heart sounding like a symphony orchestra inside her until the cab driver would pull over and say, "*Ni-ana ta, day.*" That was before her visit to the doctor.

In the middle of the afternoon, she thought of the article she had to finish editing. It was due the next day—a piece on why people garden, what kind of people chose to move among plants in prayerful parts of the day? She thought gardeners were old souls, quiet creatures of rest and peace, even of love. She had to finish this story, her boss had said, so that the anthology could move on to composition the next morning. But who cared about any of this now? She was beginning to feel a weight bearing down on her. She couldn't pay attention to the voice at the back of her mind that in the past always put her back on track whenever she strayed. There was her own book. She had to work on it first. She would turn in her resignation so she could go back to her book.

When it was time to go see the doctor, she had the usual difficulty finding a cab. She looked around and was amazed at the way people criss-crossed streets, hurried along home. No one, but no one, thought what he'd do if the world deflated like a balloon. Where would everybody be while the balloon blew out its top? She remembered the day when she was fifteen. It had been her birthday and the party had just ended. She'd been so pleased about the day. She had gone to bed still very alert, her mind reviewing over and over again everything that happened in the previous hours. Then she thought of her next birthday, and the next, until she couldn't stop counting. In the dark room, she realized with a jolt that life was short; it terrified her.

Someone in a hurry bumped into her and brought her back to the sidestreet where she waited for a cab. Yes, she needed that ride badly. Any other day, she would let the hours pass until the traffic eased, before she'd go home. Today, getting a cab was harder because it was a novena Wednesday. She couldn't stand an hour of waiting. She'd probably walk to the doctor's clinic, if it came to that. Then she saw a cab at the corner of Salvador Street and rushed to it, only to find its passengers disembarking because the cab had conked out. No matter, she knocked on the tinted window and called to the driver from the outside, "*Noy, puede?*"

The man, preoccupied with the ignition switch, rolled down the window, sized her up, then turned back to the ignition switch and said without looking at her, *"Sigi, day, basin pag moandar ni."* After the driver worked on the switch a few times, the engine finally growled, then purred. He grinned at her and said, *"Sigi, sakay na."*

The doctor's office wasn't very far from her work place but she felt she was taking the longest ride in her life. She sat in the air-conditioned cab in silence, listening to the soft squeaking of a loose bolt somewhere on her side of the back seat. Yes, it was the pain she was most afraid of, but let it come, she resolved. She felt relaxed now, as though the things she had been thinking about in the past hours had been sifted carefully and reduced to their simplest form. This was it, utmost simplicity. Why think at all of finishing her book—on time for what? From the cab, she looked at the traffic outside as if it were a pantomime on a stage and she were the audience seated far up in the balcony. The old, tenacious dream of succeeding as a writer, where was it? How empty it was now, like a shell abandoned by a mollusk. How easily she could now brush it aside when so recently it was bone-deep, a cherished dream that would not wear off. Who cared, really? Instead, how could she forgive herself now if she didn't make up with her mother? Anna, too. And the others who had been part of her life. Oh, for a last chance to come close to them and feel them breathe, feel them quiver out of the sheer fullness of life! Oh, to be in touch with them truly, in spirit! What peace of mind and heart that would give her.

It was still cold outside but the rain had stopped by the time she came out of the doctor's office. She knew where she would go. The maternity house was just around the corner and she negotiated the crowded sidewalk in no time at all. She ran upstairs to Room 201, to see the baby in the arms of her friend Glenda, a new infant, moving, kicking, vigorous, his eyes like brown windows through which life announced itself. "What's his name?" she asked softly, touching the baby's feet.

"Timothy."

"Beautiful name," she said, then she laughed as she picked the baby up and held him firmly in her arms.

Section VI   Roots

Roots

Conchitina R. Cruz

Mama teaches me roots one summer,
taking me across mountains
to my Grandmother's house.
I enter the arms of a stranger
with familiar eyes. Her fingers
brush my hair like twigs and move
with the breath of a dialect
unlike mine. In the middle
of her garden, we all stand.
Mama speaks like a child, her arms
imitating the height of trees
grown old with her absence.
I look past their leaves
to the blue morning sky.

The days move so slowly.

Tonight, Mama and Grandmother
recall stories while I sit
on the garden swing to pass time.
I watch the sky fill with stars
as the swing creaks like a voice
gone hoarse, flaunting its share
of memories. Mama recalls
her father, coming home drunk
and whipping the air. His hands
send Mama hiding behind trees,
her tears falling like leaves.
Grandmother, tired of nights
like this, awaits him once
with a piece of wood to hit him first,
over and over. Only the eyes
of stars watch as she drives
him away.

They sigh. I stop the swing,
laying my feet on the ground.
Grandmother smiles at me
and the lines on her face
deepen, reminding me of bark.
I see her withered fingers
strong on my hands,
and somewhere inside me,
a tree takes root. Above,
the sky displays its stars
with pride. Tonight, I know
the many stars are bruises
bleeding starlight.

Daughter

Conchitina R. Cruz

This is the last day.
Sunlight breaks
through the blinds
and bathes her bed.
Flowers fire
the white walls
with their flames.
She knows, pries
her eyes open
to take in
one final memory.

Her soul begins
to slide past
the machine's heavy
fingers, following
her breath
into the air.

I hold her
as she slips past
the last light
of earth.
Only silence
punctuates
our parting,
so unlike
the sound
of her first cry,
upon being born.

Vigan

Cecilia Manguerra Brainard

When I was ten, a year after my father died, my mother decided to return to Vigan, back to her grandmother who had raised her after her parents died. We left Manila for the sleepy town with crumbling stone houses, cobbled streets, watchtowers, and other vestiges of colonial days. Vigan boasted of having been founded in the sixteenth century by Juan Salcedo, the Spanish conquistador who conquered Manila. In its heyday, it was the port of entry of the Spanish galleons coming from China and headed for the Walled City of Intramuros. The ships sailed up the river and moored at the edge of Old Town, near the Cathedral and Archbishop's Palace. The merchants' houses and warehouses clustered near the river. Here, traders exchanged indigo, cotton, silk, pearls, tobacco, porcelain, and hemp for silver and gold.

Our family house sat in the middle of a row of ancient merchant houses, crumbling relics of limestone blocks and wood, built like small forts. Our house had massive wooden double doors fronting the street, which my great-grandmother said allowed carriages in and out of the family compound during Spanish times. The lower portion of our house had a shed with two pigs, four chickens, and one mean-spirited goat. A section in the back served as the servants' quarters, but since my great-grandmother had only one servant who slept upstairs, this section was unoccupied and was in total disarray. An elaborate staircase led to the second floor, which had the kitchen, dining room, living room or *sala*, the music room, library, a veran-dah, and bedrooms. There were four bedrooms, but huge, with high ceilings that allowed the air to circulate, cutting the oppressive tropical heat. Except for the room occupied by my great-grandmother, the other bedrooms had several four-poster beds, lined up dormitory-style and covered by yellowing crocheted bedspreads.

I'd only heard about this house from my mother. We had never visited it when Papa was alive. So even though I was unhappy about our move, I was impressed by the surprises the house offered. The walls of the rooms, for instance, had hand-painted murals: musical instruments were painted all around the music room, the dining room had a border of grapes on a vine with a hunting scene on the wall nearest the dining table, and the bedroom my mother and I shared had a picture of Cupid sitting on a cloud and shooting his arrow at a young woman in a forest. Although the paintings were flaking and faded, my great-grandmother, whom my mother and I called Lola, was very proud of them.

What interested me most was the coffin at the foot of the stairs. An old sheet covered it and on top were all sorts of junk: newspapers, empty glass jars, and a huge vase with dusty fake flowers. I had mistaken the coffin for a table until Lola removed the sheet to reveal a bronze casket with gold decorations. She struck the metal with her fingernail and declared it was our family coffin. Apparently old families in the area kept family coffins, which were used only for the wake. For the actual burial, the corpse was wrapped in an Ilocano woven blanket and buried directly in the family vault. The coffin was cleaned, then stored, in this case at the foot of the stairs, ready for its next temporary occupant.

The idea sent me into hysterics, considering my own father was buried in his own bronze casket—cost had been no object as far as his parents were concerned. He had been their only child.

I asked my great-grandmother what happened when two family members died, like my mother's parents, for instance. She said they lay side by side.

"But what if more than two die?" I persisted.

"It's never happened," she said. By that time, she was clearly annoyed with me, and so I kept quiet. Lola had not liked my father and his family, and I suspected that dislike extended to me. People said I looked a lot like my father. He was tall and thin and had a lot of Chinese blood, unlike my mother's family, which had a lot of Spanish blood.

Even though Lola spoke enthusiastically of the house (this remnant of our family's glorious past), I found it depressing. There were cobwebs everywhere, and at night, I dreaded going to the bathroom because I usually ran into the sticky strands. There was dust all over the old furniture. Ceiling plaster was peeling, the wooden floors creaked, and there was one section near the kitchen with woodrot. I could peer through the holes and look down at the animals. Sometimes I would spit on the goat that had butted me once.

Before we came, Lola's solitary companion was another old woman named Manang Gloria. I was never sure who took care of whom because half the time, my great-grandmother was the one in the kitchen cooking bitter *ampalaya* to strengthen Manang Gloria's blood. There were men workers who came during the day to take care of the animals and yard, but by late afternoon, they were gone.

By six in the evening, the only sounds I heard were the two old women rattling around in the kitchen, some crickets outside, and my mother sighing by the window. Times like that, I would ache for my father and my old life.

⌒⌒

My mother had never worked in her entire life. After college, she'd married Papa and moved into his house. In Vigan, she spent many nights crying, cursing my father for dying, and wondering how she could support the two of us. We had left Manila in the first place because she and my father's parents did not get along. They disliked her from the start, accusing her of being pretentious. It was true that my mother carried with her an arrogance that old families from Vigan had, even if their ceilings had caved in and their floors rotted. My mother, likewise, scorned my father's family, calling them "new rich" and accusing them of having no culture. While my father was alive, he kept the two warring parties apart, but after he died, nothing stood between his parents and my mother. Like cats and dogs they went after each other; of course, my mother was always on the losing end. After a year of strained silences, sharp words, doors slamming, and countless tears, my mother grew tired of the quarreling, took whatever she could, and we left.

It was Lola who suggested that Mama open an antique shop downstairs. "Manang Gloria knows some carpenters who can make replicas," Lola said. "Have them copy our antique furniture. Price them low. City people will buy them." She was right. Antique dealers traveled far to buy Mama's bentwood chairs and love seats, drop-leaf tables, armoires, chairs, and wooden statues of the Virgin Mary and Jesus on the cross. The most popular item was the plantation chair, an enormous lounging chair made of mahogany and rattan, that harked back to days of sitting around the verandah, a leg resting on one arm of the chair and a drink on the other.

⌒⌒

I did not like school. I did not fit. I was used to the stimulating environment of my school in Manila. The school in Vigan was dull and provincial. I spent most of my time in Mama's antique shop, doing my homework on the table, reading old books from the library, rearranging the display in the showroom, or bothering the workers who were carving the reproductions in the back. "Look at that," I would say, "antiques made to order."

I was there the afternoon Ramon arrived. He was a dealer from Manila. I overheard him ordering a lot of furniture and so I was not surprised when Mama invited him for dinner. Mama's clients usually stayed in one of the four hotels in town, none of which served decent food. When Mama invited clients to dinner, Manang Gloria would come to life and prepare local recipes, crispy mouth-watering beignets, steamed prawns, fried fish, and that bitter vegetable stew that local folk loved so much.

Ramon praised Manang Gloria's food, and she giggled like an idiot. She was really quite fresh, behaving more like a peer than our servant. When I tried to put her in her place, Lola defended her, saying she was the fourth generation to work in our house.

Lola ate and left the dining table early. When she was gone, the conversation between Mama and Ramon livened up. It seemed they had mutual friends in Manila, and they discussed them one by one, Mama gushing over the good fortune of some of them and clucking at the misfortune of others. Later (they must have forgotten I was there) Ramon talked about his wife. He had married his college sweetheart, a journalist who had gotten involved in the anti-Marcos movement. She had written many daring exposes of the oppressive dictatorship. She even wrote articles about the "disappeareds" until one night she herself disappeared. Ramon spent years looking for her until his family convinced him she had been "salvaged" so not a single trace of her body could be found. Ramon had gone into seclusion until Cory Aquino came into power. He said that after the EDSA Revolution, he discovered he was still alive after all. "I found out," he said, "that I could laugh again."

My mother grew teary at Ramon's story, then told Ramon about Papa. She described how Papa started dropping things, that we thought he'd had a stroke, but that it turned out he had brain cancer. The doctors had said he had six months to live, and they had been right almost to the date. She did not tell Ramon of her quarrel with my paternal grandparents. When he pressed her about why we left Manila, she said Lola needed her.

It was just a conversation, nothing more, but I was disturbed by it. I hated how she shared a piece of our lives with him. I hated being reminded of Papa and our old life, and I hated how happy Mama seemed with Ramon.

∾

Ramon would come around every two weeks. He would talk to Mama at great length—"business," they called it. He would dine with us; sometimes he and Mama would ride off someplace. I would interrogate Mama as to where exactly they went, and reluctantly she would confess they visited the old church and rectory in Santa Maria, or the beach of Vigan, or the Luna Museum in Ilocos Sur, or the open market to buy Ilocano blankets. She said this blithely, as if I should not care. But when I thought of the two of them in these places, I would feel a heaviness in my chest, a sorrow that lingered for days.

Ramon tried to befriend me, bringing me books, which he recognized as my weakness, but even though I hankered to read them, I would deliberately abandon them in the shop, on the same table he had set them on, so he could see, so he could understand that he could never bribe me.

Once he told me, "You are very different from your mother."

I glared at him. "I am my father's daughter," I said, thinking I sounded very smart.

My mother blushed when she heard me, and later that night she scolded me for being rude. I told her I wanted to go home.

"There is no other home," she replied softly. "This is it. Those people don't want us. They have cheated us of your father's inheritance."

She was crying now. "They are the people who killed Ramon's wife. They were cronies of Marcos; that was how they made their money. They killed her, and I suppose we are guilty too."

Her hair was disheveled; her makeup smeared. I saw how much older she had become since Papa died. I saw how vulnerable she was, how spineless, and I told myself I would never be as weak as she was.

∾

In the middle of that summer, when the heat left you breathless, my great-grandmother decided she was going to die soon. She called Manang Gloria and instructed her to have new satin lining made for the family coffin. After inspecting the shiny pink lining and checking the hinges of the coffin, she went back to bed and refused to get up.

In a few days her legs started cramping, and it became my job to massage her with Sloan's Liniment. I would pour the liniment into my palms, vigorously rub my hands together, and massage her spindly legs. That was when I learned about my mother's bad luck.

Lola said, "There are some people who attract bad luck, and your mother is that way. When your mother was four, her parents died in a car crash on the zig-zag road to Baguio. Then of course your father died. It's just bad luck, that's all. There is no other explanation."

I felt kinder to my mother after that—until I caught her and Ramon kissing. It was afternoon, and Lola had told me to call them to the verandah for *merienda*. I ran down, paused by the family coffin, and lifted the sheet so I could feel the coolness of the bronze. Then I went to the door of the antique shop. I caught them locked together in a tight embrace—my own mother with this man. Ramon saw me, pushed her away, and cleared his throat. Calmly I told them Lola had hot chocolate and pastries waiting for them.

Mama closed the front door of the shop and headed for the stairs. "Are you coming, Rosario?" she asked.

I shook my head. "I have to finish something. I'll be there."

I waited awhile then I opened his briefcase and went through his things, looking for something, I was not sure what for exactly. Just when I was putting his papers back into the briefcase, a picture fluttered out. It was Ramon and Mama standing happily in front of the town plaza. I took the picture and stuffed it into my pocket.

I had heard Manang Gloria talk of Sylvia, a *mangkukulam* who lived on the edge of town. When Manang Gloria was twenty, Sylvia had read her cards. The witch had predicted that a man would fall in love with her, but that they would be separated. A young man did come along, and for a long time, Manang Gloria tortured herself by wondering when the man would drop her for another woman. The man, however, was steadfast and asked her to marry him. They picked a date, made preparations; Manang Gloria had her white gown made. The night before their wedding day, the man walked by a *sari-sari* store where two men were fighting. He tried to stop the fight, but in the scuffle, ended up dead.

Aside from reading cards, Sylvia made potions. The most popular were love potions and potions for revenge. She could also cure sick people by catching their illness and transferring it into a rooster whose head she would chop off. If convinced it was right to do so, she could harm people. She could even turn herself into a ferocious black dog at night, which was why people avoided walking around after dusk.

One Saturday in June, I went to Sylvia's house. I was afraid; I did not know what to expect. I found her planting seedlings in front of her hut. At first glance, she appeared ordinary-looking, with a simple native dress and her gray hair tied in a knot. When she looked up, I noticed her sad, sad eyes. I told her I knew Manang Gloria. She stared at me with those sorrowful eyes, until I too felt like crying. I was about to leave when she invited me in.

She led me in front of an altar with numerous statues of saints and burning candles. She took my hand, turned it over so she could see my palm. "One day," she said, "a man will fall in love with you, but you will be separated."

This sounded like Manang Gloria's fortune; I felt disappointed.

"I'm here," I said, "for my mother."

She said nothing.

"I have to save her."

"Ah, does your mother need saving?"

I nodded.

"And whom are you saving her from?"

"From a man. A wicked man. I have a picture of him. Do you want to see?"

She glanced at the picture. Her eyes became darker and sadder still. "A handsome man. Once, I knew a handsome man...." She trailed off, but then recovered. "Handsome men...well, what can I say? Yes, they can be dangerous. Tell me more."

"He is hurting her. He is hurting us. I want him to go away. I want him to stop seeing her."

She sighed. "Your father is dead," she said. "You miss him."

This pronouncement impressed me, and I wondered how she divined this truth.

"Everyone talks in this town. You and your mother live in the Pamintuan Mansion, with Doña Epang."

Again I felt disappointment.

She stared into my eyes until my eyes burned and I felt like blinking.

"I can give you something that will attract good. You can give this to your mother, so only good will go near her. If this man is bad, he will stay away."

"Mama's a bad-luck woman. Lola says so. Nothing you can give her will attract good. I need something so he will never come back. He is evil. He has hurt her; he has hurt me."

She turned her sorrowful eyes to her altar. "All right," she finally said, "just because of Manang Gloria, I will help you." She went to a corner and returned with a bottle of Coke, only it didn't have Coca Cola in it, but some amber-colored liquid with herbs and flower petals. "The morning after the full moon, rinse with this. Then go to Mass and pray that he will no longer return. Pray hard, especially when the bells ring at the Consecration."

"Is that all?" I asked.

"That is all. Leave your money in the pot near the door."

❧

Back home, I hid the bottle in my closet and left it untouched until the first storm. Mama was in bed staring at the Cupid painted on the wall. She whispered, "It is so cold to be alone in bed."

I found a calendar and figured when the full moon was. I bathed with Sylvia's water, went to Mass, and prayed as she had taught me. When the bells tinkled at Consecration, I stared hard at the white host and repeated: "God, keep Ramon away from Mama, keep him away from us, drive him away, separate them, God, please, God, please. You've taken my father away, I'm asking you now, God, to keep him away from us. You owe it to me, God, because Papa's gone and not only have you taken him, you've taken me away from my house and planted me in this miserable place, the last place on earth I'd like to live in God. I have no friends, no one, except my Mother. Please, God, don't let her leave me too because when she's with Ramon, that's how it feels, God, like she's left me too."

On and on I rambled, venting my sorrows and miseries, and pinning them all on Ramon, blaming him for them, and wishing for him to disappear from our lives. When I left the Cathedral, my hands were shaking and I felt flushed. My mother and Lola asked me if I was all right. I kept quiet. Something had shifted in me and I knew that things would be different.

It did not happen right away. From the time I saw Sylvia in June until December, Ramon continued to visit Mama every two weeks. When I saw his happy face, my chest would tighten. He would smile, white teeth flashing, and he'd give Lola a box of American chocolates or a bag of hot chestnuts and he would kiss her on both cheeks. And Mama, standing by Lola's bed, would beam proudly at Ramon as if he were some genius-child who had done his homework right. He would greet me too and give me a book or puzzle. With a stony face I would thank him, then put his gift down and run off to wash my hands, scrubbing them hard until my skin hurt.

When he was around and I felt desperate, I would beg Manang Gloria to tell me the story of her dead lover once again. Other times, I would go to the family coffin, remove the things on top, open it and run my hands on the pink satin lining, feeling its coolness, imagining the dead people that had occupied this coffin, and thinking that one day it would hold Lola, Mama, and even me. Once I climbed into it and lay down as if I were dead, with my eyes closed and my palms together as if in prayer. I was drifting off to sleep when Manang Gloria happened to see me and screamed so loud, Lola ran down the stairs. "You are a strange, strange child," she said. "You must take after your father's family."

And so time passed in Vigan, until finally it happened, in December. Ramon arrived with Christmas gifts. By this time, I had almost forgotten my visit to Sylvia, and I must admit, I'd gotten used to his visits. Lola's house was so dark and full of decay, and Ramon's visits added some sparkle to our lives. Manang Gloria would cook, Lola would use her Sevres China and Baccarat crystal, and Mama would dress up and look happy and young.

He insisted that we open our gifts right away: an expensive bottle of French perfume for Lola, a sweater for Manang Gloria, a pearl necklace for Mama, and an antique music box for me. We were like children, fingering our gifts, and I saw him beaming happily that he had found the right gifts for us. Lola and Mama kissed him on the cheek. Manang Gloria kissed his hand, as if he were a "patron" of colonial days. And since everyone was looking my way, I went to him and planted a kiss on his cheek. He looked surprised and stood there for a long time holding his cheek where I had kissed him.

We were happy that night. Lola walked with us to the Cathedral for Midnight Mass. Later we had the *noche buena* meal at home. Numerous carolers stopped by our house, singing about Christ, love, and joy. It was a clear and beautiful night. From the verandah I looked up at the stars, and I could feel my soul expanding. Since Papa died, I had not felt happiness like that.

It was almost dawn when he said he had to drive back to Manila to have Christmas dinner with his parents. After a lengthy farewell to the women, he said good-bye to me. I felt a flutter at the pit of my stomach. "Ramon," I started, then lost my words. "Merry Christmas," I finally said.

In bed, I thought of Papa in the hospital and how he struggled to speak but could not. I thought of our big house in Manila. I thought of the malls that my friends and I used to frequent. I remembered my third grade nun who lectured once about charity being the most important virtue of all. I knew that I had done something terribly wrong. I wept silently in bed; even my mother did not hear me.

Years later, my mother blamed herself for Ramon's death, saying she was bad luck. His car had turned turtle on the highway, heading back to Manila. I did not tell her that in this matter, she was wrong.

What Ditas Left

Justine Uy Camacho

My mother left bangles
in her jewelry box,
poems that my father
can no longer find,
paintings of birds breaking
free from cages and
umbrellas catching
raindrops.

She painted me
looking over a butterfly-
sleeve and my brother
in blue and orange
with a look of awe.

My mother left me
a little trail of things:
pictures of her
beautiful, wide-eyed
saying "wow"
over and over,
a gold pendant,
a set of books etched
all over with her analysis
of characters,
bright, bold declarations
as though I would debate
with her over time.
I recognize my own writing
in her staccato style.

Sometimes when I read
what she scrawled at the
back of her photo album
I cry:
Life is full of sound and
fury, yes.
But full of significance
too. Just you wait and
see, just you wait and
see, just you wait and
see

only three
years with
you, Mommy.

I have a hand-
ful of gifts now,
things you never
thought
would mean so much.

You left me
your eyes,
your wonder,
you left me
my name.

Bahay Kubo (little house)

Melissa Aranzamendez

It isn't like he promised
The lawn is tiny
and turns brown in the cold season
Out front a putrid man
lies sprawled
on a street once rumored to be
paved with gold
My mother's purse is heavy
with a dozen keys
for each lock on the door
For climbing we have
not trees but four floors
to get to our apartment
which I first thought
was just the elevator car ride up
He said there would be
a playground in the yard
He said there'd be a pool
with a slide and a diving board
He said we would have
a hundred channels on TV

And I believed him.

I want to go home
so that I can stay out and play
bahay kubo with the neighborhood kids
outside until dark
I want to go home
so that I can climb the *aratilis* tree
and dream about life in the land
Where the seasons are more than two
and snow falls during Christmas time
Where the roads are wide and open
Where machines do all the dirty work
I want to go home so that
I can believe him again.

The Mango Summer

Lilledeshan Bose

Here there is no electricity after six o'clock. When it gets dark, we use Coleman lamps that you pump to get going; they look like ovens. And the water doesn't come out of faucets, but from a rusty red pump that makes scary gurgling noises. We live right beside the church; that's how we know when the electricity is about to go off—always before the *angelus*. My *yaya* says we have no electricity because Marcos is president, and my sister wants to know if that's why there's no Jollibee, either. We can only buy cheez curls and *halo-halo* in the stores. For one peso we can get ten pieces of *tira-tira,* brown sugar sticks that make my tongue sandy when I suck on them too long.

I am a little girl of maybe eight, nine, or ten; I forget the exact years. My family is at the beach, in mango country. It is summer, and there is a sticky fibrous sweet smell around the house. The mangoes come from our farm; there are baskets and baskets of them around the house. All these mangoes, with black imperfect marks, are faded yellow green. They are the exact color of yellow green on my seventy-four piece Crayola box—not green yellow, which is a different color entirely, but yellow green. They're blemished with *pigsas*. There is nowhere to put them, so they're lined up above the cupboards of our house. But there is not enough space on the cupboards so they're also lined up on the kitchen floor, above the bookshelves, on my *lola*'s *tukador,* on the living room table, and on the sofa ledge. Sometimes, if we don't eat the mangoes fast enough, we line them up on the balcony outside.

We are surrounded by this color, yellow green. Juice dribbles down our cheeks and hands when we're eating mangoes, and all our white vacation shirts are stained yellow green. The maids stopped bothering to take the stains out a long time ago, but whenever we peel open a mango my *yaya* still says, "*O yang* T-shirt *mo ha, mamamantsa nanaman yang mangga.*" I eat by biting off the skinny mango tip and peeling off the skin in a circle, making little spirals and piles of chewed-up mango seeds.

My hundred-and-one-year-old great-grandma, who owns this house, is crinkled and flat like Japanese paper. She moves like a kite, breezing through her house of kids and books and mangoes. She is also deaf, and she always asks me if I can hear the national anthem playing out loud. Usually, it is so silent I can hear cloud formations moving in the sky if I want to.

One day, she takes us to the farm to get the mangoes, even though we still have a lot in the house. We walk past the church, past the cockpit where the feathers flying around make me sneeze, past the rice laid out in the streets to dry like *banigs*. It takes us forever to get there. We reach a river and cross a bridge that is broken in the middle.

My brother, who is a year older than me and nasty, tries to push me into the brown *ilog*, and I run to my *yaya*. "Niko, *wag kang tikis,*" she tells my brother. "Carry," I whine to my *yaya*, stamping my foot. She doesn't think Niko will push me in the river, but I know my brother. My *yaya* picks me up and carries me to the end of the bridge. I stick my tongue out at my brother. I'm glad my little sister Ana was too little to tag along; otherwise my *yaya* would've carried her and not me. They're always carrying Ana even though she's old enough to steal my Barbie dolls and twist off their heads. Along the way a *carabao* is pulling on a *caritela* with just one wheel. The *carabao*'s nose is brown and crusty. It looks like dried shit, like the pies that we saw on the way over. Everything is covered with dust and flies. When my *yaya* puts me down, I complain. "Carryyyyy..." I whine.

"Lola," I ask, "what do we need more mangoes for?" She smiles and says, "*eh, baka maubusan tayo.*" I make a face. We'll never finish all the mangoes in the house. We're going to start keeping mangoes on our beds and we'll have no place to sleep. If we sleep in mango beds, we'll squish most of them and stain our clothes some more. Yaya wouldn't like that, I think.

There are stacks of hay at the farm, used to feed the *carabaos*. My brother and I roll down the hay. When we get bored, we play hide-and-seek by the mango trees. I'm hiding behind a water pump when he calls out to me. "Marra, O! *Tignan mo to!*" I rush off to where he is. "An anthill?" I ask. Mesmerized, I watch the ants moving in and out in straight lines until my brother pushes me onto the anthill. "Gotcha," he says, running to the base. Ants spread over my feet, biting like they're trying to make new hole-homes in my toes and ankles. I start crying and my *yaya* carries me home. My feet are swollen for two days.

I am eight, or nine, or ten, and my mother has left us here with the maids while she works in the city. My parents have just split up, I think. My mother is concentrating on being alone. Or maybe she wants to be away from her children because she is seeing someone new and pretending to be single. I forget the details. Maybe I never really knew. But I am here with my brother, my little sister who still sucks her thumb, my *lola* who is old and barely alive, and a passel of maids who follow us around with nothing better to do. And my *yaya*.

Every morning, we walk through town in our swimsuits to go to the beach. The other kids who really live here stare and follow us to the beach. They never wear bathing suits—the boys wear shorts and the girls swim with their shirts on. Littler kids wear nothing at all and they're brown and skinny like slippery worms.

The water is really clear in the mornings. Sand doesn't crumble under my feet, pebbly but smooth. Nothing here is pretty, even though tiny brown translucent fish swim around my ankles, except for the sky and the white haze of clouds that sometimes floats through it. Brown seaweed is everywhere, and grainy air. The drying saltwater sticks my hair together like mango dribble.

I don't like the beach, so what I do is wade by the shore and look for pretty stones. Sometimes I can even dive underwater for them. There are flat and smooth white stones, rough stones with pink and purple stripes, and some that crumble when I clutch at them too hard. I like to show my brother but he's always swimming. He's turning brown and skinny like the boys who live here. He doesn't need floaters like I do, so he doesn't have white stripes on his upper arms like me.

One time my brother goes, "Hey, Marra, watch this." Kicking off into the ocean, he swims a straight line from the beach through the parts of the sea that change color from aqua to deep green to navy blue. I squint my eyes to see where he is. His head is the size of a Mongol eraser before my *yaya* notices he's gone. She yells, "Niko! *Ang layo mo na!* Come back here!" Then he looks up and swims back, in the same straight line. Ever since, he's done that every day, like it's a funny joke. Sometimes my *yaya* pretends not to see him until his head is the size of a pencil tip. She panics anyway and then yells and yells till he looks up and swims back, always in that same straight line.

Because there's no electricity, my *yaya* can't watch her favorite *Flordeluna* at six o'clock. She hates missing it; Janice de Belen has just discovered she is really a rich girl and her father just had a heart attack. But no one here has TV, so my *yaya* makes us all go to sleep right after dinner.

We all sleep on a huge mat laid out on the living room floor. Me beside my brother beside my sister beside our *yaya*. There are no screens on the huge *capiz* windows; we all sleep under a *kulambo*. My *yaya* and I sleep at the edges because my brother is scared of the slither-tongued, half-bodied *aswang* waiting for him. Also because I sometimes still wet the bed.

It is one of those nights. Everyone is asleep, except my brother, who nudges me, "Marra, you awake?"

"aNnnnhhh...what..."

I see the Coleman lamp dying in red, lizards on the walls hiding in the shadows. My brother presses his body close to mine, puts his hand on my stomach under my T-shirt, then sticks his tongue in my mouth. My brother smells like mangoes and sweat. I stare at the lizards, which are now bigger with the dying Coleman light. My brother takes my hand and puts it between his legs. It feels hard, like those smooth white stones we pick up at the beach. "TuK-Oowww," clucks the lizards. Like a warning.

His hand is on my stomach, sliding it up. My stomach is moving in waves: it is clear, and then aqua, and then deep, deep green. He brings his hand down, in the same straight line, between my legs, and he sticks his finger in.

"Ow!" I cry out. It hurts.

My *yaya* wakes up, asking, "Marra? *Ano yan?*" My brother jerks his hand away, fast. He closes his eyes, pretending to sleep. I bite my lip and curl over. "Yaya," I moan, "my stomach hurts." Yaya gets up and feels my forehead, which is not hot. She gets the Efficassent Oil and rubs it on my stomach till I fall asleep.

The next day it hurts to pee. My panties have brown stains on them. My *yaya* thinks that I made poo-poo in my sleep. I know I didn't. I am not sick because we had too much *pastillas de leche* yesterday, like she thinks. The whole time at breakfast, my *lola* scolds her, "You can't feed the kids *pastillas* and mangoes! *Sinto-sinto ka ata eh!*"

Lola makes me stay home today too. "Don't go swimming *na*. You rest in my room." I make a face. Lola doesn't empty out her *urinola* until it's full to the brim, so it smells of urine. But I like my *lola's* bed, made of heavy metal. It has long *T*s on each side so the maids can hook up the *kulambo* and tie it to the metal edges of the *T*-hooks. I had my own private force-field in her bed. I imagined automatically electrocuting people who bothered me in bed.

Today, though, I feel worse. I stare at the ceiling counting lizards while waiting for my brother and sister. There are eleven lizards in my *lola's* ceiling running around, and they're making me dizzy. Before I know it, my stomach is lurching, and I run to the bathroom and throw up.

In the toilet bowl I see the blue *katchawang* we had for dinner last night, the *malunggay* leaves, the tap water that is kinda brown. I am retching and retching and then I am throwing up mangoes. Wave upon wave of yellow green rising from my stomach, sticking to my throat, then cascading out of my mouth. Bile spatters all over my hair and all over the bathroom.

"Yaya," I sob. My *yaya* rushes to the bathroom with a towel and warm water to clean me up. She wipes the yellow green from the sides of my mouth with a face towel and carries me back to my *lola's* room. I doze on and off all day, in my *lola's* force field.

It is the next day when I wake up, still in my *lola's* room. Everyone has already gone swimming. I want to go to the beach, too, so Lola makes one of the maids go with me. When we get there, my brother and my *yaya* are already doing their daily routine. My brother is in the seagreen layer of the sea, swimming in a straight line. Then he disappears. I move to the water slowly and look for pretty stones. Nothing is wrong today. Nothing happened. I turn around to see where my brother is now. While I look for him, saltwater drips into my eyes. I don't see his head bobbing up and down anymore. I can't see him. My mouth wants to scream and hangs open, but the wind is bringing sand down my throat. My brother hasn't come up for air.

"Niko! Niko!" My *yaya* screams. She takes off her slippers and goes into the water, but she can't swim. Nobody else is moving. Then I see my brother's pin-sized head by the aqua part of the sea. He is swimming back to the beach in a straight line, and when he gets to the shore, he laughs at my *yaya*. "Nikoooo, Nikoo!" he mimics in a high-pitched voice. I try to swallow, but there is dirt in my throat, and I can't speak properly. I go back to looking for shells, looking through the water, but my toes are silting up sand. "Bad boy *ka talaga!*" my *yaya* slaps my brother on the seat of his trunks. Niko just wiggles away and runs back into the water.

After that summer we all go back to school, and I forget what mangoes taste like. In art class, teachers always think I am drawing farmers plowing fields in their bathing suits. That is so strange. "Don't you see?" I try to explain. "These people are swimming." I always run out of yellow green crayon.

To a Merchant Seaman
Who Has Forgotten His Name

Jean Vengua Gier

For my father, Nick D. Vengua (Narvaez)

This is how I imagine
heaven: memories

suspended clean
in mid-air, like the wash

In a dream I see you
standing in the hallway

dazed, like an animal
a little frightened

afternoon light slants down
on the familiar wallpaper

It will not hold you

We keep ourselves busy
folding the laundry
putting it away

you say to secure the

hatches, and I am very
particular about this

otherwise the salt water
will blow in and you
will have ruined
the ensign's dinner

There is a rule for this
and for every rule a knot
to be loosened

I saw you *well* recently
as if you had never died

sometimes words, whole
sentences, songs, come out

of your mouth. This time
there is just the sound

and that is enough.

TV is a constant, dust
and lead are constant

I've learned to say *something*
so that it sounds like *nothing*

Like you, I am going to travel
anywhere, I am going to escape

you say hand me those goggles
there is a big light exploding
on the island of Eniwetok

and you are its only witness

Is it true about heaven
and is any of it true

There are signs you say
everywhere and there are four
horsemen and a fabulous beast

I think of the hard crunch
of snow on the road
to Shiprock, the cold

embarkation, the immense
distance from Zamboanga
to the notch
in Picacho Peak

I think I can travel
anywhere, I can escape.

A sea of snow and horses
these belong to me

for now

a scrap of paper, a memory
a word for *exile* and *home*

I divide the heavens
tracing a line with my fingertip

Big Dipper to Eniwetok
Manila to Naples

saying everything, even
Nothing

has a name.

Tending the Earth

Elda Rotor

the slight curve of my breast lies firm and rises
with a faint inhale of hope
a small slope underneath my fingertips
I press down to feel terrain small spheres
of cells neighboring each other
making sure there are no unwanted guests
and my blood remains pure
a traffic way carrying wastes and poisons out
leaving breath years life light radiance

I am supposed to raise my arm at different degrees and angles
to see how the geography changes
to better assess what is foreign
my right arm reaches above my head
fingertips press lightly against the cement bedroom wall
cooler to the touch than my skin on a late August night
my body knows how to steal heat
my black hair can fry eggs

at twenty-six this is my body
I wonder how close I will mirror her
her sharp glances of anger
the number of friends she kept
she married rather late at twenty-nine
at thirty-three her hands found one small intruder
asleep in the shade but still dangerous

this sphere here is mine inherited or not
I must work like the groundskeeper to live in this home
tending to the earth the roots and leaves
growing underneath
a sun the shape of faith

my fingers press firmly around as if patting down moist soil
securing the tree's roots
ready to steal heat and water and life
hoping some time
to be named

ancient

Once We Were Farmers

Elsa E'der

Once we were farmers
and we measured time
in distant moments
of new life

and our hopes dwelled
welled up through sweat and skin
unspoken and sacred

and on the rocks we let lie in the fields
we stenciled language
and fed the rainfall upon our stories
and moments circled above the earth

    till now

    unspoken is our passion
    our passion is the moon
    lying down
    in these moments
    in the fields O pen ing
    and in the rhythms of stillness
    we were life anew

we were farmers and midwives
and blood spilled towards the future
in rituals of ancient powers

we leaned toward the cries
of children who gave sound
to rocks we let lie in the fields

We sing
we sing with eloquent hunger.

Talk Story

Jean Vengua Gier

I was born in the French Hospital
just off Geary, taxied through
Chinatown, bundled past vegetable bins,
chicken crates, split hogsheads
and Woey Loey Goey's basement eatery

to the hotel above Woolworth's
where the front door displays traces
of my father's gold-leaf lettering,
where my mother crossed and re-crossed
the dark fourth floor landing to the shared
kitchenette to heat my bottle,
stir the boiling rice

Where my first clear memory is of light
shafting down on a boxing ring,
two figures dancing at each other
through the cigar smoke, black shape
of a man turning to face me,
growling: *why don't you shut up kid*
let your parents watch the fight

Six years later, in a one-room bachelor flat
I learn to listen while my father
and Ninong Gonzalo sing
that other life: my father's dream
of artistry become sacking potatoes
in Oregon, harvesting chard and spinach
in the Salinas Valley; his dream of home
become exile on a merchant ship,
long years away, distances
unrecoverable

And my mother's story: the endless,
queasy voyage across the Pacific,
the disappointment of the Virginia Hotel,
the shirt factory, cannery, laundry

I got the art lessons and piano lessons,
the books and the library cards,
the eroding signs of progress and plenty
as if these were given properties
of the land

In Gonzalo's room, the grimy windows opened
onto an alley, which opened on Vallejo Street's
fragrant kitchens and sewers, grandmas
shuffling down Columbus avenue, poets
chanting bitter news

where, forty years later I walk, jostled
by memory, buying *pok loi* and sweet
sausages, bean cake and *bagoong*

And something weighs upon
yet eases my flesh, bitter and sweet
like that first glimpse of light
and what it illuminated: two men
circling each other in a ring,
as with the tools of their fists
they hammered out a life.

Move from that moment to this;
knowing that a word might strike
tinder, to signal what flew before
and what dark bird still
sings after.

balikbayan box

Virginia Cerenio

not like *chismis*
more like an urban myth
how the pilipinos
when receiving a
balikbayan box
gather *pamilya—lolo* to *bunso—*
around the box like a hearth,
basking in the imagination of cool   ness
a brisk autumn day
a clean ocean breeze
without manila's sooty heat.
it is not the gifts inside the box—
air jordans, T-shirts, magazines, candy bars—
but that moment
cutting through the package tape
when the stiff cardboard is folded back
and the scent of America steps into the room
no Spanish lace
brazen with confidence
and for a downbeat, we imagine
America can come in a box.

The Power of Adobo

Leny Mendoza Strobel

Garlic, lots of garlic
Will scare off the *aswang*
Who would spin a curse
On a newborn
On a young virgin
On the other woman
But such nonsense
Mother said, is only for fools.

Garlic is for *adobo*
Its twin—vinegar, *paombong*,
preferably
And crushed peppercorn
Bay leaf for perfume
A touch of soy,
Simmered with cubes of pork
Untrimmed
So much the better.

Keep the lid off and let the flavors
Engulf the house to its rafters
Better yet open the doors
And windows, let your
Nosy neighbors envy you
of the delights
Of *adobo*

That nurtures your roots
Keeps them moist and
Always on the verge of new
Creations in the land
Where you smuggled
Grandma's recipe
Like a charm, *anting-anting*
To ward off the evil motives

Of hungry ghosts who
Would deny you and curse you
Because they don't have
Grandmothers and mothers
With long memories.

Adobo is of the hand-made life
The sticky juice of pungent cloves
Clings for days
Clings to your hair and collar
To your pillow and sheets
Carries over into your dreams
Of Home.

Contributors' Notes

These notes serve as an index. The title, genre, and page number in this anthology follow each biography.

Editors

Marianne Villanueva is the author of *Ginseng and Other Tales from Manila* (CALYX Books) and an untitled collection of short stories forthcoming from Miami University Press. Her writing is anthologized in *Charlie Chan Is Dead, A Southeast Asia Anthology, Tilting the Continent,* and others. She is published in *CALYX Journal, Zyzzyva, Threepenny Review,* and *Puerto del Sol,* among others. She was a finalist for the O'Henry Prize and received a Bread Loaf Writers Fellowship and California Arts Council Fellowships. She teaches at Notre Dame de Namur University and Foothill College. ("Introduction," p. 11; "Picture," prose, p. 139)

Virginia R. Cerenio was born in California and is a second-generation Filipino-American whose parents emigrated from the Philippines. Her poetry collection, *Trespassing Innocence,* was published by Kearny Street Workshop Press, 1989. Her poetry and short stories are published in various anthologies including *Returning a Borrowed Tongue* (Coffee House Press), *New Worlds of Literature—Writing From America's Many Cultures* (W.W. Norton), and *Making Waves* (Beacon Press), among others. She owns a management consulting firm. ("Introduction," p. 16, "my father has stopped eating," poetry, p. 208; "*balikbayan* box," poetry, p. 292)

Contributors

Merlie M. Alunan is the author of *Hearthstone, Sacred Tree* (Anvil Publications, 1993) and *Amina Among the Angels* (University of the Philippines Press, 1998); they contain all her works that were awarded the Carlos Palanca Memorial Awards in poetry 1985-1998. She received the 1997 Gawad Balagtas Award. Her latest work, *Fern Garden Anthology of Women Writing in the South,* was nominated for the National Book Award by the Manila Critics' Circle, 1999. She lives in Tacloban City, Leyte, Philippines, and teaches literature and creative writing at University of Philippines (UP) Tacloban College, in the Visayas and in the UP Likhaan Creative Writing Program. ("Odysseus Cripple at Bantayan Island," poetry, p. 73; "Poet Traveling Over Water," poetry, p.134)

Shirley Ancheta co-edited *Without Names: Poetry Anthology of Filipino Americans* (Kearny Street Workshop Press, 1985; revised, 1997). Her work is published in *Poems in Premonitions: Asian Poets of North America* (Kaya Press, 1995), *Bamboo Ridge Anniversary Issue* (Honolulu, 1999), and *Quarry West* (Fall 1999). Her erotica has been published in *On a Bed of*

Rice (Anchor, 1995). She is the mother of two sons and makes her home in Watsonville (CA). ("Going Home to a Landscape," poetry, p. 47; Kristine," poetry, p. 153)

Melissa Aranzamendez was born in Manila, Philippines. Her work is included in the anthologies *Contemporary Fiction by Filipinos in America* (Anvil/PALH, 1998), *Sunlight on the Moon* (Carpenter Gothic Publications, 1999), and *New To North America: Writings by Immigrants, Their Children, and Grandchildren* (Burning Bush Publications, 1997). She lives in New Jersey. *("Bahay Kubo / little house,"* poetry, p. 276)

Malou Babilonia writes poetry and fiction based on family "fact." Born in Manila, schooled in "Manilatown," L.A., she divides her time between Berkeley and the Philippines. She writes for Philippine Print News and produced documentaries for Bay Area Filipino television. Early poems were published in *Broad Topics Journal*. She earned a BA in English literature and film theory at University of California (UC), Berkeley, and an MFA in creative writing from Mills College (Oakland, CA). She is a founder of Pusod, a center for arts, culture, and ecology in Berkeley. She collaborated with the late artist Santiago Bose on a book entitled *Body Parts and Other Crash Debris, a Recovery Of* (2001). ("Baby Brother Grown," poetry, p. 227)

Michelle Macaraeg Bautista was born, raised, and educated in the San Francisco Bay Area. She has performed her work with Teatro ng Tanan and for Kearney Street Workshop, *maganda*, and Cocojam Productions. Her work is published in *Babaylan* (Consortium Books, 2000), *Unfaithing U.S. Imperialism, Eros Pinoy* (Anvil, 2001), the *Asian Pacific American Journal*, and *maganda*. She is an instructor in the Filipino martial art of Kali, and her essay on "Kali and Poetics" will be published in *Pinoy Poetics* in 2004. She dedicates her piece to the women of her clan who have inspired her. ("In Whispers," poetry, p. 131)

Arlene Biala is a Filipina poet and performance artist born in San Francisco. She authored *bone*, her first chapbook of poetry (1993), and *continental drift* (West End Press, 1999). She received an MFA in poetics and writing from New College of California and had an artist residency at Villa Montalvo. She taught and performed in the Manikrudo poetry and performance workshops of the CSU Summer Arts Programs in Long Beach and Humboldt (CA). She has performed at La Pena Cultural Center (Berkeley) and SOMArts Center (SF). She lives in Sunnyvale (CA) with husband Carl and two sons. She is working on her next manuscript, *to want to be a saint*. ("Grandma Sakamoto's Gun," poetry, p. 126)

Merlinda Bobis is a Philippine bilingual writer (poetry, prose fiction, drama) and performance artist now living in Australia. Her radio play, produced by the Australian Broadcasting Company, won the prestigious international radio fiction award—the 1998 Prix Italia, the 1998 Australian Writers' Guild Award, and the 1995 Ian Reed Radio Drama Prize. Her fourth book of poetry, *Summer Was a Fast Train Without Terminals* (Spinifex Press), was short-listed for the 1998 The Age Poetry Book Award. She published a book of short fiction, *White Turtle* (Spinifex Press, 1999). She is writing her first novel, *Fish-Hair Woman*, and teaches creative writing at the University of Wollongong. ("White Turtle," prose, p. 99)

Lilledeshan Bose graduated from the University of the Philippines and worked as the features editor for *Seventeen Magazine Philippines*. She has one book, *Una & Miguel* (Adarna House), and her essays, poetry, and stories have been published in anthologies around the world. She sings and writes songs for the rock band The Velvet Ash. ("The Mango Summer," prose, p. 278)

Cecilia Manguerra Brainard is the author and editor of eleven books including *When the Rainbow Goddess Wept* (University of Michigan Press, 1999), *Acapulco at Sunset and Other Stories* (Philippine American Literary House, 1995), and *Journey of 100 Years* (PALH/PAWWA, 2000). She is the recipient of several awards including an Outstanding Individual Award from her birth city of Cebu, a California Arts Council Fellowship, and a Brody Arts Fund Award. She has lectured and performed in many academic and arts institutions including UCLA, University of Connecticut, University of the Philippines, De La Salle University, and Ateneo de Manila University. She lives in Santa Monica (CA) and visits the Philippines regularly. ("Vigan," prose, p. 264)

Holly A. Calica is a third-generation Pilipina born and raised in the Bay Area and mother of four children. She teaches art to middle school children in San Francisco and studies Brazilian dance and traditional Pilipino kulintang music. She is a visual artist and also expresses herself through poetry, dance, and music. She has recently incorporated text and poetry into her artwork. ("Pinay Pioneers," poetry, p. 43)

Justine Uy Camacho was born in 1975 in Cebu City. She was named after the first book in the *Alexandria Quartet* (Lawrence Durrell). She grew up tracking books, pictures, paintings, and letters her mother left behind (who died in 1978 from childbirth complications). Her poetry has been featured in Likhaan anthologies published by the University of the Philippines Creative Writing Center and in the anthology *A Habit of Shores: Filipino Poetry and Verse from English: 1960s to the 1990s* (University of the Philippines Press). She works for a telecommunications firm in the Philippines and is pursuing an MA in English literature at Ateneo de Manila University. ("What Ditas Left," poetry, p. 274)

Catalina Cariaga is a poet and the author of *Cultural Evidence* (Subpress Collective/'A'A Arts,1999). She is a contributing editor of *Poetry Flash* and received her MFA from San Francisco State University. She has taught on the adjunct faculty of New College of California. She works in Berkeley and lives with her husband and young son in Oakland (CA). In her spare time, she plays and collects vintage ukuleles. ("In Late," poetry, p. 167; "No Sleep," poetry, p. 169; "Excerpts from *Bahala Na!*," poetry, p. 185)

Alison M. de la Cruz is a poet, performer, cultural worker, and *ate*. She has performed her successful one-woman show "Sungka" throughout the U.S. and will begin touring her second show, "Naturally Graceful," in early 2004. She is featured on the LA Enkanto CD, "In Our Blood: Filipina/o American Poetry and Spoken Word from Los Angeles." She has served as artist in residence in Los Angeles at Visual Communications, Fil Am ARTS, Great Leap, Inc., and Shakespeare Festival/LA's Will Power to Youth, among others. ("That Age," poetry, p. 30)

Conchitina R. Cruz is an instructor in the Department of English and Comparative Literature, University of the Philippines (UP), Diliman. She has attended the UP National Writers Workshop in Baguio and the National Writers Workshop in Dumaguete. She received a Palanca award for her poetry and is currently pursuing an MFA in writing at the University of Pittsburgh. ("Cartographer," poetry, p. 55; "Mermaid," poetry, p. 130; "Roots," poetry, p. 261; "Daughter," poetry, p. 263)

Erma M. Cuizon has two collections of essays, *Time of Year* (Giraffe Books, 1999) and *Vital Flow* (University of Santo Tomas Publishing House, 2001), and a compilation of short stories, *Homecoming and Other Stories* (University of Santo Tomas Publishing House, 2000). She is editor of the Sunday magazine of the *Sun Star Daily* (Cebu City). She is published in the *Philippines Free Press* and *Panorama*, and anthologized in *The Quill*—the Asian Writers League Journal (1991), *Cebuano Harvest* (New Day Publishers, 1992), and *Centering Voices* (1995). In 1996 she received the Manguerra Literary Award, a Cebu-based award for a body of literary work. She graduated from the University of Santo Tomas with a major in journalism. ("Another Day," prose, p. 251)

Mabi Perez David works at the Filipinas Heritage Library, an electronic research center on the Philippines in Manila. She helps manage a small book shop and organizes history lectures and writing workshops. She is a regular contributor to a local women's magazine. She is a graduate of the University of the Philippines in creative writing. ("Cloister," poetry, p. 154)

Rocio G. Davis is associate professor of American and postcolonial literatures at the University of Navarre, Spain. Her recent publications include *Transcultural Reinventions: Asian American and Asian Canadian Short Story Cycles* (Toronto: TSAR, 2001) and *Asian American Literature in the International Context: Readings in Fiction, Poetry, and Performance* (co-edited with Sami Ludwig, LIT Verlag, 2002). ("Foreword," p. 9)

Alma Jill Dizon was born and raised in Honolulu, where her father's family has resided since 1924. She studied at the University of Hawai'i in Manoa and in Spain before completing her BA at UC, Berkeley. She received a PhD in Spanish literature at Yale, writing her dissertation on Rizal's novels. She currently resides on the West Coast with her family and five dogs. When not teaching or writing, she likes to spend time with them, gardening, throwing frisbees, and watching old movies. ("Cicada Song," prose, p. 75)

Elsa E'der's poems are published in several anthologies and journals, including *Returning a Borrowed Tongue* (Coffee House Press, 1996), *Liwanag, Amerasia Journal,* and *The Wild Good: Lesbian Erotica.* As a Rockefeller Humanities Research Fellowship recipient, she did primary research on Filipinos and Social Change in Hawai'i. She earned an MA in radio and television at San Francisco State University, with an emphasis in script writing. Since 1993, she has worked with various film festivals in the San Francisco Bay Area and plans to advocate for and help create diverse programming in transnational broadcasting, cable, and satellite systems. ("Once We Were Farmers," poetry, p. 289)

Susan Evangelista was born in Michigan and educated at Swarthmore College (PA). She joined the Peace Corps at the age of 21 and was sent to the Philippines, where she has lived "most of the time" since. She married Oscar Evangelista, a professor of history from the University of the Philippines, and has taught English, nonviolence, creative writing, and the creative process at the Ateneo de Manila University. She has done workshops with teachers all over the Philippines and taught in Japan, Nigeria, Cambodia, and a Burmese refugee camp in Thailand. She is now retired from the Ateneo and lives with her husband on the outskirts of Puerto Princesa, Palawan, where she writes and teaches part-time at Palawan State University. ("Fools," prose, p. 177)

M. Evelina Galang is the author of *Her Wild American Self*, a collection of short fiction from Coffee House Press (1996). She has been widely published and her collection's title story was short-listed by both *Best American Short Stories* and *Pushcart Prize*. During 2002, she was a Fulbright Senior Research Scholar in the Philippines where she researched *Lola's House*, a book of essays based on the lives of surviving WWII Comfort Women. Her other works in progress include a novel, *What is Tribe;* a screenplay, *Dalaga;* and an anthology of Asian American art and literature called *Screaming Monkeys* (forthcoming from Coffee House Press). Galang teaches in the MFA Creative Writing Program at Miami University (OH). ("Excerpt from Chapter Six of *What Is Tribe,*" prose, p. 26)

Jean Vengua Gier was born in San Francisco and raised in Santa Cruz. She lives in Berkeley with her husband, photographer Eugene Gier. She has been (or is), variously: a mother, housewife, secretary, temp worker, commercial artist, fine artist, performing artist, scholar-researcher, and teacher. Her poems are published in numerous journals and anthologies, most recently in *Returning a Borrowed Tongue* (Coffee House Press, 1996). Her essays are published in the journals *Critical Mass* and *Jouvert* (with Carla Tejeda) and the anthology *New Immigrant Literatures of the United States* (Greenwood Publishing Group, 1996). She enjoys working in collaboration with other artists/scholars. ("To a Merchant Seaman Who Has Forgotten His Name," poetry, p. 284; "Talk Story," poetry, p. 290)

Victoria Sales Gomez was born in Calabangga, Camarines Sur, and raised in Madrid, Spain. She came to the U.S. in 1980 and works as an ICU nurse at Saint Francis Memorial Hospital in San Francisco. Her publications include book reviews for the *Seattle International Examiner* and translations of poems from Spanish in *This Wanting to Sing* (Contact II Publications, 1991), a collection of Asian South American poetry. The title character of her story, "Mang Tomas," is based on the many Filipino veterans who have passed and continue to pass through St. Francis Memorial Hospital. ("Mang Tomas," prose, p. 51)

Cristina Pantoja Hidalgo has been a teacher, writer, and editor in Bangkok, Beirut, Seoul, Yangon, and New York City while traveling with her husband to his postings as a UNICEF official. She has six collections of essays, four collections of short stories, a novel, and two collections of literary criticism. *Recuerdo* (University of the Philippines Press, 1996) won the Carlos Palanca Grand Prize for the Novel. Her latest book is a novel, *A Book of Dreams* (Anvil Press, 2001). She edited *Pinay: Autobiographical Narratives by Women Writers, 1926-1998* (Ateneo De Manila University Press, 2003). She has a PhD and teaches literature and creative writing at the University of the Philippines and is Director of the University of the Philippines Press. ("The Painting," prose," p. 111)

Luisa A. Igloria is a poet, fictionist, and essayist who published five books under the name Maria Luisa A. Cariño: *Cordillera Tales* (New Day, 1990), *Cartography* (Anvil, 1992), *Encanto* (Anvil, 1994), *In the Garden of the Three Islands* (Moyer Bell/Asphodel, 1995), and *Blood Sacrifice* (University of the Philippines Press, 1997). Her work is published in many journals, including *Poetry, TriQuarterly, Blackwater Review, Hayden's Ferry Review, The Asian Pacific American Journal, Bomb,* and *Black Warrior Review.* She received a 2001 Fiction Fellowship from the Virginia Commission for the Arts. She teaches in the Creative Writing Program and the English Department at Old Dominion University (Norfolk, VA). ("Chinatown, Moon Festival," poetry, p. 48; "Longing," poetry, p. 145)

Noelle Q. de Jesus lives in Singapore with her husband and two children and works in advertising. Her stories have been published in a number of literary magazines, among them *Puerto del Sol* and *Feminist Studies.* She has been a recipient of the Philippines' Palanca Award for the short story and has an MFA in creative writing from Bowling Green State University (OH). ("Cold," prose, p. 87)

Sherlyn Jiminez moved to California from Pangasinan, Philippines, when she was ten. She has a BA in psychology from UC, Berkeley, and an MFA in creative writing from San Francisco State University. She is currently pursuing a doctorate in clinical psychology at the University of Connecticut. She has read in the New Writer's Series at Intersection for the Arts in San Francisco and is published in *Liwanag II* and *Fourteen Hills*. ("Bandit Banjao #2," poetry, p. 235)

Lewanda Lim came to the U.S. in 1978 and lives in Westfield Township (OH). She has a BFA from the University of the Philippines, where she taught for several years before immigrating to Canada in 1976. She received an MA in studio art from the State University of New York, Albany. Her art works have been exhibited in Pennsylvania, Massachusetts, New York, and Ohio. She started writing poetry in her forties, and two of her poems are included in *From the Listening Place* (Astarte Shell Press, 1997), a collection of writings by women on intuition and creativity. ("An Expatriate to Her Sister," poetry, p. 199; "Prayer Rug," poetry, p. 201)

Maloy Luakian was born in Manila and graduated from the University of Toronto. "Piranhas in the Kitchen" is her first published story and she would like to thank her parents, Jane and Mike, her siblings, and Kevin Cheung for their inspiration. She promises that the bodies will never be found. The story is dedicated to Professors Allen Hepburn and Donna Bennett. She currently lives in Hong Kong. ("Piranhas in the Kitchen," prose, p. 236)

Dawn Bohulano Mabalon is a third-generation Pinay, born and raised in Stockton (CA). She lives in San Francisco, where she tells stories as a poet, writer, and Filipina/o American historian. She co-directed/produced the video documentary *Beats, Rhymes and Resistance: Pilipinos and Hip Hop in Los Angeles* (2000). She received an MA in Asian American studies from UCLA and a PhD in history from Stanford University. ("For the Women," poetry, p. 22; "A Poem/Tribute for Olivia Malabuyo on Her 22nd Birthday," poetry, p. 39; "April in Stockton," poetry, p. 50)

Reine Arcache Melvin is the author of *A Normal Life and Other Stories* (ORP, Ateneo de Manila University, 2000), which won the 2000 Philippines' National Book Award for fiction (the French translation *Une Vie Normale* was published in 2003). She received first prize in the Philippine Graphic Literary Awards (2001) and a Standard Chartered Bank Fellowship to the Hong Kong International Literary Festival. Her short stories are published in many literary reviews and anthologies in the U.S., France, and the

Philippines. She has been a journalist, translator, and editor for various international publications and edited an anthology of contemporary Philippine poetry. She lives with her husband and two daughters in Paris, where she works for the *International Herald Tribune*. ("Homecoming," prose, p. 58)

Maiana Minahal is a queer Filipina American poet and teacher who was born in Manila, raised in Los Angeles, and lives in San Francisco, where she teaches poetry workshops. She studied poetry at UC, Berkeley, with June Jordan's poetry collective Poetry for the People. In 1995 they toured the New York City poetry scene and won the Nuyorican Poet's Café Poetry Slam. Her work is published in June Jordan's *Poetry for the People: A Revolutionary Blueprint* (Routledge, 1995), *Take Out: Queer Writings from Asian and Pacific America* (Temple University Press, 2001), in *maganda* magazine, and in the anthology *inVasian: Asian Sisters Represent*. Her first book of poetry is forthcoming in 2003 from Monkey Press. ("Tired," poetry, p. 94)

Veronica Montes lives in the San Francisco Bay Area with her husband and three daughters. Her fiction is published in the literary journals *Prism International*, *Furious Fictions*, and *maganda*, and in the anthologies *Contemporary Fiction by Filipinos in America* (Anvil, 1997) and *Growing Up Filipino* (Philippine American Literary House, 2003). ("Apollo & Junior Grow Up," prose, p. 171)

Fran Ng is a children's book writer and illustrator based in Manila. She graduated from the Ateneo de Manila University in 1996 with a degree in interdisciplinary studies. Her picture book, *The Brothers Wu and the Good Luck Eel* (Tahanan Books for Young Readers, 2000), won first place in the Carlos Palanca Awards in 1998 and a National Book Award from the Manila Critics Circle. She has been a fellow of the National Writers Workshop and the University of the Philippines Writers Workshop. Her poems are anthologized in *Intsik: An Anthology of Chinese Filipino Writing* (Anvil, 2000) and *Love Gathers All: The Philippines-Singapore Anthology of Love Poetry* (Singapore, 2002). ("Summer Rains," poetry, p. 86; "Haze," poetry, p. 133; "Notebook," poetry, p. 136; "Dream," poetry, p. 203)

Henrietta Chico Nofre was raised in downtown Los Angeles and attended Hampshire College in Amherst (MA). In addition to fiction, she also writes plays and was awarded a Garrett H. Omata Scholarship at the David Henry Hwang Writer's Institute at East West Players Theatre. Henrietta is currently a doctoral candidate in cultural and social anthropology at Stanford University. ("Tall Grasses," prose, p. 128; "Christmas," prose, p. 232)

The Pinay M.A.F.I.A. (Mad-Ass Filipinas Infiltrating Amerikkka) is a collective that wrote "The Dozens—Pinay Style" totally via E-mail. The poem is based on the urban tradition of a round of verbal jousts, in America called "The Dozens" and in the Philippines called "*Balagtasan.*" Contributors include Filipina American poets, performance artists, teachers, students, and activists from Los Angeles, San Francisco, Stockton, Cerritos, San Diego, Seattle, and Honolulu, including Emily Porcincula Lawsin, Stephanie Velasco, Dawn Bohulano Mabalon, Allyson G. Tintiangco, Myra Dumapias, Alison de la Cruz, Faith Santilla, Rikka Racelis, Maya Santos, Darlene Rodrigues, Lilyann Bolo Villaraza, and Pamela Gil. The Pinay M.A.F.I.A. thanks Irene Suico Soriano for allowing them to perform "The Dozens" at the PinaySista's Speak! event she coordinated for the 1999 Festival for Philippine Arts and Culture in San Pedro (CA). ("The Dozens—Pinay Style," spoken word, p. 33)

Isabelita Orlina Reyes is an assistant professor at the University of the Philippines, Diliman, where she teaches creative writing courses and Philippine literature in English. She was one of the Associate Editors of the on-line magazine, *LegManila* (http://www.legmanila.com). She has one book of poetry, *Stories from the City* (University of the Philippines Press, 1998). ("The Stone," poetry, p. 84; "Invasion by Jack Fruit," poetry, p. 165)

Barbara J. Pulmano Reyes was born in Manila and raised in the San Francisco Bay Area. She received her BA in comparative ethnic studies at UC, Berkeley, and is currently an MFA candidate at San Francisco State. Her poems are published in *Liwanag* (Kearny Street Workshop Press), *Babaylan* (Aunt Lute, 2000), and *Eros Pinoy* (Anvil, 2001), and she has new work forthcoming in *Filipino Writers in the Diaspora* and *Invasian: Asian Sisters Represent.* Her first book is *Gravities of Center* (Arkipelago Books Publishing, 2003). ("Kauai 1 and 2," poetry, p. 56)

Terry Rillera received her bachelor's degree in English literature from the UC, Berkeley, and her Masters in writing from the University of San Francisco. She lives in California. ("Meteors," poetry, p. 95)

Elda Rotor's poems are published in *The Literary Review, New Digressions, The Asian Pacific American Journal,* and *Dialogue,* and in the book anthologies *Flippin': Filipinos on America* (Asian American Writers' Workshop, 1998), *The Nuyorasian Anthology* (Temple University Press, 1999), and *Turnings* (Women's Studies at ODU, 2000). For five years she published and edited *New Digressions,* a co-founded art and literary magazine that encouraged emerging artists and writers under thirty. She was a finalist in the "Discovery"/ *The Nation* 2000 poetry competition. ("Ironing," poetry, p. 218; "Tending the Earth," poetry, p. 287)

Nadine Sarreal has moved many times in her life. She considers Baguio, Philippines, and Willimantic (CT) to be the homes of her childhood. She writes fiction, usually short stories, and some poetry. She likes to cook without following recipes and often mentions food in her stories. She graduated from the Vermont College MFA program in creative writing. Currently, Nadine is writing a novel about Filipino women working in Hong Kong. An excerpt from this novel, *Putsero*, is published in the spring 2000 issue of *The Literary Review*. ("Eureka 2000," prose, p. 187)

Maria Stella Sison was born in Quezon City, Philippines, and immigrated with her parents to the U.S. when she was four. She spent 21 years in California, went to UC, Berkeley, and worked in several media organizations in the Bay Area before her first visit back to the Philippines, where she earned a master's degree in international studies at the University of the Philippines, Diliman, and worked on a human rights project. She has since moved back to San Francisco and works in community development in Oakland. This is her first creative writing publication. ("The Big I Am," poetry, p. 21)

Lakambini A. Sitoy's story "Touch" won First Place in the Philippines' prestigious Don Carlos Palanca Memorial Awards, Short Story Category, in 1998. Her collection of short stories, *Mens Rea*, won the Philippines' National Book Award for Fiction in 1998. She has two other Palanca awards, also for her fiction. Her stories and essays are published in various magazines in the Philippines and abroad. She has worked as a journalist, editor, and teacher and lives in Quezon City, Philippines. ("Touch," prose, p. 211)

Leny Mendoza Strobel is an assistant professor at Sonoma State University (CA). She is the author of *Coming Full Circle: The Process of Decolonization Among Post-1965 Filipino Americans* (Giraffe Books, 2001) and one of the co-editors of *Encounters: People of Asian Descent in the Americas* (Rowman & Littlefield Publishers, 1999). Her writings are also published in *U.S. and Postcolonial Theory: Race, Ethnicity, and Literature*; *Filipino Writers in the Diaspora*; *Filipino Americans: Transformation and Identity* (Sage Publications, 1997); *Amerasian Journal*; *Paterson Literary Review*; *Pleiades*; *The Toronto Review*; *The Other Side*; and *Filipinas Magazine*. ("The Power of *Adobo*," poetry, p. 293)

Eileen Tabios has released a poetry CD and written, edited, or co-edited eleven books of poetry, fiction, and essays, which include *Beyond Life Sentences* (Anvil Press, 1998), winner of the Philippines' 1999 National Book Award for Poetry; *Black Lightning: 20 Poetry-in-Progress* (Temple University Press, 1998), which received a Witter Bynner Poetry Grant; and, as editor, *The Anchored Angel: Selected Writings of Jose Garcia Villa* (Kaya Press, 2000), which received a PEN/Oakland Josephine Miles Award. She was editor of the *Asian Pacific American Journal*, 1996-1999. Her most recent book is *Reproductions of the Empty Flagpole* (Marsh Hawk Press, 2002). She is the recipient of the 2002 Potrero Nuefo Fund Prize. ("The Color of a Scratch in Metal," poetry, p. 202)

Grace Gamalinda Talusan was born in the Philippines and raised in the U.S. She attended Tufts University and UC, Irvine. She taught at the University of Oregon's Program in Creative Writing and currently teaches at Tufts University. She has published fiction in anthologies and nonfiction in *The Boston Globein* and *The San Diego Reader*. She is a recipient of a 2002 Massachusetts Cultural Council Artist Grant and a board member of the Writer's Room of Boston, an urban writer's colony. ("Smoky Mountain," excerpts from a novel in progress, p. 220)

Angela Narciso Torres was born in Brooklyn (NY) and grew up in Manila. She graduated from Ateneo de Manila University and the Harvard Graduate School of Education, where she obtained a Masters in psychology. Her poetry is forthcoming in the *Asian Pacific American Journal* and the *North American Review*. She lives in Northern California with her husband and three sons. ("We Go Back to Manila in 1999," poetry, p. 71; "Tango," poetry, p. 207)

Katrina Tuvera graduated with an AB art history degree from the University of the Philippines. She began writing fiction and essays in 1994. Her work is published in *Philippine Graphic, Chimera, The Evening Paper, The Weekly Mirror, Sands and Coral,* and *LegManila,* an online magazine where she is an associate editor. Her first collection of short fiction is *Testament and Other Stories* (Anvil Press, 2002). ("Testament," prose, p. 155)

Bunny Ty is passionate about children, writing, and everything else in between. After graduating from the Ateneo de Manila University (AB psychology), she obtained an MS in counseling from California State University at Sacramento. She has taught preschoolers and written a column for children in an online magazine. Currently, she is a teacher-therapist and one of the directors of the SchoolRoom, Inc., a private center in Manila that provides early childhood education and counseling. ("Some Women," poetry, p. 42)

Linda Ty-Casper writes novels set in critical periods of Philippine history. Among these are *The Peninsulars, The Three-Cornered Sun* (Cellar Book Shop, 1979), *Ten Thousand Seeds* (Ateneo de Manila University Press, 1987), *DreamEden* (University of Washington Press, 1997), *Dread Empire* (Heinemann, 1982), and *Awaiting Trespass* (Readers International, 1985), a Top 5 Women's Fiction Choice at the UK Feminist Book Fortnight, 1986. Her latest novel is *The Stranded Whale* (Giraffe Books, 2003), set in the Philippine-American War of 1899-1901. Her work is cited in the *Best American Short Stories*. She received a UNESCO Prize, a Philippine P.E.N. prize, the Filipino American Women Network Award, the SouthEast Asia, WRITE Award, and, most recently, the PAMANA Award. She is published in many anthologies and cited in *Contemporary Authors, Encyclopedia of World Literature, Survey of Long Fiction,* and others. ("Loreto, Alone," prose, p. 147)

Glossary

adobo pork or chicken stewed in garlic and vinegar, often considered the Philippines' national dish

agay ouch

alamang shrimp paste sautéed with garlic and eggs

alam mo you know

almirante admiral

ampalaya bitter gourd, a vegetable

"Ang imong auntie, *nitawag usab. Ang mama ni Anna."* "Your aunt (the mother of Anna) also called up."

anak child

Añejo popular Filipino rum

angelus six o'clock prayer to one's guardian angel

"Ang layo mo na!" "You're so far away already!"

"Ano yan?" "What is that?"

anting-anting talisman

aratilis a common type of tree bearing a small round red fruit, similar to a cherry

aswang witch

ate sister

aysus ay, Jesus (abbreviation: an expression)

babaylan Visayan priestess-poet

baboy pork

bagoong paste made of fermented fish or shrimps

Bahala Na leave it to fate

"Bahala na sa Diyos" "It's in God's hands"

"Baka maubusan tayo" "We might run out of something"

bakya wooden clogs

baliga woof stick used for weaving (Ilokano)

balikbayan Philippine-born emigrant; literally, one who returns. A generic term for all Filipinos living abroad.

balut raw duck egg, a delicacy

Banaue province in the mountains of northern Luzon

bangus milkfish

banig woven floor mats

barong a formal type of men's shirt, often with elaborate embroidery

barrio small town

Bicolana a native of Bicol province in the Philippines

boang crazy (Visayan)

bunso youngest child in a family

caimito star apple

calabasa squash

capiz translucent shell, used in window panes

carabao water buffalo

caritela   karetela, a two-wheeled horse-drawn wagon (still used as public transportation in some remote areas)

Cebuano   A native of Cebu

chica   girl

chismis   gossip

Cordilleras   mountain range in northern Philippines

dalaga   transitional period between girlhood and womanhood, sometimes used to denote a young unmarried woman

"El unico problemo es que no es guapo."   "His only problem is that he isn't handsome."

estero   estuary, drainage canal

ewan ko   I don't know

Flordeluna   a popular soap opera

gago   stupid

gumamela   hibiscus

halo-halo   Philippine version of an ice cream sundae: ice cream with a mixture of sweetened preserved fruits and beans, custard, shaved ice, and milk

haole   white, as in Caucasian

hapa   mixed race

hayop   you animal

hoy boang   hey, crazy

huwag   don't

Ilocano   a native of the Ilocos, a region in the northern Philippines

ilog   river

Ilonggo   a dialect spoken in the central islands of the Philippines

inchik   Chinese (derogatory term)

Jollibee   chain fast-food outlet—the Philippine version of McDonald's

kalabasa   squash

kalamay   sweet conserve (toasted and ground rice cooked with coconut mild and sugar)

kamote   sweet potato

kapatiran   similar to brotherhood or sisterhood but with no gender bias

kapuna   elders, ancestors

kare kare   oxtail stewed in a crushed peanut and toasted rice sauce

karetela   see *caritela*

ka talaga   you, really!

katchawang   sword fish

kaya pala   so that's why

kuchinta   sweet rice cake

kulambo   mosquito net

kumusta   how are you

"Kung mo-telephone ug usab, ingna nga mobisita ko tomorrow igpadulong nako sa trabaho. Bisan kinsay motawag..."   "If she calls again, tell her I'll visit her tomorrow. I'm on my way to work, tell anyone else who calls..."

lahi   race

langka   jack fruit

lawanit   sheets of plywood

lecheflan   dessert similar to French crème brûlée; a rich custard steamed in pans coated with caramelized sugar

lola   grandmother

lolo   grandfather

lugaw   rice porridge

lumpia   spring roll

Makati   commercial district of Manila

malunggay   leaves from the horse radish tree, used in soup

mananambal   Visayan word meaning sorcerer

manang   elder sister, term of respect used in addressing older women

Mang   equivalent to "Mr."

mangkukulam   a native witch who does voodoo or casts spells

manong   elder brother, a term of respect used in addressing old men

masamang babae   bad woman (implies a woman with loose morals)

merienda   snack, usually served mid-morning or mid-afternoon

mestizo/mestiza   person of mixed race

mongo   a kind of dried bean—resembles lentils

municipios   municipalities

"*Nasakit kono, ate Bib.*"   "She said she was sick, Ms. Bib." *(Day* is an abbreviation of *Inday,* a Visayan form of address, a respectful way of addressing a lady.)

"*Ni-ana ta, day.*"   "We are here."

ninong   godfather

nipa   palm thatch

noche buena   the feast immediately following the traditional Christmas midnight Mass

Noy, puede?   Boy, are you available? *(Noy* is a Visayan form of address, usually for young boys.)

opo   Yes, Sir, or Yes, Ma'am

palay   rice grain

pamilya   family

pancit, pansit   noodle dish

pan de sal   salt bread in small loaves

pangyaw   friend (corruption of the Cantonese)

panocha   a kind of native brown sugar, a round hard candy made from brown sugar and roasted peanuts

paombong   type of native vinegar

pastillas de leche   sugar-coated milk candies

patis   sauce made from salted fish or shrimps

patotoo   bearing witness, testimonial

pigsas   boils

pikake   jasmine

pikot   forced to get married (usually as a result of unforeseen pregnancy)

Pilipinas/Pilipinos   Filipina/Filipino

Pinay/Pinoy   Filipina/Filipino

pinipig   lightly toasted green rice, used as food topping, particularly in desserts

po   term of respect, like "Sir" or "Ma'am"

probinsiyana   person from the provinces (feminine form)

putang ina, putang ina mo!   your mother is a whore; similar to "son of a bitch"

puti   white

queso de bola   a type of round cheese, usually served at Christmas feasts

'ros caldo   rice porridge with chicken broth and ginger

salamat   thank you

sari-sari   a small neighborhood store that sells sundry items (literal translation: mix-mix)

sebo de macho   ointment made from tallow or fat, said to lighten scars

"Sige, kaputi ngani..."   "Go on, touch it."

"Sige na"   "Come on, let it be."

"Sigi, sakay na"   "Go ahead, get in."

"Si Glenda nitawag, ate Bib. Nanganak na siya ug baby boy!"   "Glenda called, Ms. Bib. She just gave birth to a baby boy."

sikwan   shuttle used for weaving (Ilocano)

sinigang   soup made with meat or fish, soured with crushed tamarind fruit

siniguelas   plum-like fruit

"Sinto-sinto ka ata eh!"   "You must be loony!"

siram sana   how delicious

Suprema   variation of "Supremo," the title assumed by the leader of the revolutionary organization, the Katipunan

Tagalog   a language of the Philippines that contains many words derived from Spanish. Tagalog spelling differs slightly from the Spanish, though in many cases the meaning is the same in both languages.

Taglish   vernacular—a mixture of English and Tagalog

talaga   really

talong   eggplant

tapis   sarong-like apron worn over a skirt

tarantado   a rapscallion

tatay   father

tayo   we/us

tenga   ear

tia/tio   aunt/uncle

'tigas   hard

"Tignan mo to!" "Just look at this!"

tira-tira brown-sugar sticks

tita aunt

torta a Spanish-style omelet with tomatoes and ground meat

tsinelas house slippers

tukador ladies' dressing table with large mirror

ube yam

ulan rain

uy Oh

Visayan a native of the Visayas (central region of the Philippines)

"...wag kang tikis" "...don't be a tease"

wahine young woman

wet market the part of an open-air market where fish is sold

yaya nursemaid

Yoruba an African tribe

Zamboangeño a native of Zamboanga, a province in the southern
    Philippines